Gifting Fire

ALINA BOYDEN

ACE
New York

ACE
Published by Berkley
An imprint of Penguin Random House LLC
penguinrandomhouse.com

Library of Congress Cataloging-in-Publication Data

Names: Boyden, Alina, author.
Title: Gifting fire / Alina Boyden.
Description: First edition. | New York: Ace, 2021.
Identifiers: LCCN 2020044418 (print) | LCCN 2020044419 (ebook) |
ISBN 9781984805485 (trade paperback) | ISBN 9781984805492 (ebook)
Classification: LCC PS3602.O9339 G54 2021 (print) |
LCC PS3602.O9339 (ebook) | DDC 813/.6—dc23
LC record available at https://lccn.loc.gov/2020044418
LC ebook record available at https://lccn.loc.gov/2020044419

First Edition: April 2021

Printed in the United States of America

1st Printing

Map design by Soraya Corcoran
Book design by Laura K. Corless

This book is dedicated to all the trans women past and present whose unapologetic visibility made my life and this book possible.

DARYASTAN
KINGDOM OF RAKHA
Rampur
Kunduz
DURRANIA
LAHANUR SUBAH
Lahanur
GHAZIABAD SUBAH
Ghaziabad
VANGA SUBAH
Surma River
Jumuna River
Lakhnauti
KHANATE OF KHUZDAR
Gelak
Shalkot
Mirpur
ZINDH SUBAH
Zindhu River
Nizam
NIZAM SUBAH
Jaigarh
Shikarpur
Bikampur
REGISTAN
Kadiro
Gwalipur
GWALIPUR SUBAH
Gulf of Arakan
Rajkot
Khambhat
MAHISAGAR SULTANATE
VIRAJENDRA EMPIRE
Devasamudra
Kolikota
Sea of Daryastan
@SorayaCorcoran

CHAPTER 1

Outside the palace of Bikampur, the monsoon rains fell in torrential sheets, the sound a constant, dull roar that filled my ears. But on this side of the marble latticework jali screens, it was warm, and dry, and safe. The oil lamps, ensconced in pierced-brass chandeliers, sent cascades of orange stars across the dark backdrop of my bedchamber's marble ceiling, and Prince Arjun Agnivansha was busy unwinding my dupatta from my head and shoulders, his full lips stretching into an eager grin.

"My lady, my lady!"

The shouting in the corridor outside gave me just enough warning to pull away, to throw the loose end of the silk fabric back over my head in some semblance of order before Shiv, one of Bikampur's court eunuchs, came striding into the room. My cheeks burned nearly as brightly as his did when he saw the state of my clothes, and just how close Arjun was standing beside me.

"Ah . . ." Shiv pursed his lips, his blush stretching all the way to his ears. "Forgive me, this is a bad time."

"No, no, it's fine," I said, because I didn't think we were going to get the mood back now anyway. "What did you need?"

"I was just making the final preparations before your household leaves for Shikarpur in the morning, my lady, and—"

"Your highness," Arjun corrected. "She's a princess of Nizam now, remember?"

I could have kissed him for that, had Shiv not been there. Royal titles weren't things that were branded on your skin. They only existed if other people believed that they did, and so Arjun's support meant everything to securing my station.

"Of course." Shiv bowed by way of apology. "Your highness, I was preparing your household as you commanded and the workmen told me they were ready to load your bed." His eyes flickered to the one that was sitting in the middle of the room, the one Arjun had been steadily guiding me toward.

"Oh. Right." My face burned even hotter than it had a moment before. It was a good thing Shiv had arrived when he had, otherwise . . .

I shook that thought from my mind. "You can have the men sent in to claim it. We'll go elsewhere."

"If you'd prefer we came back later . . ." Shiv offered, but I shook my head.

"No, no. The household needs to leave as soon as possible since they'll be crossing the desert on foot and camelback rather than through the air. Best they take it now."

I forced a smile I didn't feel, made sure my dupatta was arranged neatly, and strode from the room, Arjun hot on my heels.

He matched me step for step, walking so close beside me that our bodies were practically touching, but he didn't put his arms around me, not here where the guards and the servants could see. Instead, he whispered, "We could go to *my* bedchamber," in a voice that was so deep and quiet that it was almost a purr. My heart jolted in response.

I opened my mouth to tell him what a brilliant idea that was, but the words that filled my ears weren't my own. They belonged to Lakshmi, my little sister.

"Akka, they took my bed!" She was shouting down the corridor at me, her arms crossed over her chest, her dark brow furrowed at the indignity. "Where am I going to sleep?"

Before I could respond, Sakshi, my elder sister, appeared beside her, clad in the same white shalwar kameez as my little sister. They'd clearly both been about to go to sleep. The workmen's timing couldn't possibly have been worse, but I knew I couldn't blame them, not when the rain had been falling nonstop for three days. It had slowed everything down.

I sighed. "We'll find a place for both of you. I'm sorry."

"It's all right, Razia," Sakshi said, her arms going around Lakshmi and holding her close. "We know that this move is more stressful for you than for anyone. Don't we?" She aimed that last question at Lakshmi, but our little sister was having none of it.

"Why do we have to leave Bikampur again?" she groaned.

"You know why," I replied. She was eleven, not five, and I'd explained it to her more than once.

"You should tell your father you're staying here," Lakshmi said. "Tell him you like it here and you don't want to leave."

I sighed so I wouldn't scream. My stomach churned at the thought of leaving yet another home, of having to start over for the third time in my life. But I knew that I didn't have a choice. If I told my father I wanted to stay in Bikampur, that I loved being Arjun's princess so much that I couldn't possibly do what he asked of me, then he'd probably send assassins to slit my throat in my sleep. Honestly, I was a little surprised that he hadn't. He'd made me the subahdar, the provincial governor, of Zindh as a battlefield concession, under duress. Now that he was safe in the imperial palace in Nizam, it wouldn't take much to dispatch an army of trained killers to find me and do away with me. Wouldn't that be cheaper and easier than getting the other subahdars of the empire to respect a hijra as one of their number?

Of course, the cheapest and easiest way to kill me would be to just bide his time until I arrived in Shikarpur and kill me there. I'd be at his mercy then, surrounded by his soldiers. Here in Bikampur, with Arjun at my side, and his father's soldiers all around us, I was as safe as I could be anywhere. That was all going to change when we left for Zindh.

"Lakshmi, we've talked about this," Sakshi said, stroking my little sister's silky black hair, taming it down where it had come loose from its braid.

"*You've* talked about it," Lakshmi corrected, stamping her foot in irritation. "I've been saying I don't want to go and you won't listen!"

I took a deep breath and let it out slowly, praying to God for strength. "We're listening. But we don't have a choice. We have to go."

"I hate your father!" Lakshmi exclaimed.

That, of all things, brought a smile to my lips. "Me too, little sister." I came forward and embraced her tightly, wishing that I could let her stay here, because that was what I wanted more than anything. We'd made a home here. I was liked here. For the first time in my life, people respected me for me. And now I was going to have to give it all up, to cross the desert to start a new life in a new city. And yes, I was going to be the subahdar, I was going to be the ruler of city and province both, but I knew better than to believe that my father's gift of a royal title and a governorship would earn me the respect of the men and women who lived there.

A hijra princess was an oxymoron, and I doubted if they'd let me forget it.

"Well, you can be sad," Arjun told Lakshmi as he came up behind me. "But I, for one, am glad we're leaving."

I was sure that my face betrayed the same skepticism as Lakshmi's.

"You are?" she asked.

"I am," he replied.

"Why?" she demanded.

"Because I like new adventures," he said, in tones that suggested he didn't think she did. "I like flying over new lands and meeting new people and eating new foods that I've never even heard of before. And I like going to new marketplaces where they have different clothes and jewelry and spices. And I love learning new songs and new games too. And Zindh is probably going to be a little bit dangerous, so I'm going to have to fly my zahhak a lot, and I might have to get into aerial duels with your big sister's enemies.

"But"—he shrugged—"that stuff is probably too exciting for you. You're probably too dainty for aerial duels."

"Am not!" Lakshmi grumbled, wrinkling her nose at that accusation.

Arjun carried on like he hadn't heard her. "Yes, it's probably too dangerous and too exciting for little girls. I can talk to my mother and see if she'll let you stay here in the women's quarters with my sister. We'll let Sakshi have your zahhak instead, since she's learning to be such a good rider."

"No!" Lakshmi exclaimed.

"No?" Arjun's obsidian eyebrows shot up to his hairline in mock surprise. "But what are you going to do with a zahhak here where it's safe and there's nothing new to explore?"

"I like new things too," Lakshmi insisted. "I'm just going to miss it here is all." Her dark eyes flickered up to meet mine. "I'm tired of starting over."

"Me too, little sister," I said, and for once I couldn't summon up any words of encouragement at all. For all Arjun's talk of excitement and adventure, I knew that he opposed this journey as strongly as any of us. I was lucky he was coming at all. Most princes wouldn't have followed their lovers to new lands when they had perfectly good ones already.

"We've all started over a lot," Sakshi said, her mahogany eyes moving from me to Lakshmi and back again. "But each time we've started over, things have gotten a little bit better, haven't they?"

Lakshmi gave a cautious nod of agreement, and though I thought that Sakshi's lecture was ostensibly for our little sister's benefit, there was a part of me that suspected she was talking to me too.

"When you ran away from your father's palace because he was mean to you, that was hard, wasn't it?" Sakshi asked.

"Yes . . ." Lakshmi admitted, and I could have given the very same answer, because it had been hard. It had been the hardest thing I'd ever done in my whole life.

"You gave up so much," Sakshi said, her arms going around Lakshmi, but her eyes looking right into mine. "You gave up your family, and your zahhak, and your place in the world."

I bit my lip hard to keep from crying as Lakshmi buried her face in our sister's silk kameez.

"And when you came to Bikampur, you found a new family, but that was hard too. You had to learn so many things. You had to become a totally different person. But it was better, wasn't it?"

Lakshmi nodded, and I found myself nodding right along with her. It had been so hard, training to be a courtesan, learning to please men, to temper my words, to keep my guard up and my mind active at all times lest I find myself in their disfavor and lose everything. And that was to say nothing of the secret training, learning to steal gold and gems in the dead of night, learning to guard my tongue lest I lose my head. It had been such a heavy weight on my shoulders that there had been times when I thought my body would just give out and crumble beneath the burden. And yet, somehow, it had still been better than being a boy in a palace.

"And then you had to leave that family too," Sakshi said, her voice going quiet, because it was a pain she shared with us. "You had to come to this palace, and at first that was hard. People weren't always nice to us. We had to be careful how we behaved and what we said so that we didn't get thrown out."

Arjun's arm fell across my shoulders and I leaned against him, taking some comfort in his warmth, reminding myself that as hard as things had been here in the palace of Bikampur, he had never once let me down.

"And you had to fight to save this home," Sakshi continued. "You had to do some really scary things to keep it from being destroyed. But you did them, didn't you?"

Lakshmi nodded again, and my guts twisted. I'd forced her to do those scary things. I'd recruited my eleven-year-old baby sister to fight in a battle, because it had been the only way to ensure victory. God, what was wrong with me?

Sakshi patted Lakshmi's back gently, though her eyes were still staring unwaveringly into my own. "We survived that too, and things got even better for a while. But now we have to go to Zindh, and that's hard because we've never lived there before, and we don't know anyone, and it might be scary or even dangerous. But I think if we work hard and we persevere, we're going to be even happier there than we have been here."

"I know," Lakshmi said, "I'm just sad to leave."

"Me too," Sakshi told her, "even though I think Prince Arjun is right. I think it will be fun to see new things in Zindh. We'll get to see a whole new palace and eat new foods and wear new clothes and fly to new places. But more importantly, we're not really going to be starting all over again."

"We're not?" Lakshmi asked, and I too wondered what Sakshi was talking about, because it seemed to me that we would be.

"No, sweetheart," Sakshi replied. "We'll never have to start over again so long as we're together." She reached out and took my hand and pulled me close to her and to Lakshmi, and Arjun was dragged right along with me.

"We'll stay in my bedchamber tonight, the four of us," he said, ruffling Lakshmi's hair with one hand, the other encircling my waist.

"Like a family?" Lakshmi asked, the hope on her face hitting my heart like a dagger.

"Like a family," I promised, letting my determination replace the tears that had been threatening in my eyes.

CHAPTER 2

My last visit to Shikarpur had come in the dead of night, the pitch darkness of a new moon hiding the splendor of the city from my eyes. Now, by light of day, the glittering cobalt-and-turquoise-glazed tiles of the city's palaces and temples told me why it had been called the Indigo City by the poets of Zindh. But as beautiful as Shikarpur was, it was the danger that awaited me there that lingered strongest in my mind. As Zindh's new subahdar, I would soon find myself the target of many jealous rivals, both within the empire and without. And that was if I even survived the coming meeting with my father, which was no sure thing.

"It's going to be okay, Razia."

Arjun's voice shook me from my thoughts. He was riding behind Sakshi atop Padmini's back. The beautiful fire zahhak was soaring almost wingtip-to-wingtip with Sultana, my thunder zahhak, her yellow belly scales and flame-colored wing feathers making her look like the living embodiment of a desert sunset. It was Sakshi doing the flying, her brow furrowed in concentration as she clutched the leather reins in a white-knuckle grip. Arjun had been guiding her, his hands resting on her shoulders, which made my insides twist with longing. I wished I was the one riding in his saddle with him, his strong hands resting on *my* shoulders. I needed the courage I felt when I was with him, today more than ever.

"Razia?" Arjun's concern was so plain in his voice that it was audible even across the fifty-foot gulf of roaring wind that separated us.

"My prince?" I asked, hoping that I'd covered up my anxiety well enough not to alarm my sisters. I hadn't yet told them that I suspected my father might just execute me on my arrival to Shikarpur. If he did, they'd never be able to stop it, and if he didn't, then there was no sense worrying them over it.

"It's not too late to go back to Bikampur," Arjun said, his voice strong and clear and determined, almost like he was speaking directly into my ear and not shouting from one zahhak's back to another's. "It will never be too late to go back to Bikampur. Say the word, and we can fly back there right now."

"Can we, Akka?" Lakshmi exclaimed, and I felt my resolve crumbling to dust. My younger sister was riding her own thunder zahhak, soaring in the wake left by Sultana's and Padmini's wingtips. It was the animal she had stolen from Shikarpur in our desperate bid to save our home from destruction. Hadn't I vowed after we'd survived all that that I'd never knowingly put her in danger again?

But turning back would be more dangerous. My father had threatened war if I didn't take up the post of subahdar of Zindh. So I had to go. And though I was sad to be leaving my home, and worried that my father might have me killed, there was a part of me that wanted to go. For all the danger, for all the fear I held of my father, becoming the subahdar of Zindh and a recognized princess of Nizam gave me my power back. It let me choose my own destiny in a way that I never could as a concubine in Bikampur. And that was what I'd craved more than anything during my years as a courtesan—the power to choose. To choose whom I loved and who shared my bed. The freedom to speak my own mind. I could have lived the rest of my life without palaces and gemstones, but of all the penalties I'd suffered for living as my true self, the loss of my freedom had been the harshest one of all. If I had even the slightest chance of winning it back, then I would fight for it with all my might.

And maybe that was why my father had made me the subahdar. Perhaps he'd seen it in my eyes, or guessed it, or just knew me better than I gave him credit for. Every other subahdar in the empire could retreat, could fall back on his soldiers and his family connections if things got too difficult. But not me. For me, there could be no retreat, no failure—not if I ever wanted to maintain my freedom.

"Shikarpur is going to be a wonderful new home for us, little sister," I told Lakshmi, and I even found myself believing it. "We're going to have a beautiful palace, and we'll get to ride our zahhaks together every day—you'll see."

Lakshmi's tentative smile made my stomach churn. She trusted me with her whole heart. I hoped I knew what I was getting her into.

"Well, if we're going, we should go," Arjun said, without the least hint of judgment. He just nodded to the palace below us, and to the patrol of four thunder zahhaks that were circling warily over the city walls, waiting for us to descend. With Arvind flying Arjun's wing, our flight of four zahhaks would have been enough to alarm any patrol, and the longer we lingered, the less we would look like guests, and the more like enemy scouts. Better to get down before the patrol decided to investigate.

I reached forward, just ahead of my saddle's high front cantle, and gave Sultana's cerulean neck scales a fond pat. "Ready to see our new home, girl?"

My thunder zahhak's beakless snout twisted slightly in my direction, so that one of her jade eyes could look straight at me. She was waiting for an order.

I gave a sharp tug backward on my top set of reins, and Sultana responded at once by pitching up into a climb. As she went, I leaned my body to the right, pulling a little on the reins in that direction. Sultana responded with perfect grace, rolling smoothly onto her belly before plunging into a sheer, vertical dive.

I forgot all about my worries as her wings tucked in tightly to either side of her body, like a pair of sickles poised to cut the wind. The air roared across my face, tearing at my flying goggles, sending my silk dupatta streaming out behind me like a lancer's pennant. The golden domes of Shikarpur's palace rose up to greet me, and I aimed myself for the ruins of the zahhak stables, still in a shambles thanks to my attack weeks before.

I put a little gentle back-pressure on the reins, bringing Sultana smoothly out of her dive at the height of the mango trees crowding the palace's outer gardens. We zipped over the parapets of the yellow sandstone wall before breaking into a hard left turn to slow ourselves down. Sultana back-beat her wings and settled onto the smooth tiles of the polished limestone courtyard with all the grace of a dancer.

Beside me, Lakshmi's zahhak alighted easily, but Sakshi, Arjun, and Arvind were slower, their bigger, bulkier fire zahhaks having taken longer to descend. They landed off to my right, just as grooms came rushing forward to take our zahhaks to the parts of the stables that were still in good repair.

I threw off the straps holding me to the saddle and dropped to the ground beside Sultana. She shoved her snout against my chest before I could so much as adjust my dupatta.

"It was a very good flight," I told her, pressing my nose to hers while my hands worked to wrap my dupatta around myself into something approaching appropriate court attire. In other kingdoms, a princess never would have ridden a zahhak, or appeared outside of the zenana without a veil, but we Nizamis hailed from the wild steppes some centuries back, where everyone, man or woman, had to know how to ride, and so we permitted our princesses more freedom than other nations.

"Can I help you, my lady?" a familiar voice asked. The tone was confused and uncertain, and the language was Court Safavian, a language I hadn't heard in years.

I looked up to find Sikander, my father's old master-at-arms, standing at the head of a group of mail-coated soldiers, their fine steel turban helms covered in golden calligraphy invoking the grace of God. He was peering at me from under the rim of his helmet, without a trace of recognition behind his dark brown eyes.

"Good morning, Sikander," I replied, pleasantly surprised to find that my own Court Safavian hadn't suffered much during my years in Bikampur. I enjoyed too the way that Sikander's gray-tinged eyebrows shot up to his hairline as he finally realized who I was.

I couldn't blame the man too much for not recognizing me. The last time we'd seen one another, I'd been sweaty and exhausted, without makeup or jewelry, wearing only a simple black shalwar kameez. Now, I was dressed in a peshwaz, the proper gown of a Nizami princess. The blue, coat-like garment was covered in golden zardozi embroidery and studded all over with fine crystals, creating patterns of twisting zahhaks and bolts of deadly lightning that sparkled in the sunlight. I'd paired it with loose cloth-of-gold trousers, embroidered in the same fashion, and a matching golden blouse, which was revealed by the peshwaz's deep, triangular neckline. With my dupatta arranged neatly on my head, my makeup artfully done, and every inch of exposed skin glittering with gold and sapphire jewelry, I must not have looked anything like my former self—which had been the whole point.

Sikander's lips pursed and his eyes narrowed as he tried to work out what emotion he was supposed to be feeling. He should have been disgusted with me, furious, just like he always had been when I'd lived in the palace in Nizam, but it was plain that he was having a hard time summoning up the necessary anger when confronted with the image of a beautiful young Nizami princess dressed in perfectly appropriate attire.

"Your highness?" he ventured, as if he still wasn't sure that it was really me.

"Yes, Sikander?" I asked, trying and failing to keep a smile from tugging on the corners of my lips. I couldn't help it. My whole life, he'd been so fierce and decisive, and now he seemed so completely and utterly disarmed that I wondered how it was that I'd lived in such terror of him for so many years.

"Your father is waiting for you," he said, clearing his throat, because the tone had come out gentler than he'd intended. When he spoke again, it was gruffer, more like his old self. "He expected you sooner."

I shrugged. "It's the monsoon. You know how hard that makes it to travel."

He grunted at that, unwilling to agree with me, but unable to deny the truth of it.

"My father is in the diwan-i-khas, I presume?" I asked.

"He is, your highness," Sikander affirmed, his voice softening again in spite of his best efforts to the contrary.

"Then please take me to him. I wouldn't want to keep him waiting."

Sikander hesitated at my pretty smile and my kind words, his brow deeply furrowed, like he was still trying to work out what trick I was playing on him. In the end, he didn't manage to figure it out. He just spun on his heel and began marching across the courtyard. I followed a few paces behind him, attended by Lakshmi and Sakshi, my only female companionship these days.

"That was a brilliant landing," I told Sakshi as we walked, mostly to keep myself from dwelling on the coming meeting with my father.

"I think I'm ready to solo, don't you?" she asked.

"I'd say so," Arjun said, laying a hand on Sakshi's shoulder before I could reply. "You timed that turn into the landing just perfectly. And it wasn't just me who noticed—Padmini could tell too. That's why she was so relaxed."

Sakshi's cheeks warmed. "Thank you for trusting me with her."

"Anything for my sister-in-law," he replied.

"Oh?" I raised an eyebrow. "Are we to be married now, my prince?"

He answered me with a lopsided grin. "What need has a love as storied as ours for marriage ceremonies?"

I rolled my eyes at that, but I didn't press the matter. What his honeyed words hid was a truth I preferred not to dwell upon. I was a hijra, so I could never give any man children. There would be no little Arjuns and Razias running around at our feet, no young princes and princesses to carry on our family lines, to serve as living proof of our love for one another. And the less I let myself think about that, the better.

"Are you all right?" Arjun asked, his brow knitting with concern. I must have let my thoughts show through on my face. He let go of Sakshi in favor of putting his arm around me and holding me close to him. "Was it something I said?"

"No, my prince," I replied, letting my head fall against his chest. His warmth and strength were a comfort, given that I was presently surrounded by my father's heavily armed guardsmen. They were ostensibly there to protect me, but I knew how easily they could be turned against me if given the order. These men would never see me as a real princess. What would it matter to them if I lived or died?

I took that cheerful thought with me into the palace's inner courtyard. It seemed strangely desolate. I was accustomed to Bikampur's lush gardens of rosebushes and mango trees, its marble fountains, and the channels of water that fed them. But here, the limestone footpaths cut straight lines across bare grass. A few old banyan trees spread their shade over stone-lined pits, which had been partly filled by the monsoon rains. Were those cisterns of some kind? They were unsightly, whatever they were.

More empty stone pits were connected to one another by means of channels, rather like the ones that had conducted water to the fountains in Bikampur, but there was scarcely a finger's depth of brown slurry coating the bottoms of these cheap imitations. The channels all met in the middle of the courtyard, their sludge flowing into an enormous square moat that surrounded a white marble pavilion, its round dome covered in fine glazed tiles of cobalt blue, turquoise, and gold.

"Why is it so ugly, Akka?" Lakshmi asked, her brow furrowing in confusion as she stared at the same empty pits that had attracted my attention.

"I don't know, little sister," I replied, putting my arm around her shoulders, acutely aware of the fact that I'd promised her a beautiful new home, "but we'll have to work on it together, and make it look nice."

"It's going to take a lot of work," she observed, and I couldn't argue with her.

I'd have said more, but at that moment I caught sight of who was waiting for me in the shade of the baradari's tiled dome. My father, Humayun, sultan of the greatest empire of Daryastan, sat atop a marble throne that was inlaid with precious gems, lapis lazuli, and obsidian, producing the most remarkable images of zahhaks dancing across its surface. I knew better than to keep him waiting.

I crossed a small footbridge over an empty stone moat, which must have once been a pond, but as I passed into the shade of the pavilion and my eyes adjusted a little, my stomach gave a lurch. I hadn't seen my father sitting on a real throne for the better part of five years, and the sight of it took me right back to being a disgrace of a thirteen-year-old prince in a palace filled with servitors who despised me.

I recovered my composure quickly, plastering a neutral expression across my face, hoping my father hadn't noticed my discomfiture. No, as my eyes flickered up to scan his face, I saw that his emerald eyes were still wide with surprise. Of course. He'd never seen me in my court finery before either, and like Sikander, it was clear he hadn't imagined I could ever look so much the part of the Nizami princess.

I allowed myself the barest trace of a smile, because for all of my anxiety, I had planned my entrance carefully. My clothes marked me as a royal Nizami woman, and my sisters, who trailed behind me, were similarly attired. Lakshmi wore her acid zahhak–inspired sari of emerald and kingfisher blue, and Sakshi was borrowing the fire zahhak lehenga that Arjun had given me for my first trip to the palace of Bikampur, which seemed almost a lifetime ago. The three of us looked like wealthy princesses from three different kingdoms, not a trio of hijras from one of Bikampur's less savory neighborhoods. And if there was one thing I'd learned in my life, it was that for all of the poets' talk about inner beauty, people's judgments were based almost solely on appearance. If you looked the part, people tended to believe you belonged to it, and I definitely looked the part of a princess of Nizam.

While Sikander went to stand beside my father's throne, I made my obeisance. I stood before my father, bowed slightly, and raised my palm to my forehead, ceremonially offering him my head. I'd grown familiar with the gesture during my childhood in the palace, but the whole thing seemed so much grislier with Sikander's gnarled hand resting on his talwar, his grim face staring into mine.

"Peace be upon you, Father," I said in Court Safavian, my head still bowed, my palm still raised. I hoped the rest of my entourage were doing the same thing—I'd certainly spent enough of the morning teaching them how to greet the sultan of Nizam properly.

"And upon you peace," my father replied, which was my signal to straighten up and to lower my hand.

My father gestured to a cushion on a dais beside his throne, the place of honor in the pavilion. "Sit."

Now that the greeting was over, he was perfectly willing to dispense with ceremony. I'd always thought the man was more comfortable on the back of a zahhak than in the fine trappings of a palace, and I could see that little had changed in the years since I'd run away from home.

I took my seat while the rest of my entourage sat on cushions arranged at the base of the throne, under Sikander's watchful eyes.

My father grunted with amusement. "I wasn't sure if you'd

have the courage to come, but I suppose you've got more ice in your veins than I credited you with."

"Not exactly a high bar, Father," I replied, unable to keep a hint of bitterness out of my voice. He had never recognized my talents.

"Well, look at you," he growled, gesturing to my peshwaz, my jewels, the way I was sitting like a proper young lady on my cushion, with my hands folded neatly in my lap.

I looked around in mock confusion. "Do you not like my peshwaz, Father? I had it made especially for this occasion."

"I still have half a mind to kill you," he replied, and this time there was no anger or bluster in his voice, which made the threat all the more frightening. His lip was curled with scorn, and I'd long ago learned that that was the most dangerous emotion I could see in a man's face.

I swallowed against the bile rising up in my throat, and tried my best to keep my face impassive. Showing him fear now would be a mistake. "Well," I forced myself to ask, my voice far calmer and more collected than I felt, "what are you waiting for, then? This is the best chance you've had in years, and Sikander looks desperate to put his sword to work."

My father shook his head, but the expression of disgust didn't leave his face. "No," he said, "that would be too easy. After what you did, killing my subahdar, slaughtering his army and his zahhaks, humiliating me in front of my enemies, I have something far worse planned for you."

My heart skipped a beat as I wondered if I hadn't underestimated my father's anger. Was he going to torture me, then? Why the ruse of making me a subahdar if a slow death had been his goal all along? Why bring me here and sit me beside his throne like he intended to follow through on his promises?

I arched an eyebrow, hoping I looked intrigued rather than terrified, and asked, "Oh? What is my fate to be, then?"

"You're going to clean up your mess," he answered, and I had to fight back a sigh of relief. He gestured to the palace around us, to the dirty pits that were half-filled with rainwater. "Did you think being made the subahdar of Zindh was a reward?"

"Far from it, Father," I replied, as I'd been thinking of nothing these last few weeks but the struggles I would face here, and I was sure there would be plenty more waiting for me that I hadn't considered. "But you didn't leave me much choice, did you?"

He smirked. "No. And now that you are a *princess*"—his tongue lingered on the word like it was a curse—"you'll find that you have precious few choices left, *Razia*." My name was pure poison in his mouth, but it was the implied threat that caught my attention—the threat of being under his thumb for the rest of my life.

"You'll need a bigger army than the one you've brought if you expect me to confine myself to the zenana like a fire-worshipper's wife, Father," I warned him, as there was no way I was going to let him force me to hide myself away in the women's quarters, seeing the world only through jali screens, forced to issue my orders through servants and handmaidens. If that was to be my fate, I would go back to Bikampur, where at least I would be safe and happy.

My father stroked his mustache, his eyes flickering over my face, still taking my measure. "You've changed."

Those weren't the words I'd expected to hear from him, and I felt my cheeks burn, but not from embarrassment. From pride. Changing myself was what I'd wanted most when I'd left Nizam four and a half years ago.

"I have," I agreed, because whatever my faults, I wasn't the scared little prince I'd been when he'd known me, not anymore.

My time in Bikampur had forged me into something altogether different.

"All the same, you're going to have your work cut out for you here," he informed me, his tone becoming more businesslike, less scornful. It was a familiar pattern. Back home he'd always alternated between rage at my effeminacy and seriousness about the practical lessons he had to impart.

"I can see that," I muttered, nodding to the empty stone pits ringing the courtyard, to the complete lack of any servants save his soldiers. This place looked more like a ruin than a palace.

"If I were you, I'd waste less time worrying over the beauty of your palace and more time worrying over the state of your province," he snapped.

It was just the kind of unfair thing he'd always said to me back home, twisting my words to make me sound like some effeminate moron. "If you have reports from scouts and from zamindars on the state of the province that are so urgent, why waste all this time with empty threats and tired insults, Father?"

"Do you even know anything about Zindh?" he demanded.

My spine stiffened and my jaw clenched. Somehow, I'd let myself forget these little tests of his. My whole childhood he'd made me parrot facts and figures from every province in the empire. He'd made me recite the history of Lahanur and the religious practices of Vanga, and woe be to me if I made the slightest error. But the anger left as quickly as it came. Those lessons had saved my life, had given me the power to claw my way out of the sewer and back into the skies. God help me, I was actually grateful to the man.

But even if I had changed, he hadn't—or at least not as much. He was still waiting for me to parrot those facts, to prove that I understood the province he had given me to rule.

I crossed my arms over my chest, letting him see how annoyed

I was at being treated like a child, but I gave him what he wanted, the summary that my tutor would have demanded from me. "Zindh is the most difficult province in the empire to protect. Safavia and Khuzdar threaten its western border, Durrania its northern one, and Registan lies directly to the east, to say nothing of the fact that it is completely open to attack by sea on its southern coastline where it borders Mahisagar. Worse, it is one of the wealthiest provinces in the empire owing to the indigo trade, but one of the least populated owing to the deserts that surround it, making its defense even more difficult."

"That's half the picture," my father agreed, my understanding of matters having tamed his temper somewhat, "but the internal affairs of Zindh are an order of magnitude more complicated. For centuries it was ruled by—"

"—its own royal family," I interrupted, finishing his sentence for him, enjoying the look of irritation that flickered across his face. "The Talpur dynasty, the members of which have long served as the—"

"—jams of Zindh," he said, speaking over me. "And many people in Zindh are still loyal to the members of their royal family and will stop at nothing to see its rule restored."

I frowned at that. "Restored? I thought you had every Talpur killed seven years ago for supporting Uncle Azam's rebellion."

"I killed Rustam Talpur, their precious emperor," my father grumbled, "but his sons escaped. I kept it quiet, but now the elder of the two boys, Ali, has reclaimed Kadiro, Zindh's only port city."

"Which means our trade revenues will be crippled until he's dealt with," I concluded, seeing then why my father had been so annoyed with me for focusing on the palace.

"Correct. But it's worse than that."

I didn't need him to spell it out for me. I could see the picture developing in my mind's eye, even without the scouting reports. "With Javed Khorasani dead, and his men gone, Ali Talpur's rebels will have their run of the province."

"And it will be your job to pull them out, root and stem, and restore order to this place," he concluded.

I frowned as I mulled over the magnitude of the task before me. Even with my zahhaks, I'd need an army to defeat Ali Talpur's men, maybe more than one, to say nothing of artillery, ammunition, food, and supplies. At present, I had none of those things.

"How many zahhaks does Ali Talpur have?" I asked, as that was the most pressing issue. With just two or three fire zahhaks or acid zahhaks at his disposal, he might make retaking Kadiro nearly impossible.

"More than thirty," my father replied, "but they're all river zahhaks." He gave a dismissive gesture with his hand.

River zahhaks. Of course. My eyes flickered to the slender, colorful animals decorating the marble throne. River zahhaks were a peculiar species native to Zindh. They lived here in such large numbers that even ordinary noblemen were expected to learn to ride them, but where most zahhaks spat fire or acid or lightning, river zahhaks possessed no breath at all, making them virtually useless in warfare outside of scouting and messaging duties. It was one fewer thing for me to worry over anyway.

"And how many men are you leaving me?" I asked.

"You think I'm leaving soldiers for you after what you did?" my father asked, his voice mild, his expression anything but.

"I think that if you expect me to fight a war without soldiers then you have a higher opinion of me than I ever imagined possible," I retorted.

"I can spare you five hundred men," he said, his words sounding strangely flat without their usual undercurrent of scorn.

"Five hundred men?" I gasped. That was what he was leaving me? Not in my worst nightmares had I ever imagined it would be this bad. I forgot our sparring match, our anger at each other, and I asked, with genuine concern in my voice, "Are there no levies left under our control at all?"

"This province has always been difficult to hold together," my father told me. I didn't know if it was a response to my sudden display of worry, or some long-buried instinct, but he wasn't yelling at me like usual. He was explaining things the way he had when I was little and he'd still wanted me to take the throne. "The local emirs, their petty lords, hate interlopers, they still worship their infernal king, and they and their levies are loyal to him."

I looked out at the nearly empty inner courtyard of the palace. There should have been courtiers, there should have been servants, there should have been more guards. I understood now why there weren't. "There's nobody left in this province but rebellious lords and resentful nobles."

I wasn't the subahdar of Zindh, I saw that clearly. I had five hundred men and six zahhaks with which to fight Ali Talpur, the rightful king of Zindh, and to quell a populace numbering in the hundreds of thousands. It was impossible. I'd be dead before the week was out.

"My father can send men, Razia," Arjun said. I didn't miss the urgency in his voice, the fear for my safety. "And I have friends I can contact, young princes of Registan who are bored sitting at home in peace, and who might enjoy an adventure in an exotic new land. They could bring fire zahhaks—at least three or four."

"Thank you, my prince," I said, though I thought we both knew that it wouldn't be nearly enough. And anyway, if Ali Talpur's men commanded the forts on the border with Registan, which I had no doubt they did, then the Registani soldiers would never be able to get through.

"We can ask Prince Karim for help, Akka," said Lakshmi, with far too much hope in her voice. It broke my heart. I'd promised her a new home, and I'd brought her to a tomb. But the pain in my heart didn't change how I felt about Karim Shah. I wouldn't ask him for his help if he were the last man in Daryastan.

"Prince Karim and the Mahisagaris have their own worries now," my father said, more to me than to Lakshmi. "The Safavians have won their war with Tarkiva. The Safavian shah, Ismail, is preparing his victorious armies for new campaigns. He wants to enlarge his territory, and for the first time in a decade, he has the freedom to do it. Karim and his father will be too worried about that to help you here."

I swallowed hard against the lump of fear hardening in my throat. I hadn't counted on a threat from Safavia. They were a larger empire even than Nizam, with massive armies and hordes of zahhaks. If they turned their sights eastward, Zindh would be the ripest target for their veteran armies.

"Father, I know you're angry with me," I said, "but I would think that this province would be more important to you than a feud with your own child. I can't reclaim Zindh with five hundred men and six zahhaks, let alone defend it from Safavia. You might as well hand it over to Shah Ismail right now."

"Welcome to being a ruler, Razia," he replied, and for the first time he was saying my name without the least trace of scorn. He didn't even sound angry with me, just tired. I saw then what I hadn't let myself see before—the dark circles under his eyes, the wrinkles creasing his face. He was getting older, and the cares of the empire were weighing on him.

"The Virajendrans heard about what happened here," he said. In a different tone of voice, it would have been an accusation, a reminder of my betrayal, but he was just stating a fact. "They've been launching raids across our southern border, probing our defenses, testing us for weakness. If I don't respond in force, there will be an invasion."

I saw it then. This was a calculated loss, a strategic withdrawal to strengthen the empire in the long term.

"If Zindh falls, we'll have a river between Lahanur and our enemies," my father said, laying it out for me. "Lahanur is one of our strongest provinces, filled with soldiers and fortresses, and unlike Zindh, I won't have to cross the most barren desert in Daryastan to resupply it. And if Lahanur becomes our westernmost province, then Registan will serve as a buffer between us and the Safavians. As rich a province as Zindh is, the difficulty in defending it makes it expensive. I'm not sure our revenues will even suffer very much.

"But if I let the Virajendrans cross the Bhima River," he continued, "they'll swallow up two whole provinces before I can stop them. Maybe more than that. I can't let that happen. Far better to content myself with the loss of Zindh than to endanger the heartland of the empire in some foolish bid to save it."

It was all perfectly logical. All except one thing. "Why the charade, then, Father? Why not just take your zahhaks back and leave me in Bikampur where you found me? Or just kill me. That would be simpler."

"I had intended to," he allowed, and my heart lanced with pain, not from fear, but from sorrow. "You're right, it would have been simpler just to execute you and be done with it. But Prince Karim of Mahisagar changed my mind."

"Karim?" Had he gone and visited my father after the battle? "What did he say to you?"

"You were there," he replied. "After the battle of Rohiri, Karim said that you had devised the plan to defeat the Firangi fleet, that you had stolen zahhaks from a heavily guarded palace, that you had devised a battle strategy that had crushed Javed Khorasani's army, and that you had killed Javed and his son in aerial combat."

I remembered that speech. It had been so out of place from a selfish bastard like Prince Karim Shah.

"It occurred to me then," my father continued, "that if anyone in Daryastan could save Zindh, it would be the girl who had pulled herself out of the gutter to become a princess."

The air went out of me in a rush. God, that was the nicest thing he'd ever said to me in my entire life. I was so confused. Why say something like that while leaving me here in this province to die? There was only one explanation that sprang to mind. "You think I can win?"

He shrugged. "I don't know anything about you, Razia. I don't know what you're really capable of. My son, Prince Salim, was a spoiled brat and an effeminate disgrace. If he were in charge of this province it would fall within the hour. But you're not him, are you?"

"No, Father," I said, trying and failing to keep my voice from crackling with emotion.

"No," he agreed. "You're not a pampered prince. You're a whore who was clever enough and ambitious enough and ruthless enough to make herself a provincial governor."

He let that hang in the air for a moment before saying, "I don't think you're clever enough to save Zindh, but I'd have to be a fool to underestimate a courtesan who somehow orchestrated the worst defeat Nizam has suffered in my twenty-seven-year reign."

I stared at the floor, torn between wanting to hug my father and wanting to murder him. I should have been so proud that I'd finally impressed him, finally made him see my worth, but it was hard when it was so clear that he didn't see me as his child at all, just a pawn in Daryastan's never-ending political game. Just once in my life, I wanted him to be a father to me like Udai was to Arjun. I wanted him to tell me that he cared about me, that he was proud of me. I wanted him to admit that I was more than just an *effeminate disgrace*. But I knew that was too much to ask.

My father stood up from his throne. "Come along, then, Razia. We'll review the men I've left for you."

"Yes, Father," I murmured. I followed him out of the diwan-i-khas, but my head was still spinning from the things he'd said about me. I was hearing them over and over again in my mind. *If anyone in Daryastan could save Zindh, it would be the girl who had pulled herself out of the gutter to become a princess . . .*

CHAPTER 3

Sixteen cobalt-scaled thunder zahhaks stood in neat ranks of four, their riders holding them steady with firm hands on their reins. It had been years since I'd seen my father's honor guard fully assembled, and the sight of them squeezed my heart with a familiar pressure of loss and longing. There could have been just one reason for all of my father's fliers to have gathered outside the palace stables.

"You're leaving now?" I couldn't keep the note of surprise out of my voice, but I thought I managed to hide the hurt. It was silly; I wasn't a little girl who clung to her father's kurta and never had been. That opportunity had been stolen from me like so many others by the circumstances of my birth. But somehow, even after all the bitter arguments, the traded barbs, the harsh insults, there was still a part of me that longed to have my father in my life. The fact that he would only spare half a day for me at a time like this only served to remind me how forlorn that hope of mine really was.

My father arched a black eyebrow at the question. Maybe

I hadn't hidden the hurt as well as I'd thought. His mustache quivered slightly as his lips tugged into a superior smirk. "Why? Are you going to miss me?"

I shrugged, letting him make of that what he would, and nodded to the flame-red orb of the sun, which was sinking below the waters of the Zindhu to the west. "It's getting late is all."

"I like night flights best," he replied.

His words brought with them a flood of memories. I could still recall my first night flight, so many years ago. I'd been so little then, small enough to cram myself between my father and his saddle's front cantle, the pair of us sharing the safety straps. His zahhak, Malikah, had nuzzled me gently with her snout, making sure I was safe and secure. And then we'd taken to the skies together, the tiny orange flames of the palace's lanterns glittering like stars in the darkness below us, the heavens bright above us, suffused with the brilliant light of a silver moon.

My eyes flickered up to meet my father's just as his lowered to meet mine. All traces of his superior smirk had been erased from his face, replaced by deep furrows in his brow. I wondered if he'd just been reliving the same memory I had. I wanted to ask him. I wanted to reach out across the gulf between us, to say something, anything that would make him understand that it wasn't my fault that I was the way I was, that I'd done the best I could, that I'd never meant to cause him any pain or shame, that my whole life all I'd ever wanted was to make him proud of me.

But I didn't say anything. I couldn't find the words in time, and I wasn't sure that there were any words left to say. And then my father spoke, and the opportunity was lost forever.

"I'm leaving Sikander with you. He will command your personal guards, and your zahhak riders."

I glanced to the man in question, my father's shadow, his chief lieutenant, his most trusted guard, and my foremost tormenter.

A myriad of competing emotions warred inside of me. I was touched. My father was leaving his most trusted bodyguard with me. That must have meant that he really wanted me to succeed. Or was it a trap? Was Sikander meant to keep me in line, to kill me if I strayed from my father's plans? Or was it petty revenge, sticking me with the man who had beaten me until my insides hurt for every imagined offense against the standards of masculinity he had set?

It was those memories that made up my mind. I couldn't imagine trusting the man who had whipped me with a cane for something as innocuous as remarking on the beauty of the flowers in the garden. After a moment of stunned silence, I opened my mouth to refuse my father's offer, but I was too late.

Sikander had dropped to his knees at my father's feet, his head bowed. "Your majesty," he said, "in all the time that we have known one another, I have never once questioned an order, but I beg you to reconsider this. What use will I be to you here when Virajendra threatens in the southlands? If this is a punishment, if I have displeased you, please tell me how I can make it right."

Anger and sorrow tightened around my heart. Of course he would think that being asked to serve me was a punishment.

My father laid his hand on Sikander's shoulder with a fondness he had never shown me. "This is no punishment, my friend. On the contrary, I would consider it a favor."

"A favor?" Sikander's deep brown eyes were pinched with worry. "But, your majesty, this is a hopeless task."

"If Zindh falls, it falls," my father answered with a shrug that filled me with a bitterness that stung the back of my throat. "But losing this province to a hijra has made us look weak. If Zindh is to fall, it must not fall too quickly, and our enemies must pay a price in blood to take it. Otherwise we would look weaker still. I need someone here who can fight like a wounded lion surrounded by hungry jackals. Can I trust you to hold here as long as you can, and to punish those who would attack us with all the strength you possess?"

I crossed my arms over my chest, the sour expression not leaving my face, but I had to admire my father's way with men. He always knew how best to stroke their egos, how to flatter them and cajole them and get them to follow his orders. He'd have made a pretty good courtesan himself, though I suspected I'd have lost my tongue for telling him so.

"I will hold here for as long as you require, your majesty," Sikander swore, just as I'd known he would.

"That won't be necessary," I said. "I can hold Zindh on my own. In fact, I'd prefer it that way."

My father's green eyes narrowed in irritation, but for once his anger was nothing when set beside Sikander's. The old guardsman stood up in a huff and glared at me, his fists tightening into gnarled, hard-used fists. The threat was obvious, and one he never would have dared aim at my father no matter what the provocation.

"Did you think I was making a request, Salim?" my father snapped, before Sikander's fists could go to work.

I wished I could have honestly said that little barbs like that didn't hurt, but they did, even after all these years. I gritted my teeth, biting back a hundred angry responses in favor of the only one that mattered.

"What I think, *Father*," I said, lingering on that word, reminding him of the relationship he had so often denied, "is that if you are going to leave me here in this province to die, you could at least let me choose a bodyguard I can trust."

My father had been on the verge of shouting something at me, but he suddenly reared back in shock and confusion. He exchanged quizzical glances with Sikander, who seemed as befuddled by my words as my father was. When my father spoke, his voice was tinged with astonishment as he asked, "You really think you can't trust Sikander?"

I looked at the man in question, who seemed genuinely surprised—and annoyed—that I doubted his loyalty. Once upon a time, I'd never have dared do any such thing. When I was little, he had held my hand wherever we went. He had led me through the markets of the city, making sure I never got lost or hurt. He had threatened with death any who had dared to look at me cross-eyed. He had driven the monsters from my bedchambers, and the fear from stormy nights. But then, one day, when I was seven, I'd worn a pretty green peshwaz that had belonged to my cousin Sidra, and she'd told the harem servitors, who had told my father. And after that day, nothing was ever the same again.

"How can I trust with my safety the man who spent most of my life beating me bloody simply for existing?" I asked, my voice colder and more measured than I would have thought possible, given the roiling emotions straining against the walls of my chest. "How can I trust his hands to keep me safe, when all I've ever known from them is pain?"

My questions were met with a deafening silence. I'd half expected my father to mock me, to deride my effeminacy all over again, to tell me how richly deserved those beatings had been, but instead he just stood there, slack-jawed, like he'd genuinely forgotten all the reasons I'd had for running away from home at the age of thirteen. And Sikander, he looked down at his hands, as I'd known he would, and saw them balled up and ready to strike. All that self-righteous anger went out of him like a deflating bellows, leaving his muscular chest hollowed and his massive shoulders slumped.

"If I'm going to have a captain for my guards, I want it to be a man who has never beaten me, Father," I continued. "I don't think that's too much to ask."

My father stood there in silence, and for a moment, I thought that I had won. But then the familiar excuses came. "Everything Sikander did, he did at my command."

"I know," I replied, looking right into my father's eyes, letting him see what I knew. My own father had hated me so much that he'd tried to have my soul beaten out of my body when I was too young to understand, let alone fight back.

"What you need doesn't matter," my father said, so dismissively that it made my blood boil. "What *I* need is a strong man to lead the soldiers here. They will not follow a whore—especially not one who was supposed to be a prince."

"Forgive me, Father," I said, managing to keep my voice steady even though my body was trembling with emotion, "but did you intend for Sikander to be my bodyguard or my jailer?"

"You are the subahdar of Zindh, but Sikander will command the men I leave behind," my father replied, which told me all too clearly whom he had intended to leave in charge.

"A subahdar with no troops is no subahdar," I hissed.

"Sikander will command the soldiers, and I will hear no more about it, especially not here in front of my men." He nodded to the soldiers, who were still sitting in rigid rows on the backs of their zahhaks. I didn't know how much they could hear of our conversation, but however much they heard was almost certainly too much. My effeminacy was no longer a closely guarded secret in the Nizami court. Everyone knew what I was. But having heard a rumor and seeing me argue with my father while clad in a peshwaz and dupatta were two very different things. If his men lost confidence in him as a leader because of me, the results would be disastrous for both of us. That was why he was leaving Sikander here. Because I was too much of a disgrace for any soldier to obey.

"For once in your life, just do as you're told, Razia," my father growled before I could reply.

I understood the points he was making, but I couldn't give in to them, not if I wanted to have a chance here. "I am the subahdar of Zindh, Father. If you insist on leaving Sikander here, then I must insist on his oath to follow *my* orders, not the other way around."

"He will command the troops, but he will obey you in everything," my father assured me. It surprised me that he gave in so easily. He nodded to Sikander. "Won't you?"

"I will, your majesty," Sikander said. He turned and bowed to me in the perfunctory way he always had back in Nizam, the gesture one of necessity rather than respect. "I swear that I will obey your orders and that I will protect you with my life, as I always have."

I didn't know what to say to that. Part of me wanted to tell him that he could take that oath and cram it in a very particular place, but another part of me remembered the way he had chased the monsters from my bedchamber, the way he had taught me to feed Sultana after she'd hatched, and it wanted nothing more than for me to forgive him, for things to go back to the way they'd been all those years ago, before anyone had realized what a disgusting creature I was.

But maybe none of it mattered. If I wanted to survive, I couldn't afford to turn down good zahhak riders. I couldn't afford to turn away good military commanders. And Sikander was both of those things. More than that, I'd never known him to lie, or to take a false oath. Whatever else I could say about him, he was honest and loyal to a fault. Sometimes that meant beating a child because his sovereign ordered it. But here it meant that he really would obey me, that he really would protect my life with his own, because he'd said he would. And if I was going to take command of a province in the midst of an open rebellion, with war looming on the horizon, I would need a man whose word I could trust, whose loyalty was unquestioned. I had one already in Arjun. And while Sikander and Arjun were as different from each other as night from day, they were alike in that one regard. They were honest and loyal to a fault.

"You're sure you won't need him against Virajendra, Father?" I asked, half hoping I might still be rid of him, even if I could see the benefits he might bring.

My father shrugged. "I have plenty of good generals. His service will mean more here."

I saw then the reason for my father's irritation with me. I may have seen Sikander as a tyrant and a thug, my father's chief torturer where I was concerned, but from my father's perspective, he was gifting me with his best friend and his most trusted soldier. He was trying, in his own way, to protect me. He may have couched that in politics and military strategy, but as he'd pointed out, he had plenty of good generals. He only had one who could be trusted not to murder me and take Zindh for himself.

"Thank you." I'd never imagined I'd say those two words to my father, but if I didn't show him that I acknowledged what he was doing, that I understood him, then we truly would never have anything between us but hate. One of us had to take the first step toward reconciliation, and I knew that it wasn't going to be him. Although, maybe that's what Zindh was to him. Maybe his idea of reconciliation was leaving me alone in a ruined province to sink or swim on my own merits. When I looked at it from that perspective, I saw that it was all I'd ever really wanted from him anyway—the chance to prove myself in his eyes.

My father cleared his throat to avoid saying "you're welcome." He gave me the same gruff nod he'd always used when confronted with the risk of accidentally showing some small sign of affection for me. "Well, Virajendra isn't going to wait for me to get my men in position before they launch their attacks."

He started to step toward his waiting men, but I reached out and took his hand to stop him. The feeling of my soft palm against his rough knuckles startled him. He stared down at me, his expression hovering somewhere between confusion and disgust, but I looked him squarely in the eyes and said, "I'm not going to fail. Zindh will hold. You'll see."

"I suppose I will," he agreed, but he didn't sound convinced. He jerked his hand free of mine and walked swiftly to the stables, where one of my five hundred guardsmen was holding Malikah by her reins. The old thunder zahhak looked just like I remembered her, just like she had on all those flights so many years ago. Her tail pumped excitedly at my father's approach, and she pressed her snout to his cheek in greeting. He stroked her scales with a fondness he hadn't shown me since that horrible day ten years before, and then he swung into the saddle, strapping himself in before trotting Malikah out into the midst of his men.

I watched as the sixteen thunder zahhaks formed up in two neat ranks behind Malikah, as she raced forward, running along the limestone path that led to the edge of Shikarpur's sheerest cliff. One by one, the zahhaks flung themselves over the edge, beating back the air with their wings, dust swirling around the tips of their primary feathers. I stood there, straining my eyes to watch the dark blue animals soaring in the gathering twilight, until there was nothing to see but empty sky.

He hadn't said good-bye, but then I hadn't really expected him to. At least the last words that had passed between us hadn't been shouted in anger. I didn't know if that was a good sign, or if I was just stupidly clinging to the fragments of a relationship that no longer existed, but I couldn't stop myself from hoping. No one wants to be despised by her parents, and no child wants to despise her father.

CHAPTER 4

"She's really mine?" Sakshi asked, stroking the thunder zahhak's scales with tears in her eyes.

I nodded, my heart swelling with pride. My father had left us with the four thunder zahhaks I'd stolen from Javed Khorasani. With Sikander's mount, and Arjun's and Arvind's fire zahhaks, that gave me seven in total, a formidable enough force, even if I lacked the soldiers to exploit any victories they might bring me. Lakshmi had already kept one of those four animals for herself, and now Sakshi was well trained enough to claim a second.

"I thought you would like this one best," I said, "because her name is Ragini."

"Ragini?" Sakshi gasped, delighted by the name, as I'd known she would be. My sister was a brilliant sitar player, and raginis were the melodic moods she drew upon to color her performances. Whoever this zahhak's first master had been, he must have had an interest in music.

The zahhak responded to her name, but she was still eyeing Sakshi warily. In truth, the bond between zahhak and rider was always forged from the moment of the animal's hatching. If a rider died before his zahhak, she could be made to serve another, but never as completely as she had the one who had raised her. I wished I could have given Sakshi a zahhak egg, as I had been given, so that she might have the joy of raising her own mount, of training it, of bonding to it properly, but eggs were difficult to come by, and it took years for a zahhak to grow big enough to ride. I needed riders now, so we would have to make do.

"For the first few weeks, I don't want you to come see Ragini in the stables unless Sultana or Padmini is there too," I warned.

My thunder zahhak heard her name and pressed her face close against mine in response. I reached up and gave her a fond pat along the ridge of golden scales that traced the edge of her sapphire neck, which could flare into a hood like a cobra's. Though Sultana was nuzzling me gently, her emerald eyes were fixed on Ragini, the less dominant zahhak held under control by threat of death at Sultana's teeth and claws. Otherwise, she might well have eaten us all.

"Will she ever care for me?" Sakshi asked, the uncertainty in her voice making my heart ache for her. She deserved a zahhak who loved her the way mine loved me.

"Yes, eventually," I said, and it wasn't even a lie. "It will take a long time, but she will grow accustomed to following your commands, to serving you. She will trust you eventually. It will never be like a zahhak you raised yourself, but you won't always have to worry about her eating you."

"Well, that's something anyway," Sakshi allowed, her lips twisting into a smile as she went back to gazing up at Ragini's big green eyes. I didn't know what my sister imagined that she saw in them, but I knew from long experience that the zahhak's expression was one of tolerance rather than affection.

"And I'll get to fly with you in battle if it comes to it?"

I glanced back at her, surprised to hear the determination in Sakshi's voice, to see the seriousness etched across her face in the hard line of her mouth and the little wrinkles between her eyebrows.

"I'm not staying behind again, Razia," she declared. "I'm not going to wait in the palace, not knowing if you and Lakshmi are ever coming back to me. If we have to fight, we do it together or we don't do it at all. Promise me that."

"I promise," I told her, and I sealed it with a tight embrace. "It'll be just like we always dreamed it would be when we were little."

If I closed my eyes, I could see it, the pair of us staring up at the night sky as we lay on the rooftop of our dera, our little hijra household. The nightmares had been so frequent then that I was often afraid to sleep, but Sakshi had always held my hand and made me tell her stories about flying zahhaks through the skies of Nizam until I got so tired I drifted off in peace. I couldn't have asked for a better elder sister.

I let her go, somewhat reluctantly, but I didn't have a choice. There was too much work to be done. "You can stay here and get to know Ragini if you like. Sultana and Padmini will protect you."

"You're not getting back to work already, are you?" Sakshi asked, her brow creasing with concern.

"This palace isn't going to repair itself, this household isn't going to organize itself, and I still don't know precisely what I'm dealing with when it comes to the local emirs, and the people here in Shikarpur," I said with a sigh. "I don't know how much more time Ali Talpur is going to give me before he strikes, but we've already been here three days. I'm sure he's heard of my arrival by now, and he must have started preparations to attack."

"Your highness, are you in here?" an unfamiliar woman's voice called from outside the stables. No, not an unfamiliar woman's voice—a familiar eunuch's voice.

"Shiv!" I exclaimed, thrilled that he'd finally arrived. I rushed out to greet him. Though he was covered with the dust of the desert, he still looked like an elegant young lady in men's clothing. He'd been cut young enough that he might have passed for one of us if he'd had any desire to do so, but he'd never once suggested that he had. I embraced him all the same, because even if he wasn't a hijra, he was family of a sort. "I'm so glad you made it safely!"

"As am I, your highness," Shiv replied, not hugging me back, but bowing awkwardly instead, as if reminding me that he was a servant and not a sibling. "We've brought the furniture, of course, and the servants, and all of your clothes, as well as cooks and implements for the kitchens."

"Thank the heavens!" Sakshi sighed, because she'd been doing the cooking these last three days and she'd had nothing but camping supplies to work with. "Point me in their direction, Shiv, and I'll get the kitchens up and running. Everyone here could do with a real meal."

"They're waiting in the second courtyard, my lady," Shiv told her, gesturing in that direction.

"See you soon, little sister." Sakshi gave me a quick hug, and then skipped off to do her duty, her lehenga's crimson silk skirts flouncing about her ankles as she went.

"Did you bring workmen?" I asked Shiv.

"I did, your highness," he replied, though he was eyeing the stables dubiously, along with the scorch marks on the paving stones and the damage to the other buildings from my attack weeks earlier. "Though perhaps not as many as I should have."

"Anything is better than what we have now," I assured him, because my father had left me with soldiers, munitions, and money, but little else.

"Do you have any specific areas where you would like the workmen to begin, your highness?" Shiv asked me.

"The stables must be our first priority," I said, because without them it would be hard to keep the zahhaks safe and happy. "Once that's finished, I think I'd like the pools and fountains in the inner courtyard repaired. I don't know why they're not working, but they're an eyesore. And it wouldn't hurt to do something about the plants. I don't suppose you brought a palace gardener?"

He shook his head. "No, your highness, but one can be hired from the locals. It would be better that way, as the climate here is somewhat different from Bikampur, and I'm sure the plants are as well."

That seemed like sound reasoning to me. "Well, I'm sure you'll do everything you can, but as a personal favor, if you could get Lakshmi's bed set up first, I'd appreciate it. I think if she has to spend one more night on a soldier's cot with Sakshi and me, she's going to launch a rebellion."

"And I would be quick to join her," Arjun declared, striding across the courtyard to join us.

I rolled my eyes at that, though I couldn't deny that I too was a little sick and tired of the lack of privacy. One glance at Arjun's smoldering expression was enough to make me bite my lip with anticipation. Tonight. Finally. It had been nearly a week.

Arjun bowed to me like a courtier. "Is there anything I can do, your highness?"

"Oh, I have a great many things in mind," I allowed, drawing a smile from his lips. "But for now, I think it's best we focus on getting the servitors settled."

"Leave that to me, your highness," Shiv said. "I will make certain everyone knows his or her duty, that the servants' quarters are neatly arranged, and that all of your belongings are in their proper places before nightfall."

"You're a treasure," I said, embracing him again.

His deep brown cheeks darkened still further as blood rushed to them. "I'll see to it at once." He bowed to me, and to Arjun, and then hurried off to do his duty.

Arjun wasted no time in pulling me close to him, one hand snaring the curve of my hip, the other brushing my cheek. "Seems that we're alone at long last."

"The palace will be swarming with servitors any moment now," I warned him, though I didn't pull away for propriety's sake.

"We could go in the zahhak stables," he suggested, his lopsided grin telling me how much he would enjoy the whispers that would follow us if we were caught there rolling in the straw. "The servants wouldn't dare set foot in there for fear of being eaten."

"The workmen will start their repair work today," I reminded him, but I didn't resist as he tugged me closer to the stable doorway.

"They'll be too busy gathering materials to look inside," he replied, his face hovering so close to mine that our lips were already nearly touching.

"And what about Sultana? She might get confused and think you're hurting me," I teased.

He reached forward to tuck a loose tendril of black hair back behind my ear. "No, she knows me better than that."

I opened my mouth to agree, but at just that moment there was a crack like thunder. Both our heads swiveled to the stables, worried that one of the zahhaks had decided to try to break free, but then there was a second pop and a third, and I realized it wasn't thunder, but musket fire.

"There!" Arjun exclaimed, nodding toward the huge arched entryway that led to the main gate of the palace and the road beyond.

I rushed with him in that direction, my mind struggling to come up with some explanation for why my soldiers would be shooting. "Is someone attacking the household caravan?" I wondered, as I couldn't imagine what else it might have been.

"Could be bandits," Arjun allowed, though his tone told me that he didn't think it likely, and neither did I. The road that led from the palace spiraled down a steep hill before entering the city of Shikarpur itself. For bandits to have reached us, they'd have had to pass through the city first. Why would the citizens let them pass? Why would the bandits attack a fortress instead of the outlying homes and shops, which would be much easier marks?

"You think it's rebels . . ." I muttered, my mind summoning the likely answer to my own questions.

Arjun shrugged, I think because he didn't want to worry me by saying it out loud, but I was plenty worried enough. His hand fell to the hilt of his khanda, the straight double-edged sword that had claimed more than one life in the short time I'd known him. My own hand fell to the handles of my katars, thrust through the sash around my waist. They too had claimed a life, though I wasn't in any hurry to do it again. Not that they would do me much good against men armed with muskets if Jam Ali Talpur's army of rebels really had arrived at my doorstep.

We ran into the palace's outer courtyard, where a huge tumult was taking place. Camels were straining against their lead ropes, their backs burdened by heavy pieces of furniture or bundles of fine cloth. Horses pranced alongside them, as the Bikampuri soldiers Arjun had sent with the caravan struggled to keep their mounts under control. Their heads were twisted in the direction of the fortress's parapets, where a haze of white smoke hung over the heads of the Nizami soldiers who were rushing to reload their toradars.

"Arjun, get your men together and join me on the parapets!" I shouted to be heard above the clatter of horseshoes against the courtyard's paving stones. If it was a rebel attack, we'd need all the muskets we could get.

"Right," he agreed, rushing off to follow my orders without a second's hesitation. So many other men would have had their pride piqued from being bossed around by a hijra, but Arjun was different. While he dealt with the men of Bikampur, I raced toward the gatehouse that protected the fort's main entrance.

A sound that was so deep and so loud that it struck me like a physical force roared out from the gatehouse as a cannon belched fire and smoke. What were we dealing with if we were having to shoot our cannons at it? A whole army? My heart raced as I took the stairs to the top of the gatehouse two at a time to find out what in the world was happening.

"Hold that volley until they show themselves again!" Sikander was shouting, his form partly obscured by the white fog of gun smoke hanging thick in the air.

I rushed to his side, near the edge of the battlements, where the wind was blowing the smoke clear, giving me a view of the dirt road that led back to the city far below us. The whole hillside seemed clear of any enemy soldiers, or any people at all for that matter. I saw nothing but green shrubs and yellow sandstone boulders. Whatever was attacking us, it definitely wasn't an army.

"What are the men shooting at?" I demanded.

"Zindhi soldiers, your highness," he replied, and he pointed across the river, where a whole army had appeared on the plain seemingly out of nowhere. There were thousands of them, all soldiers mounted on horseback, ready for battle. More had already crossed the river on boats, and were moving through the town.

A guard shouted, "Your highness, zahhaks!" and my mouth went dry. Sixteen thunder zahhaks were flying straight at the palace, and I knew they weren't my father's.

CHAPTER 5

"We meet them in the air!" I exclaimed, racing for the stables with Arjun and Sikander hot on my heels. I got Sultana saddled in record time, fear surging through me as I feared we'd never get up in time to save ourselves. I strapped myself into the saddle, lowered my goggles over my eyes, snapped the reins, and she took off at a run for the cliff at the garden's far end. I was followed closely by Arjun, Arvind, and Sikander on their own animals. That gave us six if I counted my patrol circling the city. We'd still be outnumbered, and our adversaries would have the altitude advantage, but it was all we could do.

Sultana leapt into the air, and I urged her into a tight, climbing turn, her wings beating for all they were worth. Sikander kept pace with me, but the fire zahhaks were slower, and Arjun and Arvind couldn't keep up. But we all climbed as quickly as we could toward our thunder zahhaks, who had spotted the danger and were maneuvering against their sixteen adversaries.

We weren't going to be able to reach our enemies' altitude before they passed overhead. I bit my lip. That wasn't good. They could just roll over on top of us, having the advantage of speed and maneuverability. They'd be able to pound us with their breath weapons, and it would be hard for us to muster any reply. It was only the two thunder zahhaks I'd kept in the air that had any chance at all of saving us. If they could break up the enemy formation, then we might be able to make a fight of it.

"What the devil are those things?" Arjun demanded, his voice loud enough to carry across the dozen or so yards between us.

I squinted to get a better look at our opponents, and I immediately felt my stomach twist. For a long moment, I was convinced that we were facing sixteen thunder zahhaks. They were the right size to be thunder zahhaks; their wings were swept back and pointed, their tails long and straight. But as I drew nearer, I saw the little details that I'd missed before. Their scales were all wrong for thunder zahhaks—black on their heads and necks, white on their bellies. Their wings had turquoise underparts rather than gold, and upper feathers that were indigo, black, and white in a blocky pattern. Their tails were colored the same way, and as they wheeled above us, I saw that they were forked like a kite's. Like thunder zahhaks, they had snouts rather than beaks, but theirs were longer and skinnier.

Even though I'd never seen them before in my life, there was something oddly familiar about them. It took me a moment to recall the strange animals I'd seen inlaid in my white marble throne back in the palace.

"River zahhaks!" I exclaimed. "They don't have breath weapons! Don't attack them!"

"Don't attack?" Sikander asked, twisting his head over his shoulder to show me how insane he thought that order was.

I pulled up alongside him. "They can't hurt us. They can't have come to fight us; it must be a parley."

He shrugged, seeing the logic in that. We continued climbing, and the river zahhaks did a funny thing. They started a spiraling dive. They were magnificent fliers. God, with those forked tails, they could change direction in a heartbeat, and their wings were longer and pointier than an acid zahhak's, but broader and less sickle shaped than a thunder zahhak's, making them swift in the dive, but quick to accelerate, and they were tremendous gliders, floating on the wind like they weighed nothing at all.

"They're so graceful . . ." I gasped, watching as their riders skillfully brought them lower and lower in a cyclone of scales and feathers.

"They are," Arjun agreed, and he was grinning too. "I can see what the Zindhi like about them."

"They haven't got breath," said Sikander, as if that had anything to do with the way they flew.

"They're heading for the palace," Arvind observed. By now, we'd reached our thunder zahhaks, and had joined with them, but the river zahhaks were ignoring us, slowly spiraling down toward the palace's inner courtyard. "What do you suppose they want?"

"Let's find out," I said.

I rolled into a steep dive, Sultana's wings tearing the sky asunder with a sound like a silk cloth being ripped in half. I easily outdistanced the river zahhaks, which were circling lazily toward the courtyard, and pulled Sultana up short of the pavilion. She fluttered to the ground, and I climbed down from her saddle before leading the way back to my throne.

All around me, my retainers landed and took their places once more—all except the two thunder zahhaks who were still orbiting high overhead on their patrol. Still, we made for quite the fearsome sight, I thought—a princess on her throne, surrounded by four zahhaks.

The river zahhaks floated like leaves on the wind, coming to rest lightly on their wing claws and slender, mango-colored hind limbs. They were taller than they should have been for their bulk, like every part of them had been stretched out. I doubted if any of them weighed as much as Sultana or Sikander's zahhak, Parisa, but they were all taller, with longer wings and longer necks and bodies to match. Our thunder zahhaks seemed squat and compact when set beside the willowy Zindhi animals.

The river zahhaks formed up into neat ranks of two and began marching across the courtyard like they were on parade. It was a pretty little display, and I had to smile at the sangfroid of their prince. He knew how to make an entrance, and he didn't seem the least bit frightened by the zahhaks waiting for him, or the guards positioned on the walls and around the courtyard, their toradars loaded, curls of smoke rising up from their lit match cords.

It was when they got about halfway across the courtyard that I realized the zahhaks weren't being ridden by princes, or even ordinary men, but by women. My eyes widened as I took in the graceful women sitting proudly in their saddles with all the competence of veteran riders.

I'd never seen female zahhak riders before, not unless I counted Sakshi and Lakshmi or looking at myself in the mirror. Was that what I looked like? They had their goggles pushed up onto their foreheads, the strap helping to hold their dupattas onto their heads. The dupattas were enormous pieces of cloth, more like saris than the shawls I was familiar with. And the silk was patterned all over with block-printed images of swirling indigo river zahhaks and bright turquoise lotus blossoms with saffron centers.

The women dismounted from their zahhaks, and I noted that they wore full skirts like a lehenga's, beaded and embroidered, the decoration following the lines of more block printing in indigo, turquoise, and saffron, with splashes of white and black so the patterns would really stand out. They didn't wear short blouses like Registani women, but rather long ones that fell to their knees, with high slits going up their sides. These too were block printed and covered in delicate embroidery and fine beadwork. Each woman had a mango-colored sash cinched tightly around her waist, into which was tucked a bhuj, a sort of stout cleaver-like dagger hafted onto a two-foot-long steel shaft. I noted that they had scabbards on their saddles, holding enormous muskets with swooping, fish-shaped buttstocks. I wondered if they used them to try to shoot other zahhaks in the air. It seemed an impossible feat, but I supposed I'd have tried anything if Sultana hadn't possessed her lightning.

The women left their zahhaks under the control of one of their number, the other fifteen marching toward the pavilion. Now one of them took the lead, and the others fell in step behind her. Was she their leader, then? She was a tall woman, with fiery streaks of copper in her dark hair, but I was most struck by her eyes. They were hazel, the olive color halfway between the brown so common to Daryastan and the emerald green we Nizamis had brought with us from our ancestral home on the northern steppes. I'd never seen anyone in Daryastan with eyes that even verged on green outside of my own family, so I wondered where she came from, and who her ancestors were.

The woman approached the throne with no signs of trepidation and bowed properly, joined in the movement by all of her followers. She raised her hand to her forehead in salute and said, "Good morning, your highness. I hope you'll forgive us for startling you, but I didn't know where else to go."

I frowned at those words, and suddenly I saw through the fine clothes and the jewels. The young woman standing before me had dark circles under her eyes that makeup couldn't hide. The hem of her long dupatta was frayed in places, and there was something about her posture that conveyed a sense of extreme exhaustion. It was a fatigue I saw echoed on the faces of her retainers.

"What's happened?" I asked. "Are you not with Ali Talpur and his army?"

The woman sucked in a sharp breath at the mention of Ali Talpur's name, and I could have sworn she was fighting back tears, though none were visible at the corners of her hazel eyes. "Ali Talpur is . . . was . . . my brother."

"Was?" I whispered, my stomach roiling. Ali Talpur was dead? How had that happened? Who had killed him? Was it the Safavians? Had they attacked already?

"Kadiro was attacked three days ago, your highness," she continued. "The city was captured and my brother was killed. I escaped with as many of our men and zahhaks as I could and fled north."

"She's lying, your highness," Sikander growled, shocking me almost as much as the poor woman standing before my throne.

"Sikander!" I hissed, horrified that he would say something like that when it was plainly obvious from the look on the woman's face that she was telling the truth.

"Ali Talpur had no sisters, only a brother, your highness," Sikander reminded me.

My heart sank. He was right. I should have seen it at once, but I'd been so wrapped up in the woman's story that I'd missed it. I was annoyed with myself for being duped, but she'd seemed so truthful. Even now, she looked offended more than frightened. Whoever she was, she was quite the actress.

"I'm not lying!" she exclaimed.

I held up a hand to forestall any more of this nonsense. "Sikander is right. Ali Talpur had no sister."

"And Sultan Humayun had no daughter!" the woman retorted.

A surge of anger welled up inside me on hearing that. I'd been mocked dozens of times for being a hijra before, but I'd never gotten used to it, and I'd be damned if I let someone do it in my own palace. "If you think that mocking me for the circumstances of my birth is a good way to live a long life in my province, you are sadly mistaken." I reached out and stroked Sultana's head scales to emphasize exactly what her fate would be if she said one more word about it.

The woman bristled at the obvious threat. "You know, your nayak, Geeta Barupal, assured me at the last jamaat that you were a lovely, polite little thing, not at all haughty in spite of the circumstances of your birth. I'm sorry to see that she was mistaken."

I jerked my hand back from Sultana like I'd been touching a hot stove. My heart fluttered in my chest. I'd missed it. She hadn't been insulting me, she'd been comparing her circumstances to mine, claiming to be a hijra herself. And the proof of it was in her words. There was no way she could have known our nayak's name if she wasn't one of us. But I could scarcely bring myself to believe it. Could she really be a hijra like me, and a royal too? Lakshmi was, but my little sister was so young, she didn't understand the dangers and the responsibilities like I did. This woman, if she really was a hijra, shared so much with me. I longed to ask her for every detail of her life, to understand if she had been through the same things I had.

"I'm sorry," I said, much to Sikander's shock, "I think maybe we've misunderstood each other. I hope you'll forgive me, and let us start again. I am Razia Khanum, princess of Nizam and subahdar of Zindh. To whom do I have the pleasure of speaking?"

"Hina Talpur, daughter of the late Jam Rustam Talpur, and sister of the late Jam Ali Talpur." Her voice cracked on those last words, and one of her retainers stepped forward, placing her arms around her shoulders to comfort her. "Forgive me, but I loved my brother very much."

"You have nothing to apologize for, Hina," I told her, wanting very much to comfort her myself, though I knew that there was little I could do to remove the hurt of a loss like the one she was describing, and I wasn't sure she'd want comfort from a stranger, a potential enemy, and someone who had threatened her like a fool. "When you're ready, I think I should hear more about what happened in Kadiro, but for now, know that you are safe here in my dera." I gestured to the palace around us.

The little jest wrested a slight smile from Hina's lips. "Thank you for your hospitality, your highness. When my brother was killed, I . . ."

I held up a hand to stop her, as she was clearly having a hard time keeping the tears at bay. "There will be time for that later. Please, sit with me." I stood up from the throne and descended the dais, instead gesturing to the few cushions we had arranged on the floor for courtiers. I looked to Shiv, who was standing just outside the pavilion, and said, "Please have refreshments brought for Lady Talpur and her entourage."

"At once, your highness," Shiv agreed, rushing off to see it done.

Hina sank gratefully onto one of the cushions, and her retainers did too. They all looked exhausted, though they struggled to keep alert enough to protect their leader if it came to it.

I gestured to them. "Are they hijras too?"

"They are, your highness," Hina affirmed. "They're my celas. I was, until recently, the nayak of Kadiro."

"They're really hijras like us?" Lakshmi asked, having watched all of this from her place with Sakshi on the dais beside the throne.

"Just like us," I told her, though I could scarcely believe it myself. Ali Talpur's sister was a hijra in command of her own army? God, it was like a sign from the heavens themselves.

Lakshmi rushed over to sit with us, and Sakshi was nearly as quick. We all sat within arm's reach of one another, us staring at our Zindhi counterparts wide-eyed, and them favoring us with much the same expressions. Never in my wildest dreams had I ever imagined that I'd meet other hijras who rode zahhaks, who did anything but sell themselves to men.

"Your highness . . ." Sikander was staring at my behavior with slack-jawed bewilderment, and he wasn't the only one. Arjun had his hand on the hilt of his khanda like he was expecting me to be murdered at any moment.

"They're hijras," I said, like that explained everything, and when it didn't, I sighed. "When you're a hijra, you're driven from your home as a child. You flee everything you've ever known or loved, and you find yourself alone in all the world."

Hina sucked in a sharp breath, because my words had inadvertently described her present circumstances so perfectly that it must have been like a dagger to her heart.

"And it's not until you find one of your own kind that you ever find peace or safety," I finished, my voice softening, my eyes looking right at Hina's, hoping she could see the promise of safety in them. All of us knew what it was like to have to flee our homes, to come to a new city, to be at the mercy of a new guru. I wanted her to know that I understood.

"Hina and her celas are fellow hijras," I told Sikander and Arjun. "They're family."

"They're strangers and foreigners, and rebels, your highness," Sikander said, his voice slow and clear like he thought I was crazy.

"They're my sisters. We share a life that no one else comprehends, and our families are connected to one another by bonds of loyalty and rivalry as long-standing as any political bonds held by your kind." I gestured dismissively at the men around me. "The deras of Bikampur and Kadiro have always shared good relations."

I glanced to Hina. "But how is it that no one ever told me you existed, let alone that you were a zahhak rider? How are you a zahhak rider? Where do you find the money to feed them? And why are you so young? Shouldn't a nayak be our grandmothers' age?"

Hina's smile was a sad one. "Well, I was only the nayak of Kadiro for a few short weeks—after Javed Khorasani's death, and before Kadiro's fall. Before that, Ali and I lived together as mercenaries, making our living as scouts and messengers on the backs of our zahhaks."

The mention of Kadiro's fall reminded me that I still hadn't asked how it had happened. "About Kadiro . . ." I began.

"We were invaded," she whispered, her fists clutching the fine fabric of her skirt in impotent rage. "We were consolidating our hold on the city when the Mahisagaris attacked, led by their prince, Karim Shah."

"Karim attacked you?" I gasped.

"No!" Lakshmi exclaimed, her horror written all over her face. "No, Akka, Prince Karim wouldn't do that!"

I gritted my teeth in fury as the realizations washed over me. Karim had known that I would be taking over Zindh as its subahdar. He'd known that Javed Khorasani's death would have left the province in shambles. He'd known that my hold would be tenuous. And he'd decided to strike at the worst possible moment, to claim my lands for his own. I felt so betrayed, and I felt like a fool for being surprised by it. Had I really believed that Karim Shah had changed? That he'd suddenly become my ally?

"That bastard is going to pay for this . . ." Arjun growled. "Does he really think we'll just sit idly by and let him get away with it?"

"But, Akka, why would Prince Karim attack us? He's our friend," Lakshmi said.

Sakshi enfolded her in a tight hug, pulling her head down onto her shoulder. "Come on. Let's go play in the garden and leave Razia to figure this out."

"No!" Lakshmi exclaimed, wriggling free of Sakshi's embrace. "I don't want to play in the ugly garden! I'm not a baby!" She turned to me. "Akka, she must be lying. Prince Karim wouldn't do that!"

I didn't know how to tell my little sister that the prince she idolized because he was a dashing zahhak rider who was kind to her was also my rapist and a ruthless pirate. But I was too stunned by the news to come up with a suitable lie. So I just said, "Lakshmi, we'll talk about this when I know more. For now, I need to speak with Hina. So go with Sakshi and practice your music lessons."

"But Akka—" she protested, but I cut her off.

"Now," I said, my tone brooking no disagreement.

She flinched a little from the harshness of it, and that made my heart hurt. I'd never been the stern disciplinarian with her, never wanted to be, but my mind was reeling, my emotions were going in ten different directions at once, and I needed a second to think.

"Come on." Sakshi pulled Lakshmi to her feet and led her away.

It was only once they were gone that I looked back to Hina, who had been watching all of that anxiously. Did she know of my connection to Karim? She must. It wasn't any great secret that I had helped him beat the Firangi fleet, that he had helped me defeat Javed Khorasani.

"I'm sorry for that," I told Hina. "My little sister doesn't know Karim the way I do."

"So he wasn't lying, then?" Hina asked.

"Who wasn't lying?" I asked.

"My brother knew Karim Shah well when we were in hiding from Javed Khorasani," she said. "We even fought for him occasionally. As I'm sure you know, he was never shy about boasting of his sexual conquests, particularly with a little wine in him . . ."

My cheeks reddened and I sucked in a breath against the memories her words brought to the forefront of my mind—memories of strong hands pinning me to a cold marble floor, of screaming into the darkness. I forced them back into the vault where I kept them, slamming that mental door shut as tightly as I could.

"I don't know what he told you," I whispered, my voice colder than ice, "but I will never forget, nor forgive, what Karim Shah did to me when I was a child of eleven years."

"Forgive me for bringing up such painful memories, your highness," Hina said, reaching forward and placing her hand over mine. She noted, as I did, the way both Sikander and Arjun drew their swords halfway out of their scabbards before they realized that she was trying to comfort me. "But that story is one of the reasons why I came to you."

"One of the reasons?" I asked. "The other reason being the life we both share?"

"And your reputation being the third," she added.

"My reputation?" As a boy, I'd had a reputation of being a pathetic prince. I wondered what my reputation was now. Harlot? Deviant? I'd certainly heard those words hurled my way more than once.

"Everyone says you're brilliant, and wise beyond your years, and kind," Hina told me, her olive eyes looking earnestly into mine.

"And what arrangement would you like to make?" I asked her, though I thought I had a pretty good idea.

"If you will swear to punish Karim for killing my brother and to throw the Mahisagaris out of Kadiro, I will recognize you as Zindh's rightful subahdar," Hina replied.

"Why not simply make an alliance with Karim?" Sikander asked. "With his men, we won't need the Zindhis, your highness."

"I can think of half a dozen reasons," I replied, my tone as measured as I could make it, but I was sure that everyone could hear the undercurrent of hate in it. "In the first place, Karim attacked *my* province, which cannot be permitted to stand. Secondly, he is a ruthless, cruel man with whom I would never ally myself except in the direst of circumstances. Thirdly, the Mahisagaris will have infuriated the Zindhi people by murdering their rightful prince, and so Karim has ensured unrest in this province until he is driven from it. Need I continue?"

"Your highness, we don't even know if this . . . girl . . . is telling the truth," Sikander said with a scowl.

"What reason has she for lying?" I demanded.

"Razia's right," said Arjun. "Hina has no reason to lie, and if she's telling the truth, then not only has she done us a great service, but she has brought us the army we need at exactly the moment we need it."

"Which is what worries me," Sikander answered. "When things seem too good to be true, Prince Arjun, they usually are."

"Usually," Arjun and I said in unison, each gazing into the other's eyes. Our cheeks blazed, as I don't think either of us had intended on sounding like such lovesick children.

"Forgive me, your highness, but there is nothing good about my arrival here," Hina said.

I frowned. "What do you mean?"

"My brother was a very kind, very thoughtful man." She sounded like she was choking back tears as she spoke. "He would have made peace with you. We were planning to meet with you, to discuss a way forward, when Karim attacked. That's why we weren't prepared. We didn't think there would really be war between us."

I realized just then how devastating Ali Talpur's loss really was. Now, not only did I not have the prospect of a quick peace with a reasonable man, I had the man I despised most in all the world holding Zindh's most important port city, with an army and a navy that I'd never be able to match. If I was going to have a prayer of preventing him from conquering the whole province, I was going to have to win over the people of Zindh. Karim had given me some help there. He had made himself the evil outsider I needed, and he had killed Jam Ali, giving me the chance to present myself as a protector of Zindh and an avenger of its royal family. Even so, it was going to be an uphill battle.

"Well, I can't promise you that driving Karim from Kadiro will be quick or easy, Hina," I told her, "but I give you my word that if you are willing to serve me, then I will protect you and do everything in my power to punish Karim for the crimes he has committed against you and against Zindh. Is this acceptable?"

"It is, your highness," Hina replied.

"Then have messengers sent to the people of Shikarpur and your men across the Zindhu that we have reached an agreement. Once that is done, I will host the emirs here in the palace, and we will determine a path forward together."

Hina's full lips stretched into the barest trace of a smile. "Thank you, your highness. You really are the woman everyone says you are."

A year ago, I'd have been offended by those words, because I never would have been able to imagine a reputation for myself beyond being a disgrace and a courtesan, but today they filled me with pride. Saving Zindh from Karim wasn't going to be easy, but with Hina's army and the emirs of Zindh on my side, my prospects were already looking better than they had that morning.

CHAPTER 6

You look pretty, Akka!" Lakshmi exclaimed as one of Hina's celas, a twelve-year-old girl named Nuri, draped a block-printed dupatta over my head and shoulders. It had taken me a few minutes to calm her down and explain to her that we would know more about the situation with Karim later, and, like most eleven-year-olds, she'd been quick to put such serious thoughts from her mind. Besides, the sight of Nuri had encouraged her, as it was rare she got to meet hijras her own age, let alone zahhak-riding ones.

"Her highness looks like Jama Sakina reborn," Nuri agreed, offering Lakshmi a smile that helped to take some of the tension out of my heart. Hina and her celas were so kind, so easy to be around, that it was easy to forget I was going to have to fight a war against Karim and his father for control of my province.

"Who's Jama Sakina?" Lakshmi asked.

"A very famous queen here in Zindh," Hina said, wrapping her arms around Lakshmi's shoulders, though her hazel eyes were fixed on me. "She was a Nizami princess, just like your akka."

"Really?" Lakshmi asked, noting the way I was knitting my brow in skepticism.

"Really," Hina assured her. "She was the daughter of Sultan Jahandar the Great. In those days, Nizami princesses rode thunder zahhaks just like their princes, and she was famous for her skills as an aerial warrior. But Sultan Jahandar needed to make peace with Zindh, because he was fighting wars against Vanga and Virajendra, so he gave his youngest daughter, Sakina, in marriage to Jam Nizamuddin Talpur, the greatest emperor to ever rule Zindh."

"Talpur?" I gasped, recognizing that name at once.

Hina nodded, grinning at my response. She must have known what I was thinking—one of my ancestresses had married one of Ali Talpur's ancestors. I was pursing my lips, thinking back to my history lessons in the palace. Jahandar really was the greatest Nizami sultan. He conquered northern Virajendra and Vanga, adding them as new subahs to the empire. I'd paid particular attention to him because his daughter Razia Sultana, my great-grandmother, had been the only woman ever to rule our empire, and my source of greatest inspiration. Had she really had a sister married off to a Zindhi emperor? This was the first I was hearing of it. But if it was true, then Hina was a distant cousin of mine. Maybe that explained the hint of green I saw in her brown eyes when the light struck them at just the right angle.

But the history was right. Jahandar had been at war with the Zindhi emperor at the same time he was fending off attacks from Vanga and Virajendra. He'd made peace with Zindh, keeping it free and independent until my grandfather's conquest of it in the years before my father was born, and had instead turned his sights on Vanga and the southern plateau.

"And what do your stories say of this Shahzadi Sakina?" I asked Hina, while Nuri put gorgeous river zahhak–inspired bangles on my wrists, their exquisite plumage rendered in sapphire, turquoise, jet, and mother-of-pearl cloisonné.

"Jama Sakina," Hina corrected. "The stories say that everyone expected the daughter of Sultan Jahandar to be arrogant and to support her father's concerns above those of the Zindhi people. They all knew she would be plotting to turn Zindh into nothing more than a Nizami subah, and that she would use any son she produced from her pairing with Nizamuddin to undermine him at every turn."

I grunted at that, not at all flattered by the comparison. "I see."

"Not yet you don't," Hina replied, her eyes flashing with just a hint of mischief. "You see," she continued, as much to Lakshmi as to me, "when Jama Sakina arrived, she came to the people of Zindh dressed in ajrak."

"Ajrak?" Lakshmi asked.

"This." Hina held up the end of her dupatta, showing off the fine indigo block printing. "Ajrak is the cloth of Zindh, made to look like our beloved river zahhaks. It's made nowhere but here, where indigo grows wild on the banks of the Zindhu."

"And Jama Sakina wore it?" Lakshmi asked.

"That's right," Hina told her. "She wore ajrak, and she showed her husband perfect loyalty and faithfulness. And when war came with the Safavians, who thought to attack Zindh while Nizam was busy fighting against Virajendra, Jama Sakina took to the skies on her thunder zahhak and helped save Zindh from disaster. They say she used the lightning from her zahhak, and the zahhaks of her handmaidens, to tear up the earth itself, changing the course of a river, using its waters to flood the Safavian camp, drowning them all in one night."

"Is that really true?" Lakshmi asked, wrinkling her nose like she didn't quite believe it.

"I don't know," Hina admitted, "but that's what the stories say.

And there is a great lake to the north of Kadiro, the largest in all of Daryastan, and we call it Lake Sakina. The stories say that's where she drowned the Safavian army and saved Zindh from invasion."

"And she looked like Akka?" Lakshmi asked, smiling at me with evident pride.

"She was your akka's twice-great-aunt," Hina affirmed. "And, like all Nizami princesses, she had jet-black hair and eyes like emeralds."

"Just like Akka's!" Lakshmi exclaimed.

"Just like hers," Hina agreed, a hint of sadness in her voice.

I understood why at once. She had hazel eyes—the remnants of the emerald green that belonged to the Nizami royal line. If Jama Sakina was my twice-great-aunt, she was likely Hina's own great-grandmother. She probably felt the same way about stories of Jama Sakina that I had when hearing stories of Razia Sultana growing up.

And it explained the clothes I was wearing. They weren't just lavish gifts from a new retainer; they would give me legitimacy in the eyes of the Zindhi people and their emirs. If I looked like Jama Sakina, then they would draw those parallels in their own minds, particularly now with their rightful king dead, and an enemy occupying their country.

"Thank you, Hina," I said.

Hina didn't reply right away. She just smiled and gestured to Nuri, who added one last piece to the costume. It was a magnificent necklace depicting two river zahhaks, each diving from my shoulders, across my collarbones, toward the center of my chest. Their sapphire wings were folded in tight crescents, their long blue topaz tails trailing behind them. Their necks were outstretched, jet scales glistening in the morning sunlight, their mouths wide, revealing diamond-studded fangs. Each was racing the other for the necklace's centerpiece, an enormous fish with emerald scales and diamonds for eyes.

"There, finished," Nuri announced, stepping back and admiring her handiwork. "I think the necklace really suits your eyes." She looked back to Lakshmi. "Doesn't it?"

Lakshmi nodded enthusiastically. "I think so!"

"Thank you, Nuri," I told the girl, giving her an affectionate pat on the cheek before turning back to Hina, who had been studying me carefully, no doubt trying to predict what effect my new clothes might have on the emirs I was meeting today.

"Do you think they'll accept me?" I asked. They'd agreed to abide by Hina's decision, but that wasn't really the same thing as being loyal to me as their ruler.

"I think they will, your highness," she said after a moment's consideration. "They know we can't win this fight on our own." Her face betrayed real sorrow at that admission. "Zindh is a land rich in indigo and cotton, but poor in zahhaks. To our east and west, fire zahhaks occupy the deep deserts of Registan and Khuzdar, but Zindh has nothing except river zahhaks to protect her."

I was struck by the bittersweet tone in her voice, and I realized then that I was wearing cloth covered in swirling block-printed patterns of river zahhaks, their brilliant colors rendered in exquisite detail by a masterful application of ink to silk. I saw then the reason for the tone in her voice, for the look on her face.

"They're beautiful animals, and graceful fliers," I told her.

"But they have no breath," she added, her voice tight, the tendons in her slender neck standing out through her skin.

I tried to put myself in her place, to imagine growing up with a zahhak that was the living symbol of my homeland, to love her and cherish her and learn to fly her, only to discover that she was incapable of battling the zahhaks of other nations, that her very existence rendered all of my training as little more than quaint entertainment. The first half of that picture was easy enough to imagine, but the latter half tied my stomach in knots. If Sultana hadn't had breath, I would still be a concubine left to pray that Arjun never lost his affection for me.

"So you need my zahhaks," I concluded.

"And you need us," she answered.

I nodded, because that was the truth of the matter, but it brought a slight smile to my face. "Does that mean we can be friends?"

She rolled her eyes, but she was grinning. "I'd like that very much, your highness."

"As would I," I said, pleased to have at least one ally in this country. With Hina's celas, and her ten thousand soldiers, I would be free of the threat of Sikander and his guards hurting me, but I knew it wouldn't be enough to drive out the Mahisagaris. For that, I would need the emirs of Zindh to rally around me, and I had to start here in Shikarpur. "I suppose we should get moving. We don't want to keep them waiting."

"No, I don't think we do," Hina agreed.

We stood up and left my bedchamber together, Hina and her celas, and me with my two sisters. By now, Sunil Kalani, the soldier I had met the night before, and Pir Tahir, the sheikh, would be waiting for me to summon them to the diwan-i-khas. Sunil was the local emir, and Pir Tahir the spiritual leader of Shikarpur's community. Without their approval, I would never gain control of my city, let alone my province.

"Do you really have your own zahhak?" I heard Lakshmi asking Nuri as the pair of them walked hand in hand behind us.

Nuri nodded. "Her name is Nalini. She's the prettiest zahhak in the whole world. You can ride her with me if you want."

"Can two people really fly on a river zahhak?" Lakshmi asked.

"They can if one of them is Nuri's size," Hina replied, giving the younger Zindhi girl a playful pat on the head. "They're lighter than thunder zahhaks and acid zahhaks, but they have bigger wings, so they can carry more weight."

The thrilled look on Lakshmi's face tugged at my heartstrings, and Nuri was growing on me too. But then I'd always loved children, especially children like me who were being given the opportunity to grow up as their true selves.

"If you two want to go flying together, or to play in the gardens, there's no reason for you to sit through a boring meeting," I told them, because I'd hated meetings when I was eleven and my father had forced them on me.

"I don't like playing here; this palace is ugly," Lakshmi muttered.

That struck a nerve. I'd dragged her all the way out here to Zindh, to a war zone, and for what? So she could live in an ugly palace with no servants. She'd been so much happier in Bikampur.

I sighed and put my hands on her shoulders. "I know it's not everything we wanted it to be—not yet. But I'm working hard to make it better, all right? Once the workmen are done with the zahhak stables, they'll get to work on the rest of the palace."

"I know, Akka," she said. "I just miss Bikampur sometimes. It was like home."

I hugged her close to me, taking deep breaths to keep the tears from flowing. Home. The word was loaded with so much meaning for girls like us, girls who had been driven from our homes, who had been forced to start over, sometimes more than once. But she was right. The palace in Bikampur had been our home, right up until I'd gone and ruined everything by attracting my father's ire.

"I miss Bikampur too, sweetheart," I whispered. I wanted to tell her that this was going to be our new home, that I was going to build something wonderful here for her, but I knew how hard it was going to be to dislodge Karim and his men from Kadiro, and

I didn't want to build her hopes up only to destroy them. I didn't want to be made a liar. So I kissed her on the top of her head and let her go, turning to Hina, who had been watching all of this, her brow knitted with sympathy.

"Sorry," I said.

"You have nothing to apologize for, your highness," she replied. "My girls and I all miss Kadiro. It's hard to start over."

I felt some of the tension in my chest ease at being so readily understood. I'd forgotten what it was like to be surrounded by others of my kind, other women who knew exactly what it was like to give up their homes and their families to be their true selves, who understood how tenuous all the good things in life could be. If God had brought Hina to me, then maybe he intended for me to win here in Zindh, because she was just the ally I needed.

I took that thought with me into the gardens, where a knot of river zahhaks had gathered together near one of the courtyard's many empty pits. They seemed to be staring into it with disappointment written on their faces. It was the kind of look Sultana gave me when she saw other zahhaks flying but didn't get to go up herself.

"What's going on?" I asked Hina, nodding to the zahhaks.

"All Zindhi palaces have fish ponds and lotus gardens," she replied. "The river zahhaks are usually left free to wander the inner courtyard, dining at their leisure."

"Ah . . ." I murmured, understanding dawning at long last. The empty pits were all reflecting pools, fish ponds, aquatic flower gardens. Once upon a time, this courtyard would have been staggeringly beautiful, filled with the splashing of fish, the bubbling of fountains, and the gentle rushing of water through stone channels. I wondered why the palace's ponds had been left in such poor repair, but only for an instant. The answer presented itself swiftly enough.

"Javed Khorasani let them fall into ruin as an insult to the Zindhi people," I murmured.

"Just so," Hina agreed.

"Well, I'll have them repaired," I promised her.

She flashed me an encouraging smile, though the gesture didn't quite reach her eyes, which were still gazing sadly into the empty pits all around us. "I know you will, your highness."

Arjun and Sikander were waiting for us, just inside the diwan-i-khas. I hurried to them, eager to summon Sunil and Pir Tahir. The sooner I took command of Shikarpur, the sooner I could begin planning for how to deal with Karim.

"You look beautiful," Arjun said, standing as I entered the marble pavilion.

"The spitting image of Jama Sakina," Sikander agreed, giving Hina a meaningful look.

"You've heard of her?" I asked, surprised by that.

"I may be a soldier," Sikander admitted, "but I've studied history like all generals, and I fought a war against Jam Rustam Talpur, who was Jama Sakina's grandson."

"A war," I murmured, remembering for the first time that Hina's father had been killed by my own. I couldn't believe I'd let something like that slip my mind. I supposed we were going to have to talk about it sooner or later.

Arjun tore my mind away from those thoughts with the warmth of his hands on my arms. "Well, I don't know anything about this Jama Sakina, but if she looked anything like you, then she must have been the most beautiful queen in all of Zindhi history."

"She was—until I was born, anyway," Hina answered, flashing us both a lopsided grin as she took her place on one of the cushions beside my marble throne.

Sikander gave a loud snort of disapproval. "If I were in your position, I would not be flaunting my disgrace, *boy*."

Hina fixed the old man with a withering glare, and she wasn't alone. All fifteen of her celas joined in, as well as Sakshi, Lakshmi, and myself. It was Lakshmi who spoke up, before any of the rest of us could. She balled her hands into little fists, stormed over to Sikander, and growled, "We're not boys!"

For the first time in his life, Sikander was totally outnumbered. Back home in Nizam, when he'd said such things about me, there had always been a dozen male courtiers bobbing their heads right along with his inane insults, but here there were nearly twenty hijras fixing him with eyes alive with anger, to say nothing of Arjun and Arvind and even Shiv, who were joining in. There wasn't a face beneath the pavilion's dome that wasn't betraying its disapproval.

"Don't waste your breath on him, little sister," Sakshi advised, snaking an arm across Lakshmi's shoulders, which were still tense with anger. "Men who like to beat helpless girls don't have any shame at all, so there's no sense in reprimanding them."

Sikander narrowed his eyes, like he intended to challenge that description of himself, but then he glanced to me, and there was a moment of hesitation as he recalled all the times he had beaten me. I could almost see him reevaluating each and every moment, one after the other. I didn't know if it brought him to the realization that I had been a helpless girl on each and every occasion in the past we'd shared, but at the very least, he seemed to have enough sense to keep his mouth shut, which was better than I'd hoped for.

"It's all right, Lakshmi," Hina said from her place on the dais. She kept her expression mild, her hands folded daintily in her lap, her eyes slightly downcast, but her tone cut like Arjun's mother on a bad day. "Men like him are natural cowards. They can't help it. They're so frightened of things they don't understand that they try to destroy them."

Sikander's temples bulged as his jaw clamped down hard, his face darkening with anger. For a man who prided himself on his battlefield prowess, the accusation of cowardice couldn't have been more carefully calculated to enrage him. "What need have I for lessons in courage from a man in a skirt?" he demanded.

"You think it doesn't take courage to wear a skirt, Sikander?" I asked him, slipping free of Arjun's grasp and strutting toward him, the silk of my own skirt swishing as I went.

He gave a toss of his head. "I do not, your highness."

"Do you think me a coward?" I pressed, looking into his eyes to divine the answer. He'd certainly called me one often enough, but he knew what I had done to steal back my Sultana, and he knew how I'd performed in the battle that had followed.

"No, your highness," he said, and I knew he wasn't lying for my benefit. "You show remarkable courage when the situation requires it. Few men would have scaled the cliffs of Shikarpur as you did."

"Know this, Sikander," I told him as I took my place on my throne. "Scaling the cliffs of Shikarpur with my bare hands, knowing that a single false move would send me plummeting to my death, took not one-tenth the courage it takes to wear a beautiful lehenga in your presence and my father's."

His eyes widened slightly with understanding, and I drove the lesson home. "Imagine what your father's reaction would have been, had you dressed as I dress, had you spoken of yourself as I speak of myself, had you behaved as I behave, and tell me again whether or not you believe it takes courage to wear a skirt.

"Or better yet," I said before he could respond, because I didn't really want his answer anyway, "remember all the times you beat me for dressing this way, remember all the harsh words and harsher blows I suffered at your hands, and tell me again whether or not you believe it takes courage to wear a skirt."

"What I did, I did for your own good, your highness," Sikander protested.

Hot anger rose up from the pit of my stomach on hearing those words, but my voice was colder than ice when I spoke. "You think so, do you?"

Sikander gritted his teeth, realizing, I thought, how perilously close he was to being executed, but he nodded all the same. "Had I succeeded in making a man out of you, we would not be in this position."

I sighed. "Has it still not occurred to you, after all these years, that it was never something that could be changed? That you can't beat a person's soul out of them?"

His gaze flickered from me to Sakshi, to Lakshmi, to Hina and all her celas, his jaw working in time with the movements of his eyes. "I thought perhaps with more time . . ."

I let him shake his head slowly, let him draw his conclusions from the presence of so many of my kind in one place. All of us had lived through the same hell, run away from our homes, fought to be recognized for who we truly were. Sikander had likely never seen so many of us before. I had been alone in the palace in Nizam, the only one like me, but here I was one of nearly twenty, and there was a strength in that. I wasn't some lone deviant, some prince who wouldn't accept his duties and insisted on acting like a girl. I was one of a larger category of person, a member of a group whose shared history lent credence to her claims in ways that no amount of tearful begging in Nizam ever could have.

To Shiv, I said, "Please have Sunil Kalani and Pir Tahir brought forward. They have been made to wait long enough."

"Right away, your highness," Shiv agreed, bowing to me with the deepest respect, and staring pointedly at Sikander before he turned and headed for the second courtyard, where the Zindhi emir and the holy man were waiting for their audience.

"Anything I should know before they get here?" I asked Hina, as she knew both of these men.

"They have already agreed to serve you, your highness," she replied. "Their loyalty is greater to me than to you, but they have accepted my decision. Treat them as you would your own retainers, and I believe their loyalty will only grow."

My own retainers? I had precious few of those. Sikander hardly counted. Arjun was my lover, not my retainer. And Arvind was Arjun's friend, a Bikampuri noble who had come to Zindh because it was an exciting adventure and he had no real responsibilities. It occurred to me that, unlike Hina, I'd never had my own retainers before in my whole life. She was the closest thing I had to such a creature, and I thought it would be the height of foolishness to treat her as such. She might have been willing to serve me, but she was the rightful queen of this land. To act as though she were merely a follower of mine struck me as a poor idea.

Sunil Kalani and Pir Tahir arrived in the diwan-i-khas before I could consider the matter further. Shiv announced them, and they bowed properly. Pir Tahir was an old man with a full beard and bushy eyebrows that had been stained orange red from henna. He wore a white cleric's robe and matching prayer cap, and might have been mistaken for any village imam, but his dark eyes were keen, and were watching me closely. Sunil Kalani was wearing mail and plate armor over his fine silk ajrak tunic, his talwar still hanging from his hip. He was younger than the cleric, fiercer, his bold brown eyes staring right into mine in a way that suggested I had not won his loyalty just yet. I knew that I needed to choose my words carefully if I was to command them. I had an idea for how I might go about it.

"Good day, gentlemen," I told them, smiling politely. "Her majesty Jama Hina has informed me that you are willing to fight alongside me to free Zindh from Karim Shah and the forces of Mahisagar."

Their eyebrows shot up to their hairlines as they realized that I had recognized Hina by her proper title, and not as some mere retainer or hanger-on. They couldn't have missed that while I sat on the throne, she sat on the cushion directly beside it, in the place of honor. So far so good.

"That was her majesty's command," Sunil agreed, making it plain that he would fight for me only so long as Hina ordered it.

"Like you, I am honored to support her majesty, my distant cousin, in her time of need," I declared.

The reference to our shared ancestry brought fresh scrutiny. Sunil and Tahir could not have missed my emerald eyes, proof of my membership in the Nizami royal family as surely as any title. They noted the ajrak I was wearing, the fine Zindhi jewelry, and I knew that this Jama Sakina of theirs had been immediately called to mind, just as Hina had intended.

I planned to play that role to the hilt. "Like my twice-great-aunt before me, I have found myself here in Zindh not as its conqueror, but rather its defender. I have sworn to Jama Hina that I will punish Karim Shah for the death of Jam Ali, and that I will drive the Mahisagaris from Kadiro, and now I swear it to both of you. I give you my solemn oath that I will not rest until Zindh is free of invaders. I ask you both for your support in this effort for as long as it lasts."

"We will serve her majesty for as long as we live, your highness, you can be assured of that," Sunil replied, pointedly ignoring my request that he also serve me.

"And we recognize that in serving her, we serve you, your highness," Pir Tahir added, no doubt to temper the harshness of Sunil's words.

"That is enough for me," I said. "I have no desire to extract oaths of personal loyalty from either of you. We have shared enemies, and we must fight them together if we wish to survive. I bring fire and thunder and money, and Jama Sakina brings fighting men. But at present our army is not nearly large enough to take Kadiro. If we wish to defeat Mahisagar, we will need far more soldiers. Do you men have any talent when it comes to recruiting warriors for battle?"

Sunil Kalani nodded. "I know every emir from Kadiro to Mirpur, and every village headman too."

"Good, then I ask that you both go out into the countryside to collect as many soldiers as you can. You will be furnished with money, and with an escort if that is required, but until we have assembled an army capable of besieging Kadiro, we cannot risk an open battle against Mahisagar. Do you agree?"

"I do, your highness," said Hina, before her men could say a word. "I believe this is a sound strategy."

"Then we will begin recruiting an army at once, your majesty," Sunil promised, bowing to her rather than to me.

Sikander squirmed, his shoulders tensing, but I gestured for him to be still. Sunil was testing my patience, but I had honed it as a courtesan, and I knew that if he couldn't find its limit he would find it all the more difficult to view me as an enemy invader. So, I smiled and said, "I thank you for your service to Zindh, gentlemen. Shiv will see that you are well supplied with money and food for your journey. I wish you both the best of luck."

CHAPTER 7

I lay in Arjun's arms for what felt like the first time in months, though it was hard to give him the attention he deserved when there was so much uncertainty swirling around us. It hung in the air like a foul odor, one that even the strong desert breezes couldn't dispel.

He traced my cheek with the back of a finger, the tingle of my skin beneath his touch driving away the dark thoughts that lingered in the back of my mind.

"Leave it," he whispered.

"Leave what, my prince?" I asked, looking up into his warm amber eyes as he rested beside me, propped up on one elbow, the other hand caressing my face.

"This province and its worries," he replied.

Leaving it sounded nice. I wanted to forget about Zindh for a few minutes, to not worry so much over armies and zahhaks and potential enemies. But the doubts could not be so easily banished. "How can I stop thinking about it, when there's so much left to do?"

"I have a few ideas in mind," he replied, bringing his lips to mine, the gentle, insistent pressure doing a remarkably good job of making me forget about being a subahdar. I reached up and ran my fingers through his hair, as his hands wormed their way between my back and the bedsheets. He pulled me close to him, until the hard, hot muscles of his chest were burning against my skin.

I let go of his hair and reached instead for the waist cord of his trousers, my fingers working it loose with two deft tugs. How often had I been made to practice that back home in Bikampur?

His hands began hiking up my ajrak skirt, but they paused as a trumpet bleated out a series of harsh notes somewhere in the distance. The cadence was as familiar to me as the steady thumping of Arjun's heart against my own breast. It was the call a lookout sent when unknown zahhaks were spotted, and it was followed by their species and their number—thunder, sixteen; acid, five.

"Sixteen thunder zahhaks could be your father," Arjun murmured, the threat of so many unknown animals in the air driving all the passion out of the pair of us. "But the Nizamis don't fly acid zahhaks."

"Our men in Vanga subah do," I corrected as I rolled out of bed, slipping my feet into soft leather slippers. "But they wouldn't be here, and my father has no reason to come back, not unless he wants to make war on Mahisagar."

"The acid zahhaks could be Mahisagari," Arjun allowed as he tied his trousers back into place and reached for his kurta. "But why would they be flying with your father instead of against him?"

"And how would they have five?" I asked. "They only had four a few weeks ago. Where would they have come up with a fifth?"

"So it's Safavia, then," Arjun reasoned, hurrying now to get his sash tied around his waist, to snatch up his flying goggles.

My heart hammered in my chest. Safavia might have got acid zahhaks from Ahura, or one of the other coastal islands. But Arjun was right, they were the only power on the continent that could field sixteen thunder zahhaks other than my father, or perhaps the Rakhans far to the north. If Shah Ismail was here now, then his army wouldn't be far away.

But it was another thought that really put fear in my heart. Sakshi and Lakshmi were the riders we had up on patrol alongside Hina's river zahhaks. If the Safavians decided to attack . . .

I ran out of the room, slamming straight into the hard mass of muscle and steel that was Sikander, who had just been coming to get me. I rebounded off of him, and would have fallen flat on the floor if he hadn't steadied me with strong arms. "Your highness—"

"I heard the trumpet!" I exclaimed, pushing him aside and racing for the zahhak stables. "We have to get airborne now, while there's still time!"

"Your highness!" Sikander grabbed my arm, holding me back.

"My sisters are up there!" I practically screamed it in his face, but no matter how I twisted I couldn't wrench my arm free from his grasp. "We have to move now!"

"Your highness, the thunder zahhaks belong to your father, I'm sure of it," Sikander said, his voice calm and steady.

I glanced up at the sky, where the sixteen thunder zahhaks were already circling high above my sisters and the four fliers Hina had sent out on patrol that morning. From so far away, one thunder zahhak looked much like another, but I knew Malikah, my father's mount, from every angle, and there was no mistaking the distinctive pattern of black barring on the golden undersides of her wing and tail feathers.

"What's he doing here?" I wondered aloud.

Sikander's hand slid free of my arm as he realized that I wasn't going to rush off in a blind panic to attack. He pointed with his other hand toward a cluster of zahhaks lower down, coming forward to make a landing approach.

The five emerald and turquoise acid zahhaks were keeping perfect formation as they flared wide their peacock-like tails, back-beating their wings to slow themselves as they overflew the walls of the palace. At their head was an animal I knew well, having flown alongside her in the battle against Javed Khorasani. Her name was Amira, and she belonged to none other than Karim Shah of Mahisagar.

"Your highness!" Hina exclaimed, rushing toward us with her celas close behind. "What's going on? Are we under attack? My fliers don't have weapons!"

"It's my father," I told her, pointing to the thunder zahhaks, which were circling lower and lower, forcing Lakshmi and Sakshi to give way, lest they put themselves in an indefensible position.

"What about the acid zahhaks?" she asked, nodding to the ones that were just now landing near the stables.

I swallowed hard, not wanting to tell her the truth, but knowing that a lie would be so much worse, and would spare her nothing. "One of them was Amira, Karim Shah's animal."

"Why would your father be with Prince Karim?" Hina demanded, her voice shrill with panic. "Was this a trick the whole time?"

I held up my hand to forestall a fight and said, "I don't know any more than you do. If I'd had the slightest inkling that Karim was showing up, do you really believe I'd have placed my sisters on patrol today?"

"I don't know," Hina answered, her voice tight with fear. "Maybe you had an arrangement with him this whole time."

"She did not," Arjun snapped. "Razia would never play you falsely. She has treated you with nothing but courtesy, and you owe her the same."

Hina crossed her arms over her chest, her mouth clamped tightly shut, though it was plain that she was close to panicking. Her celas were gathered close around her, hugging one another, their fear palpable. Karim had murdered their king; they'd exhausted themselves fleeing him. They had come here in the hopes that they might escape the same fate, that they might find some way to get their revenge, and now it looked as if they'd been played for fools all along, that it was all for nothing, that they would be slaughtered.

I went to Hina and put my hands on her shoulders. "I don't know what's going on, but what I do know is that you protected me when I needed you, Hina. I'll do the same for you. I swear to God, whatever happens, no one is going to hurt you or any of your people. I give you my word."

She nodded, but her mouth was a hard line, and tears were spilling down her cheeks as she fought to get her emotions under control. I couldn't blame her. I was furious and afraid too, and Karim hadn't killed my family members. I kept my arms around Hina as I waited for my father and Prince Karim to arrive.

"What are your orders, your highness?" Sikander asked.

"Have our trumpeters order my sisters and Hina's fliers to descend to the diwan-i-khas and land there. I don't want them anywhere near the Mahisagaris," I said. I flickered my eyes to meet Hina's, took a deep breath, and added, "And I want guards in the middle courtyard, a lot of them. When Prince Karim lands, he is to be arrested, disarmed, and brought before me as a prisoner."

"I'll see to everything, your highness," Sikander promised, but then he added something that I wished he hadn't. "Unless your father countermands it."

I grimaced, but nodded. I couldn't very well ask Nizami men to go against their sovereign, and Sikander knew as well as I did that my father must have had a reason for traveling with Karim rather than simply knocking his zahhaks out of the sky.

But we weren't the only ones drawing that conclusion. Hina and her celas were glowering at the descending zahhaks, and I had to admit that their arrival didn't do much for my mood either, because try as I might, I couldn't work out what Karim and my father would have been doing flying together. Karim had attacked one of our cities. How could my father possibly let that stand? Shouldn't he have dealt with Karim when he had the chance? And anyway, the five acid zahhaks landing in the middle courtyard told me that Karim's father, Ahmed Shah, was here too. With all of Mahisagar's nobility at our mercy, with the entire male royal line here in our province, why not just kill them all and take Mahisagar for ourselves? That idea must have occurred to my father, so why hadn't he done it? It wasn't like him to hesitate at times like this.

Well, whatever my father wanted, I didn't have to abide by it. I had soldiers now too, and with Sikander gone to deal with Karim and the Mahisagaris, I was free to issue whatever orders I liked to those men I controlled who were not ultimately beholden to my father.

"My prince," I said, turning to Arjun, "I want Bikampuri musketeers on the parapets of the inner courtyard, as many as you can muster, before Karim or my father can get here."

"Right," he agreed, and he took off at a dead run to see it done.

To Hina, I said, "Get as many Zindhi men in this courtyard as you can. Whatever my father is planning, it's obvious he hasn't killed Karim and the Mahisagaris. If he means to ally with them, I must have the means of refusing him."

Hina nodded, her expression grim. "I'll see to it."

She started to leave, but I grabbed her before she could take a step. "But my father cannot be killed. I want to make that clear from the start. We can't fight Nizam, and killing him would make everything worse."

"I understand, your highness," she assured me. I let her go, and she went with her celas to see to the disposition of their soldiers.

Trumpets blared, and my sisters were quick to descend toward the diwan-i-khas. I ran to meet them, hoping that this wasn't what it looked like, that my father hadn't cut some deal with Karim and Ahmed, granting them control of Kadiro, but I couldn't think of another explanation.

I reached the diwan-i-khas at about the same time that my sisters landed with Hina's fliers. Lakshmi came running toward me right away. "Akka! Akka! Did you see? It's Prince Karim!"

She sounded excited, which made my insides twist. Karim had always been careful to be kind to her, to use all of his considerable charms on her. He was nothing if not experienced at grooming young girls to be abused later, and the fact that my little sister came from a coastal city where handsome men rode acid zahhaks had made her even more vulnerable. I'd tried to explain to her that he was a bad man, but she wasn't old enough to understand manipulation.

"I saw," I said, letting my tone tell her how unexcited I was to see Karim. "We are going to wait for him here." I nodded to the baradari, and to my throne. "He attacked us in Kadiro, and he killed Hina's brother, remember?"

"I don't think he would do something like that, Akka," Lakshmi told me.

"He did!" Nuri exclaimed, the young girl from Hina's ranks having flown right alongside Lakshmi on patrol. She was still holding the reins of her river zahhak, and her fury made the animal turn its head toward Lakshmi in alarm.

"We stay calm when we are around zahhaks, Nuri," I reminded her, my voice gentle. The last thing we needed was to get in a shouting match.

"But it's true," she insisted, her voice softening nonetheless.

"I know it's true," I assured her. "I will see to everything; I've given Jama Hina my word. For now, we must wait, all right?"

Nuri nodded, as did the older celas arrayed around her. I took Lakshmi with me to my throne, collecting her thunder zahhak's reins along the way. Sakshi and Ragini joined us, for which I was wholly grateful. I wished more than anything that Sultana was beside me, rather than in the stables, but two obedient thunder zahhaks and hundreds of loyal soldiers would be protection enough against my father and Karim and whatever they were planning.

As I sat on the throne, Bikampuri musketeers took up their positions all along the walls, led by Arvind. Arjun was striding across the courtyard to join me, followed closely by Hina and half a hundred Zindhi soldiers, to say nothing of her celas. The young women were keenly aware of the precariousness of the situation, and they gathered around her, all armed with the long-barreled rifles with fish-shaped stocks that were so popular here in Zindh.

The Zindhi contingent took up their positions all around the diwan-i-khas, their weapons at the ready. They used the banyan trees and the marble columns for cover, their faces grim beneath their steel helmets. They expected to be attacked. For a moment, I regretted my decision to bring them here, as so many armed men full of fear increased the odds of something going wrong. But I wasn't going to let my father dictate his terms to me as he had before. I may not have had as many soldiers within the palace walls as Sikander did, but I had enough to make a fight of it.

Prince Karim, the heir to the throne of Mahisagar, strode through the gates of my courtyard with all the swagger of a conquering hero, though to my eyes he looked more like a plundering pirate in his silk dhoti, with his curved firangi sword swinging from his hip. It was the little details that marked him out as a prince—his perfectly coiffed black hair that glistened in the sunlight, his carefully trimmed beard, the fat jewels on the rings that graced his fingers. And his attitude, which could only have belonged to a prince as well. Though he was in a foreign city, about to meet a ruler who had every cause to murder him, he was smirking, not an ounce of fear evident in the haughty gaze of his dark eyes.

I wondered how much of his confidence was owed to my father's presence here, and how much to misplaced arrogance. Though, watching his entrance, I noted that he was followed closely by four Mahisagari men wearing flying goggles on their heads, and not one of them was Ahmed Shah. I recognized Jamshid, the man who usually flew on Karim's wing, but the other three were completely new to me, which was strange, as I'd met all of Mahisagar's zahhak riders not two weeks before. Where had they suddenly come by three more trained fliers? Could it be that Mahisagar had more zahhaks than I'd realized?

The thought chilled me. If Karim had more than five zahhaks to draw upon, then his father might well be ensconced in Kadiro with God only knew how many animals. Had they made an alliance with Virajendra against us? That might explain why my father was here, why he hadn't killed Karim. But I couldn't quite work out why Virajendra would favor Mahisagar with an alliance when they had long been rivals. Something wasn't adding up.

But whatever the case, if Ahmed Shah was still in Kadiro with his army, then that complicated matters. Killing Karim here wouldn't end the war, though it might serve to weaken the Mahisagari position. But while Karim was many things, stupid wasn't one of them. He wouldn't have come here like this if he'd thought I would kill him. He must have had some trick up his sleeve to preserve his life.

Sikander and my father came into the courtyard behind Karim, along with eight thunder zahhaks ridden by my father's men, and nearly two hundred Nizami guardsmen. Sikander must have realized that I would bring my loyal men to this meeting, and now he had evened the odds—maybe more than evened them, with the presence of those thunder zahhaks.

"What is this, your highness?" Hina demanded from her place beside me on the dais.

"I don't know," I told her, so earnestly that she couldn't help but believe me. "But we'll sort it out with words if we can. Fighting is a last resort—they have us outnumbered. So keep the weapons down for now."

"For now," Hina ground out through clenched teeth, but her fist was bunched tightly around the long hilt of her bhuj ax, and I knew that she was aching to drive the blade through Karim's skull for what he'd done to her brother. I couldn't blame her. Every time I saw Karim, I wanted to stick something sharp right between his eyes too.

Karim reached the baradari and showed not the least hesitation in entering it, still smirking insufferably, still standing straight and tall, his hand resting lightly on the hilt of his firangi, all in spite of the presence of Hina's enraged celas, and the murderous looks of the Zindhi soldiers who flanked the building. He began a grandiose bow, but paused halfway through it as his eyes landed on Hina.

"So this is where you ran off to?" He grinned. "I should have considered that."

"You should have considered many things before you attacked my province and killed one of my allies," I replied, not wanting to let Hina and Karim get into a shouting match.

He shrugged, the smile remaining on his face. "You have to admit the timing was perfect."

"It was," I agreed, before Hina could blow her top. "But now you've made the fatal misstep of appearing here, and unless my father gives me a very good reason to the contrary, I'm going to have you executed for your unprovoked attack on my subah, and for the cold-blooded murder of Ali Talpur, one of my subjects."

Karim didn't look the least bit frightened. He said, "Where I come from, it's frowned upon for a girl to execute her own fiancé."

"My what?" The words tumbled from my mouth unbidden, as I struggled to comprehend what I'd heard. My fiancé? Karim Shah? The thought of it made my skin crawl and my stomach knot. It was the most preposterous, idiotic . . . brilliant thing I'd ever heard in my life. Of course. That was why my father hadn't killed him. Karim had offered him a marriage alliance, and in return, Mahisagar would keep Zindh safe and a part of the empire. It would be a dowry of sorts. And my father wouldn't have been able to resist such an offer, not when it neatly settled all of his problems. Zindh would be protected, a man with military experience and a reputation as a prince's prince would be left in charge, trade with Mahisagar would be enhanced, the port would be secure, and with Mahisagar's soldiers to draw upon, the revolts could be put down in short order.

And if my father had agreed to it, then he would do everything he could to enforce it. That was the reason for the thunder zahhaks still swirling overhead, for the eight of them standing in a line across from my throne, for the hundreds of soldiers pouring into the courtyard at Sikander's command.

"This is a sick joke," Arjun growled.

"Oh, it's no joke, Arjun," Karim replied, his smirk widening.

"Your highness, give the word, and we'll shoot him dead," Hina told me, her hazel eyes narrowed as she glared daggers at Karim.

"As will my men," Arjun agreed.

"You will do no such thing." That was my father speaking. He was backed by hundreds of bodyguards, all armed with toradars, all wearing armor and carrying swords, with Sikander himself leading them, to say nothing of the zahhaks. One look at Sikander's face told me that if he had to, he would give the order to kill me to protect my father.

"Give me one good reason why they shouldn't, Father," I demanded. "If your plan is truly to marry me off to Karim Shah, then why should I not tell my men to open fire and let fate decide which of us lives and which of us dies?"

"You would do that with your precious baby sister caught in the cross fire?" Karim taunted, clucking his tongue with disapproval. "What happened to those maternal instincts of yours, Razia?"

He was right, God damn him. Sakshi and Lakshmi were seated right beside my throne. If I fired on my father's men, they would fire on me, and while I was prepared to die rather than marry Karim, I wasn't prepared to let Lakshmi die in my place.

My father didn't understand me, but he knew an opportunity when he saw one, and he smirked at my hesitation. "Enough bluster, Razia. Have your men stand down."

"I can't do that, Father," I said, because I wasn't yet ready to cede the field to him. Marrying Karim filled me with such dread that I wouldn't surrender to it unless it was my absolute last resort. Right now, with friendly soldiers all around me, we hadn't reached that point.

"Stand them down if you want your sisters to live," he repeated, his voice taking on a sterner edge.

"They don't obey her, they obey me," Hina growled, "and I'm not about to order them to stand down, not when I have the bastard who murdered my brother in my sights."

"Who is this girl?" my father asked, his emerald eyes searching her face, but betraying no signs of recognition.

"Hina Talpur, daughter of Rustam Talpur," Sikander answered. "She's a hijra and she serves her highness as an adviser and general."

"That's why we couldn't find the second son . . ." my father murmured, stroking his mustache as he stared at Hina, scrutinizing every inch of her, no doubt looking for some sign of her past written into her body. I'd been on the receiving end of that same gaze often enough to recognize it.

"Hina is under my protection," I said. "She is not to be harmed."

"She's a rebel and a traitor and you should have put her to death the moment you discovered her identity," my father replied.

"Oh? And that's why Karim Shah is still alive after he invaded our province, is it, Father?" I countered.

My father shrugged, because he couldn't deny that he was being hypocritical, but then he'd always had a soft spot for ruthless, cold-hearted men who took advantage of others when they were weak. I supposed it was the only kind of person he really understood.

"I was going to kill Karim for what he did in Kadiro, but he made me a better offer."

"And what offer was that?" I asked, though I thought I already knew. I was just praying that I was wrong.

"Your hand in marriage," Karim said, his eyes roving up and down my body with a lingering lasciviousness that turned my stomach.

Even after all that he had done to support Bikampur in our fight against Javed Khorasani, the truth was that I could scarcely stand to be in the same palace as Karim Shah. Just the sight of him was almost enough to make me vomit up everything I'd eaten that day, to say nothing of the queasiness I felt at this ridiculous notion of a marriage. I tried to suppress a shudder, but didn't quite manage it, and I was sure my disgust was plain on my face as I said, "I'm never going to marry you, and imagining sharing your bed is making me sick to my stomach."

Karim clucked his tongue. "Oh, come now, Razia, you don't need to imagine it, you just need to remember it."

I set my jaw against the torrent of emotions that flooded my body at the explicit reference to my rape. If I'd thought for an instant he would obey, I'd have ordered Sikander to murder Karim right then and there, but I knew he would refuse, and then I would look weak. Hina would shoot, but with toradars already aimed in every conceivable direction, the slightest movement would set off a fusillade that would kill us all. No, I had to keep myself under control, for Lakshmi's sake if not for my own. She was still seated beside the throne, with no way to escape the cross fire.

"Let me make this plain, Karim—I will never marry you. It's a stupid idea, and I can't believe you were foolish enough to bring it to me like this."

"It doesn't look stupid from where I'm standing," my father said. "If you ask me, it solves all of my troubles. Mahisagar's army is strong enough to control Zindh and to discourage an invasion. A marriage alliance between my own daughter and Sultan Ahmed's heir will unify our two kingdoms, growing Nizam's strength. And your offspring with Karim will command the most powerful empire in the world."

"Offspring with Karim?" I raised an eyebrow at that, wondering just how ignorant my father was in matters pertaining to hijras. "Father, you must know I'm not capable of bearing children."

"No," Karim agreed, "but your cousins are. I've heard they're pretty enough, and they'll serve the purpose."

I frowned, confused now. "You're going to be marrying one of my cousins, then?" That made more sense, but it didn't explain all this nonsense about his being my fiancé.

"No, I'm going to sire an heir off one of them, and then we'll adopt the child as our own," Karim said. "It's not perfect, I don't think any of your cousins is as clever as you are, but maybe there's enough of you in their blood to make it worthwhile."

"Uncle Shahrukh would never permit that . . ." I murmured. The idea of treating a princess of Nizam like a broodmare was horrifying, even to me. Not even my cousin Sidra deserved that.

"He'll permit it, so long as his grandson is the heir to the throne of Nizam," my father replied. "And if he insists on a marriage, then so be it. There is no law limiting a man to a single wife."

I saw the genius of it then, though I wished I hadn't. "It would solve all the squabbling and infighting between the two of you . . ." I whispered, realizing that if I were raising Uncle Shahrukh's grandson, he'd be far less inclined to try to take my father's throne by force, though all bets were off where his sons, Tariq and Rashid, were concerned.

"Just so," my father agreed, looking proud of himself. "It solves everything neatly and cleanly."

"Except for one thing," I said.

"And what's that?" he asked.

"I'm not marrying Karim!" I fairly shrieked it at him, heedless of the muskets still raised all around us. "He raped me! Have you forgotten that?"

My father shrugged. "All the more reason for him to make an honest woman out of you, then."

I made a sort of strangled choking sound, I was so furious with him for saying something like that. I was half-tempted to order Hina's soldiers to kill him, and they looked like they were on the verge of doing it anyway, but if I did that, then my father's men would have no choice but to fire, and we'd all die—Lakshmi included. She was still sitting beside my throne, taking this all in with wide, horrified eyes.

There would be shooting. I saw that now. If my father insisted on forcing me into a marriage with Karim, I would let Hina's men kill him instead. And if I did that, then we would all perish. I needed a way to remove our negotiations from the courtyard, where all the men could hear. I thought I could make my father see reason if I could only get him alone.

"Enough of this," I said, gesturing to the armed soldiers on both sides. "If you want to discuss this plan with me, Father, then let us discuss it in private, rather than holding toradars on one another like petty bandits."

"Just the two of us?" he asked, raising an eyebrow at the notion.

No, that wouldn't work. Leaving Karim and Hina together was a recipe for disaster. But if I brought Karim, then between him and my father, there was a chance they might simply take me hostage, and then I would have to surrender. Arjun was the obvious choice to bring with me. As good as Karim was in a duel, I thought Arjun was better, and having an important Registani prince at my side would remind my father that I possessed powerful allies still.

"You, me, Karim, and Arjun," I said. "The four of us will retire to my chambers to discuss this."

"If you agree to marry him, I'll kill you," Hina warned me.

"If I agree to marry him, I'll let you," I replied, drawing a trace of a smile from her lips, if only for a single instant.

My father considered that for a moment, and he must have decided that Arjun and I didn't pose enough of a threat to his life to worry himself over, and he probably realized how foolish it would have been to leave Karim and Hina together. So, he nodded and gestured toward my chambers. "Lead the way, daughter."

Now he called me his daughter? I scowled, but I stood up from the throne all the same. To my sisters, I said, "Sakshi, take Lakshmi out of here, please."

"You will not," my father said, wagging a finger at her. "Sikander, if those two try to leave, they are to be shot."

Sikander's nod was instantaneous. "Yes, your majesty."

He would do it. I knew it with the same sick certainty that had informed all of my encounters with him in the palace of Nizam. My fists clenched, but they would do me no good here; only my mind could get me out of this. I couldn't let anger rule me, but it was hard not to be furious when my father was using my sisters as hostages. For Lakshmi's sake, I kept my voice calm. "Sakshi, keep Lakshmi close. I'll be back soon."

"We'll be right here waiting," Sakshi assured me, hugging Lakshmi so that I would know my little sister was safe.

I gave a gruff nod and stalked off to my chambers, Arjun right beside me, my father and Karim trailing close behind.

CHAPTER 8

Years ago, I'd have been fuming over Karim's proposal, so angry at his betrayal that it would have been hard for me to focus on anything else, but living as a courtesan in Bikampur had changed me. I was still furious, of course; my training hadn't robbed me of my emotions, but it had allowed me to act in spite of them, to set them aside, and to act with cold calculation. So, rather than fuming, I was scheming. There had to be some way to change my father's mind, and I fully intended to find it.

"If you think that speaking to me privately is going to change my mind, you're very much mistaken," my father warned me from his place on the cushion opposite my own.

"I wanted to speak without risk of getting all of us killed, Father," I replied, keeping my tone neutral for the time being. "Surely you can agree that it's better to avoid a bloodbath if we can."

"So long as you do your duty as a princess of Nizam and marry the man I have chosen for you," my father allowed.

It rankled, hearing him suddenly talk about me as a princess with genuine enthusiasm. He'd made it plain what a disgrace he thought I was. Our last conversation had left me with few illusions as to why I had been brought to Zindh. He thought perhaps I was clever enough to do him some good, though he was well insulated from the possibility that I would fail. But nowhere in that conversation had he wholeheartedly embraced me as his daughter the way he was doing now. It was such a transparently self-interested manipulation that it made my throat tighten with anger, and with other emotions besides. How I had longed for him to recognize me as his daughter, and now he was using that childhood hope to destroy my life.

"Give me one good reason why I should marry Karim, Father," I said.

"I can think of at least sixteen good reasons," he answered, nodding toward the ceiling, indicating the thunder zahhaks still swirling overhead, and the ones in the courtyard besides.

"We might lose this fight," I allowed, forcing myself to shrug like it didn't matter, "but if you're going to take away everything I care about anyway, then what incentive do I have to surrender to you?"

"Do you really hate me so much that you would see Lakshmi dead?" Karim asked.

"If you gave a damn about Lakshmi, or me, you'd never have invaded my province and put me in this position," I shot back, my voice just as icy cold as I could make it.

But my words were like water off a river zahhak's back to Karim. He smiled at me. "I think you're just angry because you've been outsmarted for a change."

"You think this is clever?" I demanded.

"I do," he replied. "While you were playing princess with Arjun, I spent the last few weeks planning this. First we took Ahura, and its acid zahhaks. Thanks to you, the island was without a Firangi fleet to protect it."

I scowled, regretting that I'd helped him and his father in their naval war against the Firangis, though if I hadn't, I never would have won back Sultana, might never have even earned myself a position at Bikampur's court. My life hadn't been my own then. I'd had little choice in the matter. Still, it rankled that I'd given Karim the zahhaks he needed to carry out his invasion of Zindh, however indirectly.

"Then I invaded Kadiro and took it, knowing that the Zindhis wouldn't be able to put up a fight." He grinned. "And once I contacted your father with my offer to protect his province and his beautiful daughter in exchange for a marriage alliance, well . . ." He held out his hands to indicate our little meeting.

"You're a fool," I grumbled.

Of everything I'd said, that seemed to hit home. Anger flashed behind his dark eyes. "Is that so?"

"It is," I insisted, though I probably shouldn't have been taunting him. "The Safavians won't let you keep Ahura. It was theirs before the Firangis took it, while they were busy fighting Tarkiva. Now that Shah Ismail has won his war against his greatest rivals, he is free to act. His first act will be to retake Ahura. If you had come to me as a friend rather than an enemy, I might have been able to use my influence in Registan, and my own zahhaks here in Zindh, to help you in that fight. But now you will face Safavia's wrath alone."

"I had considered that," Karim said, the anger having left his face. "But it occurred to me that you might not be willing to start a war between Safavia and Nizam to help my father keep an island. However, after our marriage, the alliance between Nizam and Mahisagar will be a formal one. If Safavia attacks us, they attack Nizam too."

I glanced to my father. "And this is acceptable to you? A war with Safavia when you're so worried about Virajendra?"

"Mahisagar's fleet and its armies more than make up for the

possibility of war with Safavia," my father answered. "With their assistance, we will finally be able to strike the Virajendrans where they live—along the coasts and out at sea. If they attack us now, they risk having their entire merchant fleet obliterated by the most fearsome pirates in all Daryastan."

"That may deter Virajendra, but it won't deter Safavia," I told him. "And with Safavia fighting you in the west, you can be assured that Virajendra will seize the opportunity to attack from the south."

"And Registan will join with Safavia and Virajendra against you," Arjun added, staring straight into my father's eyes with such a ferocious determination that he put me more in mind of a tiger than a man. "We rarely fight outside of our own borders, but if Safavia and Virajendra go to war, so will we."

"You are the prince of Bikampur, not Registan," my father scoffed. But I noted that Karim wasn't scoffing; he was shifting uncertainly, tugging nervously at his mustache.

Arjun leaned forward, so that scarcely a handsbreadth separated his face from my father's. "If you think you can take Razia from me, you are very much mistaken."

"If you value her so highly, you should have offered her marriage, as I have," Karim snapped. "You made her a concubine. I'm treating her like the princess she is."

"As a creature to be bought and sold in exchange for an alliance, you mean," I corrected.

"That's what a princess is," my father retorted.

"If that's what will solve this, then I will marry her," Arjun said. "My father will approve. I only held back because I thought you would refuse me."

"And you were right, I do refuse you," my father told him. "Bikampur is not Mahisagar. You have no fleet. Your army is smaller. You have far fewer zahhaks."

"But if one Registani city is attacked, we all defend one another," Arjun reminded him.

"Zindh is not Registani, nor will it be," my father pointed out. "The maharajas of Registan will not march to the defense of Kadiro or Shikarpur—you know this, boy."

"They would march for Razia," he said, and though he sounded like he really believed that, I wasn't sure that I did. I had helped Udai, and I had defeated Javed Khorasani, but the other lords of Registan owed me no real loyalty. Maybe they would help me and maybe they wouldn't, but a war with Safavia was something that had the potential to destroy them all. They wouldn't enter into that lightly—certainly not for a hijra, even if she was the wife of one of their princes.

My father shrugged. "Whether they would or wouldn't is immaterial. I would be a fool to cast aside an alliance that I know will hold in the hopes of gaining a far more tenuous one. And it ignores the reality on the ground. Mahisagar holds Kadiro with fifty thousand men and a hundred ships and thirteen acid zahhaks."

"Twelve," Karim corrected. "The thirteenth is a wedding gift."

"You're gifting me an acid zahhak?" I asked, startled by that. Zahhaks were uncommon gifts, even when sealing alliances. They conferred far too much power, and they tended to be far too closely tied to their masters. Zahhak eggs were different; they were the most valuable of all trade goods, and a single zahhak egg might seal an alliance lasting decades.

"I am," Karim told me. He leaned forward, reaching out to take my hand, but I snatched it away before he could touch me. He forced a smile to cover his irritation. "This is to be a real marriage, Razia. You will be my first and primary wife. You will be my queen. Has any man ever offered you so much?"

I felt bile rising in the back of my throat, but managed to choke it back down before I gagged. Karim wasn't wrong—no man had ever offered to make me his queen—but being Karim's queen was an offer it was all too easy to refuse. Just the thought of it made my skin crawl.

"Have you forgotten what you did to me?" I hissed.

"That was six years ago," he said. "We were different people."

"Yes, I was a different person then," I agreed. "I was a helpless child. Well, I am not that helpless child any longer, Karim. I have zahhaks, and I have soldiers, and I have power now, and I will use it if I must." I looked my father straight in the eyes and said, "I will not marry him. Either we fight to the death or you go back to Nizam and leave the management of my province to me. It's your choice, Father."

My father shrugged. "Fine. We'll shout to our soldiers to start the shooting. Your sisters can be the first casualties in this war." He got up and headed for the door.

I managed to roll to my feet, putting myself between him and the doorway, stopping him from getting out of my chambers to give Sikander the orders that would see my sisters killed, but it was a mistake. He was wearing armor, and I was wearing a silk blouse and skirt. He grabbed me with both hands and threw me up against the wall hard enough to rattle my brains in my skull.

Arjun was up in an instant to defend me, but Karim was just as quick. The pair of them drew their swords, but I could already see that it was hopeless. Karim was between Arjun and my father, and my father had my arms pinned up against the wall to keep me from getting to my katars.

"If you were a man, you could stop this," my father taunted, his gauntleted hands locking around my forearms until I felt like the bones would snap. He was leaning all of his body weight against me, pressing me against the cool marble wall. If he'd wanted to end this fight, he could have driven a couple of knees into the pit of my stomach and left me gasping for air on the floor. I'd seen him do it to enough men in training. But he just held me there, his face tight with anger. For all his taunts, he wasn't enjoying this. I wondered what that meant.

"Let me go, Father." It wasn't an order, but I wasn't quite begging either. When he didn't listen, I said, "You're right, I'm not going to sentence my sisters to death, so let us sit and talk."

"There's nothing to talk about," he told me. "You will do your duty as a princess of Nizam and that is the end of the matter. I will tolerate no more of this nonsense from you. Your whole life you told me you were a princess and not a prince. You minced around in skirts, and you shamed me." Those last two words came out with so much pain that it made my own heart hurt.

"And you told me that if I'd just treated you like a woman, you never would have shamed me, you would have been the perfect little princess." His hands squeezed tighter around my arms, forcing me to clench my jaw against the pain. "And now I have recognized you as a princess, and you are going to shame me again by refusing to act the part? Maybe the problem wasn't how you were born. Maybe the problem is you."

Those words hit me like hammer blows. Some part of me wilted inside. It was my worst fear made manifest. He was right. I'd always held on to this idea that if I hadn't been born a boy, I'd have been his perfect little princess. I'd always believed with my whole heart that but for the circumstances of my birth, my life would have been charmed; I would have had a place in the world and a family that loved me and treasured me. But what if that wasn't true? What if I was just a terrible, worthless child, whatever form I took?

"Don't listen to his lies, Razia."

I glanced up to see Arjun holding his khanda at the ready in case Karim attacked, but he was looking at me, and there was a warmth in his amber eyes that I'd never seen in another man's.

"Your father is a fool and a coward," Arjun declared.

My father looked back at him with hate smoldering in his eyes. "Is that so, boy?"

"It is." Arjun met his glare without the least sign of fear. "A real father would never marry his daughter to her rapist. He would gut the man for his crimes. You're no kind of father to her, and no kind of man either."

"If my daughter put herself in a position to be raped, then how can I fault a man for doing it?" my father asked.

"She didn't put herself in that position," Arjun replied. "You failed to protect her, and then you punished her for your own failures."

"He was a boy!" my father roared back, his face reddening. "And his conduct afterward, whoring himself out to any man he met, makes plain whose fault it was!"

My heart ached far worse than my body, in spite of the way my father was pressing me against the wall until it felt like my bones would snap. There was a part of me that believed him, whatever Arjun said to the contrary. I had run away from home to become a hijra, and I had sold my body to the highest bidder for years. Any princess who had done such a thing would have so disgraced herself that she would have been killed at best, left to live in the gutter as a common whore at worst. She certainly wouldn't have been entertaining marriage offers, not even from men as slimy as Karim Shah.

"It was your fault," Arjun said, his fist clenching around the hilt of his khanda until his knuckles turned white. "You knew who she was, you knew what she was, and rather than protecting her, you beat her, and tormented her, and left her exposed to men like Karim. You did it on purpose. You let him rape her on purpose."

More than Arjun's words, it was my father's reaction that shocked me. His eyes widened; his grip slackened. It was true. It was all true.

"You let him do that to me on purpose?" I asked, tears threatening at the corners of my eyes. Never in my whole life had I imagined that my father had orchestrated what Karim had done to me, but now I saw what I'd been too young and too blind to notice before. I had screamed. I had screamed in a palace full of servitors. I had fought as best I could. No guard could have failed to hear me. But no one had come. And when I had told Sikander what had happened, he hadn't been surprised, he'd just beaten me for being such a weakling, but he had never once asked me for details, never once asked me where and when it had happened. Because he'd known all along.

My father let me go with a snarl of frustration. He stood there, his face reddening, whether from shame or anger I couldn't have said. At last, he threw his arms wide. "I thought it might teach you a lesson! I thought if he used you as a woman, you wouldn't want to be one anymore!"

"And this lesson?" I asked, gesturing to Karim, and to him, with arms that were already turning purple from where he'd grabbed me. "What is this meant to teach me, Father?"

"This is a political decision," he said, his tone actually softening for once. "Ahmed Shah holds Kadiro. You won't be able to take it back from him. I cannot afford a war with Mahisagar, as it would only embolden Virajendra. So, we make peace. The price of peace is your marriage to Karim. It will strengthen both of our kingdoms, and it will ensure the safety of Zindh—and your safety too."

"You think marrying me to my rapist ensures my safety?" I gave a hollow laugh at that, wondering how the man could be so deluded.

"I'm sorry for what I did six years ago, Razia," Karim said, "but things are different now. You will be my wife. I will care for you, and for your sisters. They will want for nothing. *You* will want for nothing. And with my armies and your brains, we can conquer the world together."

"Ah." That was what Karim wanted. With me as his wife, he would eventually be sultan of Nizam, the most powerful man in Daryastan. And with me at his side, directing his every move, he reckoned that he would grow the empire even more than my father had. The worst part was, I wasn't sure that he was wrong. I was ambitious, maybe more ambitious than I wanted to admit. For all the talk of living with Arjun in Bikampur, I'd chosen to become the subahdar of Zindh. Why? For freedom? Or for power? I didn't even know anymore. If this was freedom, it certainly didn't feel like it.

I walked past Karim to where Arjun was standing, and I embraced him tightly, pressing my face into his chest.

"Razia," he warned, one arm going around me to protect me, the other still keeping his khanda pointed at Karim.

"He's not going to hurt you, my prince," I told Arjun. As if to prove to me how reasonable he could be, Karim sheathed his firangi and held up his hands to show Arjun that they were empty.

Arjun pulled me back toward the far wall of the chamber before sheathing his khanda and holding me in his arms. We just stood there for what seemed like both a long time and no time at all. My mind was racing, struggling to find a way out of this mess, but I wasn't seeing one. Not unless I could convince my father that this was wrong, that whether it was politically expedient or not, it was unfair and horrible and cruel. I didn't think those arguments would sway him, but I had to try.

I turned to face him, surprised to see so much uncertainty on his face. Maybe there was a chance after all. "Father, please don't do this to me."

He reared back, shocked that that was the angle I would take. "We have Karim here; we have nearly half of Mahisagar's zahhaks at our mercy," I told him. "Let us take him prisoner and make a bargain with Ahmed Shah. He leaves Zindh, and never comes back, and his son gets to live. They will be too busy fighting Safavia in Ahura to strike back at us. And I will have united the Zindhi people by then. I will be able to hold this province. With Arjun's help, I already have seven zahhaks to fight against their twelve, and more could be brought from Registan. They won't take those odds, not against me. And Safavia would rather fight for its own island than for my province. It would be far easier for them to risk a war with Mahisagar than Nizam."

Karim's eyes widened as he realized for the first time just how much danger *he* was in. "If you do that, your majesty, my father and I will make an alliance with Virajendra, and I swear to you not a single ship will ever set sail from Kadiro's harbor again. Our fleet will make sure of that."

"So we don't return Karim to his father," I said. "If he doesn't want peace, we kill him, and we take his zahhaks. We rally the Registani fire zahhaks to fight alongside us, we burn the Mahisagari fleet to ashes, we obliterate their army, and we retake Kadiro. With your thunder zahhaks and the fire zahhaks Arjun could supply us, it would be an easy matter, Father. And then we could conquer Mahisagar, and gift Ahura to Safavia in exchange for peace. Let Durrania and Khuzdar face Safavia's armies for a time, while we build our strength."

Karim could see the cogs turning behind my father's eyes, and his hand fell to the hilt of his firangi. "Virajendra would join with us. They would rather fight a war of annihilation than let Nizam control Mahisagar, and my mother, she is a Yaruban princess, her brother is the emir of Jesera, and he is rich in fire zahhaks. If you murdered her son, then my uncle would join us against you."

"You would have Registan's support in this, your majesty," Arjun said, cradling me protectively.

"I would, no doubt," my father agreed, crossing his arms, looking at me rather than the rival princes. "If I agreed to this, I would have allies with which to fight a massive and costly war against Mahisagar and Virajendra and Yaruba, and perhaps Safavia too, though perhaps they might join us instead." He shrugged. "Tens of thousands of men would die, perhaps hundreds of thousands. Trade would be interrupted across an entire continent. Zahhaks would fall from the skies by the dozens. It would be a war like none we have ever witnessed before."

My heart sank. I knew what was coming next, even before he said it.

"But if I give you in marriage to Karim Shah, as I have promised, there will be no war. Virajendra will be too frightened of Mahisagar's fleet and the might of my zahhaks. Registan will not march outside of its borders for a foreign princess. And Safavia, while they might retake Ahura, or even attempt an invasion of Zindh, will be checked by Mahisagar's newfound power in the air, and by your own thunder zahhaks. There will be peace. Trade will flourish. Countless thousands of lives will be not only spared but enriched."

"Not mine . . ." I whispered, my voice catching in my throat.

"No, not yours," my father agreed, his voice tinged with something approximating regret.

"This is your final decision?" I asked him, hoping against hope that he would find it somewhere in his heart to change his mind.

"It is," he replied.

I took a deep breath and let it out as a slow hiss, because that was the only thing keeping me from screaming in anguish. My mind was working furiously to come up with some way out of this mess, but if the plan I had spun for my father hadn't worked to change his mind, then nothing would. He would force this marriage on me, even if it meant killing my sisters. They were nothing to him when set beside me, and he was willing to throw me to my rapist for a treaty, so I had no illusions about what would become of Sakshi and Lakshmi if I refused him. If only I had left them in Bikampur, I would have gone out shooting, I would have let myself die in a bloody battle rather than going meekly to Karim's bed. But I couldn't kill my sisters. God help me, I couldn't let them suffer for my mistakes.

"I need some time to make arrangements with Arjun and with Hina," I said. "In private."

"Razia, you're not going to surrender, are you?" Arjun asked, holding me close to him.

"We don't have a choice, my prince," I replied. "My father will kill my sisters if I refuse him. I can't let him do that."

"And you think we're going to give you a chance to plot your way out of it?" Karim scoffed. The mask of affection had dropped—not that I could blame him; I had nearly convinced my father to murder him, after all.

"I need an hour, Father, to determine suitable terms and to present them to you," I said, hoping that he would at least extend me that much courtesy.

"You have an hour," my father said, and he held up a hand to forestall Karim's objections. "You are getting what you want, and I have held fast to the terms of our arrangement. You will give my daughter the time she needs to see to the disposition of her household."

Karim shrugged. "Fine. One hour."

CHAPTER 9

One hour. Was that really all the time I had left with Arjun? God, it hurt so much I could hardly stand it. I was clinging to him like a baby, still standing in my bedchamber, while Karim and my father waited in the courtyard, giving us some semblance of privacy.

I was sobbing quietly in spite of myself, my shoulders shaking as Arjun held me tightly against his chest with one arm, the other stroking my hair gently.

"We could still fight . . ." he whispered.

I shook my head. "There's no way to keep Sakshi and Lakshmi safe. The moment I tried to move them, Sikander would kill them. I know it."

"Do you really think any of you will be safe with Karim after everything you said?" he asked.

Those words were exactly the last ones I wanted to hear. I felt my courage crumbling, and I choked back a thousand desperate pleas. I knew that if I asked Arjun to lay down his life for me, he would. I knew that if I asked him to charge into the courtyard with his khanda to cut down Karim, he would. But then he would die and all hope really would be lost.

No, I had to use my brain rather than give in to my basest impulses. Karim wasn't wrong. An hour was enough time for me to ruin his plans. I just had to stop crying like an infant and get to work.

I wiped the tears from my face with my dupatta and took several deep, fortifying breaths. I had work to do. I had to have everything in place before I surrendered. After that, there would be no chance at all.

"I love you with my whole heart, my prince," I told Arjun, placing my palm against his rough cheek, savoring the sensation, not sure when I would ever experience it again.

"Razia . . ."

"I need you to listen to me," I said. "There isn't much time. We have to make the best use of the time we have left."

He understood at once. "You have a plan?"

"Not a good one," I confessed, the ridiculousness of it making me smile in spite of all the pain that was pressing against the walls of my chest. "But so long as you love me, I will have hope."

"I will always love you," he declared, which was what I'd expected him to say. What I hadn't expected was for him to hold me close and to look into my eyes and to say, "Whatever happens next isn't your fault. I know how women are judged in this world for circumstances that are beyond their control, but I will never judge you for what comes next. You do what you have to do to survive. So long as you are alive, I will always love you. Nothing that Karim Shah does will ever change that."

I felt my resolve crumbling, because as much as his words gave me hope, as much as they reassured me, they also filled me with dread. Neither of us was naive. We knew what would come next. We knew what Karim would do to me once I was under his power. Arjun was giving me permission to survive it, but I wasn't sure that I really wanted to survive it. I wasn't sure I had the strength to face it again. But for my sisters, I would. For them I would have faced anything.

"You will have to return to Bikampur." I could scarcely choke the words out through my too-tight throat. "You and Arvind will have to go back, and you will have to convince your father and as many Registani noblemen as you can to fly for you against Mahisagar when the time comes."

"I can do that," he assured me, hugging me fiercely. "If that's what you need, then that's what will happen."

"We will need to find some way to communicate," I said, my mind working frantically for the answer, but I hit on it quickly enough. "Shiv. I can send messages through Shiv. He can relay them to loyal Zindhis in the town, and they can relay them to Sunil Kalani. He has river zahhaks. They can act as go-betweens."

"You think he'll still work for you after you agree to marry Karim?" Arjun asked.

I shrugged, tears spilling down my cheeks as I imagined the way I would be viewed by the Zindhis now, as some foreign whore, willing to sell them out at the first opportunity. "If I can convince Hina that I'm not betraying her, then I think so. I hope so. But I don't know. I can't be sure." Admitting that was so painful, but I had to consider the possibility that they wouldn't. "If they don't, messages will flow more slowly, but I'm sure Shiv will find a way."

"He will," Arjun assured me, whether he really believed it or not. He cradled my face in his hands, brushing away the tears with his thumbs. "So we have messages worked out. And I will get you fire zahhaks. I can't promise sixteen, but I think I can get at least eight."

"Eight would be enough . . ." I murmured. "How long will it take?"

"At least a fortnight," he replied. "But once they've agreed to fight, it will be better if the battle takes place sooner rather than later."

"A fortnight . . ." I didn't know if that was enough time for Sunil to rally the Zindhi countryside to arms or not, but I supposed it would have to be. And I would need Safavia to attack as a distraction. It wasn't absolutely necessary, but it would help. But in order to even get that far, I was going to have to convince Hina to trust me, and I was going to have to find a way of keeping her alive and safe. I thought I could keep her alive, but getting her to trust me? That was going to take work.

"Go and tell Shiv of my plans," I told Arjun, "and send Hina in here. Take command of the troops yourself, so that Sikander doesn't get any ideas."

"I won't let him hurt your sisters," Arjun promised. But he didn't let me go right away. He clutched me to his chest and pressed his face into my hair, drinking in my scent like he was trying to commit it to memory. I closed my eyes and pushed all the pain and the fear and the planning from my mind so that I could remember what it felt like to be held by him. I didn't want to forget, and I didn't know how long it would be until I felt it again.

At last, Arjun let me go. He left the bedchamber, and I collapsed on my bed, curling up into a ball, with my knees hugged to my chest and my back pressed against the headboard. I cried then in earnest, because there was no one there to see my weakness, no one there to think any less of me for the anguish that was spilling out of me in a torrent of tears.

I had intended to let myself have a moment, and to find my control again before Hina reached me. But she was at my bedside before I realized she was there. I looked up, startled by her presence, and one look at the fury in her hazel eyes told me that my plans were pointless. She wasn't going to let Karim leave this place with his life, not after the way he had killed her beloved brother. She didn't know me, and if she had ever trusted me to fight back, I'd lost that faith now, letting her see me this way, sobbing like a child.

"I . . ." I didn't know what to say. I frantically wiped my face with my dupatta, knowing it was too little, too late.

"Arjun told me your plan," she said, her voice taut with anger.

"I can't let them kill my sisters, Hina." I was pleading with her, more like the subordinate than the ruler. "I can't . . ."

"He killed my brother," she reminded me.

"And he will pay for it."

She rolled her eyes, and I couldn't blame her. I must have looked so pathetic, crying like that, but the scorn I saw on her face lit a fire inside me. The tears dried up as a familiar rage rose to replace them.

"He *will* pay for this," I declared, looking her right in the eyes so she would see the truth of my words. "I did not let myself be fucked by every rich bastard in Bikampur for it to end like this. I did not risk my death or mutilation every night, stealing from them, for it to end like this. I did not climb a cliff and steal back my zahhak just to give up now. But he has us outmaneuvered for the moment. It would be idiotic to fight him here, on the ground of his choosing. You never let the enemy choose the time and place of battle. So, we make a tactical withdrawal. We let him think he has won. And then, when the time is right, when the place is right, we kill him, and his father, and we make sure that no Mahisagari soldier ever dares set foot in Zindh again."

"All right," Hina allowed, and she smiled slightly. I thought maybe we finally understood each other. "So how do we kill him? What is this plan of yours?"

"Arjun will gather fire zahhaks in Registan. To communicate

with him, I will need Sunil Kalani's men, loyal river zahhak riders. Karim would never permit them to come and go as they pleased, but the eunuch here, Shiv, is trustworthy, and he would have access to servants and workmen. He could pass messages for us. Meanwhile, Sunil will continue to raise the levies of Zindh, gathering the army we need to fight."

"How do you intend to escape and reach this army?" she asked.

"I don't," I said. "I intend to fly as part of Karim's aerial armada. I will need an external threat, some force that will look foreign enough that Karim will believe that I will fly for him. And while he is busy with the invaders, we will strike him from all sides, and kill him, and his father with him."

"It could work," Hina allowed, "but how do you intend to ensure this external threat arises? What if nobody tries to invade Zindh?"

She had a point. We all thought Safavia would try invading before long, that they would strike at Ahura or Kadiro, but what if they didn't? What if Ismail was distracted by something else? And even if he did attack, where was the guarantee that he wouldn't just kill me too, once Karim was out of the way?

"Haider . . ."

Hina quirked a copper-tinged eyebrow. "Who?"

"Prince Haider of Safavia," I said, my heart beating a little faster. "When I was little, he was a very close friend. One of my uncles rebelled against my father, and there was a civil war. It looked for a time like my father might lose, so I was sent to the Safavian court to keep me safe. I lived with Prince Haider of Safavia and Princess Tamara of Khevsuria for two years. They treated me very kindly. If I could get a letter to Haider, I think he would come for me."

"You think?" Hina asked.

I shrugged. "It was a long time ago. We were children then,

and he's a man grown now. But I think he would. Especially if I offered him Ahura."

"And what is my place in all of this?" Hina asked.

"You'll be kept safe," I replied. "The Zindhis will fight for you and no one else, so you must live. Sending you to Bikampur probably makes the most sense. Arjun could ensure you are well protected until the time is right."

"No." She gave a toss of her head. "No, I'm not leaving Zindh. This is my home. I will stay here until the fighting is done."

"Do you have a fortress? A place the Mahisagaris can't find you?"

"No, you're not understanding me," she said. "I'm not leaving you. I'm staying with you, to make sure that you don't forget your promises."

"I would never forget them," I replied. "And if you think for one second that I want to marry Karim after what he did to me . . ."

She held up a hand for calm. "I get that. But you can't fight if you're dead. You'll need bodyguards you can trust. You'll need friends."

"I have my sisters. Karim won't hurt them, but if you stay, I can't guarantee your safety," I replied. "I can negotiate it, but Karim and Ahmed can always go back on their word."

"I'll take my chances," she said. "If this plan doesn't work, I want to be close enough to stick a dagger in Karim's back. The only way to do that is to stay close to you. So, you will negotiate a place for me as one of your handmaidens, or I won't agree to help you."

"I can do that," I said, "but I can't promise Ahmed and Karim will honor it once my father is gone."

"I understand," she replied. "All the same, I want to stay with you. And if I die, I want your word that you will kill Karim in my place."

"You have it," I assured her, taking her hands in mine. "I have no intention whatsoever of being Karim's wife. I will kill him and kill myself before that ever happens."

"Then we have an agreement," Hina said. "But you're sure this is how you want things to play out? We have the troops now to just kill them and be done with it."

"They would kill us too," I reminded her. "And then Ahmed Shah would have free rein in Zindh, and possibly in large swaths of Nizam too. Is that what you want? For Mahisagar to rule Zindh for all time?"

She scowled. "It's just hard to surrender now, when we have weapons and zahhaks, and to believe that things will be different once we're under Karim's thumb . . ."

I nodded my agreement. I was terrified that this plan would fail, terrified that I was making a miscalculation. But Karim had outmaneuvered me, loath as I was to admit it. My love for my sisters prevented me from ordering my soldiers to fire with the same callous cruelty my father and Karim himself would have shown. Did that make me weak? Unfit to rule? My father would have said so.

"If you don't believe I can succeed, then I urge you to go with Arjun, or to find some other prince who will protect you," I told her. "There is no shame in living to fight another day."

Hina didn't even consider it. "No, I will stay close to Karim. You may have managed to overturn fate and find yourself in a position of power, but such things are so rare as to be unheard of. I would be a fool to believe that life would offer me the same chance."

"Then I will speak with my father, and with Karim," I said. "I want you to go and pass a message to Sunil Kalani telling him all of this. I don't care how you do it, but do it now. Speak to a workman, a soldier who won't be missed, anyone."

"I'll get on it," she agreed. She gave me a pat on the shoulder. "Courage, your highness."

"Thanks . . ." I whispered, forcing myself to smile until she was gone. Then I let my shoulders slump, let myself give in to the dread, if only for a moment. I was going to have to agree to marry Karim Shah. God, I wasn't sure I had the strength to do it, even with the plans I had put in place. Hina was right. I had soldiers and zahhaks now, but I would have nothing at all once I surrendered. Did I really think I would be better placed to fight back once I was stripped of everything than I was at this moment?

No. That was the truth of it. I wouldn't be better placed to fight, but I would have the opportunity to move my sisters out of the cross fire. That was what I needed to do to regain my freedom; I needed to get them out of the way, someplace safe, where Karim and my father couldn't use them as hostages to guarantee my behavior. Sending them away with Arjun seemed the smartest option. If I could manage that, I could fight with a freer hand.

I stood up from my bed and staggered to the door, my legs feeling like lead, my heart pounding from all the nervous tension that was coiled up inside my chest. My father and Karim were outside, sitting in the shade of a banyan tree, waiting. Sikander was still standing with the men near the baradari. Arjun had been standing opposite him, but now he made his way back toward me, leaving Arvind in charge of the Bikampuri and Zindhi soldiers, while Hina conferred with some of her men, no doubt relaying the information to as many soldiers as possible so that at least one could get the message out. That was smart.

"Finished plotting?" Karim asked, his dark eyes narrowed with suspicion.

"I was making arrangements to end all of this without bloodshed, your highness," I whispered, keeping my voice soft and my eyes downcast and trying to make myself look as small and helpless as possible.

"Spare me the delicate maiden act," Karim snapped. "I've seen you kill a man, and I won't forget that you tried to have your father murder me half an hour ago."

I shrugged. "You want me to forget what you did to me in the past, but you won't extend to me the same courtesy?"

"What I did to you was six years ago, not half an hour," he retorted.

"And what I did to you didn't hurt you, your highness," I reminded him. "If it made you feel afraid then consider how I must feel at this moment, knowing what comes next."

He scowled, but there was enough uncertainty on his face to tell me that my words had hit home. I didn't know if that would spare me his wrath, but I thought if I conducted myself like a frightened princess for the remainder of these negotiations, it might tip the scales in my favor.

"Do you need anything, Razia?" Arjun asked me, having arrived at my side.

So many things sprang to mind. I wanted to embrace him again, I wanted to make love to him again. But we couldn't touch each other, not now, not with Karim watching, not if I wanted him to honor the agreements I would force him to make.

"No," I said, my voice too tight, but I wasn't crying, so that was something. I looked to my father. "I'm ready to discuss the terms of this arrangement, Father."

He glanced up at me, his green eyes peering from beneath dark, hooded brows. His mouth was a hard line of worry. I didn't know whether that was a good sign or a bad one, but I supposed it showed that he still felt something for me. He'd shown that in our negotiations. Of course, he'd also admitted to letting Karim rape me in the hopes of curing me of my deviancy. How could I possibly reconcile myself with that?

"Sikander!" my father bellowed as he stood up from his place beneath the banyan tree. "You are needed! Leave Bilal in charge and join us."

Sikander shouted his assent and rushed over to us, leaving his junior officer in command of the musket-armed men who were still staring down their Zindhi counterparts. If only they'd had an ounce of loyalty to me, I could have prevented all of this, but I knew that they didn't, especially not with my father here.

I returned to my bedchamber so that if the negotiation soured, the men wouldn't see it and take action. I had to keep my sisters safe above all.

We all took our seats, my father, Karim, and Sikander on one side of the room, Arjun and me on the other. I took a deep breath, steeling myself for the coming discussions, not sure whether I could win even a single concession from my father. But I had to try. Everything depended on it.

"I will have my forces stand down, Father, and I will accept this engagement," I gasped, nearly choking on the words in spite of my best efforts to the contrary. "But I have conditions."

He motioned for me to get on with it. That was a good sign. He wasn't demanding an unconditional surrender, and neither was Karim, in spite of the harsh words we'd exchanged earlier.

"First, Arjun and Arvind and the men of Bikampur must be permitted to return home safely," I said.

"No argument," my father replied.

Karim nodded. "We want no war with Registan."

I took a deep breath, because the next ask was going to be harder. "I would like my sisters to be permitted to return to Bikampur with Arjun. They were happy there, and safe."

"No." Karim spoke before my father had a chance. "They will remain with you."

"As what?" I demanded. "Hostages? Is that what you think a marriage should look like?"

"If you intend to marry me as you claim, then why send your sisters away?" Karim retorted. "If you intend to make your home with me, why would you not bring them with you?"

"Because I'm afraid you'll hurt them, to punish me," I replied.

"Punish you for what?" he asked.

"I'm sorry," I said, "have you already forgotten how angry you are with me for trying to convince my father to kill you?"

He scowled. "Your sisters will not be harmed, but neither will they be left behind."

I bit my lip, annoyed, but not surprised. It would be easier if they were safe in Bikampur, but I supposed I was going to have to find some way to keep them safe here. Part of that would be with zahhaks. I looked to my father. "I wish to be permitted to keep my zahhaks, at least Sultana and the two my sisters use as their mounts."

"You are a princess of Nizam, you will keep your zahhaks," my father declared, without so much as glancing in Karim's direction.

Karim gave his opinion on the matter all the same. "You may keep them, but the three of you may not fly together. I do not trust you not to run away from me, Razia, and until I do, I will have one of your sisters left behind at all times as a guarantee of your return."

I had expected that much, and didn't complain. I needed to seem reasonable. "I'm sorry you find that necessary, your highness, but I do not blame you, and I will agree to your terms."

Karim's expression softened ever so slightly, which was just what I'd been praying for. I continued, "I have made a promise to Hina that she would be safe with me, that no harm would come to her, and I must ask that you all agree to honor it."

"As long as she lives she is a threat to our rule in Zindh," Karim declared.

"She wishes to serve me as my handmaiden, your highness," I said. "Surely having her as a hostage will do more to ensure Zindh's stability than executing her."

My father was nodding along, seeing the wisdom in that. Karim was pursing his lips, though, like he suspected a trap. I let him mull it over, let him analyze it, try to work out how it might hurt him. In truth, I wasn't sure that it did. Sending Hina to Bikampur or letting her go free would have raised the specter of revolt, but letting Karim keep her under his thumb would make it far more difficult for a Zindhi army to move against Mahisagar without the threat of execution hanging over their queen's head.

"Fine," Karim said at length. "Hina and her celas may serve as your *unarmed* handmaidens."

I'd expected that much, and I nodded to show that I agreed to it. "But they must be permitted to keep their zahhaks. They're only river zahhaks, after all . . ."

Karim waved away my concerns. "Yes, yes. That's acceptable. But they will not fly them without my express approval. And when they do fly them, they will explain in detail where they are going and when they will return. I will not have you using them as an army of spies against me."

"It will be as you say, your highness," I replied.

If I'd thought that would win Karim over, I was wrong. He scowled. "You're plotting something. I don't know what it is, but I'll find out."

I shook my head. "You said it from the beginning, your highness. You have outmaneuvered me. I am surrendering. That's all."

"I may not be as clever as you are, Razia, but I'm not stupid," Karim warned me. "You *are* plotting something, and rest assured I will find out what it is and ensure that it fails."

My heart leapt in my chest at the threat, because I was plotting something, but he couldn't know that for certain, not if I didn't let on. Pretending to be demure and obedient would be my only defense from here on out. "If you will never trust me to be your wife, then why do you insist on marrying me?"

"Trust takes time," he replied. "If you behave yourself, if you are useful to me, then we will see about trust. Until then, I will watch you closely."

"As your highness wishes," I said, because I knew better than to protest my innocence.

"There are other conditions," my father said, which surprised me. I wasn't expecting him to weigh in on the matter.

Evidently, neither was Karim, because he asked, "What conditions?"

"In the first place, there will be no marriage until all of Zindh is secure, and I am certain that it will remain so," my father replied.

"Nothing in life is certain, your majesty," Karim pointed out.

"All the same, if Zindh is calm, and the tax revenues are good, then the marriage may proceed," my father said.

"Tax revenues?" I perked up a little at that. "But the harvest was brought in more than two months ago, and next year's crop won't be sown for another two or three months."

Karim scowled. "You expect me to wait the better part of a year before the marriage is made official?"

"I do," my father said. "I will leave my daughter in your care; she will be wife to you in all but name. You will have control of her subah, you will have her mind, which you told me was your real desire in marrying her. But you will not be her husband until I am certain that you and your father can live up to all that you have promised me."

Karim grunted at that. "Very well. So long as she remains with me, in my household, I will not complain."

"There is another condition," my father added, feigning not to notice the tension it brought to Karim's face. "Sikander will remain as Razia's bodyguard and chaperone. As a princess of Nizam, she is not to be dishonored before her wedding night."

Karim snorted. "She has opened her legs for every man in Registan, what honor has she got left?"

"If you think so little of her, then why are we here?" my father asked, his tone suddenly going cold and hostile. "Why should I not take my daughter up on her plan to destroy you instead?"

Karim realized he'd made a mistake, though he seemed as confused by my father's response as I felt. Was the man defending me, after all this? Why?

"My daughter is a princess of Nizam and she will be treated as such; that was our agreement from the beginning," my father reminded Karim. "If you do not believe her to be worthy of that respect, then there will be no marriage and no alliance. We will have war instead."

Karim held up his hands for calm. "Forgive me, your majesty, I was wrong to say what I said. I will honor your daughter as a princess of Nizam, as was agreed. She will be permitted whatever chaperones and guards you think fit."

"And you will not touch her before her wedding night, or there will be war," my father added.

"As you wish, your majesty," Karim agreed, though I could see in his dark eyes that he knew as well as my father did—as well as I did, for that matter—that once my father was gone, he wouldn't necessarily know what became of me, not even with Sikander there to watch.

My father looked to me and asked, "Is there anything else?"

He was giving me a chance to make other demands? I hadn't expected that. Maybe Arjun's rebuke had finally gotten through to him? I didn't know if I could really believe that after being disappointed by him so many times over the course of my life, but I wanted to believe it. I wanted to be stupid and naive and to believe that my father loved me in spite of all evidence to the contrary. I wanted to imagine that he was helping me, giving me the time I needed to avoid my fate, to come up with a plan to free myself of this engagement. It was easier than believing the alternative, that he didn't much care what became of me, that I was just a pawn to him, not his only child.

I thought for a moment about what else I might want, but I had secured everything I needed to carry out my plan. Though there was something else that was weighing on me, something personal, and something that might be the key to escaping all of this.

"I'd like a moment alone with Sikander before we announce the arrangement to the men," I said.

"Of course," my father replied. He stood up, and waited for Arjun and Karim to do the same. The three of them left the room, and then it was just Sikander and me, as I'd requested, the pair of us sitting across from each other.

My father's old guardsman looked a bit confused that I would request a one-on-one audience with him. His brown eyes were scanning my tear-streaked face with something that verged on concern, though I didn't detect in them any of the affection he had held for me as a child. Maybe, after four years apart, and more years being beaten by him, it was too late for that, but if he was to be my only real protection from Karim, then I had to see where I stood, and now I knew the question to ask.

"I just have one question for you, Sikander," I said, my voice quieter than it had been these last few days, my heart pounding at the memory I was about to conjure.

His brow furrowed with alarm. "Ask it, your highness."

"Did it bother you?" I wondered. "Even a little?"

"Did what bother me, your highness?" he asked.

"When Karim raped me," I said, every muscle in my neck straining to push the words out. "I must have screamed your name a hundred times. I begged for you. I thought you didn't hear me, but today I learned that you did, that Father had ordered you to let it happen. So did it bother you, hearing me scream your name while he did those things to me?"

A few tears escaped the corners of my eyes as the magnitude of the betrayal washed over me, as I remembered how much I'd trusted and loved him in spite of everything, how hard I had fought to please him. He had been my protector, the one person I was supposed to be able to trust to keep me safe from my enemies. And he had just let Karim do what he'd done.

Sikander's face turned the color of ash as the blood drained from it. His brown eyes got big and round. So it had bothered him. Good. I could work with that.

CHAPTER 10

I left Sikander there to stew on what he had done to me, and walked out into the courtyard where my father was waiting with Karim and Arjun. Hina had gone back to the baradari to sit with my sisters. The soldiers on both sides seemed to have relaxed a little, realizing that our negotiations were taking too long to lead to a battle. I went to my father, head bowed.

"I presume you'll be leaving immediately for Nizam?" I couldn't imagine that the man would stay with me once the marriage negotiations had been concluded.

"No, I will remain here to fortify this city," my father replied, and for a moment I felt a profound sense of relief wash over me. He was staying with me? I wouldn't be living directly under Karim's thumb? God, that was so much better than I'd feared.

"You will be coming with me to Kadiro immediately," Karim informed me.

"Kadiro?" I hadn't considered that possibility. If we flew to Kadiro, then I would be surrounded by Mahisagari soldiers. I would have no bodyguards save Sikander. I would have no help from the local Zindhi populace. Shiv wouldn't be able to deliver my messages. God, nothing would go according to plan.

"That was the arrangement," Karim said.

"Sikander will be going with you," my father told me, which was cold comfort. I was surprised when he stepped forward and put his hands on my shoulders. When was the last time he'd touched me in a way that didn't hurt? He looked into my eyes, and though his expression wasn't exactly warm, it wasn't hostile either. "If Karim mistreats you, you are to tell Sikander at once, and he will inform me, and I will come for you. You are my daughter, and no man may harm or dishonor you without harming and dishonoring me." He aimed that last statement at Karim, but I felt the full weight of it in my heart. It wasn't exactly the acceptance I'd longed for my whole life, but it was something.

"And you will permit Arjun and his men to return to Bikampur safely?" I asked, wanting to reassure myself of that.

"I will. And the Zindhi soldiers currently under arms will be permitted to return to their homes, provided they do not take up arms against me," my father agreed.

I nodded, taking a deep breath to steel myself against the pain of going off with Karim as his betrothed. "Thank you, Father."

He frowned, which could have meant anything. I had another good-bye to say before I left, though.

I looked to Arjun, wishing I could embrace him, but knowing I would pay for it if I did it in sight of Karim after agreeing to marry him. So, I just choked out, "Good-bye, my prince," and left it at that.

Arjun came to me and wrapped his arms around me. My eyes flickered to Karim's glowering face, and I said, "My prince, we can't . . ."

"Karim knows what we've meant to each other all this time," Arjun said, loudly enough that every man heard. He leaned down and brushed my forehead with his lips, letting them linger just long enough to leave a warm glow on the surface of my skin. When he pulled back, he whispered, "I will always love you. No matter what."

I wanted to make the same promise to him, but I couldn't. Uttering those words now, with Karim listening, would just deepen his suspicions of a plot to escape. So I bit down on my lip against the pain of this parting, and I bowed my head, praying that Arjun would know what I was thinking, that he would know I loved him as much as he loved me, that he wouldn't hold it against me for not feeling safe enough to say it out loud.

"Remember what I told you," he whispered, and I knew in that moment that he understood. I knew what words he was referencing. *Do what you have to do to survive.*

"I will, my prince," I whispered back, my voice catching in my throat.

Arjun stepped away from me, and Karim stepped closer, his jaw clenched tightly. He glared down at me, his dark eyes wide with fury. "I permitted that as a courtesy, but from now on, no man touches you but me. Do you understand?"

"Yes, your highness," I replied, keeping my voice calm and subdued, removing from it any traces of the anger and hatred I was feeling. "With your permission, I would like to explain the situation to my sisters and to Hina and her celas. They must be very nervous by now."

"Yes, fine." He gestured to the baradari. "But be quick about it. I want us in Kadiro before nightfall."

"As you wish, your highness," I agreed.

I tried to project an image of calm as I made my way back to my throne, where Sakshi and Lakshmi were waiting. I knew that my older sister would be under no illusions about what was happening, but I didn't want Lakshmi to be scared. Karim was a horrible man, he was evil, and cruel, and he had raped me when I was

Lakshmi's age. I wanted her nowhere near him. But that wasn't a choice that I had, so the best I could do would be to shield her with my body and my mind, and hope that it was enough.

"It's true, then?" Sakshi asked as I stepped beneath the pavilion's domed roof. Her collarbones were standing out from her skin as she sucked in a tense breath to steel herself for my response.

"We will be flying to Kadiro with Karim Shah, all of us," I said, nodding to Hina and her celas so that they would know they were included too.

"Kadiro?" Hina asked, not missing the fact that we hadn't planned for this. "Is your household not coming with you?"

I shook my head. "It is not."

She said nothing, not here, not where others might hear, but the grim expression on her face spoke volumes. It asked me all the questions I was already struggling with—how would we get our messages out without Shiv? How would we contact Sunil Kalani to let him know where we were? How would he contact us? How would we get a letter to Haider to ensure that Safavia attacked? My plans were already falling apart, and it had only been an hour since I'd made them.

I didn't have answers to those questions, not yet. I knew that platitudes like "We'll think of something" were worthless here. We might well not think of anything. It might be that Karim kept us as virtual prisoners in the palace. But I did have some good news. "There will be no wedding before the tax revenues are assessed next year. That gives us some time to make preparations."

Hina nodded. She saw what a relief that was. Our situation had changed drastically in the course of a single day. Months could shift the balance of power back in our favor, if we were careful, if we used our time wisely.

"Are you really going to marry Prince Karim, Akka?" Lakshmi asked. She didn't sound disgusted at the prospect, just confused.

"I am," I lied, because I didn't want her to know about our plans; I didn't want to risk her telling anyone. And if she believed that I would marry Karim, then maybe it would help convince him and his men that I was serious about it.

"But don't you love Prince Arjun?" she asked.

"I do," I admitted, my heart aching for him already, "but my father arranged for me to marry Karim instead."

"I thought you didn't like Prince Karim," she said.

"It's complicated, little sister," I told her, reaching out and running my hand over her jet-black hair. "We'll have plenty of time to talk about it, but for right now we need to fly with Karim to Kadiro."

"And Nuri is coming too?" Lakshmi asked, nodding to indicate Hina's twelve-year-old cela.

"She is," I agreed. "All of Hina's celas are coming with us. But we all must be unarmed. They're not going to be soldiers and bodyguards anymore, but handmaidens and companions."

Lakshmi frowned. "But they'll still get to be zahhak riders?"

"Yes, we all get to keep our zahhaks," I assured her, as well as Hina's disciples.

Hina surrendered her weapons to one of her soldiers and had her celas follow suit. All sixteen of them gave away their fish-tailed Zindhi rifles and their bhuj axes, and in a flash they were reduced from a troop of women warriors to a retinue of pretty handmaidens as you might find in any palace in Daryastan. Seeing that strengthened my resolve to beat Karim. I wasn't going to let Karim strip us of everything that made us special and powerful. He had won this battle, but the war was far from over.

I returned with my sisters and Hina and her celas to where my father was still standing with Arjun, though I noted that Karim and his men were gone, and Sikander too. That worried me.

"Where are Karim and Sikander, Father?" I asked.

"Fetching the zahhaks from the stables," my father answered. "I'll be sending Sikander and two fliers with you."

Two fliers? That didn't make sense. I'd stolen four thunder zahhaks, including my Sultana. That meant that I needed at best one Nizami flier, not two. Was he gifting me zahhaks from his personal retinue? If he was, then that would bring my numbers up to six thunder zahhaks. With so many flying on my side, I would have Karim outnumbered on the flight back to Kadiro. Why not use that to my advantage and kill him?

Or was my father sending extra men to keep me under closer guard, to even things out in the event I decided to attack Karim's five acid zahhaks with my sisters? That made a certain amount of sense too, but I doubted very much if any Nizami soldier would kill me to protect a foreign prince. So why the show of force?

Before I could finish puzzling it out, the men returned, mounted on their zahhaks. Sikander was riding Parisa, his personal mount, and two Nizami men followed him, riding zahhaks I had taken from Shikarpur, while leading Sultana and Ragini by the reins.

"Akka, why is he riding my zahhak?" Lakshmi asked, pointing to the soldier who was mounted on the back of the animal she had chosen for herself.

"I don't know, but we won't let him keep her," I assured her.

Karim followed close behind Sikander and his men, mounted on Amira's back, the brilliantly colored acid zahhak strutting across the palace grounds, her bright red eyes and her hooked beak giving her a menacing aspect. He was attended by three of his men riding acid zahhaks of their own, but a fourth man was leading a fifth acid zahhak by her reins. Was this the gift Karim had promised me?

"Mohini?" Lakshmi's voice was filled with hope and doubt as

she stared at the acid zahhak that was trotting dutifully behind the man holding her reins.

"No, sweetheart," I told her, patting her on the shoulder. "It couldn't be."

But Lakshmi wasn't listening to me. She shouted, "Mohini!" and tore free from me, the skirt of her sari threatening to trip her as she raced across the courtyard.

"Lakshmi, no!" I ran after her, terrified that she was going to get herself devoured. The last thing you wanted to do around a strange zahhak was make sudden movements, and a girl as small as Lakshmi would be an easy morsel, even for an acid zahhak.

But the acid zahhak being led by the Mahisagari soldier perked up at the sound of Lakshmi's voice. She tore free of his grasp and galloped across the courtyard toward my little sister, springing with her wing claws, her crane-like rear legs kicking furiously at the paving stones.

Before I could stop her, Lakshmi had run straight up to the massive zahhak, and the animal buried her beak in my sister's chest. I ran, horror gripping my insides, waiting for the spurt of blood as the creature tore my baby sister apart in front of me, but the blood never came. The zahhak was pushing her head up against Lakshmi's chest, sniffing at her, nuzzling her. Lakshmi was clinging to the animal's massive skull, running her hands over the brilliant blue feather crest atop her head, all the while crying, "Mohini!" over and over again.

The acid zahhak saw me coming and pushed Lakshmi aside, using one wing to protect her, like she might her own hatchling, and leaned her head low, her beak widening to reveal razor-sharp teeth. She hissed at me like a snake, and I froze in place, suddenly aware of the fact that I was the one breaking all the rules by running up on a strange zahhak like a crazy person.

For an instant, I thought I was going to be bathed in acid, but at that moment, there was a fluttering of wings, and a huge blue and gold form appeared out of nowhere, dropping from the sky to land in front of me, roaring a warning. It was Sultana. She'd pulled free of the man holding her the moment she'd seen me in danger.

"Mohini, no!" Lakshmi exclaimed, and I was shocked when the zahhak turned her crimson eye to look at the little girl for permission.

"You don't eat my akka!" Lakshmi chided, her harsh words making the zahhak bow her head in submission.

For my part, I had put my hand on Sultana's neck to calm her, and though she kept one emerald eye on Mohini, she nuzzled my body with her snout, taking in great sniffs of me to make sure I was okay.

"Thank you, my friend," I told her, giving her a big kiss on her snout, and rubbing her cobalt scales with great affection.

"Akka, come see my Mohini!" Lakshmi called, now that both of our zahhaks were under control, even if they were eyeing each other warily.

"Be nice," I told Sultana as I slowly approached my little sister, watching Mohini for any signs of aggression. She regarded me suspiciously, but since Lakshmi was walking toward me with no signs of fear, she kept her wing claws and her razor-sharp beak to herself.

My sister was grinning from ear to ear, her face wet with happy tears. "Can you believe it, Akka? My Mohini came back to me!"

"She's my wedding gift to your big sister," Karim declared from his place in Amira's saddle. "I traded a zahhak egg to your father for her."

My hackles went up at once. Was this gift meant to be some grand gesture to me, or a way of earning Lakshmi's undying favor? Was he grooming her, as he had groomed me? The possibility of it roiled my insides. I could never let the two of them be alone together, no matter what happened. I wasn't going to let him do to her what he had done to me.

"Thank you, Prince Karim!" Lakshmi exclaimed, tears continuing to stream down her cheeks as she petted Mohini, as the two of them nuzzled each other, as she clung to the zahhak's emerald neck scales. It should have been such a joyous moment, but I felt nothing but hatred and fear at my sister's reunion with her zahhak. If I'd entertained any doubts about the sort of monster Karim was, they were gone now.

"You're welcome, Princess Lakshmi," Karim replied, bowing gracefully in the saddle, favoring her with a charming smile.

"Your father really traded a zahhak egg to his rival, the zamorin of Kolikota?" I asked dubiously.

Karim shrugged. "We have plenty more where that came from. The Firangis were using Ahura to build up a force of acid zahhaks, as it's a nesting ground. When we captured the island, we captured their acid zahhaks, and a cache of eggs. Soon, Mahisagar will have a force of acid zahhaks to rival even Virajendra."

"That's wonderful news," I said, and I thought I even managed to sound sincere, though in reality my mind was churning, trying to work out just how strong Karim's position really was. I supposed when we reached Kadiro, I would find out for myself. I bowed my head. "Thank you for this magnificent gift, your highness. It warms my heart to see my little sister so happy. I could have wished for nothing more than this."

"I really get to have my Mohini back?" Lakshmi asked me, her face full of tears of joy.

"Yes, you really do," I assured her. I came forward slowly to embrace her, and though Mohini kept a scarlet eye on me all the while, she made no aggressive movements, though she did press her snout against Lakshmi all the harder, as if trying to prove to the girl that she loved her even more than I did. Normally I would not have imagined myself a rival for a zahhak's affections, but where my little sister was concerned, I didn't think even a zahhak's fabled loyalty was worth very much when set beside my own.

"Is it safe to come closer?" Sakshi asked, standing a few paces away, looking nervous.

"She won't hurt you!" Lakshmi promised, and she made sure of it by being the one to go to Sakshi and embrace her, rather than the other way around. "Isn't my Mohini the prettiest zahhak in the whole world?"

"She is," Sakshi agreed, though for my part I didn't think I would ever view an acid zahhak in the same way I viewed my Sultana. I reached up and ran my fingers across the paler blue scales on the underside of Sultana's neck, my thunder zahhak still hovering protectively over me, just in case the shorter acid zahhak got any ideas about eating me.

Now the math made sense at least. My father had known about this gift, and had accounted for it. I would have three thunder zahhaks flown by Sikander and two of his men, plus Ragini, Mohini, and my Sultana. Six animals: five thunder, one acid. It wasn't enough to defeat all of Mahisagar in battle, though it was more than enough to defeat Karim's four acid zahhak riders, I thought. If I attacked en route, would Sikander's men join me, oppose me, or sit back and watch?

"If you're finished getting reacquainted with Mohini, Lakshmi, dear," Karim said, "we should mount up and get moving. You and your akka will be flying with me back to Kadiro now. Sakshi and Sikander have to stay here to finish making preparations, but they will join us in a couple of hours."

He was smirking at me, letting me know that he'd already considered the possibility that I might attack him on the way to Kadiro. But with Lakshmi and me flying alone, the odds were too badly stacked against us to risk a fight. And my father and Sikander would kill Sakshi if I rebelled. It was clever. The bastard had thought of everything.

"And what about me?" Hina asked. She was already mounted on her zahhak, Sakina, along with all fifteen of her celas on theirs.

"You and half your fliers will come with Razia and Lakshmi," Karim told her. "The other half will follow with Sikander."

"As you wish, your highness," Hina said, and she even managed to keep the hate and the rage out of her voice, though God only knew how. The tension in her shoulders betrayed her anger, though her face was a carefully composed mask of neutrality.

"I'll see you in a little while," Sakshi told Lakshmi, hugging her tightly. Then she turned to me and said, "I'll be all right here with Sikander, Razia, don't worry about me."

"See you soon, then," I replied, because when I was already leaving Arjun, and this new home in Shikarpur, I didn't have it in me to say any more long good-byes. I swung into Sultana's saddle instead, and steeled myself for the flight to Kadiro, wondering what horrors awaited me there.

CHAPTER 11

Karim and his three fellow acid zahhak riders kept about two hundred yards above us and fifty yards behind us the whole flight south to Kadiro. It was an aggressive posture, designed to give them a clear shot if I tried anything, though I didn't see why it was necessary when I only had Lakshmi flying my wing.

Hina's eight river zahhaks floated in and out of the formation, but Karim's men ignored them, as they lacked breath. If only they'd had thunder or fire, we could have flown up to meet Karim in battle, and defeated him. But I supposed if river zahhaks had breath, Zindh would be one of the great powers of the world, and not a backwater province of Nizam.

Still, in spite of all my disadvantages in numbers and position, I was tempted to simply wheel Sultana around and send a bolt of lightning straight into Karim's face. But I knew that biding my time was the smarter move. When I struck, I wanted it to be a completely devastating blow that destroyed Mahisagar, and secured Zindh. I wanted to give myself an unassailable position that would force my father to acknowledge my supremacy over Zindh, and dissuade him from ever dreaming of marrying me off to any man against my will again. The trouble was, I didn't have the slightest idea how I was going to do that now that Shiv was back in Shikarpur, unable to deliver messages, and Karim seemed wise to all my tricks.

"It'll be all right, your highness," Hina said.

I looked up, having been staring at the waters of the Zindhu below me, completely lost in thought, and found that I was flying alone with Hina—the rest of the formation having floated off to our right, out of earshot.

"I know it looks grim now, but we'll get through this together," she said.

I shook my head, marveling at the generosity of her words. She'd just lost everything and she could still spare a thought for my feelings? I wasn't sure I'd have been able to be so gracious in her position.

"Thank you for supporting me," I said. "If you'd left . . ." I trailed off, not sure what I would have done had she withdrawn her allegiance. I couldn't have blamed her if she had. I'd surrendered to Karim after I'd promised I wouldn't.

"It's not the return to Kadiro that I'd imagined," she confessed, looking over her shoulder at the Mahisagari acid zahhaks hovering above us and behind us, their peacock-like plumage blending in surprisingly well with the bright blue sky. "But I couldn't just leave you, not after everything that happened. Nobody deserves to be forced into a marriage with that monster."

"Do you think Sunil will be able to recruit enough men to really challenge Mahisagar's army?" I asked, because if he couldn't, then I wouldn't have a prayer of avoiding this marriage.

Hina shrugged. "I think a lot will depend on Prince Arjun and the Registanis."

Arjun. My heart hurt just thinking about him. But I remembered his words of support, remembered the permission he'd given me to survive, and I kept those words close. He would never blame me, whatever it took to get through this, and that meant the world to me.

"You know, I never did get the chance to thank you, your highness," Hina said.

"Thank *me*?" I screwed up my face in confusion at those words. "For what? Getting you into this mess?"

"For saving my life," she replied. "First when you took me in, and again when you defended me from your father and Karim. And I suppose a third time, when you talked me out of just shooting him and trading my life for his."

"I half wish I had let you shoot him," I muttered.

She shook her head. "No. You made the right decision. If we're going to survive this, we need to be smart about it, we need to have a plan. Let's not throw away our lives now just because we're scared."

"You're scared too?" I asked her, because there was no sign of it on her face. Even when Karim had arrived, her expression had been one of rage rather than fear.

"We all are," Hina assured me, but then her eyes flickered over to where Lakshmi and Nuri were flying a mock dogfight in the middle of the formation of river zahhaks, giggling loudly enough that we could hear them from where we were sitting. "Well, except them."

It was a remarkable thing to watch. I'd never seen river zahhaks growing up, so I knew little of their capabilities, beyond what I'd seen since coming to Zindh. But as Nuri and Lakshmi fought their mock duel, I noted that the river zahhak's flight was far more buoyant than any other species I'd ever seen before. Nalini's wings didn't seem to beat with the same strength of purpose as a thunder or acid zahhak's, giving her flight a lazy character to it, but each wingbeat lifted her higher in the air than a beat from Sultana's wings would have done for her. And while Nalini didn't have Mohini's raw speed, and her long, pointed wings couldn't roll quite as quickly as the acid zahhak's shorter, broader ones, when the pair of them circled in the sky, it was the river zahhak who turned tighter, her long, forked tail twisting sideways as her wings dug so hard into the air that they sent little wisps of white smoke corkscrewing off their tips.

"They're such magnificent fliers," I said, more to myself than to Hina.

"Yes, they're going to be so ferocious when they grow up," Hina agreed, mistaking my meaning.

"No, not Lakshmi and Nuri," I said. "Well, yes, them too. I meant your river zahhaks. I've never had the pleasure of watching them fly before. They're exquisitely maneuverable."

"And if they had breath, Zindh would be free," Hina lamented. "That's what my brother used to always say. If we could just give a river zahhak the fire of a fire zahhak or the lightning of a thunder zahhak, Zindh would be the most powerful kingdom in all the world."

I grunted at that. "How many river zahhaks are there in Zindh anyway?" Hina had sixteen of her own, and I knew that Sunil had more besides, but I hadn't been in Zindh long enough to get a rough idea.

"Altogether?" Hina shrugged. "I don't know. But before Mahisagar's invasion, my brother and I had forty-eight animals at our command. Now there are just thirty-two left. The other wealthy zamindars in Zindh have zahhaks of their own, but they'll be reluctant to fly for us when they know they haven't got a prayer of winning a fight in the air."

I shrugged. "I'm less worried about river zahhaks than I am about soldiers. Arjun can bring fire zahhaks from Registan, and if

I can get word to Haider, he might bring thunder zahhaks from Safavia. But without soldiers, we'll never recapture Kadiro."

"Speaking of which, we're getting close now," Hina said, gesturing to the farmlands in front of us.

I didn't see what was so different about them from the ones we'd been flying over for the last three and a half hours. Flat fields of freshly planted rice and cotton were broken up here and there with tall sugarcane stalks reaching the midpoint of their growing season. The farms lined the banks of the Zindhu in a strip of green leaves and black furrows about ten or fifteen miles wide, before the land turned to yellow dust, too arid for farming, and bereft even of much tree cover.

"How can you tell?" I asked.

"Because we're reaching the delta," she replied, pointing to little ribbons of water branching off the main channel of the river, spreading out before us like a fan. "Kadiro is there." She pointed across the desert to our right, though I couldn't yet make out any signs of a city in that direction.

Still, Hina had lived in Kadiro and its environs for the whole of her life, so I trusted her as she banked Sakina in that direction, the indigo-winged river zahhak quickening her pace as she too recognized the landscape near her home.

I followed Hina, noting that the other Zindhi fliers had already started their turns for Kadiro, drawing sudden movements from the acid zahhak riders behind us, none of whom really knew Zindh very well, and who had been content to follow the winding course of the river to the city.

Personally, I'd have rather taken the scenic route to get to Kadiro. The longer I put off my arrival, the longer I could pretend that none of this was really happening, that I wasn't engaged to Karim, that I wasn't going to be forced to live in a strange palace surrounded by foreign soldiers, ruled over by men who wanted to strip me of my freedom and command me like a slave. And the closer we got to Kadiro, the more aware of my fate I became, and the more I worried that I wasn't smart enough and strong enough to change it.

But all too soon, the city of Kadiro hove into view, and my heart climbed into my throat. It was a bigger city than Shikarpur, and had served for centuries as Zindh's traditional capital. Nizam had made Shikarpur the capital of the subah because it held the strongest fortress, but Kadiro was the great port at the mouth of the Zindhu's delta, a hub of trade all along the coast, and one of the two endpoints of the river trade that flowed up and down the Zindhu.

My eyes were struck by the bright blue tiles mingling with yellow sandstone bricks, by the domes of turquoise and gold, and by the stout city walls protecting Kadiro on its landward side. Its harbor was a natural lagoon, guarded from wind-driven waves by a barrier island that paralleled the seashore. The entrance, a narrow channel, was guarded by twin forts, small but stout, and bristling with cannons. The bulk of the city formed a crescent around the bustling harbor, but I noted that Hina was flying us not toward the walled city but toward a fortress that seemed to rise straight up out of the waters of the lagoon.

It was only as we drew closer that I realized the fortress wasn't a fortress at all, but a palace of gleaming marble. On its northern side, a pair of retaining walls stretched out like arms, encompassing a harbor that was a miniature reflection of the city's. The still waters served as lotus gardens, blue-petaled flowers standing out like stars against the deep green of the lagoon. Gleaming marble walkways and pavilions capped with cobalt-and-turquoise-tiled domes led from small docks to the first courtyard of the palace, where dozens of buildings sat nestled amid date palms and enormous banyan trees, their marble facades connected to one another by means of golden sandstone walkways that stood out in sharp contrast to the bright green of the manicured lawns and well-tended rosebushes.

"Akka! It's so beautiful!" Lakshmi shrieked, pointing at the marble palace buildings, at the bright lotus gardens, at the scenic lagoons and the thoughtfully placed shade trees.

"It is!" I agreed, offering her a smile that was utterly at odds with the sick sense of dread that was settling like a pall over my heart.

"Maybe it won't be so bad living with Karim," she said, her tone so hopeful that it hurt me to hear it. She wasn't old enough to understand that what she saw as a beautiful home was actually a gilded cage. So long as she was safe, reunited with her zahhak and living with her family, nothing else mattered. But I knew the truth. If we were going to live in this palace in safety, I would have to give up everything that I had become. I would have to let the man I despised most in all the world touch me whenever he pleased, and I would have to raise his children as my own. And all the while, I would be watched by his agents day and night. No, I didn't think I could subject myself to that—not even for Lakshmi.

As we approached the palace, I spotted a pair of acid zahhaks winging their way across the lagoon toward us. They weren't moving with much urgency, not when they could so clearly see Karim and his acid zahhaks behind us and above us in the position of advantage, but the patrol kept its height nonetheless, circling in behind us, joining Karim and his fliers, creating a six-strong formation of acid zahhaks in the perfect position to kill us all.

It went against every instinct I possessed as a flier to just sit on Sultana's back and watch that happen. It went against Sultana's instincts too. The poor thing kept craning her neck back to get a look at Amira and the other acid zahhaks, her hood flaring slightly from anxiety. She'd been in enough battles to know that giving up her tail feathers to an acid zahhak was a good way to get killed, even if she could never have articulated it the way a human mind could.

"It's all right, sweetheart," I lied, stroking the smooth cobalt scales of her neck. "We're going to be just fine."

"Razia!" Karim called, Amira flapping her wings until they were turquoise blurs on either side of her body as she raced to catch up. He pointed to the outer palace's courtyard, and a particular marble baradari that must have served as the diwan-i-khas here in Kadiro. "My father is waiting for us there."

"Of course, your highness," I replied, and I forced myself to smile in spite of the anxiety eating a hole in my stomach. I steered Sultana toward the building in question, focusing my attention on bringing her in for a smooth landing on the sandstone path that led to the baradari's bright white steps.

Beside me, Mohini settled to the ground, and Lakshmi was quick to throw off her saddle straps so that she could better reach forward and hug her zahhak's emerald-scaled neck, shouting words of praise and encouragement. Hina landed an instant later, and within seconds, I found myself surrounded by the eight Zindhi fliers so effectively that Karim and Amira couldn't find a way through the cordon.

He and his fellow Mahisagari fliers landed a short distance away, where they were soon joined by close to fifty musket-armed soldiers—or what passed for soldiers in Mahisagar. The men wore loose dhotis, and some hadn't even bothered putting on their kurtas, letting their bare flesh take the force of Zindh's harsh sun instead. With long, curved daggers thrust through their sashes, and battle scars marring their faces and arms, I thought they looked more like bandits than royal guards, but I knew from long experience that whatever they lacked in order or discipline, the Mahisagaris were the best fighters at sea to be found anywhere in Daryastan.

More Mahisagari men approached from the other end of the garden, followed by three acid zahhak riders whose mounts pranced like proud horses, their keen red eyes taking in the river zahhaks around me with a predatory eagerness that sent shivers down my spine. One glance at the river zahhaks told me that they were nervous. I wondered if they were often made prey for acid zahhaks in the wild, on account of their lack of breath, or if these river zahhaks just remembered their last encounter with the acid zahhaks of Mahisagar a few days ago.

Whatever the case, the hundred soldiers and seven zahhaks resembled not at all the usual welcoming party for a new bride arriving in her husband's home. It was a completely unsubtle reminder of the fact that I was a prisoner, dragged here against my will, whatever pretty words Karim might try to spin to the contrary. But Sultan Ahmed of Mahisagar had never struck me as a particularly subtle man. I thought that was to my advantage, because I was going to need to outwit him if I was going to get myself out of this mess, and he was already starting the match with the deck stacked heavily in his favor.

I sat uneasily on Sultana's back, waiting for Karim and his men to dismount, but they hadn't yet.

The tension was broken by the arrival of about two dozen women dressed in chaniya cholis with bright embroidery and delicate shisheh mirror-work covering every inch of fabric. Their wrists and ankles were festooned with golden bangles and their faces hidden by the diaphanous silk of their dupattas. Like Hina's celas, they were unarmed, and from the quality of their jewelry and the fine silk of their clothes, I suspected that these were the royal women of Mahisagar. Their arrival calmed some of the fears that had been gnawing at the back of my mind. I didn't think the court women would have been present had Karim and his father intended to harm me.

Karim swung down from the saddle as the women approached, and he came forward to embrace one of them in particular. As her saffron dupatta was covering her face, I couldn't make out her identity, but her words gave me the answer. "Welcome home, son."

"Thank you, Mother," Karim replied, with a politeness that I wasn't used to seeing from him.

"How was the flight?" she asked, her tone suggesting that she was either totally oblivious to the presence of so many zahhaks and so many armed men, or so accustomed to it that it bothered her not in the slightest. Wasn't she the least bit worried that I might use my thunder zahhak to murder her and her son? She couldn't be ignorant of our history, could she?

"The air was smooth as glass," Karim told her, "and we weren't battling too much of a headwind. But it's been a long day, and I'm sure that we'll all be eager to get some rest before long."

Karim's mother turned to look at me, and made her way over, followed closely by her son and her handmaidens. She kept her dupatta covering the majority of her face for modesty's sake, which made me feel a little exposed, as I had but loosely wrapped mine over my hair. I wasn't used to hiding my face, not when it had always been part of what my clients had paid to see.

"There's nothing to be frightened over, dear," Karim's mother said.

"Frightened?" I asked, wondering what had made her choose that word.

She gestured to me, still sitting atop my zahhak, and said, "It's normal to be nervous when coming to a new home, but there's nothing to be worried about. My husband and I are very happy to welcome you into our family. Karim has told me so much about you."

"Has he?" I asked, wondering just what stories he'd told his mother about me. Had he forgotten to mention that I was a hijra and had spent years living as a courtesan? Those were typically not the qualifications most sought after in a primary wife. Most men would never consider marrying a courtesan, let alone a hijra.

"He has," she assured me. "And so has my husband. He's eager to see you again."

Eager to see me again? Somehow I doubted that, but the woman's smile, barely visible through the thin silk fabric of her dupatta, was enough to convince me that I wouldn't be immediately murdered if I dismounted. I unstrapped myself from the saddle and slid down to the ground, taking a moment to smooth the wrinkles from my ajrak clothes.

As soon as I dismounted, Karim's mother stepped forward, letting her dupatta slide just enough that I could make out her face, though it was still kept hidden from the men on account of Sultana and Sakina, the two zahhaks almost completely blocking us from view. She looked like Karim, after a fashion. Her eyes were the same nearly black color as his, the ideal sought after by so many courtesans even in Nizam, and their corners were creased with laugh lines that made it seem that she was accustomed to smiling—not the expression I typically associated with Karim and his father. Her skin was several shades darker than mine, a fine, deep brown that matched well with her lustrous hair, which was still a uniform black, without the slightest trace of gray, though I knew she must have been nearing forty.

"My name is Asma, but you may call me mother-in-law," she said.

Though her words were mild, I felt like this was a test of sorts, and I was eager to pass it, to help take some of the suspicion off of myself, to help hide my true feelings after I'd done such a poor job of it back in Shikarpur. So I said, "Thank you for welcoming me into your home, mother-in-law."

Asma's ruby-red lips pulled back into a brilliant smile, suggesting that I'd given a suitable response. "No thanks are necessary; it is my pleasure and my honor to welcome my son's bride into our home."

I felt something warm and soft brush my hand, and I looked over to find that Lakshmi had come to stand beside me, her hand clutching mine, her eyes downcast like a properly shy princess. She'd even draped her sari so that the pallu covered her hair demurely. It was the acid zahhak sari I'd bought for her in Bikampur, paired with the acid zahhak jewelry that had once been mine, but which was now effectively hers.

"And you must be little Lakshmi," Asma said, bending over a little so that she was at her eye level. "You're even prettier than my Karim said you were."

Lakshmi's cheeks reddened at the compliment, and she lowered her big brown eyes still further beneath her thick lashes. God, she really had learned her trade well from Ammi's tutors in Bikampur. Another two years, three on the outside, and she would have been one of the most sought-after courtesans in Bikampur. As it was, she looked every inch the young Virajendran princess, which worried me. If Karim had noticed her beauty already, then I was going to have to make good and certain that I never gave them a moment alone together.

"Did my son's gift please you?" Asma asked Lakshmi, her eyes darting in Mohini's direction.

Lakshmi bobbed her head, her earrings jingling in time with the movement. "I'll never be able to thank him enough for bringing my Mohini back to me! I missed her so much."

"Well, you're quite welcome, dear," Asma said. "My son, Karim, has told me that he considers you to be like his own daughter, and so I will consider you my own granddaughter. How's that?"

"I'd like that very much," Lakshmi said, with such longing that it tore open a whole host of scars across my own heart that I'd almost forgotten were there. The desire to be accepted for myself, and to have the family I was robbed of by dint of my birth, was so strong it was almost overpowering. And either this woman was far kinder than her son, or she knew something about the pain we'd experienced and she was using it to manipulate us. I supposed time would tell which it was.

"If you'll come with me, I will take you to my husband," Asma offered. "He's waiting to meet you in the diwan-i-khas." She gestured to the building in question, and now that I was standing on ground level, I could see more clearly past its colonnaded facade, to where Sultan Ahmed was sitting atop a marble throne not at all unlike the one in the palace of Shikarpur.

"Normally we ladies do not have much cause to visit the outer palace," she said as we walked, her maids moving to surround us on all sides, "but given that you were arriving in the company of so many men, my husband thought it appropriate to receive you here, and to permit me to join him."

To permit her to join him? I resisted raising an eyebrow at that phrasing, but it still sent a chill through my heart. Were they planning on sequestering me away in the inner palace, then? I supposed I was about to find out.

Hina and her celas joined us as we made our way to the diwan-i-khas. They filtered through the handmaidens until they had effectively boxed them out, positioning themselves close to me and to Asma as well.

She regarded the newcomers with the same smile she had shown me. "And who might you be?"

"That's Ali Talpur's little sister," Karim said, having moved to stand in front of us, flanked on either side by at least a dozen Mahisagari musketeers. "She's here as Razia's handmaiden."

"Oh!" Asma gasped, holding her hand to her mouth in horror.

I expected her to run and hide behind her son, knowing that Hina likely wanted her and every other Mahisagari in the palace dead, but instead she reached out and took Hina's hands in hers and said, "I'm so sorry for your loss, dear. The wars men wage are such dreadful things, and too often we women are the ones left to bear their consequences."

Hina seemed as startled as I was by Asma's behavior, but the older woman plowed ahead as if she didn't notice, patting Hina's cheek gently. "Whatever you may be feeling now, you have my word that you'll be safe here."

Hina bristled at the older woman's touch, and the muscles behind her temples bulged as she worked her jaw, struggling to muster a response to Asma's words. In the end, she just gave a stiff nod, but I noted the way her olive eyes darted to Karim, standing just a few paces away, and I knew she was thinking of all the ways she'd like to murder him for what he'd done to her brother. Her self-control in coming here like this was almost superhuman. I didn't think I could have done it.

I put my hand on Hina's shoulder and whispered, "Thank you for coming with me. I can't tell you how much it means to me."

"It's my pleasure, your highness," Hina replied, but her voice was stiff and wooden, and her eyes were still staring unblinking at Karim and his men. There were more of them now, almost three dozen, blocking our path to the baradari.

For a second, I wasn't too worried by that, as I was confident that Karim and Ahmed had no intention of murdering me, but then I realized that wasn't necessarily true for Hina. If they killed her, I could protest, I could scream and shout and complain, but I was powerless to stop them. That realization made my stomach churn.

"Is there something wrong, your highness?" I asked Karim, my voice betraying the fear that was coursing through me as I worried that I had delivered Hina's head on a platter to her enemies.

"No, there's nothing wrong, Razia," Karim replied, and his voice was gentler than it usually was, more like it got when he was talking to his zahhak. To prove it, he made a gesture with his hand and the men parted, clearing the path for us, though their presence was a clear reminder of who held the power here. As if I needed another.

"Come along, then, ladies. My husband won't keep us long, and then I can help you settle into your chambers," Asma said.

So it was their plan to keep me in the inner courtyard. I mulled over whether or not it was worth fighting them over that point. I supposed that it didn't much matter at the end of the day. Until I could work out a way to send messages out of the palace, which particular courtyard I was confined to was of no great consequence.

As we stepped into the baradari, my heart quickened its pace. There were no courtiers here, none of the leading men of Mahisagar. All the men had been kept to the edges of the pavilion, and they were all armed guards. More guards followed us in, taking up their positions on the stairs, effectively blocking us from our zahhaks. But it was difficult to protest, as Karim's fliers had stayed outside the baradari too. He and his father were the only men present, apart from a pair of armed and armored soldiers with shields and spears standing at the base of the throne.

While I felt like I technically outranked the sultan of Mahisagar as the princess of Nizam, I decided that politeness outweighed precedence, and I bowed properly to Ahmed Shah as we reached the throne.

"Welcome, daughter," he said, his tone betraying no small amusement at the situation.

"Thank you, father-in-law," I replied, keeping my eyes downcast, my voice quiet, my posture submissive. I didn't want him to see the least seed of rebellion in me. He'd be suspicious enough without my giving him cause for it, and if I wanted to keep any power of my own, I was going to need to play the part of the proper princess to assuage his doubts—particularly after the way I'd tried to negotiate his destruction with my father in Karim's hearing.

"Father," Karim said, "Razia has had a difficult past few days. I think it would be best if we concluded matters here quickly, so that she can rest."

"Yes, of course," Ahmed agreed. To me, he said, "As my son's fiancée, you will be treated as my own daughter. You will be given a suite of apartments in the inner palace, as will your sisters and your maids." He gestured dismissively to Hina and her celas. "However, there are certain rules you must abide by, just as any daughter-in-law must when entering her husband's home."

"Of course, father-in-law," I replied, still the picture of filial submission.

"I keep a conservative home," Ahmed said. "As such, you will remain in the inner palace, and will not leave it without a proper escort. If you do need to make public appearances, you will veil yourself appropriately. Needless to say, as a princess in the heart of my palace, you will have no need for weapons of any kind, and neither will your maids."

"My father did send Sikander and two bodyguards to serve as my chaperones, father-in-law," I informed him. "I trust they will be permitted to remain armed?"

"They will be," Karim said, answering for his father, and Ahmed dipped his head in acknowledgment.

"You will be provided with every comfort in the women's quarters," Ahmed continued. "We will give you a generous allowance of clothing and jewelry until your father sees fit to send your dowry. You will be permitted to go anywhere in the inner palace you like, and to send and receive letters to and from your family. Simply hand them off to any of the guards, and they will have them sent via my own couriers. If you need to procure anything from the markets, tell a servant, and we will have one sent to fetch it for you."

"Yes, your majesty," I replied. It was going to make sending messages to Arjun all but impossible if I couldn't find a way to get someone out of the women's quarters with my letters, but I didn't want to press the case too hard now, lest I make them more suspicious than they already were.

"If there is nothing else, I am sure you're tired owing to the long flight, and my wife is eager to show you to your chambers," said Sultan Ahmed.

"I would be most grateful, father-in-law," I agreed, as getting a sense of the palace layout would be crucial if I was going to find some way around these restrictions they had placed on me.

"If I may make a suggestion, your majesty," Hina offered, bowing her head to Asma. "I think the rooftop chambers along the southern wall will suit her highness best. There is usually a strong breeze coming in from the sea, and the view is magnificent."

"I think that's a lovely choice," Asma agreed. "I'll let Hina take you there, and I will join you later."

"I look forward to it, mother-in-law," I replied, meeting her smile with one of my own. I still wasn't quite sure what to make of her, but all things considered, I didn't think I had fared too badly in this first encounter with Karim and his family. I didn't exactly have my freedom, but I thought I had enough of it to work with if I could just find some way of sending my messages out of the palace.

CHAPTER 12

I understood at once why Asma had agreed so readily to Hina's recommendation when I had been led to my new chambers. Perched high atop the palace's southern wall, they looked out over the calm waters of the lagoon and the barrier island to the south, with the sea visible beyond as a dark blue smudge that stretched out until it met the sky. It was a remarkably beautiful view, and true to Hina's words, a cooling breeze flowed through the marble jali screens, driving out the worst of Zindh's heat.

But the beautiful view and the comfort of the sea air came at a price. My chambers were as far from the docks that led off this island as they could possibly be. They were as far from the zahhak stables as any rooms in the palace. If I ever wanted to get out of this place, I would have to cross the palace's innermost courtyard, where every servant and every guard could see me. Then I would have to pass through a heavily guarded gateway, into the central courtyard of the palace, where more open gardens would leave me exposed to the sight of more servants and more guards, before finally reaching the zahhak stables. And if I wanted to take a boat?

Well, then I would have to pass through a second gateway, a third courtyard, and then reach the docks under the watchful eyes of more Mahisagari soldiers than I could count.

"What do you think?" Hina asked as I paced the yellow sandstone patio that projected out from the palace walls. It let me look down at the waters of the lagoon, with only a knee-high decorative railing standing between me and a fifty-foot fall.

"I think we have our work cut out for us," I muttered, keeping my voice low, though Hina's celas were guarding the entrance to my chambers, so I knew that no servants would be able to overhear us.

"These are the most secure rooms in the palace," she explained, gesturing to the long drop to the water below. "But they're also the most remote. If Karim wants to bother you, he'll have to do a lot of walking to get here."

"That's something anyway," I allowed, because the thought of Karim visiting me in my bedchambers sent a shiver of dread running through me.

"And choosing secure chambers will help you to avoid suspicion," she added. "That'll be important if we're going to continue with the plan." She hadn't phrased it like a question, but I sensed the tension in her voice. She was worried that I was giving up.

"The plan stands," I assured her. "I presume that if I can find us a reliable messenger, you know men in Kadiro to whom we can send our missives?"

"I do, your highness," she replied. "But it won't be easy to find a loyal messenger here. Who could we possibly trust with letters to Arjun or the Safavians?"

"I don't know yet," I confessed, "but we have a little time to figure it out."

"Not much," she warned. "Arjun said that it would be best if we attacked within a fortnight, and he wasn't wrong. Sunil will be able to piece an army together, I'm sure of it, but it won't hold for long, not without money and supplies. And the longer the Mahisagaris remain here, the stronger their control over Zindh will become. Better we push them out soon, your highness."

"I don't want to wait any more than you do," I said, "but if we move too quickly and too clumsily, we will be caught. You will be executed, and I will be married to Karim for the rest of my life, kept a prisoner in his palace to be used as he pleases." Just saying those words out loud made my stomach tie itself in knots, made my fists clench with fear and frustration. "Believe me, I am going to do everything in my power to get us out of this mess, Hina."

"I believe you, your highness," Hina said, resting her hand on my shoulder. But then she added something that I wished she hadn't. "I hope it's enough."

What if it wasn't? That was the thought that was gnawing away at the back of my mind. Karim had me right where he wanted me, trapped in his palace, separated from my zahhaks and from Arjun and from any friendly guards or soldiers. He had won my father's support in this marriage, which meant that Sikander couldn't be trusted to take my side in this dispute, not unless Karim violated the terms of the marriage agreement. And while I was accustomed to dealing with opponents who had all the advantages, I was also accustomed to being underestimated. Karim wouldn't make that mistake, not after everything he had seen me accomplish in Bikampur.

I sighed and leaned up against one of the golden columns that supported the patio's roof, my fingers wrapping themselves around a decorative rosette of blue-glazed tile, made to resemble the lotuses that grew in the palace's water gardens. It was one of many, running in equally spaced bands around the fluted sandstone column. More such rosettes had been affixed to the outer walls of my chambers, to provide a splash of color to the otherwise uniform yellow-brown sandstone blocks.

Hope went through me like the electric jolt I sometimes got when Sultana was about to unleash a bolt of lightning. I rushed to the knee-high railing at the edge of the patio, moving so quickly that Hina actually grabbed my wrist to stop me from going over.

"You can't give up that easily, your highness," she told me, her voice stern.

I shook off her grip with a deft twist of my arm—a wrestling technique I'd picked up in Nizam. "Relax. I'm not going to kill myself just yet."

Instead, I knelt down and leaned over the railing as far as I could, to get a better look at the walls of the palace beneath me. The yellow sandstone was festooned with carved floral motifs, with stylized zahhaks and checkerboard patterns, with vines and leaves, all covered with turquoise-, cobalt-, and white-glazed tiles, creating belts of raised decorations that ran the length and breadth of the walls all the way down to the calm waters of the lagoon some fifty feet below. The lip of the patio projected about five feet beyond the walls, which would make things a bit more difficult, but the sandstone buttresses supporting it were carved and decorated too, so it wouldn't be that tricky, I didn't think.

"Is everything all right?" Hina asked, still hovering cautiously beside me, just in case I really was suicidal and about to throw myself over the ledge.

"How far is it from the palace to Kadiro's docks?" I asked.

She raised a mahogany eyebrow, her lips twisting with concern. "How far?"

"To swim," I said. "How far of a swim is it?"

"You wouldn't survive the fall, your highness," she warned me. "The water is shallow here around the island. You'd hit bottom and break every bone in your body—if you weren't killed from the impact with the water itself. And even if you somehow did survive the fall intact, every guard in the palace would hear the splash."

I stood up and dusted off my skirts. "Humor me."

She rolled her hazel eyes. "I suppose it's about half a mile. But if you think I came all this way, gave up all my weapons, and placed myself under Karim's control just to watch you hurl yourself into the lagoon, you are sorely mistaken."

Half a mile. I could manage that. I was a strong swimmer, or had been, when I was living in Nizam. I hadn't had much cause to swim in Bikampur, the desert city not affording me many opportunities to practice, but I hadn't forgotten the lessons I'd learned as a young prince in Nizam, or the times I'd gone swimming with Haider and Tamara during those two glorious summers in Tavrezh, Safavia's glittering riverside capital.

"Are there any odd currents that might drag you out to sea?" I wondered, as that was the real danger.

Hina crossed her arms over her chest and said nothing, convinced that I'd lost my mind. I couldn't even blame her, not really. To anyone else, my new home probably looked like an impregnable fortress, but I had scaled more difficult walls in Bikampur, to say nothing of the cliffs of Shikarpur, which had towered two hundred feet above the desert, the natural rock providing nothing as secure for handholds and footholds as the raised decorations that studded every inch of this palace.

"Did no one tell you how I stole the thunder zahhaks from Javed Khorasani?" I asked her.

"People said you scaled the cliffs of Shikarpur with your bare hands . . ." she murmured, but her eyes were still narrowed with skepticism. She hadn't been there, hadn't seen it for herself.

I walked back to the column that had provided my inspiration, and I scampered up it, using the big rosettes for handholds, shoving the tips of my slippers into the gaps in the tile work to lever myself upward as easily as if I were walking across solid ground. In an instant, I was fifteen feet in the air, my legs wrapped around the column's capital. I bent over backward, letting my body hang, my arms crossed over my chest, my braided hair spilling down until it was nearly touching the top of Hina's head.

"If there are no powerful currents in the lagoon, then I think I have found our messenger," I declared.

CHAPTER 13

Her highness is resting!"

A man's deep, gruff voice echoed off unfamiliar marble walls, jarring me from my sleep. I sat up with a start, my heart pounding, my eyes flickering across blue lotus tile work set into bright white marble and golden sandstone. The sound of the sea was droning in my ears, the waves crashing on a beach somewhere in the distance providing the backdrop to the louder lapping of calmer waters against the stout stones of the palace walls nearby. The raucous calls of seagulls were loud overhead, and a few tiny fish zahhaks, no bigger than crows, were chattering away from their perches on the marble railing of my patio.

It took my mind a moment to assemble the pieces of my memory, to recall yesterday's horrible events. Kadiro. I was in Kadiro, trapped within the walls of Ahmed Shah's new palace, and the voice I heard outside my chambers, thick with sarcasm, was Karim's. "Calm down, Sikander, I'm sure my wife-to-be will be *thrilled* to see me."

I sat up, a thin silk sheet sliding off my body into my lap just as Karim came striding into the room. Sikander walked close beside him, one hand on the hilt of his talwar.

"Sleep well, your highness?" Karim asked, his lips following the upward curve of his mustache as he smirked at me, his eyes taking in the thin white kameez I wore, making me acutely aware of how sheer the fabric was. My cheeks burned, and I pulled the silken sheet in front of myself, though I knew I must have looked ridiculous.

"So modest?" It was a taunt, but the husky note in his voice betrayed him. He liked it.

"I'm sorry," I said, remembering that I needed to play the role of the beaten and submissive girl if I was going to keep him from guessing my plans. I bowed my head. "Was I supposed to be up earlier, your highness?"

"My father and mother would like for you and your sisters to breakfast with us in the garden," Karim explained. "I've come to collect you."

"I'll need a few moments to get dressed, your highness," I told him, not letting the silk sheet drop. I knew how little good it would do me if Karim wanted to touch me, but I couldn't help myself; it was the only defense from his roving eyes that I had, and it helped to keep my revulsion from overwhelming me.

Karim stepped closer, and were it not for my years of training as a courtesan, I'd have flinched. As it was, I kept perfectly still, my breathing a bit shallow, but not noticeably so. I didn't gasp or shy away or cringe. I sat there, eyes downcast, not moving a muscle, waiting to see what he would do, every fiber of my being praying that he wouldn't touch me.

Karim sat on my bedside, just inches away from me, and I didn't know if he was testing me, or if he was just unaware of how viscerally horrified I was to be sitting so close to him, with no weapons, and no one to protect me other than Sikander. But he hadn't stopped Karim the first time, and he hadn't kept him out of my room this time. I'd thought maybe after the things I'd said to him yesterday that he would have been at least willing to keep Karim at arm's length, but I supposed I'd just been imagining his regret.

"Do you remember when you came to the palace in Rajkot with Arjun?" Karim asked.

My mind drifted back to that night, not so long ago. I'd been wrapped in Arjun's arms then, and Karim had been staring at me with hungry eyes, offering money for a night with me. And I'd refused him. I'd had the power then to refuse him. How bitterly ironic it was that after everything I'd been through, after everything I'd worked for, I didn't have that power now.

"I remember," I whispered, wondering if he was bringing it up now only to gloat.

"I behaved foolishly that night," he said, the apologetic tone in his voice taking me completely by surprise. "I didn't understand your worth then. But I do now. That's why I made this marriage alliance, that is why I will honor you as my first wife, even though you cannot bear me any children."

He'd phrased it as if it were an act of kindness on his part, as if an ordinary marriage was far too good for a barren hijra like me. But I said nothing, because I didn't have it in me to thank him, not after everything he'd done, and I knew that showing the anger I was feeling would just make everything so much worse. So I sat there in silence, head bowed, waiting for him to finish saying whatever it was that he wanted to say.

"You may not have chosen me," he allowed, "but you're a smart girl. I know that eventually you will realize that this is best for you, and best for your sisters. Someday soon, I will be the sultan of Nizam and Mahisagar, and you will be my sultana, and with your mind and my sword, we will soon find ourselves rulers of all Daryastan."

I didn't miss the meaning of his words. Ruling all of Daryastan meant conquering Virajendra, but Registan too. It meant conquering Bikampur. It meant killing Arjun. If he thought for one second that I would fight against Arjun for him, then he had lost his mind.

"And while my dream is that one day we will work together in harmony, until you come to your senses and I can be sure that I can trust you, I will keep a very close eye on you," he warned, at last showing me the real reason for his visit. He reached forward and brushed back my hair with his fingers, and though I found his touch repulsive, it was gentle. "But I'm not going to hurt you, so there's no need for all of this fear."

I frowned, wondering what he meant by that, realizing only upon reflection that my entire body was as rigid as a marble statue, that I had scarcely drawn breath since he had entered the room, that my heart was hammering hard enough in my chest that he must have seen my pulse in the veins in my neck. My cheeks burned. I'd thought I was doing a better job of hiding my emotions than I had been.

"I'm sorry, your highness," I said.

"For what?" Karim asked. "Trying to have me killed yesterday, or being afraid of me now?"

"They're connected, are they not, your highness?" I replied.

He chuckled at that. I was scanning his face frantically, trying to work out what emotion was lurking behind those dark eyes of his. He was smiling at me, and he seemed amused, but it was so hard to tell sometimes with men like Karim. I'd had quite a few clients like him, clients whose moods could change in a flash, and who took special pleasure in hurting the girls who offended them.

"I don't hold it against you," he said, which I believed not at all.

"You're headstrong, and you're usually able to win these little contests. But I'm not Arjun, and I'm not your father. I'm not going to lose. The sooner you accept that and make your peace with it, the happier we will both be, my darling."

He leaned forward then and kissed me on the cheek, and Sikander lifted not a finger to stop him. I didn't know if I was grateful for that or not, if stopping him from kissing me would make my life harder or easier. I just knew that I hated it, and I didn't want it, and I was powerless to stop it on my own.

"I'll leave you to get dressed. My father and mother are eager to see you this morning." Karim stood up, bowed to me like a courtier, and breezed from the room.

I let out a sound that was half sigh and half whimper the instant he was gone. I hugged my knees to my chest and buried my face in them, my whole body shaking with fear and disgust. So this was what I had to look forward to every morning from now on? God, if not for the hope I had in my plans, I'd have killed myself from despair.

"I'm sorry, your highness."

I glanced up at Sikander, whose mouth was a hard line, his brow knitted with worry. I hadn't expected him to apologize to me. He never had before.

"For what?" I asked.

His jaw tensed, and so did his fists, but he wasn't angry with me, I didn't think. If I'd had to guess, I'd have said he was angry with himself.

"I'm sorry I didn't stop him from entering your chambers or touching you, your highness, but I thought it would make things worse," he said.

"You were probably right," I replied, though that didn't make me feel any better. But if Karim was going to make it a habit to roam this part of the palace, then whether or not he touched me was the least of my worries. Sikander couldn't stop my husband-to-be from kissing me. But he could stop Karim from doing other things.

"I want your men posted outside my sister Lakshmi's door from now on," I told him, noting the way his eyes widened with alarm. "She has caught Karim's eye, and she is eleven years old—the same age I was when Karim attacked me."

Sikander's face flushed crimson with rage. Had he not remembered how old I had been? Or perhaps he had never conceived of me as being as small and helpless and naive as Lakshmi. He stood there, frozen in place, staring at me, his mouth half-open, his hand gripping the hilt of his talwar so tightly that his knuckles had turned white. So the regret wasn't false. That was something.

"Sikander, whatever strife there has been between us, I want your word that you won't let him hurt my little sister," I said.

"You have it, your highness," he replied. "I will have men posted outside her door day and night, and I will not permit any man to enter her chambers for any reason. I swear it."

"Thank you," I told him, and I meant it. It was a huge relief to know that Karim would have to fight his way into Lakshmi's bedchamber if he wanted to hurt her. I didn't think he would do that; it would create too much trouble, even in a household where he had all the power. No, rapists like him thrived in environments where their behavior went unchallenged, where people made excuses for them and swept their misdeeds under the rug.

"Your highness." Sikander bowed stiffly, and left the room. I heard him issuing new orders in the hallway, though his words were too muffled to make out.

With Lakshmi's security taken care of, at least insofar as I was able, I decided it was time to get out of bed and get dressed, lest Karim return in a fouler temper. I threw aside my silk sheet and stood up, stretching out my arms and legs, just as Hina and two of her celas came striding into the room, already fully dressed in ajrak skirts and long blouses, carrying wooden boxes of clothes and jewels like proper handmaidens.

"It was never my intention for you to serve me in your own home, Hina," I said, my cheeks heating as I realized that I was occupying her favorite bedchamber, and she had arrived to wait on me hand and foot.

"I knew what I was volunteering for, your highness," Hina replied. "And anyway, I wouldn't trade places with you for all the gems in your father's palace." Her eyes drifted back toward the corridor, back to where Karim had been, and I caught her implication at once.

I shuddered involuntarily as I remembered Karim's kiss on my cheek. God, I wanted to take the longest bath in the world. I wanted to scrub my skin until it bled to get the feeling of him off of it, but I didn't have time for that. I had to face Karim and his parents at breakfast.

"We'll need an excuse to fly our zahhaks today, your highness," Hina informed me in a low voice as she and her celas began dressing me in my thunder zahhak–inspired peshwaz, with its matching jewelry. "If you are to be our messenger, I want to point out the havelis of the most trustworthy emirs of Kadiro. They will have zahhaks, and will be willing to use them to carry our messages."

I nodded, as that made perfect sense. I would need to get a sense of the city's layout if I was going to sneak through it at night, make contact with one of the emirs, send the messages, and get back to the palace safely. It was ridiculous, that I could so easily secure my own freedom by simply disappearing as I had that night four years ago in Nizam, but that my sisters, and my zahhak, and my place in the world held me back from doing it. So, I could slip away from the palace at night, but I would have to return before morning, lest everyone I loved suffer in my stead.

"There's something you should see, your highness," Hina said as her celas put the finishing touches on my makeup and my jewelry.

"What's that?" I asked.

She motioned to the patio, and I followed her out, our presence startling the fish zahhaks from their perches. They let out shrill cries and beat the air back with their indigo wings, looking for all the world like miniature river zahhaks as they raced away from the palace, skimming the water with their belly scales. But as my eyes followed their movements, they caught sight of the fish zahhaks' much larger cousins.

A pair of fire zahhaks were flying several hundred feet above us, making a lazy circuit of the lagoon. Their yellow underparts made them vanish into the rising sun, only to reappear a few moments later as a splash of fiery color against the blue backdrop of the morning sky. As they banked into their turn, I got a better look at the crimson, flame-orange, and even purplish hues of their neck and back scales, my eyes squinting to try to make out a familiar pattern. Were they Registani animals? Was it Arjun and Arvind? My heart soared at the possibility, though I knew it would cause me nothing but trouble if they had arrived here alone, without an army or an aerial armada to support them.

"Do you recognize them?" I asked Hina.

She shook her head. "I was thinking that you might. Are they your friends?"

"I don't know," I murmured, studying them carefully, watching the way they flew. They were too far away to really make out properly, but more and more I didn't think they were any zahhaks I knew. "I don't think that's Padmini. I told Arjun to stay away until I sent for him. He wouldn't just show up here, not without a very good reason."

"Then maybe Mahisagar has fire zahhaks now," Hina muttered, her face darkening.

I shook my head. "Where would they find them?"

"I don't know, your highness," she replied. "I only know what my eyes are showing me."

As if to prove her right, a pair of acid zahhaks swooped down and joined the fire zahhaks in a single formation for a short time, the riders chatting with one another cheerfully, before they broke apart, orbiting Kadiro's harbor in opposite directions. They were definitely patrolling together. However unlikely it may have been, Karim had gotten his hands on fire zahhaks.

I sighed, wondering just how many animals they had now. With twelve acid zahhaks, and at least two fire zahhaks, their numbers stood at fourteen. If I could convince Sikander to fight alongside me, which was no certain thing, then I'd have just six zahhaks with which to oppose Karim, maybe as many as twelve or fourteen if Arjun was very successful at recruiting his fellow Registani princes to his side. But fighting a battle with even odds wasn't the cleverest of strategies, and I thought everyone would balk at the prospect. Zahhaks were rare and expensive and represented every kingdom's wealth and prestige and power. To wager all that on a hijra was asking too much. I needed some way of tipping the balance of power in my favor, or there would be no battle, regardless of how many messages I sent.

Haider and Tamara might be able to help me, but I didn't know how many zahhaks they would bring, or if I would be inviting disaster by asking for Safavian and Khevsurian assistance here. What if they just decided to take Zindh for themselves? I didn't think Haider or Tamara would do that to me, not when we'd been such close friends as children, but Shah Ismail was a different matter. He was a man cut from the same cloth as my father. If he saw an opportunity to grow his empire, he wouldn't care who it hurt.

"Razia, are you ready yet?" Karim called from just outside my chambers.

"I am, your highness," I replied, forcing myself to smile as I said those words, because I knew that would help to disguise the dread in my voice. I glanced over at Hina, who gave me a sympathetic pat on the shoulder, her hazel eyes betraying a sentiment that I could only describe as "better you than me."

I hurried from my chambers, joining Karim in the hallway. He looked me over and nodded his approval, which annoyed me a little, as I certainly hadn't asked for it, but I knew better than to make a scene. I was going to have to accept these patronizing gestures from him for the time being. I had learned patience as a courtesan, and though I'd been spoiled by Arjun ever since I'd met him, I hadn't forgotten what it was like to put my desires aside in the moment in order to gain what I wanted long-term. That was the game I had to play with Karim, and it meant not antagonizing him or giving him any signs that I despised him. I didn't have to look happy to see him, not yet—that would have made him suspicious—but I couldn't look completely miserable either.

I settled on a cautious smile, as if I was hoping that I would meet his approval but was still worried and frightened nonetheless. It seemed to be the right note to strike, because it was met at once by a smirk on Karim's part.

"You look very beautiful this morning," he informed me as we walked toward the sandstone stairwell that led down to the gardens.

"Thank you, your highness," I replied, bowing my head demurely.

I was fortunate that the gardens were relatively close by, so I didn't have to make any more small talk with Karim before arriving at the pavilion where Ahmed Shah was taking his breakfast at the head of a large rectangular cloth. He was sitting cross-legged on a silk cushion, flanked by his wife, with spaces open beside them for Karim and myself. My sisters were already seated in their own places, along with a man I didn't recognize. He looked vaguely like Karim, though he was somewhat darker skinned and stockier of build, and he wore a beard that was fuller, less carefully trimmed.

"Good morning, dear," Asma said as I sat with Karim on our cushions beside hers.

"Good morning, mother-in-law," I replied, keeping my eyes properly downcast, my hands folded neatly in my lap. I knew that she was watching my every move carefully, and I didn't want to give her the least cause for complaint. I wasn't sure how much power Asma held here, but I knew that the primary wife could often be the tyrant of the zenana in any royal family. She would have more cause to interact with me than any of the men. She would see more of my behavior than they would, and one word from her could curtail my freedoms in an instant.

"You look like a proper Nizami princess," she observed, taking in my thunder zahhak jewelry, and my clothes, which shared those animals' coloration. "We'll have to have new clothes made for you now that you are to be wed to my Karim. I think it's only fitting for a new bride to wear the clothing of her husband's people, don't you?"

I noted that she was wearing a turquoise chaniya choli, the blouse and skirt festooned with tiny green-tinted mirrors that served as the scales of embroidered acid zahhaks writhing their way across the surface of the fabric. I thought Karim had said she was Yaruban, and while I had never been to Yaruba, I knew that they didn't wear clothes like these. She had adopted Mahisagari fashion herself. So did that make her recommendation the sort of friendly advice an older wife might pass to a younger one, or was it something more?

"I do, your majesty," I replied, bowing my head to her, forcing myself to smile. "I hope you will forgive me, but I had no time to prepare for this journey, nor to procure suitable attire."

"There is nothing to forgive, dear," she assured me, smiling brightly. "We'll simply have to bring tailors to the palace to see to the matter."

"I'd be most grateful, your majesty," I lied. The last thing on earth I wanted was to dress up like a Mahisagari bride, but if it would keep their suspicions at bay, then it was a small sacrifice.

"Akka, you should see my new room, it's so beautiful!" Lakshmi exclaimed from her place beside Sakshi.

"It really is," Sakshi agreed, smiling at me, though I saw the concern in her red-brown eyes as they searched my face for some sign of how I was feeling. "We're very grateful to have been given such magnificent chambers."

"Nonsense, you are my daughter-in-law's sisters," said Asma, waving away Sakshi's words of gratitude with a swipe of her palm. "I wouldn't dream of giving you anything less than the very best this palace has to offer. Though once we return to Rajkot, your chambers will be more glorious still."

My eyes perked up, but I fought to keep my alarm from showing through on my face. "Are we going to Rajkot?" I glanced from Asma to Karim, searching their faces for an answer.

"Not right away," Karim said, placing his hand over mine, the heat of his rough palm on my skin making my insides twist. "But as soon as the marriage is concluded, we will discuss it. Though I might prefer to have you with me here in Kadiro, or even in Ahura. Much will depend on how Shah Ismail reacts over the coming weeks to our presence there."

"Well, if he decides to fight, we stand ready to defend you, cousin," the young man I didn't know told Karim.

"Thank you, Rais," Karim replied, and he seemed to realize that I didn't know who Rais was, because he said, "Razia, this is my cousin Rais, my uncle Nasir's firstborn son."

"The emir of Jesera?" I ventured, hoping that I'd remembered Karim's lineage properly.

"That's right, dear," said Asma, looking quite pleased with me for knowing the name of the city. "My brother is the emir, and my nephew Rais was kind enough to join us with a few of his friends, to help keep Kadiro safe."

That explained the fire zahhaks. Yaruba was a great, vast desert land, richer in fire zahhaks than almost any other nation in the world. And Jesera was the most prosperous and powerful of Yaruba's many competing city-states. Much like Registan, Yaruba was a land divided among a large number of kings, known as emirs, but one that came together to oppose outside threats. I didn't think even a man of Nasir's prominence would be able to convince the other city-states of Yaruba to join him in fighting for Mahisagar, but the prospect of facing Yaruban fire zahhaks changed things. Now, even if Arjun was able to bring a substantial number of men from Registan, they would merely offset the numbers Karim could call upon from Jesera.

"Akka, can I fly Mohini after breakfast?" Lakshmi asked. "I want to practice dogfighting with Nuri again today."

It was the perfect chance to ask Karim for permission to do some flying of my own. I smiled and said, "I don't know, sweetheart, that's up to Prince Karim." I looked to the man in question and asked, "Would it be all right, your highness?"

"Of course it would be," Karim answered, looking directly at Lakshmi with a smile that made me want to slap him. "Someday you'll be called upon to fly in Mahisagar's defense, just like all of our other acid zahhak riders. So you'll have to be very good at dogfighting."

Lakshmi nodded eagerly, rushing to eat the rest of her breakfast so she could fly as soon as possible. The idea of her flying for Mahisagar made my blood boil, but how could I blame her? From her point of view, Karim had given her back her beloved zahhak, he doted on her, and I had brought her to this place, in effect giving it a mark of approval.

"Sakshi also needs to work on her skills, your highness," I informed Karim. "And I was hoping that I might supervise matters with Hina, to make sure that Lakshmi and Nuri are staying safe."

Karim raised an eyebrow. "We talked about all of your sisters flying at the same time, didn't we?"

"We did, your highness," I allowed, dipping my head in acknowledgment, "but I was hoping that you and your cousin might fly with us, and perhaps your mother too, if she is amenable."

"Me? Fly?" Asma asked, and I noted a flurry of competing emotions flickering across her face. There was genuine surprise, followed by suspicion, but also eagerness. She wanted to go up almost as much as Lakshmi did.

"Well, I don't know what saddles Rais has brought, and I certainly don't want to make any offers on his behalf," I replied, bowing my head to the Yaruban prince and keeping my eyes carefully downcast, "but before I recovered my Sultana, I would often fly in a double saddle with Prince Arjun of Bikampur atop his fire zahhak, Padmini. I thought perhaps if you hadn't flown in such a fashion before that you might enjoy it, your majesty, though I wondered if perhaps you hadn't done such things in Yaruba before your marriage to Sultan Ahmed."

"My brother used to take me up on flights when I was little," Asma recalled, a bittersweet smile playing at her lips. "We would fly through the canyons west of Jesera together on daredevil flights that would have made my father furious had he ever found out about them. He taught me to handle his zahhak, Zahira, though I think my father would have killed me had he ever caught me taking her out alone."

"I learned to fly with Father on Zahira's back too, Auntie," Rais told her. "If you'd like to come up with me, I have a double saddle, and I'm sure Farida would be honored to bear you aloft."

Asma looked hopefully at her son, realizing after an instant that I had brought her around to being completely in favor of a flight over the lagoon that permitted me and my sisters some measure of freedom. Her kohl-ringed eyes narrowed slightly, but I thought I detected in her smile some measure of reluctant admiration for the way I had handled things.

Karim stared at me for a long second, as if he was trying to work out what angle I was playing, but after a moment he shrugged his shoulders. "Yes, I think that sounds like a lovely idea, Razia. I'll bring Jamshid and a few others along to serve as adversaries for your sisters, and to give them whatever advice they can."

I knew that the real reason for the extra fliers was to keep us from trying to run off, but since I wasn't trying to run away today, I didn't care. I was able to say, "Thank you, your highness," with such genuine enthusiasm that Karim couldn't have mistaken it for anything else. It didn't exactly get him to lower his guard, not yet, but I had definitely won this battle, and I didn't think he even realized it.

CHAPTER 14

"You pleased me today," Karim said, his arm wrapped tightly around my back, pulling me close beside him, his fingers absentmindedly rubbing at the sleek, soft fabric of my peshwaz's silk sleeve.

The heat of Karim's body against mine, the feeling of his hands on me—it was enough to make bile rise in the back of my throat, but I was already getting better at fighting it down. Another day or two, and I'd probably not feel it at all, though I knew that nothing would change the sense of dread I got in the pit of my stomach whenever we were alone in a room together. Standing there on my balcony, watching the sun set behind desert hills, framed perfectly by the twin forts that guarded the entrance to Kadiro's harbor, I tried to pretend that it was Arjun's arm around me, his body pressed close to mine, but my heart wasn't so easily fooled.

"I am glad, your highness," I said, hoping that I managed to sound sincere.

I must have missed the mark, because he asked, "Are you?"

A ripple of uncertainty ran through my body, and I knew he

must have felt it, but I thought that hiding my fear and my dread was the wrong move. One day wouldn't change our relationship. He wouldn't believe that. And anyway, I had reason enough to be afraid beyond our past history. It was normal for a girl dragged into a marriage she hadn't wanted, whatever the circumstances. And besides, I thought, the more uncertain and helpless I sounded, the more easily I would be able to shed Karim's suspicions that I might be planning to undermine him.

"I thought you just said that I had pleased you, your highness . . ." I whispered, my voice quivering with anxiety.

He rubbed my arm a little harder, not painfully so, almost like he was trying to reassure me. "You did. But it makes me wonder why."

"Because I don't know what else to do," I replied, letting my shoulders hunch a little, my body shrinking in his grasp.

He arched an eyebrow, his lips forming an unreadable line beneath his curled mustache. "Do you really expect me to believe that you've given up so easily?"

I stared down at my slippers and said nothing. That was what a cowed woman would do, wasn't it?

"You will answer me when I ask you questions, Razia," he said, and I couldn't have missed the warning note in his voice.

"I don't know what you want from me, your highness," I replied. "You've said many times now that you've outmaneuvered me, that you have planned for all eventualities, that you won't be beaten by me. And you said this very morning that the sooner I realized those facts and accepted them, the better it would be for both of us."

"That's all true," he agreed, "but I know you. You would never give up so easily."

"Why not?" I asked, looking up into his eyes—helplessly, I hoped. "If I can't see any way out, then why should I keep fighting? Why should I risk something horrible happening to me, or God forbid, to my sisters, if it's hopeless?"

Tears welled in the corners of my eyes. I'd expected that it would take some effort to conjure them, but with Karim's arms around me, with the tension of my first attempt at passing messages before me, it took no effort at all. They just appeared, and began streaming down my cheeks. I looked away from Karim, like I was afraid that crying would upset him. I hunched my shoulders, like I was expecting him to hit me for them.

I felt the uncertainty in Karim's hand on my arm. It had stopped moving, like he didn't know whether to grab me or pet me to calm me down. After a moment, his grip tightened. "This is a trick."

"Please don't hurt me." I breathed the words, letting my body tremble in his grasp. His hand loosened once more, and I knew that I had him confused, that I had to really sell this. "If you don't want me to try to please you, then please tell me what it is you do want from me, your highness.

"Shall I try to escape?" I asked, looking up at him with tears streaking my face and blurring my vision. "Shall I try to sneak to the zahhak stables with my sisters? I'd only have to pass through two courtyards filled with servants and guards, after all. Child's play for someone like me," I scoffed.

"Or shall I try to kill you?" I suggested, encompassing with a gesture the way his body engulfed my own, the way he towered over me. I nodded to the firangi he wore at his hip. "I killed a sleeping guardsman once with my katars, so I'm sure killing you barehanded would take me no effort at all."

"Razia . . ." Karim sighed.

"Or maybe I'll send messages to my allies through all the loyal servants and courtiers I have in this palace," I said. "And I'll bide my time and wait while all the maharajas of Registan rise up to fight a bloody battle in defense of a hijra who helped Bikampur once. I'm sure they'll be appearing on the horizon any day now to rescue me, when my own father wouldn't do the same."

Karim shifted uncertainly, my words having some effect.

"Is it a crime to not know what to do, your highness?" I asked him. "Because if it is, then I'm guilty, but that is the only thing I'm guilty of."

He held me close to him, one hand pressed against my lower back, the other stroking my hair gently.

"Four years . . ." I whispered.

"What?" he asked.

"That's how long I spent living as a whore in Bikampur." I buried my face in his chest, my body shaking with genuine sobs. "Where were my brilliant plans then?"

"Forget about all that. You're safe here now," he said, with none of the bitter irony I felt on hearing those words. "I'm sorry that I've been so suspicious, but how can you blame me with the way you acted in Shikarpur?"

"I loved Arjun, that's all," I told him, careful to use the past tense. "I've never made a secret of that."

"But you expect me to believe that you don't anymore?" he asked, sounding completely unconvinced.

"Of course I do," I replied. "But I love my sisters more. Keeping them safe has always been the most important thing. I'm not going to get Sakshi and Lakshmi killed over a man. And even if I wanted to, I can't. You and my father have made sure that there are no options left open to me. So, I'm going to do my best to survive, like I always have. And maybe that's not the honorable thing to do, maybe it makes me pathetic, and weak, but you were counting on it, weren't you?"

"I don't think your talent for survival makes you weak and pathetic," Karim said. "It's the reason I wanted you to be my wife."

"Well, I'm sorry to be such a disappointment, your highness," I told him. "I know you must have been expecting some brilliant plan to overthrow you. I'm sorry I couldn't deliver it."

He gave a snort of laughter. "I forgive you."

"Thank you, Karim," I said, my voice softening with feigned relief, my body sagging a little against his, like the tension was finally draining out of it.

He kissed me on the top of my head. "You should get some sleep, my wife-to-be. These past few days have been trying for all of us."

"I'll do that," I lied.

He stroked my hair one last time, and then let me go. "I'll be back in the morning."

"Thank you for being kind to me, your highness," I replied.

His mustache quivered as his lips offered me the briefest of pitying smiles. "You're welcome, Razia."

I waited until I was sure he was gone before sighing with genuine relief and wiping at my face to clear away the tears.

"Well, you had me convinced," Hina quipped as she joined me on the balcony. With Sikander watching Lakshmi's chambers, she and her celas were my makeshift guards now.

"Good," I said. "He's not a complete idiot. His suspicions won't be banished by one conversation, so we have to make sure he never gets wind of our plans."

"Which means no one can see you tonight," Hina warned.

"I'm aware," I said, and I managed to smile in spite of everything. "I'm accustomed to that kind of danger anyway. When I used to steal from clients for the dera, I was always risking execution."

"Well, here it'll be our necks on the line," she reminded me.

"I know," I said, looking her right in the eyes to show her the determination in my own not to fail her. "I'm sorry that I couldn't fulfill my promises the way I meant to, but I'm not going to let you down. We will get through this."

"Let's get you ready, then." She motioned for me to follow her back into my bedchamber, where her celas were waiting for me with fresh clothes and a very interesting pair of slippers.

Hina handed me the shoes, saying, "We managed to reinforce the soles the way you asked, but I'm not sure if they're going to be very comfortable to wear, or if they'll even work."

I examined them, noting the subtle curve to them, the stiffness in the toe and the arch of the foot, the reinforcement at the heel. They weren't exactly proper climbing shoes, but they were far better than the soft slippers I was wearing. They wouldn't be comfortable for walking long distances, but I could take them off while sneaking through the city and put them back on when I needed to climb something.

I slipped them over my feet with some effort, because they were tight, just like I'd asked for. "Where did you get the materials?"

"We asked Lady Asma for them," Hina replied. "We said we needed to mend our clothes and our shoes, and she was happy enough to provide everything required."

"Did she see you working on them?" I didn't know if Asma understood climbing shoes, but I didn't want to take any chances.

"No, we were careful," Hina assured me.

I stood in my new shoes and found that they were definitely too curved to make for comfortable walking, but when I approached one of the columns near my veranda, and put my toe against a tile rosette, I grinned. "Oh, these are good . . ." I scampered up the column much faster than I had the day before, feeling like a mountain goat thanks to the way the reinforced toe of the shoe hooked each and every crevice in the stonework.

I dropped down, and hurried to trade my peshwaz and fine

silk trousers for a simple cotton shalwar kameez, the ajrak pattern consisting mostly of dark indigo dye, with splashes of lighter blue, white, and saffron. Ordinarily, I didn't like wearing white at night, but I thought the little irregular patches of it would actually help to make me harder to see, because it would break up my silhouette, and I'd look less like a human-shaped shadow to prying eyes.

Hina stuffed a pair of ordinary slippers into the pockets of my shalwar. "I wouldn't take anything else with you. If you're caught it's best that you can deny the worst accusations against you."

"If I'm caught, we're all finished," I replied, because I knew better than to believe I could ever win Karim's trust if he discovered that the whole time we'd been talking on the veranda I'd been lying through my teeth. He'd never believe another word I said.

"So don't get caught," Hina said, offering me a gentle pat on the shoulder.

"I won't," I promised.

"You'll want to give my name to the man at the door to Sanghar Soomro's haveli," Hina said. "Tell him you're one of my celas and that you have a message for Sanghar. That should earn you an audience. After that, it will be up to you to convince him to help you rather than kill you or take you hostage."

"Sounds like fun," I muttered, hoping that this man was as loyal to Hina as she claimed he was. Otherwise he might well earn favor with Ahmed and Karim by handing me back to them. But I would worry over that when the time came. I had to try to send a message, and if Hina thought this was the best way, then this was what I would do.

"May God watch over you," Hina said.

"And all of you," I replied.

"Oh, we'll be having a restful night's sleep in your bed," she assured me, flashing me a grin that was confident enough to wrest a smile from my own lips in response.

"Don't get too comfortable," I warned. "I'll be back soon."

She nodded, her jaw tensing. "You'd better be."

I decided that I could say good-bye all night, but that was just putting off the inevitable, so I turned and walked out onto my balcony, looking carefully into the darkness along the walls for any signs of guards or servants or curious palace women who might be able to see me from their own verandas or through their jali screens. I positioned myself in what I thought was something of a blind spot to the rest of the palace, but I'd be careful to move quickly and suddenly when the time came. That way, if someone was watching, they might think I'd simply gone back into my chambers. The less time they had to watch me climbing, the better.

So I flung myself over the railing, grabbing at the bottom edge of the marble floor with my fingers, kicking my hooked toes into crevices in the decorations on the buttresses below, and I hung there, holding myself close to the stonework, listening for cries of alarm from guardsmen, or shouts of surprise from palace women. But all I heard was the gentle lapping of the lagoon's waters against the sandstone bricks below me.

CHAPTER 15

Most people would have been afraid of descending a fifty-foot fortress wall in the dead of night, but it wasn't the climb that was eating away at my mind. I'd scaled enough havelis on moonless nights in Bikampur to be comfortable feeling along the wall with my hands and feet, searching out solid holds before testing my weight on them, and easing myself down. It was methodical, almost meditative. I'd have found it relaxing if not for the worries weighing on my mind. If I were caught, or if someone discovered I wasn't in my bed, the punishment would be swift and severe, and I knew that I wouldn't be the one suffering it. It would fall on someone I loved.

Hina would be first, I thought. Karim would kill her in front of me, and her celas too. He would know that he could do that and let the threat hang over my sisters, and that I would fall in line to preserve them. Just as I was sure that he knew if he touched one hair on my sisters' heads, I would be his enemy for all eternity. He would save them for last. But Hina first. Nuri second. I saw it so clearly that my hands and feet froze in place on the wall, unwilling to move. If anyone discovered that I wasn't in my bed . . .

No, I couldn't let my doubts control me. I forced myself to find another good toehold, to put my weight on it, to lower myself down. Maybe Karim would find out what I was doing. Maybe he would kill Hina and Nuri and my sisters and me too. That was possible. I wasn't stupid; I knew the risk I was taking. But I would never forgive myself if I didn't go through with this, if I sat there like a helpless princess from one of the storybooks, contenting myself with my lot in life. Karim thought he could enslave me? Because for all the talk of marriage, that's what this was, enslavement. He wanted to use my mind to his advantage, to keep me under his power for the rest of my life. Well, I would show him what happened to men who tried to use me in that fashion, or I would die trying.

I let my hands and my feet worry about finding holds, keeping my eyes on the palace guards. They were visible in their domed chhatris, the pavilion-capped towers standing one at each corner of the southern wall. Though there were hundreds of guards in the palace, there were just two who might have spotted me. In a way, I was lucky to be sequestered in the women's quarters. It meant that there were no guards manning the walls on this side of the palace, because unrelated men weren't allowed here. So this entire stretch of wall was protected by a pair of sleepy-eyed sentries in towers dozens of yards away, where their best views were of the eastern and western approaches. Still, if one of them happened to turn and look this way, my whole plan might be undone before it could begin.

I tried to focus on the climb, to push thoughts of failure from my mind. I couldn't control whether or not someone came into my bedchambers and realized that the girl in my bed wasn't me but one of Hina's celas. I couldn't even really control whether or not a guard saw me. That was in God's hands. What I could control was getting off this wall as quickly and silently as possible.

It was tough to tell just how far away the water was below me. That was always a danger when climbing—jumping down only to find that you were twenty feet up, not five. With the darkness of the night, and the starlight playing across the rippling surface of the lagoon, it was even more difficult than usual. So the first sign I got that I had made it was when my foot got wet while it was trying to feel out another crack in the masonry.

I breathed a little sigh of relief. So far so good. No guards had spotted me yet, though I knew that my swim would be the dangerous part. If I splashed, the noise would draw the eyes of every guard in every watchtower. And I would have to keep low, my head just barely peeking out above the water's surface, otherwise my silhouette might give me away.

As I slowly lowered myself into the water, another thought occurred to me—were there crocodiles in this lagoon? I suddenly wished I'd asked Hina about that, though I supposed maybe it didn't matter. I didn't have any weapons with which to fight back, so if a crocodile attacked me, I'd get eaten. It was as simple as that. Or at least that was what I told myself, but as the waters of the lagoon swallowed up my knees, and then my hips, I imagined a crocodile the size of Sultana gobbling me up, and my heart started to pound.

I forced myself to take a deep, calming breath, and then I let go of the wall and slid soundlessly into the water. It was shallow enough that if I stood on my tiptoes I could walk across the bottom and keep my chin just barely above the surface of the waves, but it was easier to just use the wall itself for propulsion. I put my hands on the stonework, letting my fingers dig into the cracks in the masonry, and glided along the base of the wall, toward the western guard tower.

I'd spent hours planning my route, thinking over every eventuality, but staying so close to the palace was a calculated risk. If the guard in the southwestern tower looked in my direction, I was sure he would spot me. He seemed impossibly close, standing in the orange light cast by the bronze lanterns hanging from the chhatri's sandstone pillars. I could make out the details of his face, the deep brown of his mustache, the lighter brown color of his eyes, the whites of them tinged yellow thanks to the lantern light. I knew I was moving in shadow, and I knew that few guards would look straight down when they had been trained to look for more distant threats, like enemy ships sailing into the harbor, but luck had always played an outsize role in these nightly escapades of mine, and I always feared that it would eventually run out.

But this was safer than swimming in the middle of the channel. Here, at least none of the servants or palace women could spot me. Their jali screens prevented them from looking straight down. So long as I hugged the wall, I would be safe from the prying eyes of Asma and the other denizens of the palace zenana. But I still felt hopelessly exposed as I propelled myself closer and closer to the guard tower. Once I got to the base of it, I would be safe, but I wasn't there yet, and moving without splashing was agonizingly slow. Though I knew it had only been a few minutes, I felt like I'd been in the water for hours.

The guard shifted his weight and turned his head, and I stopped breathing, but I didn't stop moving right away. I slowed down, letting myself drift to a gradual stop. Sudden changes draw a person's attention. If you don't want them to catch sight of you, you can't do anything abruptly. The guard was looking right over my head, I thought, staring at his compatriot in the eastern tower behind me. He reached up his hand, and I braced myself for the cry of alarm, for the guards to come pouring out of their barracks, but he was just scratching his nose. He played with his mustache for a moment, sighed, and turned away.

I waited a long moment before taking my first stroke with my arms, fighting down the urge to sigh, to breathe hard, to give the tension in my chest some audible release. I couldn't risk his hearing me, not now, not when I was so close to escaping his notice. I pressed on, dragging myself right up to the base of the tower. My heart slowed a little, and I felt myself begin to relax. I was far enough away from the eastern tower that I didn't think the man there could spot me, and unless the guard in this tower bent over and looked straight down, I was safely out of sight.

I worked my way around the tower, fighting down the urge to rush. Impatience was always the biggest danger. Every fiber of my being was screaming at me to just go as fast as possible, to just get it all over with, but that was a surefire way to get caught. No, in spite of the fear that was surging through me, I had to take everything in a plodding, methodical fashion. I had to be sure of each grip with my hands, of each gentle pull to move me through the water. I had to time my movements with the waves so that I wouldn't accidentally bump up against the tower, or cause one of the ripples to break early and create a splash.

I paused as I reached the far southwestern corner of the palace. Once I rounded this bend, I would be on the western side. There would be more guards here, standing along the parapets, manning at least one more tower to my north. But once I got past them, I'd be able to swim straight toward Kadiro's harbor.

I shook my head. This was madness. After all this, I still had another wall to swim past, and then a half-mile swim through the lagoon, all while praying that not a single guard saw me. The waters were dark, it was true, and it would take sharp eyes to notice me, but I couldn't help but feel completely and utterly exposed. There were no pillars or rosebushes or statues to hide behind here, like there had been in the wealthy havelis in Bikampur. There were no alleys I might vanish into. And if an alarm was raised, even if I could swim away and escape the musket balls they would surely shoot at me, Karim's first move would be to check my bedchamber, and then everything would be undone.

But it would be stupid to turn back now. I might well be caught climbing back into my bedchamber, without anything to show for it. That would be the worst outcome of all. So I steeled myself against the agony of uncertainty and turned the corner, pulling myself along the wall with slow, steady movements, gritting my teeth against the urge to turn around and go back to bed. If I didn't get these messages out, then someday soon, Karim would be lying in that bed with me. When set beside that horrific prospect, getting shot by a guardsman's toradar didn't seem half-bad.

The western wall was crawling with guards. Every crenellation in the battlement above me was highlighted by the red glow of a toradar's burning match cord. The tower in the distance had four men standing in it, each one looking in a different direction. God, did Karim know what I was doing? Had he been expecting me to try something like this? I should have scouted things out better, should have spent a night or two observing the guards' routines before running off like an imbecile.

None of the men was looking down; that was to my advantage, but I couldn't imagine trusting it to chance. All it would take would be one random glance, one guard staring at his feet at the wrong moment, and then all would be lost. This wasn't like breaking into a haveli with a couple of servants armed with clubs. This wasn't even like our assault on Shikarpur. At least there the guards had all been half-trained peasant conscripts, the bulk of the army having already left to attack Bikampur. No, these men were Sultan Ahmed's best, and they were all awake and alert. What had I got myself into?

I clung to the wall for a moment, weighing my options. The men seemed so clear to me because they were standing in torchlight, or holding burning slow matches whose soft glow illuminated their faces. But the water was pitch black. I'd sneaked past guards before, trusting the darkness to shield me, but never so many, nor so well armed. I took a slow, quiet breath, inhaling as deeply as I dared, and then I lowered myself until only my eyes were above the water, and I moved.

I could almost feel their eyes on me. My skin was tingling with anticipation, my chest was tight, and I had to fight the urge to shut my eyes, like that would somehow make me invisible. I paused every now and again for air, being careful to breathe normally, not to take great gasping gulps, in spite of the burning in my lungs. Noise was my greatest enemy. If the guards heard something moving at the base of the wall, they would all stare until one of them spotted me.

I made it to the base of the northwestern tower and stopped for a moment to catch my breath. I was about to undertake the most dangerous part of the journey thus far. I was going to have to swim north, toward the harbor, moving away from the protective shadow of the palace walls. I wanted to do as much of it as I possibly could underwater, so I needed to make sure that I had enough air in my lungs to see me safely outside the range of the guards' vision, though I didn't really know how far that was.

I moved with the utmost care around the circumference of the tower, hugging the stone wall with my body, my nose just a hairsbreadth above the surface of the water, the lapping waves washing completely over my face every few seconds. There was no way they would be able to make out my black hair against the darkness of the water. At least I hoped they wouldn't.

I stopped when the city of Kadiro came into view, its domed dargahs and tall havelis mere shadows illuminated by the orange glow of torches and bronze lanterns. I was separated from those pinpricks of light by a vast expanse of perfect, liquid blackness, like someone had spilled a pot of ink across the face of the world. It was now or never.

I took a deep breath and pulled myself beneath the surface of the lagoon, fumbling along the alga-covered surface of the wall with my palms until I was certain I was low enough that I couldn't be seen from above. I aimed myself at the city, and I kicked off the wall, scrambling with arms and legs, praying that I could get myself to a safe distance from the tower before I surfaced.

My lungs burned like fire, creating an urgent pressure that demanded to be released. But I didn't go up for air. I kept fighting for more distance, kept thrashing my feet behind me, keenly aware that the baggy shalwar I was wearing were slowing me down. I made long, powerful strokes with my arms. I fought for every last inch until there was no denying the need to breathe any longer.

My head broke the surface of the water and I tried not to gasp, tried not to sputter, tried not to make too much noise, but my breath sounded impossibly loud in my own ears, like the roar of some great beast. I twisted to look behind me, back in the direction of the fortress, and was horrified by how close it seemed. I thought I could reach out and touch its sandstone walls, but there were no shouts of alarm from the men atop the towers, and after one or two terrifying moments, I realized that it was farther away than it seemed.

I turned back around, intent on paddling for Kadiro's distant harbor, but before I could move, something huge and black loomed out of the darkness and hit me like a giant fist. I felt pain first and then terror, as the only possible explanation surged to the forefront of my mind—crocodile.

CHAPTER 16

I twisted in the water, holding up my hands to ward off the beast's jaws, when I realized that what I was facing was far worse than any mere crocodile. A riverboat bristling with small cannons and filled with armed men had plowed straight into me on its way toward the palace. Now I was looking up into the eyes of startled men who were rushing to bring their toradars to bear. I held up my hands helplessly as cannons swiveled on their mounts, orange match tips glowing brightly, poised to fall into touchholes primed with powder. I knew with a sick certainty that twisted my insides that I was going to be turned into so much mush by the volley that was surely coming.

The men hissed to one another in a language that was like Daryastani, but not Daryastani. Was it Mahisagari? I strained my ears to find familiar words, but they were speaking too quietly and too rapidly for me to follow. I knew that if I wanted to live I had to say something before they decided what to do for themselves. There was only one thing I really could say.

"I surrender. Please, you don't have to kill me."

My voice was quiet, because we were still near enough to the guard tower, and I didn't want to draw their attention. Maybe the men in this boat were Karim's, but even if they were, the last thing I needed was a commotion from the guards on the walls making them panic. And if they weren't Karim's men, if they were Zindhis, then maybe I'd be able to strike a deal with them that would keep me alive and enable me to deliver my messages.

A man barked an order, and this time I caught the words well enough—"Get her in the boat." It wasn't Mahisagari, it was Zindhi.

Strong arms reached down and snatched my wrists, pulling hard. I was lifted free of the water without too much noise, and thrown into the bottom of the boat, my shoulder slamming into the soggy wood with a dull thud. The boat started to move, but I couldn't make much sense of where we were going, because one of the soldiers was pinning me down to keep me from sitting up, and a second had plastered his grimy hand across my mouth, pressing hard enough that I was sure I was leaving imprints of my teeth on the insides of my lips.

My eyes flickered in all directions, trying to get as much information as I could, but the only things I could see clearly were the men holding me down, and the legs of the men sitting on the benches all around me, poised with their fishtail-stocked rifles, like they meant to shoot. Had they been intending to attack the palace? To what end?

They kept silent as three men in the back of the boat worked a single, enormous sculling oar, propelling the vessel silently across the shadowy waters of the lagoon. Wherever we were going, I didn't think it was toward the palace. My sudden arrival must have spooked the men and made them change course. That, or they thought I was a worthy enough prize to take back to their lair, wherever it was. I couldn't imagine that these men kept an armed ship in Kadiro's harbor right under Ahmed Shah's nose. They must have had a hideout somewhere.

Wherever it was, I didn't get to see it. The captain of the vessel, a man whose proud nose and high forehead gave him a strong silhouette even so far from any sources of light, knelt down beside me and tied an ajrak scarf around my eyes, totally blindfolding me. In Daryastani, he whispered, "If you're a good girl, and you keep quiet, there's a chance I won't kill you. If you scream or try to move, we'll club you over the head and leave you for the crocodiles."

So there were crocodiles in this lagoon. I didn't know why that thought came to me, when I'd just been threatened with murder, but I had fully intended to keep quiet anyway, so I didn't feel that threatened. Whatever this man did to me, I didn't think it would be as bad as being Karim's wife. He could have pulled out my fingernails with a pair of tweezers and I still would have considered it a step up in the world.

When he saw that I wasn't going to say anything, the captain muttered, "Good." I heard him move away from me, but I didn't know where he was going, or what he was planning. The man who had been keeping his hand on my mouth finally let me go, as did the man holding my limbs down.

I knew that I'd been ordered not to move, but I rubbed the life back into my arms all the same, trying to knead out the bruises the Zindhi sailor had surely left there. Nobody seemed to mind, because I wasn't clubbed over the head and left for the crocodiles. I resisted the urge to sit up, or to give any appearance of looking around. It was difficult, because the longer the boat wobbled in time with the movements of its sculling oar, the more I worried that I was being taken too far from the palace to get back before morning. If I wasn't back in bed by the time Karim arrived to escort me to breakfast, all would be lost.

But I'd been told to keep quiet, and I was fairly certain that the captain intended to make good on his threat if I disobeyed him. He didn't know who I was or what I was worth, and until I knew who he was, I wanted to keep it that way. So that meant staying put and keeping my mouth shut and hoping that I could get back before sunup.

I heard movement all around me. There was the sound of metal clunking against wood, of cloth being moved. I felt something heavy land on the timbers on either side of me, and then my whole body was covered in a thick canvas cloth. It was draped loosely enough that I could still breathe, so I didn't panic, but I thought I understood what was happening. These men did live in Kadiro, and they were hiding their weapons as they returned to the port, just in case a sharp-eyed Mahisagari guard caught sight of their boat. The silhouette would look like a fishing boat, not an armed gunboat.

I didn't really think that would be enough to save them, not when they were out so late with so many men packed into the vessel, but I supposed they had to take every advantage they could find. It couldn't have been easy sneaking out into the harbor with weapons, not when the Mahisagaris were such natural sailors, and so accustomed to watching harbor traffic.

The boat bumped into something. Men started piling out. They were moving quickly, but quietly. I felt their movement more than I heard it, as the boat slowly rose higher in the water as it was relieved of its burden. The cloth came off next, and I was grabbed an instant later by strong hands around my arms that hauled me to my feet. I hadn't yet had the chance to change out of my climbing shoes, so it was hard for me to walk, but even through the reinforced soles of my slippers, I could feel that I was walking on stone rather than wood.

"May I change my shoes?" I asked, because the man holding

me was marching me along at a pace that made it almost impossible to keep up.

He stopped for a second, and though I couldn't see him, he must have looked down at my feet to check them. He let me go, and asked, "What are those things?"

"Climbing shoes," I replied, kneeling down and peeling them off my soggy feet, replacing them with the slippers I'd stuffed in my pockets earlier. I shook out the climbing shoes, trying to get rid of as much of the water as I could before I stuck them in my sodden pockets and stood up once more.

The captain, for I had recognized his voice, took hold of me once more and we continued our march along the stone path. I didn't know whether I was inside or outside, but the floor was so level and so smooth that I had to imagine we were indoors. "Where are you taking me?" I asked.

"Enough questions," he replied, his voice harsh enough that I knew better than to push my luck. I just shrugged instead, and kept walking.

We ascended a stairwell, which must have been quite an impressive one, because the steps were shallow, and made of smooth stone, and after we reached a landing, we had to turn and keep climbing. We must have been in a haveli of some kind. There was a lot of light streaming through the ajrak cloth wrapped around my eyes, not enough to see by, but enough to know that there were torches or lanterns hanging at regular intervals along the wall, visible as dull halos through the indigo fabric.

We turned a sharp corner and came to a stop. Somewhere in front of me, a man's voice demanded in Zindhi, "What's this?"

"I don't know, my lord," the captain replied in the same language. Then he said a bunch of things I couldn't follow, though I thought he was referring to me, because I heard the words for "water" and "boat." But Zindhi was even more different from

Daryastani than Mahisagari was, and I'd never spent much time in this province. And anyway, Daryastani wasn't even my first language, Court Safavian was, and it was even more removed from the tongues of the common people.

The lord, whoever he was, said something in Zindhi. His tone made it plain that it was a question, but I didn't understand anything of it. There was a long pause, and then he asked a different question, in a slightly gruffer voice, and I knew it was Mahisagari, but I couldn't follow that either.

I sighed. "If you wouldn't mind speaking in Daryastani, I'd rather not stand here all night until you've exhausted your linguistic repertoire."

He chuckled. "You're educated. Who are you?"

"Razia Khanum, princess of Nizam," I replied, pulling off the blindfold so that he could see my green eyes, which were nearly proof enough of my identity in these lands, though they were so much more common on the steppes where my people hailed from.

I had to squint against the brightness of the light pouring from half a dozen brass lanterns. It took my eyes a moment to adjust, to really let me see the figure standing before me. He was a tall, fit man, though I suspected he was at least twenty years my elder. His dark black beard hadn't yet started to become speckled with gray, nor had his full head of hair, which was mostly covered by a heavily embroidered Zindhi cap. He wore an ajrak kurta of fine silk, depicting block-printed river zahhaks racing across a background of pale indigo, the color calling to mind the waters of the sea on a bright day.

His dark brown eyes met mine, studying them carefully. He examined my soaking-wet shalwar kameez, the ajrak pattern not so far removed from the one he was wearing. He pursed his lips as he considered the possibility that I was telling the truth. "Do you have any proof of that?"

"Aside from my eyes?" I asked.

He smirked. "Yes, aside from those."

I switched into Court Safavian, because I knew it wouldn't be common here in Zindh. "Do you speak the language of the Nizami court?"

His eyes widened a little, and he nodded. "Some." His accent was unpolished enough that I heard it even from that one word. It would have got him laughed out of the diwan-i-khas in Nizam, but I supposed for a provincial lord it wasn't terrible.

I returned to Daryastani so as not to embarrass him. "Would you be kind enough to grant me your name, sir?"

He worked his jaw, considering his answer. I knew he must have heard what had happened to me by now. Word of a marriage alliance with Nizam would have made its way through the ranks of the common soldiery of Mahisagar like wildfire, and from there the common people of Zindh would have heard the rumors too. If he believed that I was Karim's willing wife, then he'd have done well to keep his mouth shut. But I had to believe that Hina hadn't left Kadiro without making her plans to ally with me known to her emirs. So didn't that work in my favor?

"I am Sanghar Soomro," he said.

I breathed a sigh of relief, scarcely believing my luck. It was hard to keep a smile off my face. "Hina said you would help us."

Sanghar Soomro quirked an onyx eyebrow at that claim. "Is that so?"

I nodded, but then I suddenly felt the weight of fatigue crashing over me, and I abruptly sat down beside a silk cushion a few paces away. I'd have sat on it, but I didn't want to ruin it. While the warm breezes of a desert night were doing much to dry my clothes, they were still sodden enough with lagoon water that I didn't think I could risk it.

"Please, sit down, your highness," Sanghar said, the ironic tone in his voice bringing a smile to both of our lips.

"Forgive me, it was a long climb down from the palace and a difficult swim, and that was before your gunboat nearly battered me to death." I rubbed the spot on my shoulder where I'd been struck—the same spot where I'd landed when I'd been thrown into the bottom of the boat. I was going to have a massive bruise there in the morning.

"And what were you doing swimming in the lagoon at night, your highness?" Sanghar inquired, once he'd taken his seat on one of his plush cushions.

"Coming to see you," I replied.

"Oh?" He didn't look like he believed that.

"Hina and I have sworn to each other that we will fight Karim Shah and his father to the death," I told him, looking him squarely in the eyes, hoping he could see the determination in my own. "To do that, we must send messages to rally our allies. She assured me that you remained loyal to her, and that you had the necessary river zahhaks to see those messages delivered with speed."

"Perhaps what you say is true," Sanghar allowed, "but perhaps it isn't. What assurances do I have that you're not simply trying to trick me into committing treason against your father-in-law?"

"Ahmed Shah is *not* my father-in-law," I growled.

Sanghar spread his hands in apology. "Father-in-law-to-be, then."

"He will not be my father-in-law," I assured Sanghar. "What he will be is a corpse. But to do that I need fighting men, and I need zahhaks, and to get those I need to send messages to my allies. Now, you can either help me do that or you can refuse me, but I need you to make your decision quickly, because if I am not back in that palace by sunup, Hina will be the one paying the price for it."

His brow furrowed with alarm, and I knew then that he was

truly loyal to Hina, that he wouldn't let anything happen to her. He pursed his lips like he'd tasted something sour. "All right, your highness, it seems I have no choice but to trust you. I will serve as your messenger. Tell me what messages you need sent, and I will have my fliers send them."

I shook my head. "They must be written in my own hand or they won't be trusted. Do you have paper and ink?"

"Pens too," he quipped, a little of his ironic sense of humor returning. He gestured for the captain to fetch them, and the man returned with a lap desk and everything I needed to compose my messages.

I pulled back my damp sleeve so that I wouldn't drag it across the surface of the paper, and picked up one of the pens. Immediately the emir raised an eyebrow. "Left-handed? Your palace tutors never corrected that?"

"There is much about me they failed to correct," I retorted, and I set about writing my letters. I dipped my pen in the ink, and then paused. I might not get another chance to send a second message, or even to receive replies. This might be my only chance of arranging my plans. I couldn't merely ask for vague help. I had to give specific instructions. I had to come up with a plan that would see Karim defeated and Kadiro liberated. That meant I had to arrange for all my allies to arrive on the same day. But what day?

I glanced up at Sanghar, who had positioned himself to read over my shoulder. "The next full moon is the brother-sister festival, is it not, emir?"

"It is, your highness," he replied, though it was plain he didn't understand what significance that had for my plans.

The next full moon was twelve days hence. It wasn't much time, especially not if I intended for Haider and Tamara to receive their letters and have a chance to act on them. If Tamara wasn't in Tavrezh with Haider, she'd be in the Khevsurian summer palace of Tamtra. I'd only been there once, and I thought it was the better part of two thousand miles away. Even a swift zahhak would need at least three days to make such a journey, and probably four was more likely, assuming the animal wasn't fighting a headwind. Then she would need time to prepare, and to return. I was cutting it close. There would certainly not be time to compose any further messages. This was my one chance at freeing myself from Karim and saving Zindh.

I had a date, but I needed a plan. I had to find some way of getting Karim and his father away from the palace in Kadiro, allowing Arjun and Sunil to assault it, without the possibility that my sisters and I might be held as hostages. There was only one way to get Karim away from Kadiro, and it would require Haider's help. If he didn't answer my call, then all would be lost. But how could I convince a man I hadn't seen since I was eleven years old to come for me in my time of need, to potentially start a war on my behalf?

I picked up the pen and began to write. *To His Royal Highness, Prince Haider of Safavia, Lord of Artavila, Victor at Vendigar, First Captain of the Armies of the Faithful, and the Elder Brother of my heart: Greetings.*

"Safavia?" Sanghar asked, his eyes widening slightly.

"Mm-hmm," I murmured, but my mind was focused on the letter. In it, I told Haider of my plight, of the arranged marriage to my rapist, of the abuse I had suffered at his hands, of the way my father had abandoned me to my fate. I told him too of the brother-sister festival, a ritual tradition in Daryastan where girls tied amulets to their brothers' wrists, binding them together, the amulet protecting the brother in return for the brother's promise to protect his sister in her time of need. And I reminded him of the amulet I had tied around his wrist seven years before, when I had lived at the Safavian court while my father fought a bitterly weighed about the same that Lakshmi did these days, and just like with Lakshmi, my arms started to burn after a few moments.

I handed it back to the sailor and said, "Bring as many of these as you can when you attack the palace. We'll haul them up with ropes and mount them from the windowsills and in the corridors. The palace guards will have us outnumbered, so we will have to use every advantage we can."

The captain grinned. "Sounds like fun."

I wasn't sure that fighting a gun battle within the confines of an island palace qualified as fun, but it would be a relief to be free of Karim and his family. Twelve days and I would know whether or not Haider had answered my call. On the thirteenth, I would either be free or facing an impossible battle.

contested civil war. I begged him, if he felt any affection for me at all, to make a diversionary attack on the fortress of Ahura on the night of the next full moon to draw off Karim and his zahhaks so that I might win my freedom. I signed it *Your little sister, Razia Khanum, Princess of Nizam.*

"Do you think he'll come?" Sanghar asked me as I set the letter aside to dry and prepared to draft the next missive.

I shrugged. "You're a man. What would you do if a princess from your childhood sent such a letter to you?"

"I think I'd attack that fortress, your highness," he replied, with a bemused grin creasing his face.

The next letter was to *My beloved elder sister, Princess Tamara of Khevsuria.* I explained my situation, in much the same terms as I had to Haider, and I begged her to come with all haste to Kadiro on the day after the brother-sister festival.

"You want my messengers flying all the way to Khevsuria?" Sanghar asked in disbelief. "I don't even think they know how to get there."

"So send him to Tavrezh first with the other messenger," I suggested. "Someone there will be able to direct him to Tamtra. Or one of Prince Haider's men might deliver the message himself."

I let Sanghar chew that over while I composed the most important message of all. *To the prince of my heart, Arjun,* I wrote, holding back tears that were threatening at the corners of my eyes, *I have arranged for Prince Haider to attack Ahura on the night of the next full moon to draw off Karim's zahhaks. The next morning, I expect he will be gone. That night, your men must be ready to attack the harbor fortresses of Kadiro, and to take the city itself. Your zahhaks must be prepared for battle. Everything depends on it. With all my love, Razia.*

The last letter was to Sunil Kalani. I told him simply to arrive the night after the full moon with his army and his zahhaks to help assault the city with Arjun. I suggested arriving by boat on the Zindhu, to avoid the city walls, especially since Karim's zahhaks wouldn't be there to attack any approaching ships on the water. I handed that letter to Sanghar and said, "I don't know where exactly he is. He might be hard to find."

"I know where he is, your highness," Sanghar assured me, taking the letter and folding it up once he'd blown it dry. "I can promise you that he will be here, ready to fight. I just hope the rest of your allies are as reliable."

"So do I," I replied, my stomach churning as I wondered whether or not my childhood friendship with Haider and Tamara would be enough to bring them thousands of miles across deserts and mountains to fight a battle that wasn't their own. It was a question that was impossible to answer, so I pushed it from my mind. There was one last arrangement left to make.

"You will attack the palace on the night after the full moon," I informed Sanghar. "Get as many gunboats as you can. Approach the southern wall under cover of darkness. That's where my chambers are. I'll throw down ropes so that your men can climb up unseen."

"And the guards on that side?" he asked.

"Just two," I said. "One on each of the southern towers. I'll kill them before you arrive. The way will be clear for you, you have my word."

"Then we will be there, your highness," he assured me. "And these letters will reach their destinations, I promise you that. Whether anything will come of them . . ."

I clapped him on the shoulder. "That is in God's hands now."

"It is," he agreed. He nodded toward the doorway, where the captain was leaning against a carved sandstone pillar. "You should go now, your highness. If you're caught, these plans will all come to nothing."

I couldn't argue with that, so I stood and hurried away, following the captain back through the palace. Now that I could see it, I realized that it straddled a canal, giving it a hidden set of docks on the bottom floor. That was why the men were able to bring weapons in and out of the lagoon without being spotted by Mahisagari patrols.

"I need a small weapon I can keep hidden on my person," I informed the captain. "I was disarmed when I was brought here, but if I'm going to kill the guards for you, I'll need something to fight with, preferably a katar."

The captain led me to a crate, and when he popped open the lid, my eyes widened. Inside were dozens of talwars, neatly packed in straw, along with daggers of various kinds and several nice katars. He gestured for me to take my pick, and I settled on a pair of katars that fit tightly together in a single scabbard. They were shorter and narrower than the ones that had been taken from me, but that would make them easier to hide. I tucked them into the waistband of my shalwar, pleased that my kameez hid them completely.

We turned back to the boat then, and I noted that the small cannons were being offloaded. They had a kind of swiveling mount with a spike at the bottom, so they could be stuck onto the wooden gunwales of the boat and shot in any direction. Each gun was about as long as a man was tall, but from the way they were being carried, I didn't think they were very heavy.

"How much do those weigh?" I asked the captain, my mind brimming with possibilities.

"Less than you do," he replied. He called one of his men over and barked an order at him in Zindhi. I didn't know what he said, but an instant later the man was pressing one of the cannons into my arms. I expected to drop it on my toes, but was surprised that I was able to bear the weight without too much difficulty. It

CHAPTER 17

"Just a week left," Hina remarked as I sat on the southwestern tower, in my favorite spot beneath the domed roof of a cobalt-tiled chhatri.

I grunted an acknowledgment, but made no reply, because thinking too much about the impending battle tied my stomach in knots and made it hard to pretend to be "finding my place here" as Karim had commanded. I couldn't control whether or not Haider came for me, couldn't control whether or not Karim would leave for Ahura as I'd planned. All I could do was sit and wait.

"It's okay to be nervous, but it's a good plan," Hina said, sinking to the cushion beside mine and taking my hands in hers. "Fate will decide what responses your letters will bring, but the important thing is that you were brave enough to send them."

I glanced over at her, keenly aware of how much strain she must have been under, how angry she must have been. She was still grieving the loss of her brother, and here she was, sitting in his conquered palace, living cheek by jowl with his murderers, and she still had the wherewithal to comfort me.

"How do you do it?" I asked her.

She didn't need me to explain the question. She just heaved a sigh that was as heavy as the ones that so frequently left my own lips these days, and said, "The same way you let Karim kiss you good night every evening."

I shuddered at the memories of his lips grazing my cheek, my forehead, even my mouth from time to time. He knew just how far he could push things before Sikander would intervene, though the old guardsman spent most of his time keeping Lakshmi safe.

"I'm sorry I wasn't able to kill him before he could drag you into this," Hina told me.

I shook my head. "It's my fault he came to Zindh at all. If I hadn't been named subahdar, none of this would have happened."

"If you hadn't been named subahdar, we Zindhis would still be living under Javed Khorasani's thumb, and that was no better, I promise you," she replied.

"He wouldn't have been subahdar if my father hadn't killed your father," I pointed out, recalling the aftermath of the Nizami civil war seven years before.

"I don't miss him," Hina replied with a shrug. "He was a terrible man. He beat me every chance he got."

"My father always left it to Sikander to do the beating," I muttered. I realized that the pair of us hadn't had much chance to get to know each other these last few days, we'd been so busy plotting against Karim. "Did you run away from home too, then?"

"He didn't leave me any choice," she said. "He despised me. He said that I would be the death of Zindh, that I was worthless, that it was lucky he had Ali, because I had no chance whatever of reclaiming our independence."

I managed a stiff nod, having more or less heard words to that effect for the whole of my life.

"Finally, when I was thirteen years old, I just couldn't take it anymore. We were in the midst of our uprising. Your father was fighting a civil war against his brother, and we sided with him, whatever his name was."

"My uncle Azam," I recalled, though in truth I barely remembered the man beyond his name, having only met him a few times. "I was nine when that rebellion started. My father sent me to the Safavian court for safekeeping. I was eleven by the time the war was over and I could finally come home."

"Just a baby," Hina teased.

"That's what Prince Haider of Safavia thought. He was thirteen when I arrived, fifteen when I left."

"Was he handsome?" she asked.

"In his own way," I said. "I mostly thought of him as a big brother, but his mother was the younger sister of the queen of Khevsuria, and like her sister, and her niece, Princess Tamara, she had flame-red hair and bright blue eyes."

"They're Firangis?" Hina asked, raising an eyebrow at that. "And Prince Haider too?"

I shook my head. "He takes after his father mostly. He doesn't have pale skin like a Firangi, and his eyes are brown, but he does have unusually red hair."

"Hm," she grunted as she imagined it. "Doesn't sound very handsome."

"More so than you might think," I replied. "And I always thought Tamara was beautiful."

"That would be the crown princess of Khevsuria?" Hina asked.

I nodded. "She was very kind to me. They both were." I pushed those thoughts from my mind before they could overwhelm me. I'd spent too many years wondering how my life might have been different had my father lost the civil war and I'd stayed in Safavia.

Maybe it would have turned out the same way, but I didn't think so. Haider and Tamara never would have let those awful things happen to me.

It was the thought of everything that had happened to me after I'd run away from home that reminded me that Hina had been in the midst of telling me her own story. "So, you were thirteen when you left home in the midst of that rebellion?" I prompted.

"Oh, right, that . . ." She grimaced, and I half wondered if she'd been letting me get sidetracked on purpose to avoid painful memories, but I kept quiet and she pressed on. "My father beat me pretty severely one night. I think he must have been upset that the war wasn't going well, but most of it was that I'd been wearing one of my mother's old lehengas, and he'd caught me doing it. He'd beaten me plenty of times before, but never like that." She shook her head at the memory, her arms wrapping around her stomach, her shoulders hunching. "It had never hurt like that. Not ever. I thought he'd killed me."

I took her hand in mine, rubbing my thumb across her knuckles in gentle circles, hoping to distract her from the memory of the pain, because I knew exactly what she was talking about. Pain is a wonderful teacher, and I had not forgotten a single lesson.

"I had to run away," Hina murmured. "But I didn't want to leave without saying good-bye to my brother. Ali had always been my protector. He'd known I was different, ever since I was little, but he'd never hurt me for it, never chastised me for it. Sometimes he would distract Father for me. Other times he would hide me in his room, or take me for a ride on his zahhak, back when Sakina wasn't old enough to be ridden. He was my only friend, and I loved him fiercely, and I just couldn't bear to go without saying good-bye."

Her voice was so thick with emotion that I thought I knew what was coming next. "And he ratted you out to your father?"

Anger flashed in Hina's olive eyes, and she glared at me for an instant before realizing that I hadn't meant to impugn her brother's character, that I'd just been responding from my own horrific experiences.

"No." She gave my hand a pat. "No, Ali was like Arjun. He never would have abandoned me—not for anything. He packed up his things, and helped me pack mine, and we took our zahhaks, and we rode off into the night sky together."

"He went with you?" I gasped, tears threatening at the corners of my eyes, because I'd wished more than anything in the whole world not to be alone that fateful night when I'd fled the palace of Nizam. God, how I'd wanted someone to come with me, but there had been no one in all the world I'd trusted—no one except for Haider and Tamara. What would it have been like if I'd had a big brother to protect me like Hina had? I couldn't even imagine it. I doubted I'd have ended up in Bikampur, serving Varsha and learning to be a thief and a courtesan. And that meant I wouldn't have my sisters or Arjun. That thought quelled whatever jealousy I'd been feeling. It was all right to dream about a past without pain, but I couldn't regret any part of my life when it would mean losing the people I loved most fiercely.

"He did," Hina whispered, and tears did spill down her cheeks, reminding me that he was dead, and that Ahmed and Karim were responsible for it. "He supported me while I got my nirvan, and then we sold our services as scouts. He told everyone I was his sister, and no one batted an eye at a young noble girl with her own river zahhak, as it's not at all uncommon here in Zindh. He recruited men, and when we had enough money, I started recruiting young hijras, training them to serve as my retainers, eventually becoming an unconventional guru, and then a nayak. If not for Ali, I don't know what I would have done. Someone would probably have stolen Sakina from me—I wasn't strong enough or tough enough to fend off an attacker, and while she's big and strong, she hasn't got any breath. And without Sakina, I'd have become a penniless orphan. I'd probably have had to join a dera and sell myself to men like a common . . ."

She trailed off, her cheeks burning as she noticed the way I was staring at the floor, because I hadn't had a brother to save me from that fate. "Forgive me, Razia, I didn't mean . . ."

"It's all right," I said, my voice tight with emotion. "I'm glad you didn't have to go through that. None of us should have to."

"I couldn't agree more." She looked down at Nuri, who was riding Nalini all around the courtyard, and I turned my eyes to Sakshi and Lakshmi, who were flying lazy circles over the palace on the backs of their brilliantly colored zahhaks. Whatever had happened to us, we weren't letting it happen to our sisters, that was the main thing.

But then my eyes drifted over to Karim and I remembered that my own suffering was far from over. He was standing in the courtyard, one hand raised to shade his eyes from the sun as he watched Sakshi and Lakshmi flying overhead, the pair of them trailed by four acid zahhaks, just to be certain that they didn't get any ideas into their heads of fleeing.

"And he killed your brother . . ." I whispered, gritting my teeth at the idea that a man like Karim Shah could continue to draw breath while Ali Talpur was dead and buried. Sometimes I wondered if there even was a God at all, the world was so full of injustice.

"He's going to pay for that," Hina promised.

"He is," I agreed, my vow every bit as fervent as hers.

"But enough of that talk," Hina said, her tone changing completely as she plastered a smile across her face. I didn't know what that was about, not until I turned and saw Asma marching across the rooftop toward us, trailed by her handmaidens.

I stood up at once to greet her, bowing my head in proper deference, though all the while I was repeating, "Seven more days," like a mantra in my mind. That was how long I had left until the full moon, how long I had to put up with this farce before bringing it to a bloody end. But for now, I exclaimed, "Mother-in-law, what a pleasant surprise!"

Asma took my hands in hers, offering me a bright smile. "I've brought something for you, dear."

"Oh?" I asked, hoping that I seemed appropriately eager, though I doubted very much if she had the slightest idea as to what stirred my heart.

"Your husband-to-be has had lovely gifts commissioned for you," she said. "He tells me that he means them to be a symbol of your engagement, and your commitment to one another. My Karim is so pleased that you seem to have found your place here so quickly."

In another tone of voice, there might have been unspoken suspicions lurking behind those words, but Asma sounded genuinely pleased with me. I bowed my head to her, and smiled prettily, and lied just as boldly as I dared, "I am grateful that my husband-to-be is pleased with me."

"You two will make such a lovely pair." She gave my cheek a fond pat, and then settled herself on the cushion I had formerly occupied in the chhatri. I took Hina's place, shunting her away, which I thought was probably a blessing, as it meant she didn't have to deal with her brother's murderer's mother directly.

Asma clapped her hands, and one of her handmaidens came forward, laying a beautiful sandalwood box at my feet. When she opened it, she removed a blouse of emerald silk fabric, with darker green embroidery creating a pattern of scales all across its surface. Turquoise beads and tiny circular mirrors formed an eye on each scale like the ones found on a peacock's tail feathers, just like on a real acid zahhak.

My eyes widened at the sight of such an exquisite garment. Lakshmi was going to be so incurably jealous when she saw me wearing it. And the skirt was just as beautiful, though rather than being green to look like an acid zahhak's scales, it was the deep sapphire of their tail feathers, carefully embroidered with turquoise eyes in a ring around the skirt's wide hem, the shisheh mirror-work making the fabric sparkle in the bright sunlight.

"This embroidery style is traditional in Mahisagar," Asma explained as she took the skirt out of the box, holding it up for me to admire.

"It's magnificent," I whispered, not even having to pretend to be impressed by it, in spite of who it was who had given it to me.

"He included jewelry, of course," Asma said, "as it seems that your little sister has taken yours."

I smiled at that. "It meant more to her than it did to me. But this I'll treasure."

A handmaiden opened a jewelry box, revealing bangles for my wrists and ankles, each one crafted from pure gold that had been cut and inset with sapphire and emerald cloisonné to form perfect tiny replicas of acid zahhaks chasing their own tail feathers. It wasn't the most creative of gifts, as I'd received similar jewelry from Arjun, but the workmanship of these pieces was exquisite—the equal of anything any princess in all the world owned.

There were matching earrings, of course, and a tall necklace that resembled a coiled acid zahhak twisting itself around my neck. The dupatta that went over my head was the larger style popular in Zindh and Mahisagar, but the fabric was the brilliant blue of lightning, marred by dark black stripes, just like an acid zahhak's mane. It was a detail that the tailors in Bikampur had missed when Arjun had dressed me up as an acid zahhak to draw Karim's eye. Just remembering that day made me wish I'd refused contested civil war. I begged him, if he felt any affection for me at all, to make a diversionary attack on the fortress of Ahura on the night of the next full moon to draw off Karim and his zahhaks so that I might win my freedom. I signed it *Your little sister, Razia Khanum, Princess of Nizam.*

"Do you think he'll come?" Sanghar asked me as I set the letter aside to dry and prepared to draft the next missive.

I shrugged. "You're a man. What would you do if a princess from your childhood sent such a letter to you?"

"I think I'd attack that fortress, your highness," he replied, with a bemused grin creasing his face.

The next letter was to *My beloved elder sister, Princess Tamara of Khevsuria.* I explained my situation, in much the same terms as I had to Haider, and I begged her to come with all haste to Kadiro on the day after the brother-sister festival.

"You want my messengers flying all the way to Khevsuria?" Sanghar asked in disbelief. "I don't even think they know how to get there."

"So send him to Tavrezh first with the other messenger," I suggested. "Someone there will be able to direct him to Tamtra. Or one of Prince Haider's men might deliver the message himself."

I let Sanghar chew that over while I composed the most important message of all. *To the prince of my heart, Arjun,* I wrote, holding back tears that were threatening at the corners of my eyes, *I have arranged for Prince Haider to attack Ahura on the night of the next full moon to draw off Karim's zahhaks. The next morning, I expect he will be gone. That night, your men must be ready to attack the harbor fortresses of Kadiro, and to take the city itself. Your zahhaks must be prepared for battle. Everything depends on it. With all my love, Razia.*

The last letter was to Sunil Kalani. I told him simply to arrive the night after the full moon with his army and his zahhaks to help assault the city with Arjun. I suggested arriving by boat on the Zindhu, to avoid the city walls, especially since Karim's zahhaks wouldn't be there to attack any approaching ships on the water. I handed that letter to Sanghar and said, "I don't know where exactly he is. He might be hard to find."

"I know where he is, your highness," Sanghar assured me, taking the letter and folding it up once he'd blown it dry. "I can promise you that he will be here, ready to fight. I just hope the rest of your allies are as reliable."

"So do I," I replied, my stomach churning as I wondered whether or not my childhood friendship with Haider and Tamara would be enough to bring them thousands of miles across deserts and mountains to fight a battle that wasn't their own. It was a question that was impossible to answer, so I pushed it from my mind. There was one last arrangement left to make.

"You will attack the palace on the night after the full moon," I informed Sanghar. "Get as many gunboats as you can. Approach the southern wall under cover of darkness. That's where my chambers are. I'll throw down ropes so that your men can climb up unseen."

"And the guards on that side?" he asked.

"Just two," I said. "One on each of the southern towers. I'll kill them before you arrive. The way will be clear for you, you have my word."

"Then we will be there, your highness," he assured me. "And these letters will reach their destinations, I promise you that. Whether anything will come of them . . ."

I clapped him on the shoulder. "That is in God's hands now."

"It is," he agreed. He nodded toward the doorway, where the captain was leaning against a carved sandstone pillar. "You should go now, your highness. If you're caught, these plans will all come to nothing."

I couldn't argue with that, so I stood and hurried away, following the captain back through the palace. Now that I could see it, I realized that it straddled a canal, giving it a hidden set of docks on the bottom floor. That was why the men were able to bring weapons in and out of the lagoon without being spotted by Mahisagari patrols.

"I need a small weapon I can keep hidden on my person," I informed the captain. "I was disarmed when I was brought here, but if I'm going to kill the guards for you, I'll need something to fight with, preferably a katar."

The captain led me to a crate, and when he popped open the lid, my eyes widened. Inside were dozens of talwars, neatly packed in straw, along with daggers of various kinds and several nice katars. He gestured for me to take my pick, and I settled on a pair of katars that fit tightly together in a single scabbard. They were shorter and narrower than the ones that had been taken from me, but that would make them easier to hide. I tucked them into the waistband of my shalwar, pleased that my kameez hid them completely.

We turned back to the boat then, and I noted that the small cannons were being offloaded. They had a kind of swiveling mount with a spike at the bottom, so they could be stuck onto the wooden gunwales of the boat and shot in any direction. Each gun was about as long as a man was tall, but from the way they were being carried, I didn't think they were very heavy.

"How much do those weigh?" I asked the captain, my mind brimming with possibilities.

"Less than you do," he replied. He called one of his men over and barked an order at him in Zindhi. I didn't know what he said, but an instant later the man was pressing one of the cannons into my arms. I expected to drop it on my toes, but was surprised that I was able to bear the weight without too much difficulty. It weighed about the same that Lakshmi did these days, and just like with Lakshmi, my arms started to burn after a few moments.

I handed it back to the sailor and said, "Bring as many of these as you can when you attack the palace. We'll haul them up with ropes and mount them from the windowsills and in the corridors. The palace guards will have us outnumbered, so we will have to use every advantage we can."

The captain grinned. "Sounds like fun."

I wasn't sure that fighting a gun battle within the confines of an island palace qualified as fun, but it would be a relief to be free of Karim and his family. Twelve days and I would know whether or not Haider had answered my call. On the thirteenth, I would either be free or facing an impossible battle.

CHAPTER 17

Just a week left," Hina remarked as I sat on the southwestern tower, in my favorite spot beneath the domed roof of a cobalt-tiled chhatri.

I grunted an acknowledgment, but made no reply, because thinking too much about the impending battle tied my stomach in knots and made it hard to pretend to be "finding my place here" as Karim had commanded. I couldn't control whether or not Haider came for me, couldn't control whether or not Karim would leave for Ahura as I'd planned. All I could do was sit and wait.

"It's okay to be nervous, but it's a good plan," Hina said, sinking to the cushion beside mine and taking my hands in hers. "Fate will decide what responses your letters will bring, but the important thing is that you were brave enough to send them."

I glanced over at her, keenly aware of how much strain she must have been under, how angry she must have been. She was still grieving the loss of her brother, and here she was, sitting in his conquered palace, living cheek by jowl with his murderers, and she still had the wherewithal to comfort me.

"How do you do it?" I asked her.

She didn't need me to explain the question. She just heaved a sigh that was as heavy as the ones that so frequently left my own lips these days, and said, "The same way you let Karim kiss you good night every evening."

I shuddered at the memories of his lips grazing my cheek, my forehead, even my mouth from time to time. He knew just how far he could push things before Sikander would intervene, though the old guardsman spent most of his time keeping Lakshmi safe.

"I'm sorry I wasn't able to kill him before he could drag you into this," Hina told me.

I shook my head. "It's my fault he came to Zindh at all. If I hadn't been named subahdar, none of this would have happened."

"If you hadn't been named subahdar, we Zindhis would still be living under Javed Khorasani's thumb, and that was no better, I promise you," she replied.

"He wouldn't have been subahdar if my father hadn't killed your father," I pointed out, recalling the aftermath of the Nizami civil war seven years before.

"I don't miss him," Hina replied with a shrug. "He was a terrible man. He beat me every chance he got."

"My father always left it to Sikander to do the beating," I muttered. I realized that the pair of us hadn't had much chance to get to know each other these last few days, we'd been so busy plotting against Karim. "Did you run away from home too, then?"

"He didn't leave me any choice," she said. "He despised me. He said that I would be the death of Zindh, that I was worthless, that it was lucky he had Ali, because I had no chance whatever of reclaiming our independence."

I managed a stiff nod, having more or less heard words to that effect for the whole of my life.

"Finally, when I was thirteen years old, I just couldn't take it anymore. We were in the midst of our uprising. Your father was fighting a civil war against his brother, and we sided with him, whatever his name was."

"My uncle Azam," I recalled, though in truth I barely remembered the man beyond his name, having only met him a few times. "I was nine when that rebellion started. My father sent me to the Safavian court for safekeeping. I was eleven by the time the war was over and I could finally come home."

"Just a baby," Hina teased.

"That's what Prince Haider of Safavia thought. He was thirteen when I arrived, fifteen when I left."

"Was he handsome?" she asked.

"In his own way," I said. "I mostly thought of him as a big brother, but his mother was the younger sister of the queen of Khevsuria, and like her sister, and her niece, Princess Tamara, she had flame-red hair and bright blue eyes."

"They're Firangis?" Hina asked, raising an eyebrow at that. "And Prince Haider too?"

I shook my head. "He takes after his father mostly. He doesn't have pale skin like a Firangi, and his eyes are brown, but he does have unusually red hair."

"Hm," she grunted as she imagined it. "Doesn't sound very handsome."

"More so than you might think," I replied. "And I always thought Tamara was beautiful."

"That would be the crown princess of Khevsuria?" Hina asked.

I nodded. "She was very kind to me. They both were." I pushed those thoughts from my mind before they could overwhelm me. I'd spent too many years wondering how my life might have been different had my father lost the civil war and I'd stayed in Safavia.

Maybe it would have turned out the same way, but I didn't think so. Haider and Tamara never would have let those awful things happen to me.

It was the thought of everything that had happened to me after I'd run away from home that reminded me that Hina had been in the midst of telling me her own story. "So, you were thirteen when you left home in the midst of that rebellion?" I prompted.

"Oh, right, that . . ." She grimaced, and I half wondered if she'd been letting me get sidetracked on purpose to avoid painful memories, but I kept quiet and she pressed on. "My father beat me pretty severely one night. I think he must have been upset that the war wasn't going well, but most of it was that I'd been wearing one of my mother's old lehengas, and he'd caught me doing it. He'd beaten me plenty of times before, but never like that." She shook her head at the memory, her arms wrapping around her stomach, her shoulders hunching. "It had never hurt like that. Not ever. I thought he'd killed me."

I took her hand in mine, rubbing my thumb across her knuckles in gentle circles, hoping to distract her from the memory of the pain, because I knew exactly what she was talking about. Pain is a wonderful teacher, and I had not forgotten a single lesson.

"I had to run away," Hina murmured. "But I didn't want to leave without saying good-bye to my brother. Ali had always been my protector. He'd known I was different, ever since I was little, but he'd never hurt me for it, never chastised me for it. Sometimes he would distract Father for me. Other times he would hide me in his room, or take me for a ride on his zahhak, back when Sakina wasn't old enough to be ridden. He was my only friend, and I loved him fiercely, and I just couldn't bear to go without saying good-bye."

Her voice was so thick with emotion that I thought I knew what was coming next. "And he ratted you out to your father?"

Anger flashed in Hina's olive eyes, and she glared at me for an instant before realizing that I hadn't meant to impugn her brother's character, that I'd just been responding from my own horrific experiences.

"No." She gave my hand a pat. "No, Ali was like Arjun. He never would have abandoned me—not for anything. He packed up his things, and helped me pack mine, and we took our zahhaks, and we rode off into the night sky together."

"He went with you?" I gasped, tears threatening at the corners of my eyes, because I'd wished more than anything in the whole world not to be alone that fateful night when I'd fled the palace of Nizam. God, how I'd wanted someone to come with me, but there had been no one in all the world I'd trusted—no one except for Haider and Tamara. What would it have been like if I'd had a big brother to protect me like Hina had? I couldn't even imagine it. I doubted I'd have ended up in Bikampur, serving Varsha and learning to be a thief and a courtesan. And that meant I wouldn't have my sisters or Arjun. That thought quelled whatever jealousy I'd been feeling. It was all right to dream about a past without pain, but I couldn't regret any part of my life when it would mean losing the people I loved most fiercely.

"He did," Hina whispered, and tears did spill down her cheeks, reminding me that he was dead, and that Ahmed and Karim were responsible for it. "He supported me while I got my nirvan, and then we sold our services as scouts. He told everyone I was his sister, and no one batted an eye at a young noble girl with her own river zahhak, as it's not at all uncommon here in Zindh. He recruited men, and when we had enough money, I started recruiting young hijras, training them to serve as my retainers, eventually becoming an unconventional guru, and then a nayak. If not for Ali, I don't know what I would have done. Someone would probably have stolen Sakina from me—I wasn't strong enough or tough enough to fend off an attacker, and while she's big and strong, she hasn't got any breath. And without Sakina, I'd have become a penniless orphan. I'd probably have had to join a dera and sell myself to men like a common . . ."

She trailed off, her cheeks burning as she noticed the way I was staring at the floor, because I hadn't had a brother to save me from that fate. "Forgive me, Razia, I didn't mean . . ."

"It's all right," I said, my voice tight with emotion. "I'm glad you didn't have to go through that. None of us should have to."

"I couldn't agree more." She looked down at Nuri, who was riding Nalini all around the courtyard, and I turned my eyes to Sakshi and Lakshmi, who were flying lazy circles over the palace on the backs of their brilliantly colored zahhaks. Whatever had happened to us, we weren't letting it happen to our sisters, that was the main thing.

But then my eyes drifted over to Karim and I remembered that my own suffering was far from over. He was standing in the courtyard, one hand raised to shade his eyes from the sun as he watched Sakshi and Lakshmi flying overhead, the pair of them trailed by four acid zahhaks, just to be certain that they didn't get any ideas into their heads of fleeing.

"And he killed your brother . . ." I whispered, gritting my teeth at the idea that a man like Karim Shah could continue to draw breath while Ali Talpur was dead and buried. Sometimes I wondered if there even was a God at all, the world was so full of injustice.

"He's going to pay for that," Hina promised.

"He is," I agreed, my vow every bit as fervent as hers.

"But enough of that talk," Hina said, her tone changing completely as she plastered a smile across her face. I didn't know what that was about, not until I turned and saw Asma marching across the rooftop toward us, trailed by her handmaidens.

I stood up at once to greet her, bowing my head in proper deference, though all the while I was repeating, "Seven more days," like a mantra in my mind. That was how long I had left until the full moon, how long I had to put up with this farce before bringing it to a bloody end. But for now, I exclaimed, "Mother-in-law, what a pleasant surprise!"

Asma took my hands in hers, offering me a bright smile. "I've brought something for you, dear."

"Oh?" I asked, hoping that I seemed appropriately eager, though I doubted very much if she had the slightest idea as to what stirred my heart.

"Your husband-to-be has had lovely gifts commissioned for you," she said. "He tells me that he means them to be a symbol of your engagement, and your commitment to one another. My Karim is so pleased that you seem to have found your place here so quickly."

In another tone of voice, there might have been unspoken suspicions lurking behind those words, but Asma sounded genuinely pleased with me. I bowed my head to her, and smiled prettily, and lied just as boldly as I dared, "I am grateful that my husband-to-be is pleased with me."

"You two will make such a lovely pair." She gave my cheek a fond pat, and then settled herself on the cushion I had formerly occupied in the chhatri. I took Hina's place, shunting her away, which I thought was probably a blessing, as it meant she didn't have to deal with her brother's murderer's mother directly.

Asma clapped her hands, and one of her handmaidens came forward, laying a beautiful sandalwood box at my feet. When she opened it, she removed a blouse of emerald silk fabric, with darker green embroidery creating a pattern of scales all across its surface. Turquoise beads and tiny circular mirrors formed an eye on each scale like the ones found on a peacock's tail feathers, just like on a real acid zahhak.

My eyes widened at the sight of such an exquisite garment. Lakshmi was going to be so incurably jealous when she saw me wearing it. And the skirt was just as beautiful, though rather than being green to look like an acid zahhak's scales, it was the deep sapphire of their tail feathers, carefully embroidered with turquoise eyes in a ring around the skirt's wide hem, the shisheh mirror-work making the fabric sparkle in the bright sunlight.

"This embroidery style is traditional in Mahisagar," Asma explained as she took the skirt out of the box, holding it up for me to admire.

"It's magnificent," I whispered, not even having to pretend to be impressed by it, in spite of who it was who had given it to me.

"He included jewelry, of course," Asma said, "as it seems that your little sister has taken yours."

I smiled at that. "It meant more to her than it did to me. But this I'll treasure."

A handmaiden opened a jewelry box, revealing bangles for my wrists and ankles, each one crafted from pure gold that had been cut and inset with sapphire and emerald cloisonné to form perfect tiny replicas of acid zahhaks chasing their own tail feathers. It wasn't the most creative of gifts, as I'd received similar jewelry from Arjun, but the workmanship of these pieces was exquisite—the equal of anything any princess in all the world owned.

There were matching earrings, of course, and a tall necklace that resembled a coiled acid zahhak twisting itself around my neck. The dupatta that went over my head was the larger style popular in Zindh and Mahisagar, but the fabric was the brilliant blue of lightning, marred by dark black stripes, just like an acid zahhak's mane. It was a detail that the tailors in Bikampur had missed when Arjun had dressed me up as an acid zahhak to draw Karim's eye. Just remembering that day made me wish I'd refused the clothes. Maybe if I hadn't worn them then, I wouldn't be sitting here now.

"I'm overwhelmed," I said, offering Asma a demure smile. "Your son is too good to me."

"He wants to make you happy," Asma replied, sounding like she really believed that, which made one of us.

"And I hope I can make him happy too," I lied.

That earned me a look of approval. Asma patted my cheek. "Karim adores you. He's so happy that you've agreed to become his bride. And you two are going to have so many wonderful children together. I know that you're not fertile yourself, but I've seen the way you are with Lakshmi. You'll make a wonderful mother for my grandchildren."

"With you advising me, I don't think it could be otherwise," I said, wondering if I sounded too dutiful and submissive even for a simpering dolt like Asma.

Her cheeks flushed with genuine pleasure, proving that she really was as simple as I thought. She wouldn't have lasted five minutes in the zenana in Nizam, but I supposed Ahmed Shah liked his women dumb and tame.

"Well, let's get you out of those clothes and into these new ones," Asma suggested.

"Now?" I asked. "Is there some special occasion?"

"No, but I think it would please Karim to see you wearing the clothes he commissioned for you," Asma said, leaving me to decide whether or not pleasing Karim was something I wanted to do.

"In that case, lead on, mother-in-law," I replied, standing up alongside her.

"I thought that might be your answer." There was something smug in her smile, though I supposed it was just because she thought I had submitted to Karim's rule over me. Wouldn't she be surprised when I destroyed them all?

Asma led me to my bedchamber, her servitors following close behind. I let them dress me in my new acid zahhak attire, and I had to admit that I liked the way I looked in it. But as beautiful as the clothes were, the fact that they came from Karim meant that they would always remind me of him, even when all this was said and done. Maybe I'd let Padmini burn them to cinders once I was free again.

Soon. That was what I told myself as the handmaidens finished dressing me. Soon Haider would attack Ahura; I had to believe that. And then with Arjun and Sunil at my side, I would take Kadiro. Once that was accomplished, I would kill Ahmed and Karim, take their lands from them, and dare my father to do something about it. But that day wasn't today. Today I had to be Karim's blushing bride no matter how much I longed to stand up to him.

As if to remind me of that fact, Karim arrived at the doorway to my bedchamber. For days now, I'd let him touch me, let him kiss me, though I was grateful it had gone no further than that. I thought I was gradually winning him over, and I needed to keep that up. I needed to remain above suspicion if I was going to be free to act when the time came. So I smiled at him, as if I were pleased to see him, and said, "Thank you for the lovely gifts, your highness."

Karim stared at me for a long moment, his eyes roving over every inch of my body in a way that made me feel like I was wearing nothing at all. He strode across my bedchamber and put his arms around me, leaning his face low, so that our noses were practically touching. I was grateful for all the training I'd had in Bikampur as a courtesan, because it kept me from flinching or showing my disgust.

"You look exquisite," he said.

"Thank you, your highness," I replied, keeping my gaze downcast, looking up at him only through kohl-darkened lashes, just as Ammi had trained me to do. The men in Bikampur had always found it irresistible, and Karim was no different.

He rubbed my arms through the thin silk of my new blouse and seemed on the point of kissing me when he remembered that his mother was present. He turned his attention to her and said, "Your handmaidens have done their work well, Mother. I've never seen my wife-to-be look so beautiful."

"It's your fine gifts that have highlighted her beauty," his mother replied. She was beaming at the pair of us, like we were a happy couple deeply in love, and not enemies brought together by conquest and political machinations. To me, she said, "Daughter-in-law, you are looking so lovely that I think perhaps it would please us all if you would dance for us this evening. I know my son would appreciate it, and it would give you a chance to try out your new dancing shoes."

"Dancing shoes?" I wrinkled my nose, wondering what she was talking about.

Even Karim laughed. "Mother, I know you're not familiar with courtesans, but they never wear shoes when they dance. It's always performed barefoot."

"Oh!" Asma exclaimed, holding a hand to her mouth, her cheeks reddening. "Forgive me, I feel so stupid . . ."

"No," I rushed to say, "it's a common enough mistake." It wasn't, but I wanted to smooth things over with her. I needed to keep things calm until the full moon.

"You're such a sweet girl," Asma told me, but her tone was all wrong. The embarrassment that I'd seen on her face had vanished in a flash. Her dark eyes seemed somehow harder and sharper. She snapped a finger and one of her servant girls came forward, producing from behind her back a pair of slippers with reinforced soles, giving them the curve needed to get good toeholds on boulders. They had wear marks, and were discolored from the waters of the lagoon, and they should have been hiding amid my clothes from Shikarpur.

Asma took the climbing shoes from her servant and held them up in front of my face. "If these aren't dancing shoes, daughter-in-law, then what kind of shoes are they?"

I was too shocked to speak. This whole time I'd thought Asma was an idiot, that she was completely naive, and the truth was exactly the opposite. She'd been playing me for a fool all along.

Karim's arm had tightened around my shoulders, but he was still plainly confused. He didn't know what kind of shoes they were. If I could find some reasonable explanation for them, I might be able to get out of this alive.

Asma had been watching me closely, and she must have seen my decision to lie written across my face, because the moment I opened my mouth to speak, she cut me off. "You see, dear, I assumed they must have been dancing shoes, because the only time I'd ever seen their like before was many years ago, back home in the mountains of Yaruba, where shoes like these are sometimes used for scaling rocky cliffs. But I can't for the life of me imagine what use you might have for climbing shoes here." She looked pointedly at her son as she finished springing her trap. "And yet . . . they seem well-worn." She tugged at the fraying fabric and worn leather on the toes with interest.

I glanced up at Karim, and one look at the black rage building behind his eyes told me that the full moon might as well have been a decade away. I wasn't going to survive another week here. I might well not survive another hour.

CHAPTER 18

"Your highness, I—"

Those were the only three words I managed to get out before Karim threw me up against the wall so hard that it drove the breath from my lungs. His hand flew up and clutched my throat, squeezing it shut just at the moment when I needed air most. My chest heaved and my body convulsed as I tried to breathe, but no air came. My vision was going gray at the edges and my legs were turning to jelly beneath me. If I didn't do something fast, I was going to faint.

The trouble was, I wasn't sure there was anything I could do. Oh, I knew how to fight, I knew where to hit him. I thought maybe I could make him let go, even though he was a lot bigger and stronger than I was, even though he was angry and ready for it. But if I did that, then what? I'd been roughed up by enough clients over the years to know that if I hit back it was always worse. They had the power, and I didn't, and they never let me forget it. And Karim had power over my sisters, and Hina too. If

I hit back, if I defended myself, he might punish them for my crime, and I couldn't bear that.

And anyway, I'd waited too long. My knees went weak. The world started to get well and truly dim. I'd been counting on him to let go, but as I hung there by the neck, all of my weight supported by the bulging muscles of Karim's arm, I realized that I'd miscalculated just how angry he was, just how cruel, just how willing to see me dead. I'd believed too much in my own value. I'd thought he wanted the throne of Nizam enough to spare my life, but maybe I'd been wrong about that too.

I woke up when I hit the floor, aware only then that I'd been unconscious. I was gasping for air, clutching my throat, which was so tender that it made it hard to breathe. I had barely managed to recover my senses when Karim grabbed me by the hair and jerked me to my feet. My scalp burned with pain, and I feared that he might tear my hair out in his rage. I kicked with my legs, getting them under me, standing on my tiptoes to take the pressure off.

He was shouting, bellowing really, sounding more like an angry beast than a man. He'd been shouting the whole time, but I'd been so disoriented that I hadn't heard a word of it. Now I did. "Where did you go? Answer me!" He was shaking me, like that would pry the answers loose.

I fumbled for a response, but my mind was moving too slowly, and Karim was in no mood to be patient. He backhanded me across the face, tearing my new nose ring from my nostril. I hit the ground like a sack of grain and clutched my face, blood pooling in my palm. But he wasn't finished. He kicked me in the ribs with his shin, sending me sliding across the polished marble floor.

Self-preservation kicked in then. I scrambled to my feet as he stalked toward me like a hungry tiger, his eyes too wide, his pupils too big and too black. I held up my hands to ward off whatever punch he threw and gasped out, "Shikarpur, your highness!"

"What?" he growled, but he paused, and that was the opening I needed.

"Shikarpur, your highness. I wore them when I scaled the cliffs of Shikarpur. I brought them with me from Bikampur when I came to Zindh, and they must have arrived with my other clothes in the same chest. I didn't even know they were here!"

"Then why didn't you say so?" he demanded.

"Because she didn't give me a chance to speak!" I exclaimed, gesturing to his mother. "And neither did you!"

Karim gritted his teeth, but a lot of the anger seemed to have gone out of him. He took a step toward me, but I backed up, flattening myself against the wall. He sighed. "Razia . . ."

I held my bloodied face in my palm, thinking of all the ways I could use this misstep on Asma's part to my advantage, when the old hag spoke up again. "I had considered that these might be those shoes you wore on your now-famous ascent of Shikarpur's cliffs, daughter-in-law."

My stomach lurched. There was something about the smirk on her face that told me there was more, that she knew more than she'd let on. God, had I underestimated her again? If she proved to Karim that I was lying about those shoes . . .

"But the fabric used to make them is the fabric I supplied to Hina and her celas to repair their clothes and their shoes," Asma said. "So, naturally, I assumed they were dancing shoes. But if they are climbing shoes like the ones you used in Shikarpur, and they are newly made, then why are they worn? Where have you been going, daughter-in-law?"

Karim looked to his mother, his fists clenched. "You can prove this?"

"I can, dear," she assured him. "I know that you love this . . . creature, but you cannot put your faith in a cross-dressing whore. He lies about everything—even his sex."

Karim whirled on me, his eyes narrowed. "I should have known!"

He stepped toward me, and there was nowhere left for me to go. But at that moment, Sikander came into the room, and I saw Hina and Sakshi hanging back by the doorway, and I knew that Hina had gone to fetch him the instant Karim had started beating me. Sikander took one look at my bloodied face, at the bruises on my neck, and he turned and marched toward Karim, his face purple with fury.

Karim opened his mouth to say something, but he didn't know Sikander like I did. When my old guardsman got that look on his face, I'd always made myself scarce, because there was no reasoning with him. I realized, as his fist smashed into Karim's jaw, that he'd never looked at me that way before. He'd reserved his true fury for men who had failed in their duties, not for those under his protection. It wasn't that he'd never beaten me before, but those had always been carefully controlled affairs. Not like this.

Karim reeled from the impact of the punch, but a second was already on its way. The Mahisagari prince blocked the second punch with his forearm, but Sikander had been expecting that. He was powerful and stocky and created by God himself for wrestling. He grabbed Karim's arm and twisted his body, dropping to one knee as he hurled Karim over his shoulder to make the throw that much stronger.

I'd never in my life heard anybody hit stone that hard before. Karim made a kind of wheezing noise as all the air was pounded out of his lungs. I expected that to be the end of it—Sikander had made his point—but he pulled back his fist, and I realized that he wasn't going to stop, that this wasn't about making a point, that he had seen me bloodied by Karim so soon after being reminded of his failure to protect me from being raped by him six years prior, and now he was going to avenge the both of us.

I couldn't have that. If he killed Karim, then I'd be killed too. We'd be the first casualties in my father's new war with Mahisagar. And much as I wanted to see Karim's face pounded into mush, I knew that Ahmed Shah wouldn't tolerate it, even if the consequence was a war he couldn't hope to win.

"Sikander, stop!" I exclaimed.

I was shocked when he froze in place, when both he and Karim twisted their heads in my direction, like they hadn't expected anyone to intervene.

"Please get off of my fiancé. This has gone far enough," I said, keeping my voice calm so that I wouldn't add any more fuel to the fire.

"But your highness, he struck you," Sikander reminded me, still clutching one of Karim's wrists in his fist, his other fist still poised to slam down into Karim's face.

"I was in the wrong," I said, shocking everyone in the room, except perhaps Asma. She was narrowing her eyes at me, waiting to see how I would spin this. The mask was off now; she wasn't pretending to be naive any longer. "Everything the sultana has said is true. Well, nearly everything. I do not lie about my sex." I glared at her for that.

"No, just about everything else, it would seem," she replied.

"I had shoes made for climbing," I said, looking at Karim. "And I used them to climb the columns in my bedchamber for practice, because I enjoy it. And I didn't tell you, because I knew you wouldn't like it. So you may punish me for that however you wish, your highness." I nodded to Sikander. "Let him up, for God's sake."

Sikander let go of Karim, but he came to stand between us, just in case Karim got any ideas about hitting me again.

"You expect us to believe that you just climbed columns for fun?" Asma scoffed.

I shrugged. "I don't expect you to believe anything I say, your majesty, but I ask you—where would I go? You keep me under close guard at all times."

"Not at night," Asma pointed out. "You might have scaled the palace walls then."

"And gone where?" I demanded. "We're in the middle of a crocodile-infested lagoon."

"To a boat you had arranged to meet you, obviously," she retorted.

"Arranged how?" I asked, and I felt vindicated when she couldn't come up with an answer, when it didn't occur to her that I was suicidally brave enough to swim in a crocodile-infested lagoon to send messages.

Karim had been listening closely, and when his mother failed to come up with any plausible way for me to arrange for a boat, he said, "I believe you, Razia."

I crossed my arms over my bruised ribs and scowled. "Why?"

"Yes, a very good question I would like answered as well," Asma agreed.

"Because it fits," he said, and he sounded pretty regretful. "It explains the shoes, and the lies, and also why you have been trying so hard to fit in here, to learn your place, why you have been working so hard to please me. I should have known you wouldn't leave all of your old self behind, shouldn't have expected it of you. But I do believe that you're trying your best to make me happy."

"Darling, women are expert liars," Asma warned him.

"I thought I wasn't a woman," I shot back.

"And courtesans lie best of all," she added, sneering at me.

"If you think her highness is a whore and a liar, then I will return her to Nizam," Sikander declared. "You have assaulted her, and insulted her, and Sultan Humayun was very clear what the consequences would be if you mistreated his daughter."

"My mother does not speak for me," Karim told him. "As I have said, I believe her."

"And yet you did this to her." Sikander gestured to my bloodied nostril, to more blood spilling from my split, fattened lip, to the bruises around my neck. "Why? Because she chose to amuse herself by climbing columns?"

"And you struck my son in return," Asma replied. "Which might well be considered an act of war."

"As was his assault on her highness," Sikander growled. "And it was not his first assault on her."

Asma's eyes widened, and I realized that, for all of Karim's boasting about it to other lords, either she didn't know or she was pretending that she didn't.

"No one told you that he raped me when I was a child?" I asked her.

"You can't rape a whore," she replied, her eyes narrowing to slits.

"Shut her mouth, boy, or I'll shut it for her," Sikander warned.

"Don't you threaten my mother, old man." Karim's hand fell to the hilt of his sword, and I realized just how close we were to starting a war that would see me and my sisters killed in its opening shots.

"Enough!" I exclaimed. "I have said that I will accept whatever punishment my husband-to-be deems fit for my mistakes. Does that not satisfy everyone?"

"It does," Asma said. "But I think you should consult with your father about the nature of her punishment, Karim. You're too smitten with the girl to see clearly on this matter."

"Very well," I said, before Karim could argue one way or the other. "I will remain here, as I have for more than a week now, and I will await your judgment, your highness. I ask only that you send for a surgeon to stitch my nose, unless disfigurement is to be part of my punishment as well."

Those words broke through whatever defenses Karim had left. He took one good, clear-eyed look at my face and hung his head with shame. "A doctor will be summoned immediately."

"Thank you, your highness," I whispered, keeping my head bowed, like a properly contrite little wife, knowing just how much it would infuriate his mother.

"Come along, dear," Asma said to Karim. "We should speak with your father at once."

He nodded, and followed along with her.

The moment he was gone, Sakshi rushed to me and began examining my face. She studied my nose intently, frowning, but after a moment she said, "I don't think it's going to actually need stitches, Razia. I think the hole just got stretched out."

"I know," I replied, keeping my voice low, lest I be overheard, "but did you see the look it put on Karim's face? And now when the surgeon says it won't need stitches, he'll be relieved."

"Well, stitches or no, you should have let me break his nose, your highness," Sikander muttered.

"No, this works better than a war where we're the first killed," I told him, though I wasn't sure how I was going to smooth things over enough that I could be sure of carrying out my role in our plans. Of course, if Sikander hadn't intervened, I didn't think I'd still be alive, so I bowed to him and said, "Thank you for protecting me."

"This time," he said, his voice soft. "But if this is the way he treats you over a pair of shoes, what will he do next time?"

I shrugged. "This is what you and my father forced me to accept. I begged with you not to do it, but you did."

"I followed my sultan's orders," Sikander protested. "You think this is what I want for you?"

"In truth, Sikander, I don't know what you want for me," I confessed.

"I want for you what I've always wanted for you, your highness.

I want for you to be safe and happy. The things I did to you when you were a child were wrong, but I did them because I believed they would be for the best. It was never my intention to harm you."

"I know," I said, surprising myself by how thick with emotion my voice was. "That's what hurt the most."

Sikander hung his head like a chastened child, and I realized that Asma had actually done me a favor by provoking Karim into beating me. I hadn't yet involved Sikander in my plans, because I knew he was my father's man, and I knew he'd be honor-bound to support this marriage. But after today, I thought it would be different. Now that he'd seen who Karim was, I might be able to get him to join me in fighting back when the time came. At the very least, I didn't think he would fight against me. If I could add his zahhak, and those of the other Nizamis, to my forces, then I'd have a better chance in the battles to come.

I was startled by how quickly Ahmed Shah came striding into the room. I'd expected a surgeon, not the sultan, not so soon. My alarm turned to terror when I saw the dozen guardsmen he'd brought with him, to say nothing of his wife, who was smirking like she'd won some great victory. Karim was there too, and one glance at his face told me that he wasn't happy with the result.

I stood and bowed respectfully. "Your majesty."

"I have heard what took place here today," Ahmed said, his voice thick with anger. "I have heard about these shoes of yours, and your excuses for them. My son believes you. I do not."

"Then we will return to Nizam," Sikander declared, before he could continue. "You have no authority to punish her."

"You are lucky you are still alive," Ahmed replied. "If not for my son's intercession on your behalf, I'd have had you executed for daring to place your hands on him."

"Your son beat the princess of Nizam," Sikander reminded him.

"My son chastised his fiancée as any man might," Ahmed said.

"But we will forget about your transgressions. We will not, however, forget about hers." He looked me right in the eyes. "You are dangerous, girl. I underestimated you when I first met you in Rajkot, but I will not make the same mistake again, not when you are living under my roof. You will be moved to an interior apartment without windows. You will be guarded whenever you leave it, and you will be attended by loyal women whose integrity my wife can vouch for. And you will not set foot near a zahhak again."

"Her highness is not a prisoner here, and she is not to be treated as such," Sikander said.

"Really?" Ahmed asked. "Because I was told that she had agreed to submit herself to whatever punishment I deemed fit."

"You were misinformed, your majesty," I said, enjoying the way his face darkened, though I knew I shouldn't have been taking pleasure in antagonizing him. "I agreed to submit myself to whatever punishment my fiancé deemed fit, as it was his right to chastise me for my actions, and it is to him I must answer."

"And he answers to me," Ahmed said, but the anger had gone out of him.

"He does, your majesty, but the punishment must be his decision, taken in consultation with you." I wanted Karim to have to set the terms. I didn't think he had it in him to be as thorough as his father in treating me like a prisoner here, not after the way he'd beat me.

"Which is precisely what we did," Asma snapped.

"Then I await my husband-to-be's decree," I told her, bowing my head and looking contrite.

"You have just heard it, girl!" she growled.

I said nothing, and for once Sikander seemed smart enough to keep his mouth shut too. I waited for Karim to speak.

He sighed. "Father, I'll handle this."

"You will not countermand my orders, boy," Ahmed replied.

"Razia, you will remain in your chambers here," Karim said, drawing his father's ire, "but everything else my father says stands." He looked to Ahmed. "She can't climb the walls of the palace while Mother's handmaidens are watching her, can she?"

"No, I suppose not," Ahmed allowed.

I noted that he hadn't countermanded his father's orders about my zahhak. I didn't need Sultana to carry out my plans, but not being able to ride my zahhak also showed that Karim had no faith in me. I couldn't have that, not if I wanted to have some freedom of action when the time came to take the palace. But I thought I could spin it to my advantage.

"How long will I be banned from seeing Sultana, your highness?" I asked, keeping my voice soft and quiet, without a hint of challenge in it, just sadness.

"Just for a little while," he said. "Until things calm down."

"Thank you for your kindness, your highness," I said, maintaining my posture of total submission, knowing that it would make it that much harder for Karim to really believe I'd been swimming across the lagoon, delivering messages.

"I'll have the surgeon brought in," he assured me, his voice unnaturally quiet.

Asma turned on her heel and stormed off, though three of her handmaidens remained behind. The Mahisagari guards positioned themselves around my balcony and at the entrance to my chambers. Once that was seen to, Ahmed left me without another word.

With so many strangers in the room, there was no way to discuss the implications of all these guards for my plans, so I just sat on my bed and waited for the surgeon to arrive, all the while wondering just how I was supposed to clear the towers of guards for Sanghar Soomro and his men now.

CHAPTER 19

Does your neck still hurt, Akka?" Lakshmi asked me as she stared at the big, ugly bruises ringing my neck in the perfect shape of Karim's palm and fingers.

"No, sweetheart," I lied. "I'm fine."

"He shouldn't have hurt you for climbing," she said, shaking her head in a way that made my heart ache. She was still trying to work out why he had beaten me, why the man she thought of as a dashing prince had attacked her big sister and bloodied her face and strangled her. "You love climbing, he knows that. He saw you climb in Shikarpur."

"He wasn't mad at me for climbing, he was mad at me for lying," I told her, appalled with myself for defending Karim to Lakshmi, but it was still another few days before the full moon, and I didn't want Lakshmi to antagonize him. "I should have told him about the shoes, and I should have told him about the climbing."

"But he should never have hit her," Sakshi added, a surprising amount of anger coloring her voice. "No man should hit his wife for any reason ever. What Karim did was bad, and wrong, and he should be the one punished for it, not our sister."

Some of Asma's handmaidens raised eyebrows at Sakshi's tirade, and I knew they'd be whispering all of that in Asma's ears before long. That was fine. Sakshi could be angry. I couldn't afford to have my words used against me, though. So I kept my mouth shut, and let Lakshmi decide things for herself.

Lakshmi just hugged me tightly and said, "I miss Prince Arjun, Akka. He never would have hurt you."

I miss Prince Arjun too. That was what I wanted to say, but I knew better. I just let my emotions go out of me as a long sigh, fighting not to cry in front of everyone. I wrapped Lakshmi in the tightest embrace I could manage. "We're going to be okay," I promised her. "You'll see."

Sakshi was frowning. She knew what I'd been planning with Hina. I'd kept Lakshmi in the dark, because eleven-year-olds are terrible about keeping secrets, but my elder sister knew everything. She knew that in just a few days there would be a battle, that all of our lives would be on the line. I wondered if that frightened her.

"Razia is right," Sakshi said, and though she reached forward and stroked Lakshmi's hair, she was looking at me. "We're going to be fine. This is all going to work out for the best. You'll see."

"How?" Lakshmi asked. She looked up at me. "Do you really think marrying Prince Karim is going to be for the best when he hits you?"

"I think you should leave those things to the grown-ups," I replied, as that was the only answer I could give her that wasn't a bald-faced lie.

"Akka, I'm not a baby . . ." she complained.

"I know you're not," I told her, "but things are complicated right now, and you have to give me a chance to work through them, okay?"

"Yeah . . ." she allowed. "But if Prince Karim hits you again, I'm going to tell Mohini to eat him."

"You will do no such thing," I chided, though my heart felt warm and fuzzy imagining Karim being eaten by a zahhak. "If you want to keep riding Mohini, you have to be good, all right?"

"It's not fair that he won't let you ride Sultana," she said. "She's lonely. She even comes up to me in the stables sometimes, because I smell like you."

That hit me like a punch to the gut. I forced myself to smile. "Well, until Prince Karim decides that he can trust me with my zahhak, you'll have to give Sultana some petting for me. Will you do that?"

She bobbed her head.

"Good." I shooed her off my lap. "Now, go play with Nuri or something. You don't want to sit here on the roof all day, do you?"

She surprised me by shrugging. "They don't let us out of the women's quarters. It's so boring. Back in Bikampur Shiv would take me to the market sometimes. I still haven't seen the market in Kadiro."

"Why don't you go flying?" I suggested, pushing down all the righteous anger I was feeling on my little sister's behalf, an anger that was so much hotter and fiercer than the one that cropped up when I was feeling abused and controlled by Karim and his family.

"They don't let us go very far," she said. "And anyway, I want to fly with you and Sakshi like we used to in Bikampur." She frowned as a realization occurred to her. "Akka, I want to go *home*."

My heart felt like it had been stabbed with a dagger. I was completely at a loss for what to tell her. What I wanted to say was forbidden, it would get us all killed, but it was all I could do to keep my mouth shut, to not tell her, "Honey, I want to go home too." I sucked in a sharp breath through my nose instead and looked at the floor, trying to think of something smart to say.

"It's okay to miss Bikampur and Prince Arjun," Sakshi told her, sparing me from having to come up with anything. "It's normal to miss people and places we love. But we live here in Zindh now, and someday we're going to love living here just as much as we loved living in Bikampur."

"No, I won't!" Lakshmi declared.

"You might," Sakshi said. "But until then, we have to make the best of things. And that means finding things here that make us happy when we're feeling sad. Do you know what I like to do when I'm missing Bikampur?"

"Play your sitar?" Lakshmi ventured, which I thought was a pretty perfect guess.

"That's right," she said.

"But you play your sitar every night," Lakshmi pointed out.

Sakshi shrugged. "I'm homesick every night."

That was too much for me to bear, plan or no plan. I stood up abruptly and started walking away, because I just didn't have room for the realization that I'd made both of my sisters completely miserable by accepting this stupid position from my father. I'd been forced into it, sure, but I hadn't tried to argue, had I? I hadn't negotiated when I'd had the chance. And now . . . now look at the mess I'd got us in.

"Razia?"

I looked up and saw Karim coming up the steps toward me, followed by his mother. Great. Just what I needed. He'd been making himself scarcer for the last couple of days, though he hadn't stopped taking me to breakfast and kissing me good night. And Asma had been even worse. She'd been keeping close tabs on me, rotating her handmaidens frequently to get reports on every word I uttered and everything I did. And now I had to pretend like everything was fine. I stopped in my tracks and bowed my head, and said, "Good afternoon, your highness, your majesty."

"Is everything all right?" he asked me, because I must have been looking pretty harried.

I decided to be honest, because he was going to hear the truth from Asma's handmaidens anyway. "My sisters are bored, your highness. Well, Lakshmi is bored. I think Sakshi is just homesick for Bikampur. She's Registani, after all."

"Well, I might be able to help with that," Karim replied, hefting a pair of cloth-wrapped bundles that I hadn't even noticed in my distress.

"What are they?" Sikander demanded. He'd been keeping watch with his men, and now he was standing right behind me, one hand on the hilt of his talwar.

"Gifts for Razia and Lakshmi," Karim answered. "I would have got something for Sakshi too, but I don't think these would suit her."

"What sort of gifts?" Asma asked, and I saw then the reason she was following Karim. She'd seen the bundles and couldn't resist sticking her nose where it didn't belong.

"You'll see," was all Karim told his mother. He gestured to the chhatri where my sisters had lately been sitting, but both of them had gotten up and were rushing over, now that I was standing near Karim. "May I?"

"Yes, of course, your highness," I replied, bowing and stepping aside so that he could precede me.

He didn't get two steps before Lakshmi came running up, though. She took my hand, protectively I thought, and stood between me and Karim. "We should go to the courtyard together, Akka."

"In a minute," I told her, because much as it warmed my heart to see her taking this turn against Karim, I needed her to play along at least a little bit longer. "Prince Karim has brought us presents."

"I don't want a present," Lakshmi declared. "I want your face to go back to the way it was before Karim hit it."

My hand flew up to my nose in spite of myself. It had taken a suture to close the wound after all, though the surgeon had assured me that there would be no scarring. I just wouldn't be able to wear nose rings for a while. I dropped my hand as quickly as I could, and put it on Lakshmi's shoulder instead, but the damage was done. Karim was standing there, grinding his teeth, and he looked on the point of leaving. I couldn't have that, not when he was clearly trying to make amends. I needed to be above suspicion when Ahura was attacked, or they might well just kill me, or my sisters or Hina, just on the off chance it had been my doing.

"Your highness, I'm sorry," I said. "She's young, and it's difficult to make her understand the situation."

"I understand everything," Lakshmi growled, tears filling her eyes as her black brows scrunched down over them.

"Come on." I took Lakshmi's hand with one of mine, and Karim's elbow with the other. "Let's sit down and see what Prince Karim brought for us."

"I said I don't want to!" Lakshmi protested.

"Well, we're going to," I replied, my voice a touch sterner, though I hated myself for it. I didn't want to teach my little sister that it was okay to let a man hit her. I didn't want to teach her that it was important to let him give you gifts afterward to make up for it. She was watching all of this, and she was learning, and I feared that she was going to take all the wrong lessons from it. If my plan succeeded, I was going to have to have some very long and honest conversations with her, but that could wait. For now we just needed to survive the next few days. If we lived through all of this, then I could worry about undoing the damage.

"But Akka . . ." Lakshmi protested.

"No more," I warned.

Sakshi showed up to help, taking Lakshmi's other hand. "Let's sit down and listen to what Prince Karim has to say, all right?"

Lakshmi scowled, but she stopped complaining, which was what I needed right then, even though she was absolutely right to point out that Karim's gifts were the hollowest of apologies for his actions.

I sat us both down on cushions beneath the chhatri's umbrella-like dome. Karim sat across from us, still looking uncomfortable, his mother claiming a seat right beside him. I forced a smile and said, "I'm sorry for all of that, your highness."

"I'm sorry," he said, and he even sounded like he meant it, which surprised me a little. How could he be sorry for beating me, when he wasn't sorry for forcing me into this marriage, or killing Hina's brother, or any of the other awful things he'd done?

"I know, your highness, as am I," I answered, because that was the right thing to say. Even Asma couldn't find fault with my words, though she did roll her dark eyes to the sky and snort with derision.

Karim set the bundles in front of me and Lakshmi. My little sister crossed her arms in front of her chest and looked away, making Karim frown, which I thought was well deserved, but I reached out and took my package anyway, unwrapping the cloth to reveal a pair of shoes. Climbing shoes. These were proper ones, with carved wood laths and grippy leather and a steep, aggressive downturn to the toes. I dropped them like they were hot.

"I don't understand," I whispered, wondering if this was some kind of a trick or a trap or an insult. "If I've done something new to offend you, your highness . . ."

"What?" His confusion helped to quell the frantic beating of my heart. "No, I just thought that you might like some. You said you enjoyed climbing. You should be able to do it. There's no reason to hide it from me. You can climb any building in the palace you like. Lakshmi too." He gestured to the second bundle, and I knew it contained a second pair of shoes, sized for her. That was brilliant. It was a way to keep her safe when the time came to take the palace, a way that we could sneak to the zahhak stables together if it came to it, or run if we had to.

I pressed the bundle into Lakshmi's lap and beamed at her. "Put them on!"

"Akka . . ." She looked hurt that I would force her to accept a gift from Karim after what he did to me, and in truth it hurt me to do it, but this was too important.

"I want to climb," I said. "Will you climb with me?"

That got through to her where nothing else might have. She bobbed her head. "If it will make you happy."

"It will," I assured her. I glanced back to Karim. "That is, if it's acceptable, your highness."

"It is," Karim said, in spite of the way his mother crossed her arms and glared at us.

I wasted no time in putting the tight-fitting shoes on, and I helped Lakshmi with hers, since she hadn't worn any so aggressive before. And then we waddled over to the nearest wall and started climbing, both of us smiling—her because she was enjoying it, and it wasn't boring, and me because it meant that Karim was showing some trust in me, all the while giving me new weapons to use against him when the moment came to strike.

CHAPTER 20

"Did you sleep?" Sakshi whispered as she came to sit beside me on my balcony to watch the sun rise over the waters of the lagoon.

I shook my head, glancing around to make sure that there were no guards standing close enough to overhear. There were some around, like usual, but they kept their distance on Karim's orders, and out of fear of Sikander, who had taken to spending more time with me, letting his men keep Lakshmi safe.

"Do you think Haider did what you asked?" She asked that question so softly that I almost mistook the sound for a gentle breeze.

"I hope so," I whispered back, glancing to the pale form of the full moon, still visible as a hazy white disc against the bluing sky. Today was the day of the brother-sister festival. I'd asked him to attack last night. We'd see whether he'd followed through on that or not.

Sakshi put her arms around me as I fought to keep the tension in my chest from spilling out where others might see. I had to act the part of the innocent girl today. I couldn't let anyone suspect that I had been responsible for Haider's attack on Ahura, if that was what he'd done. Asma would blame me. Ahmed might too. Playing innocent was the only thing that would keep me alive today.

"I think he did," Sakshi told me.

"You think who did what?" Hina asked, having come to join us. She kept her voice low enough not to be overheard by Asma's handmaidens, who were lurking in my bedchamber, just out of sight, but I knew they were there by the rustling of their skirts.

"Haider," I murmured, covering my mouth with my hand like I was yawning to disguise it.

"Ah." That was enough for Hina to understand the whole conversation. I was sure that she'd done nothing the whole night but wonder too.

"Do you remember when you first arrived in Bikampur, Razia?" Sakshi asked.

I wondered what had brought that up, but I nodded all the same. "I don't think I'll ever be able to forget it." It was one of the most important memories of my whole life. I'd been near death, sickly, starving, and I'd found a home that accepted me and a big sister who cared for me.

"When Ammi brought you into the dera, you were so skinny and so weak from hunger and fever that I really didn't think you were going to survive," Sakshi recalled.

"And you never left my bedside." I smiled and took her hand in mine. "I knew from the first moment I saw you that I'd finally found somewhere I could be safe."

"Is that how you remember it?" she asked, raising an eyebrow. "Well, I shouldn't be surprised, you were half-delirious with fever, after all."

I frowned. "What do you mean? That's the truth."

She shook her head. "No, Razia, the truth is that after three days of watching over you, and caring for you, I got tired, and I fell asleep. When I woke up, Ammi said you'd run away, that you were talking nonsense, but that it wasn't worth it to go after you, not when you were probably going to die anyway."

"I ran away?" I asked, searching my memory, but finding nothing of that. Then again, as indelible as some of the memories of my arrival in the dera were, many of them were fainter. I'd been so sick that sometimes I hadn't known what was real and what wasn't.

"You did," she affirmed. "I ran out after you, despite what Ammi had said. I asked around, and you were easy enough to find. You were staggering down the western road outside of town, barely able to put one foot in front of the other."

"I was walking into the desert?" I asked, wondering what could have possessed me to do something so stupid. There was nothing beyond Bikampur in that direction except dunes until you reached Shikarpur. But that was too far to travel on foot, even for a healthy adult. Especially without food or water.

"I caught you, and started dragging you back to the dera, but you fought me," Sakshi said, her hand reaching up to stroke my hair. "The whole time you were screaming that you had to get to Safavia, that you wouldn't be safe until you found your big brother, Prince Haider."

My cheeks warmed, and my heart ached. I didn't remember any of this, but I knew it was true. "That was where I'd been going. That was why I ran west. I never told anyone, I thought."

"I told you that if you kept saying things like that your father would catch you and kill you," Sakshi said. "And then you fainted in my arms, and I carried you back home. When you woke up, you never spoke of it again, so I've always wondered if you remember it or not."

I shook my head. "No. All I can remember is you caring for me."

"Well," she murmured, holding me tightly, "now we'll get to see what sort of man your big brother Haider really is."

"I suppose we will," I agreed, though that did nothing to quell the tension in my heart. I had such fond memories of Haider.

"I've been wondering about that myself," Hina admitted. When I looked a question at her, she clarified. "What made you so certain that Prince Haider would fight a war to help a hijra. You said that you were childhood playmates, but you were a prince then, not a princess."

"Some of the time," I allowed. "For formal functions and audiences and the like. But when I met Tamara, and told her how pretty her clothes were and that I wanted to wear clothes like hers, she let me. And Haider caught us. I thought he was going to beat me the way that Sikander would have, but he didn't. He just smiled and told me he thought I looked beautiful. And after that, whenever we were together, I was Princess Razia. It was the best two years of my life. I never wanted that civil war to end."

"And none of that ever got back to your father?" Hina asked in disbelief.

I frowned, because of course it had. "Why do you think he and Sikander let Karim do that to me? Why do you think it occurred to Karim that I might be a girl and not a boy?"

Sakshi rubbed my shoulders, but Hina was sitting up a little straighter, almost like she'd been pleased by what I'd said. I shot her a dark look and she immediately seemed more apologetic, but she said, "Forgive me, your highness, it's just that Karim wasn't shy about telling that story."

My spine stiffened. "I am aware, thank you."

"Well, did it ever occur to you that it might have got back to Haider all those years ago?" she asked.

That thought brought a smile to my lips too. If Haider had heard what Karim had done to me back then, then to be reminded of it now might make my plight seem all the more dire. At the very least, it added to our chances that he had struck Ahura last night.

"How long do you think it will be before we hear word?" Sakshi asked.

I shrugged and glanced to Hina, as she'd know better. I'd never been to Ahura myself.

"It's an eight-hour flight at top speed over open water," she mused. "Safer would be flying north to the coast and then following it to Kadiro. That would add at least an hour, maybe two. If they left last night under cover of darkness, then they'd have taken the safer route, I'd expect. But if they left this morning at first light, then they probably chose to fly directly. Either way, we should know something by this afternoon at the latest."

"I hope it's sooner," Sakshi said, and I felt a little bit of the nervous tension in her fingers as she rubbed my shoulders.

"Me too, elder sister," I muttered, though there was just nothing to do but wait either way. Well, wait and prepare. We had a few crucial hours left to us, I thought. And I knew better than to waste them. I leaned closer to Sakshi and whispered into her ear, "Tell Lakshmi to keep her climbing shoes in her pockets today."

Sakshi nodded, her mouth becoming a hard line of worry. She knew that there would be no escaping the palace for her. No one had ever taught her to climb. I reached up and placed my hand atop hers on my shoulder. "I would never leave you."

"I know, Razia," she replied. She slipped away and went off to deliver my message to Lakshmi.

"Which of your celas has the katars today?" I asked Hina, grateful that I hadn't been stupid enough to leave them in my chest with my clothes and the climbing shoes. They'd been passing them around among themselves, just in case any of them got searched by the guards, and they'd been careful not to ever let

Hina have them, because she was under more scrutiny than her disciples.

"I have them," she told me. "I'll pass them to you tonight, if and when the situation demands it."

"Fine," I agreed. "I want you to get your celas together and bring them to my chambers. I want to distract Asma's handmaidens and the Mahisagari guards so I can get my climbing shoes in my pockets without them noticing."

"With pleasure, your highness," Hina agreed, and she was smiling the first genuine smile I'd seen on her face in an age as she hurried off to collect her disciples.

I looked west, watching the gray horizon lightening toward blue as the sun rose behind me. I was searching for any green scales or blue feathers that might hint at the approach of an acid zahhak from Ahura, but the sky seemed totally clear save for the morning patrol wheeling over the lagoon. It would be smarter to watch them than the horizon. They had a better view than I did, though they didn't know to be especially watchful for a messenger today. Still, they flew in lazy circles, giving me no sign that there were any approaching zahhaks from the west.

I stood up and stretched, feeling at my still-sore neck. The bruises had largely faded now, and it wasn't so tender. My nose was almost healed too, which was a welcome surprise. Seeing the mess Karim had made of me in the mirror had been a bit disconcerting. I didn't like to think of myself as vain, but I'd spent most of my life making my living on my looks, so I was a little protective of that particular asset. After all, for everything I'd accomplished with my brains, I'd never met a man who had hired me for them.

Save Karim maybe. The irony of that wasn't lost on me as I entered my bedchamber, and Asma's handmaidens rushed to seem like they were sweeping or arranging my bedclothes—anything but spying. I laughed a little at that. "I know why your mistress places you here. You don't have to pretend; it's not a secret."

They all bowed their heads and kept their mouths shut. I rolled my eyes and waited impatiently for Hina to get here with her celas so I could hide my climbing shoes in my pockets. If I was caught doing it, it would look suspicious, but if Ahmed and Asma managed to cast doubt on whether or not I had anything to do with the attack on Ahura, I might be moved to more secure quarters, and then I'd never be able to take care of the tower guards tonight like I'd promised Sanghar Soomro—not without some means of escape. I would need my shoes and my katars, and I couldn't leave that to chance.

Hina wasn't long in returning, and when she did it was with all fifteen of her celas. They filled the room in a crowd of ajrak skirts and dupattas, gathering around me in a semicircle that immediately rendered me invisible to the handmaidens, who stood up and craned their necks, trying to see what was going on. But Hina seemed to have concocted a plan, because she clapped her hands twice and said, "Let's get her highness prepared to meet her mother- and father-in-law for breakfast! I want her looking perfect!"

And the next thing I knew, all sixteen of them burst into action. Hina was making me stand in one particular spot in the room where a pillar blocked me, while her celas rushed in every conceivable direction. There was so much frantic movement going on in so many different places that my eyes didn't know where to look. Someone was fetching my chest of clothes, another my jewelry boxes, a third was for some reason bringing over the pillows from my bed while a fourth was snatching my cosmetics case, and at least two others picked up the mirror from its stand on the floor and started marching toward me with it.

Clothes were pulled out of the chest seemingly at random, and

I was made to put on my ajrak skirt, but it felt oddly heavy, and it seemed to weigh even more once the blouse was thrown over the top of it. They put jewelry on my wrists, ankles, neck, ears—they even stuck hairpins in at a speed that frankly worried me. In a matter of moments, I was completely bedecked from head to foot like a Zindhi princess, as I had been that first day Hina had come to the palace in Shikarpur. I was aware, after the flurry of activity had settled down, that at some point, either before or after I had put it on, the hidden pockets of my skirt had been stuffed with my climbing shoes, their presence hidden by means of the large number of petticoats I wore with it. And at another point, my katars had been slipped into the waistband of my skirt at the small of my back, their handles hidden by the long Zindhi-style blouse. Had I been wearing the shorter, Registani variety, they would have been plainly visible, but between the blouse and the long, shawl-like dupatta, there was no chance at all of anyone spotting them.

Hina was smirking, enjoying the bewildered looks on the faces of Asma's handmaidens. She guided me to the pillows her celas had set down and had me sit on one of them while she personally applied my makeup, being careful to hide my bruises and to mask the split in my lip and the suture in my nose.

"There," she said once she was finished. "You look like a proper princess, your highness."

"I feel like a proper princess," I replied, knowing that she and her celas would understand that I was referring to my climbing shoes and katars, but that the words would seem innocuous enough to Asma's handmaidens.

We exchanged a secret smile, and I stood from my cushion, smoothed out my skirts and my dupatta, making the gestures seem natural, though in truth I was ensuring that wherever Karim put his hands, he wouldn't feel the weapons or the shoes through my clothes. He tended to like to touch my arms, sometimes my hips, but the small of my back and my thighs were usually safe enough. I just hoped he wasn't feeling particularly eager this morning, otherwise I was going to have to be careful to use Sikander as a chaperone. The last thing I needed was for Karim to discover katars on my body just hours before word reached him of an attack on Ahura by unknown forces.

I had just finished composing myself when Asma came breezing into the room, trailed by one of her handmaidens, who must have rushed out to warn her that something unusual was going on. I forced myself to smile, because that was how the game was played, even with our hatred of each other out in the open now. "Mother-in-law, how lovely you look this morning."

"And you as well, daughter-in-law," she replied, plastering on a fake smile of her own. "Your makeup is so expertly applied, it makes that mutilated nose of yours look almost normal."

"Thank you," I replied, my eyes flashing with malice. I strutted over to her, enjoying the look of surprise and fear on her face. I reached over and tugged at the silken hem of her blouse. "This is so beautiful. Is it new?"

"Yes, I had it made just this week." Asma preened.

"I thought so," I said. "Your tailor has cut it so perfectly. It's so much more slimming than your other ones."

Asma's maidservants gaped at me in mute horror as the old woman's cheeks darkened with embarrassment. The hate I saw in her eyes made the whole thing worth it, and I was sure I returned it tenfold.

"Razia," Hina said, coming to stand beside me, "you didn't get a chance to finish the story you were telling me earlier. How many men was it you killed in the assault on Shikarpur?"

"With my zahhak or with my katars?" I asked, not taking my eyes off Asma's face. Her eyebrows shot up. Had she forgotten that?

"I only count men I kill with my own hands," Hina replied, giving Asma a death stare of her own.

"Just the one, then," I confessed. "But I did put my katar right through his neck, in one side and out the other." I let my eyes flicker from Asma's face to the hollow of her throat and back up, one side of my mouth quirking upward in a lopsided grin.

"Is everything all right in here?"

I looked up as Karim stepped into the room. He was noticing the way that Asma and her handmaidens had more or less squared off against myself and Hina.

"Everything is fine, your highness," I said, before Asma could muster any words at all. "I was just admiring your mother's new blouse. It's very becoming. She has a very fine tailor." I turned my eyes from Asma to Karim, and pretended to stare and grin. "As do you, your highness."

His shoulders relaxed, and he came to greet me as he always did in the morning, taking my upper arms in his hands, rubbing them through the silk fabric of my blouse. "And you've decided to be a Zindhi today?"

"Well, I am the subahdar, your highness," I reminded him, my voice slightly mocking, like I knew better than to really believe I was in charge here.

"You are," he agreed, in much the same tone. *What a delightful joke.*

"Do you suppose there will be any pomegranates at breakfast this morning, your highness?" I asked, leading Karim from the room, totally ignoring his mother—and the best part was that he didn't seem to notice, because he was too busy staring at my chest.

"Are they your favorite?" he asked.

"This time of year," I allowed, "though I prefer the mangoes from Nizam. My servants used to keep great bowls of them in my bedchambers, and the air would be filled with their sweet aroma day and night."

He smiled, and I could see him filing that tidbit away in the back of his mind for next year. It would make a lovely gift for the next time he beat me so badly that I needed stitches. Well, I didn't intend for Karim to survive until the next mango season. I should have felt more conflicted, holding the arm of a man I intended to murder, but I didn't, not really. He was a threat to me and a threat to Lakshmi, he was a rapist, he had killed Hina's brother, and he was holding me prisoner. Whatever little baubles he gave me could erase none of those facts.

We strolled together along the walkway that ringed the palace's innermost garden, the roof over our heads keeping the worst of the sun's heat at bay, though the evening breezes had stalled overnight, leaving the air still and sticky, like it was most mornings. That was probably why Sultan Ahmed had four servants with fans beating the air for him as he sat on his cushioned dais in the garden's central baradari. My sisters were there already, waiting for me, and Sakshi's smile told me that she had dealt with Lakshmi's climbing shoes, just as I'd asked. Sikander stood behind them, acting the part of the proper guardian.

Sultan Ahmed narrowed his eyes at me as we approached, but only for a brief moment, before directing his attention to his son. "Is your mother not coming?"

"Mother? She's right—" Karim turned and looked for his mother, only spotting her a moment later, far behind us. I saw the color come to his cheeks as he realized he'd just left her behind, and I allowed myself a small smile. If I couldn't take pleasure in the little things, then what was the point in living?

Karim stood there shamefaced until his mother had caught up, and he said, "Sorry, Mother, I thought you were right behind us."

"Oh, is that my place?" Asma asked, arching an eyebrow, her expression absolutely savage.

"No, of course not, Mother," Karim replied, while she took her place beside her husband.

"It's all right, dear," Asma told him, smiling sweetly. "You're a young man, and young men are wont to be *distracted*." She emphasized that last word while looking pointedly at me.

"She is *very* distracting," Karim agreed, rubbing my back gently, right between my shoulder blades.

I felt his hand starting to drift lower, toward the handles of my katars, and I pulled away, taking his arm in both hands, grinning. "Well, forgive me, your highness, it was never my intention to distract! Let us sit, so that your mother and father need wait no longer for their breakfast."

Karim was still smiling, evidently not having taken my sudden movement for an insult. I supposed my big smile and my girlish exclamation had sufficed to dispel any suspicions he might have had as to my feelings about having his hands on my body. How I had managed to suppress so many shudders over the last few weeks was a mystery even to me.

We had started to sink to our respective cushions when a trumpet blast made the both of us freeze and turn our eyes skyward, searching for the source of the sound. I looked west by instinct, and spotted the onrushing acid zahhak first, pointing at it. "Your highness, look!"

Karim stared after my finger, stopping on the zahhak a second later. Ahmed was standing and searching for it too as the trumpet blasts continued to ring out. It was an alarm call of some kind, though I hadn't been privy to the trumpet calls of Mahisagar, as they were a closely guarded secret lest their enemies use them against them. Whatever the call, it changed the mood immediately. Karim and Ahmed looked at one another with worry, and I noted from Asma's narrowed eyes that she understood the call too.

"Your highness, is that an alarm call?" I asked.

"Something's wrong," Karim said, rubbing my shoulders absentmindedly as he watched the rider's approach. Squinting, he stared at the zahhak's feathers, at the pattern of scales on its belly. "Father, I think that's Faris's animal."

"If it is, then it can only mean one thing," Ahmed replied. "Safavia has attacked Ahura."

CHAPTER 21

My heart was in my throat as the emerald, turquoise, and sapphire wing feathers of the acid zahhak fluttered over our heads, the rider making a tight turn to bleed off speed before settling down on the paving stones of one of the garden's wide paths. Haider had answered my call. He'd attacked Ahura. That must have meant that Tamara had agreed to do her part too. And Arjun would be coming. Tonight. God, I hadn't let myself think of it, but tonight we would be reunited at long last, and I would be free.

It was all I could do to struggle to look confused and concerned rather than triumphant as the messenger climbed down from his zahhak to approach the sultan. Already I could see the signs of exhaustion on his face, the sweat soaking his hair, and his wrinkled clothes. He'd been flying all night, there was no question of that. Haider must have attacked at dusk. It was so hard not to smile as I imagined Safavian thunder zahhaks sweeping out of the graying twilight sky, raining lightning on my enemies. I'd never realized just how sweet revenge could feel.

"Forgive me, your majesty," the messenger said as Asma rushed to cover herself with her dupatta, like anybody really wanted to get a better look at her. She glared at me, hissing, "Daughter-in-law, you will show a little modesty!"

I rolled my eyes, but wrapped my dupatta around my head and let it fall across my face, because it helped to hide my expression, and I was having a very hard time not grinning in triumph.

The messenger cleared his throat again and bowed to Ahmed. "Your majesty, Ahura was attacked last night by thunder zahhaks. We don't know how many, but a number of men were killed, and some fires were set. The fortifications are holding, but if this is a prelude to a Safavian invasion, we won't last long without assistance."

"Did you see what kingdom these thunder zahhaks came from?" Ahmed asked.

The man shook his head. "No, your majesty, it was too dark to see the riders, and one thunder zahhak looks much like another. We think they must be Safavians, as the Tarkivans wouldn't risk venturing out so far when rumors say they're embroiled in their own civil war. And the Nizamis are the only other thunder zahhak riders, but they are our allies, are they not?" His eyes flickered over to me as he asked the question.

"We are," I declared, before anyone could suggest otherwise.

"So far as we know," Asma muttered.

"If my father wanted to break our alliance, he would not attack Ahura, he would attack Kadiro," I replied.

"Enough," said Ahmed, motioning for both of us to shut up. "I don't need women's prattle distracting me at a time like this. It is the Safavians; we've expected their attack for some time. And now we must meet it."

He looked to Karim's cousin Rais, and asked, "Is your father ready to join us in Ahura as promised?"

"He will be, Uncle," Rais replied. "I can fly straight to Jesera and we can be in Ahura by tomorrow morning at the latest."

"Good, then go with God, boy," Ahmed told him.

"Yes, Uncle." Rais was grinning as he got to his feet. He walked over to Karim and the two clasped arms before hugging and pounding each other on the back. "Tomorrow we'll show Shah Ismail what our family is made of, cousin."

"Tomorrow," Karim agreed.

I frowned. I hadn't expected for Jesera to be prepared to join Ahmed Shah in battle. That meant we might be facing an aerial assault of not only a dozen acid zahhaks, but potentially a large number of fire zahhaks besides. I wondered how many Jesera might bring to the battle. If it was more than Arjun brought from Registan, then we would likely be outnumbered, unless Haider had brought a fair number of thunder zahhaks from Safavia. I supposed I would soon find out the answer.

Once Rais was gone, Ahmed said to Karim, "We'll leave immediately for Ahura with all of our zahhak riders. We can't risk leaving a single man behind."

"You should leave at least two to serve as messengers, my husband, just to be safe," Asma suggested.

"If we're going to make a show of force, we need as many men as possible, dear," Ahmed answered.

"Shall I have Sultana saddled, then, your majesty?" I asked him, bowing my head politely. I didn't want to go, because that would ruin my plans, but not offering seemed foolish, especially when I knew there wasn't a chance that he would actually bring me along. He didn't trust me, and he would know of my connection to Haider. That would be enough to see me left here to command the attack on Kadiro I had arranged.

"No, you're staying here," Karim said without a moment's hesitation, which meant that they must have discussed this eventuality and settled on their answer already.

I pretended to be confused all the same. "But, your highness, if Safavia is attacking, you'll need more than a dozen zahhaks to defend Ahura. I have five thunder zahhaks, plus Lakshmi's acid zahhak, at my command. That is no small force."

"And if you could be trusted to use it in our defense, you would be coming, girl," said Ahmed, "but you cannot."

I stared at Karim through the thin fabric of my dupatta. "You don't think you can trust me, even now, after all of this? Why? Because of a pair of shoes?"

"It has nothing to do with the shoes, Razia," Karim said, putting his hands on my shoulders gently. "But if Safavia is attacking us, who would likely be leading that attack?"

I frowned, as if suddenly coming to the same realization they already had. "Haider . . ."

"We know of your affection for him, and his for you, girl," Ahmed declared. "So, you will remain here, where you cannot add your numbers to his."

"I have not seen Haider in seven years," I protested.

"All the same, you will remain here," Karim told me. "My father and I have already discussed this. And it will give you a chance to prove your loyalty to this alliance. We know Sikander and his men will fight for Nizam's interests, so we will leave Kadiro in your hands, just in case the Safavians choose to attack here as well."

"You're leaving me in charge of Kadiro?" I asked, surprised by that, and certain that I'd misheard him.

"We're leaving you here under my wife's guardianship," Ahmed corrected, and I felt my stomach twist. I hadn't been expecting that. "If necessary, you will use your zahhaks to defend Kadiro."

"Do you really expect me to permit this girl to ride zahhaks while you are away in Ahura, my husband?" Asma demanded.

"If it is necessary for the defense of the city, yes," said Ahmed, and he held up a hand to forestall his wife's indignant protests. "But we will ensure that she does not get any ideas into her head." He looked at me, and the malicious smile creasing his lips made my blood run cold. "As you have said, we need more zahhaks, and I must leave two here to serve as messengers at my wife's request, but your sister Lakshmi flies an acid zahhak. We will take her with us to help in Ahura's defense and to make up for the messengers left behind."

I felt like someone had suddenly pulled the earth out from under my feet. Lakshmi in Ahura? No, I couldn't let that happen. If they took her, and got word that I'd rebelled in Kadiro, they would butcher her! And I couldn't call off the attacks. The messages had already been sent, the men were already on the way, and with Asma in charge here in the palace, I'd never be able to get new messages out to call off the assault. It was going forward tonight whether I liked it or not.

"She is a child!" I exclaimed, turning to Karim, my desperation plain in my eyes. "Your highness, she's so young. Please, she's all I have!" I clung to his arm, and for once none of it was a carefully calculated act.

"Which is why she will ensure your cooperation," said Ahmed, and the bastard looked like he was enjoying himself.

My mind was spinning frantically to come up with a solution to this. God, if they took Lakshmi, then she was as good as dead. And even if I found some way to get her back before Ahmed found out about the attack, or if I found some way to call off the attack, then I'd still have to worry about Karim being alone with her, at night, in a faraway fortress. What might he do to her? I'd seen the way he looked at her. I couldn't forget that I'd been the same age when he had raped me. And there would be nobody there to protect her, no one at all. They would laugh and let it happen; I was sure of it.

"No." I shook my head. "You are not taking her."

"You think you have the authority to give me orders here?" Ahmed asked, and it was impossible to miss the hard edge to his voice, the tone that warned of more punishments to come.

I was shocked when Sikander stepped forward and said, "Princess Lakshmi is her highness's younger sister, and thus is a princess of Nizam."

"And you think your sultan would agree with that logic?" Ahmed scoffed. "No, he barely views that creature"—he gestured to me—"as a relation. I am certain that he would not shed a tear over the fate of some hijra child."

I looked to Karim. "Say something. Please."

"I'll keep her safe, Razia," he said, and I felt fresh hatred welling up within me. He was going to let his father use Lakshmi as a hostage?

"You can't promise that," I retorted. "If there's a battle, anything can happen in the air. You know it as well as I do."

"There's not going to be a battle," he assured me, his hands rubbing my arms gently to try to calm me down. "It's just a show of force. Once Safavia sees the numbers we can bring to the fight, they will back down. Ahura isn't worth it."

I wondered how many zahhaks that was, but I knew better than to ask, and anyway, it did nothing to quell my fears about what was going to happen to Lakshmi, because the real threat wasn't from Safavia, it was from me. When my forces attacked Kadiro, her life would be forfeit.

"Is there nothing I can say to make you reconsider, your highness?" I asked, and I was surprised when tears burst from the corners of my eyes, but I couldn't help it. I was panic-stricken at the thought of Lakshmi in Ahura in the hands of my enemies while my attack went forward here. There would be no saving her at all.

"Don't be swayed by false tears, my son," Asma warned. "She just doesn't like being brought to heel."

"Shut up, you spiteful old hag!" I exclaimed. I regretted the words as soon as they were out of my mouth, but I couldn't help myself. This was Lakshmi's life that was at stake.

"There, you see, Karim?" Asma asked. "She shows her true colors."

"*My* true colors?" I growled. "You have not given me a chance here, though I have tried my best to abide by every rule." I turned to Karim. "Your highness, I have been treated most unfairly in my time here, but I have accepted it. I will not accept this. I will not let you put my baby sister in danger for no reason except your parents' hatred of me!"

"Guards," Ahmed called, and a dozen men answered him, marching to surround the baradari on all sides.

"Father, that's not necessary, I can handle this," Karim told him.

"Then handle it, boy," Ahmed replied.

Karim planted his hands on my shoulders. "Razia, I will keep Lakshmi safe. You need to calm down, and accept that this is the way things are. After the threat from Safavia is defeated, and we have returned, we can talk about the way you are treated here. But this wild behavior of yours is doing you no favors."

My body slumped as my heart sank through my feet. There was nothing I could say. I saw that. They were going to take her, and the certainty of it was making me tremble with fear. I couldn't think straight. I took one deep, gasping breath after another, fighting down the panic that was rising up from my chest to overwhelm me. I had to figure something out. I couldn't let it end like this. I couldn't let Lakshmi die because I wasn't smart enough and brave enough to save her.

Maybe there was a way. They'd arrive in Ahura at night. I might be able to reach it before dawn if the battle in Kadiro went fast enough. Then, I'd have a chance of saving her. She had her climbing shoes. If I climbed the fortress, I might be able to get her out. But I'd need to know which room she was in. I'd need to be able to go straight to her and get her straight out. It was the only chance. There was no other way now.

But I couldn't let Karim be in the room with her. God, for so many reasons I had to keep them separate now. And that meant she couldn't go alone.

"Sikander, you will go with Lakshmi and you will protect her with your life," I commanded.

"I will, your highness," Sikander agreed, before anyone could say otherwise.

I looked at Karim. "You will need all the zahhaks you can get, so a thunder zahhak will be helpful, and will still leave me with four here in case Kadiro needs to be defended."

He was quick to nod his approval. "If that makes you feel better, then of course Sikander can come along to protect her."

I turned to my sisters and saw the tears streaming down Sakshi's cheeks as she clung tightly to Lakshmi. She knew as well as I did just how badly stacked the odds were against our ever recovering her. But I had a plan, and I wasn't going to let it fail. I couldn't let it fail. I went to them, and I took my dupatta off and I handed it to Lakshmi, pressing it into her little hands. "This is for luck, okay?"

"I'll be fine, Akka, I'm a good flier," she told me, not seeing the reason for all the tears, because she didn't know our plans, didn't know how much danger she was in.

"I know you are, sweetheart," I replied, squeezing her so tightly that she let out a little cry of protest, but I kissed her on top of her head for good measure, and then I went to Sikander, fighting against every instinct I had to yank my katars from their hiding place at the small of my back and start killing Mahisagaris until I was dead or all of them were. It wouldn't work. I needed to stick to the plan.

I surprised Sikander by embracing him, but that was just an act to let me whisper where no one else could hear. "Tonight, hang the dupatta from her window so that it can be seen from the outside. Stay in the room with her. Do not let her leave, and above all, do not let Karim enter. Is all of that clear to you?"

"It is, your highness," he whispered back. Louder, he said, "You have nothing to fear. I will let no harm come to her."

He didn't know how much danger he was in. Poor man. I wondered if he'd have been so quick to follow my orders if he'd known that I was essentially sending him into an enemy fortress at the outbreak of a war. Probably. The man had never lacked for courage of the military kind; I could grant him that at least.

When I was finished speaking to Sikander, Karim approached me, taking my hands in his. I wanted to slap him, but I held back. I couldn't risk antagonizing him now. So I bit my lip and hung my head, and waited for him to make whatever pathetic promises he was going to make.

"We'll be back in a matter of a couple of days, not more than a week," Karim said. "I will make sure that Lakshmi is kept safe. You have my word on that."

I managed a stiff nod. "Thank you, your highness. She means the world to me. You know that."

"I do." He hugged me, pulling my head against his chest like that was a comfort and not a horror. "I'm sorry that this is necessary, but I think once it's over, we'll be able to move forward with more trust."

"I think so too, your highness," I replied, because once this was over, I was going to be moving forward in a world without him or his filthy parents in it.

"Enough time wasted on the girl," said Sultan Ahmed. "Let's get moving. Safavia won't wait for us to assemble before they attack." He gestured for a guard to grab Lakshmi, but the man stepped right into the point of Sikander's talwar, the sharp tip pressed up against the hollow of the man's throat. The move had been so swift and so deft that nobody had seen it coming.

"You will not touch her," Sikander growled, and the fear I saw in the Mahisagari guardsman's face gave me some small satisfaction.

I went to Lakshmi and hugged her again, pulling her close to me in just such a way that I could feel her climbing shoes in her pockets, assuring me that they were there. "Do what Sikander tells you, okay?"

"Okay, Akka," she agreed.

"I'll see you soon." I kissed her forehead, and breathed in the delicate aroma of coconut oil from her hair, my fury and my sorrow mingling together in a way that energized my limbs for a fight that was nowhere to be found. I settled for squeezing her tightly one last time before letting her go.

"Look on the bright side, Akka," she told me. "I get to ride Mohini all day!"

"You do," I agreed, and tears rolled down my cheeks. She had no idea how much danger she was in.

"She'll be safe, your highness," Sikander said, but he didn't know how much danger they were in either. Still, it made me feel a bit better when the big man took Lakshmi by the hand and led her toward the stables, without any Mahisagari guardsmen harassing them.

I turned away, and found Karim standing close behind me. Bastard wanted a good-bye kiss. He reached down and took my tear-streaked cheeks in his hands, tilting my head up before planting his lips on mine. It lasted way too long. When he finally had the good grace to pull away, he wiped my tears with his thumbs and said, "I'll be back with Lakshmi, and we'll talk about your place here moving forward. You have my word."

"Be safe, your highness," I replied, like I didn't want him dead.

"Always," he said.

I was grateful when he finally let me go and walked off with his father toward the zahhak stables, though my emotions were still in far too much turmoil to feel relief. With Lakshmi in Ahura, and Arjun attacking tonight with Sunil Kalani and Sanghar Soomro, I wasn't sure how on earth I was going to get there in time to save her. And that was if we even succeeded in our rebellion. Even with Karim and Ahmed gone, there was every chance we would fail, especially with two acid zahhak riders ready to attack any forces we brought into the lagoon.

"Guards!" Asma called, once Karim and Ahmed were out of sight and out of earshot.

I looked up, horrified that I hadn't seen this coming, but she was grinning mercilessly. Sikander was gone. My other Nizami guards were close by, but there were just two of them, and there were close to thirty Mahisagari men already ringing the baradari. Even with Hina and her fifteen celas, we were badly outnumbered, and the women weren't armed.

"Is taking my sister from me not enough?" I demanded.

"For a spiteful old hag like me?" she replied, arching a black eyebrow. "Not even close."

I gritted my teeth, wishing I had kept a better guard over my emotions, but I hadn't expected to lose Lakshmi like that, and my fear for her had overwhelmed everything else. I shrugged, because I knew that I had lost this round of things. The only question that remained was how badly.

"What will you do with me?" I asked, my mouth dry as I wondered if she was planning to just kill me and get it over with, or if she was going to imprison me so thoroughly that I would have no chance of fulfilling my promises to Sanghar Soomro and his men.

"Nothing," she answered, still smirking. "I will keep you safe and under control until the men return from Ahura. But as I cannot trust you, I will be keeping you in your chambers until then. The guards will ensure that you do not leave them, and my handmaidens will ensure that you want for nothing."

"And my sister and my handmaidens?" I asked, wondering whether she intended to keep us together or apart.

"They will stay with you," she declared, "lest they get any ideas into their heads about sneaking off and trying to fan the flames of rebellion while my husband and my son are away."

Idiot woman. Having them with me was just precisely what I needed, but I didn't let that show on my face. I bowed my head. "Well, I'm not in any position to refuse."

"No," she agreed. "You are not. You will return to your chambers now, and you will take your sister and your handmaidens with you. If you remain there like a dutiful daughter-in-law, then there need be no violence, but if you attempt to leave, for any reason, we will revisit that decision."

"Then I will go, and I will remain there, your majesty," I replied, bowing to her.

She snorted derisively. "I was warned about you, you know. Everyone said you were so dangerous and so clever. But you're really nothing more than a pretty whore who tricked a prince into thinking too highly of her."

I let my spine stiffen, like her words had hurt my feelings. She didn't know the half of how dangerous I was, but she would see. Tonight I would show them all, and I would find some way to get Lakshmi back. I swore it as I marched under heavy guard back to my chambers.

CHAPTER 22

"No appetite, your highness?" Fatima, Asma's chief handmaiden, taunted as I sat on the floor of my bedchamber in front of an uneaten thali. There were a dozen Mahisagari soldiers all around me, leering at me. They didn't usually get to visit the women's quarters of the palace, and they seemed to be enjoying having a woman to intimidate. Of course, they didn't know that I wasn't so easily intimidated.

"No, as a matter of fact," I said, glancing out my jali screen at the deep gray sky. The sun was just setting. I didn't know how much longer I could wait before making my move. Arjun was on his way, and so was Sunil Kalani. If they attacked as soon as it was dark, then that would alert the Mahisagaris, and I'd be killed before I could get Sanghar Soomro's men inside the palace. I had to make my move now.

"In fact, I'm tired," I declared, shoving the thali away like a petulant child. "I would like to sleep. Please have these men removed so that I may change into my nightclothes."

Fatima grinned and shook her head. "No. The men stay. Lady

Asma was very clear about that. Besides, you're a man anyway, what do you care if they see you?"

It was a stupid thing to say when surrounded by eighteen hijras, but Fatima didn't seem to care. She must have felt pretty invincible with all of the guards gathered around her, knowing that Asma hated me and would reward her for hating me in turn.

I bit back any sharp replies and said, "Please send one of your girls to Lady Asma to relay my request that I be permitted privacy to undress. What harm is there in asking?"

"No," Fatima replied, grinning at me from behind the sheer fabric of her yellow dupatta.

I leaned closer to her, keeping my voice low, and said, "You are serving your mistress well. That's good, you'll earn her favor that way. But Karim intends to make me his wife, and that is also what Lady Asma intends. So, someday I will be the sultana, and Lady Asma will be dead. You're younger than she is; you may yet be a servant in the palace when that day comes. What do you think I will do to you then? I have a long memory, Fatima, ask anyone."

She frowned, seeming a lot less sure of herself then. I watched as she worked the puzzle out in her mind, folding her arms across her chest, trying to decide if honoring my request would be enough to forestall the fate I had outlined for her. In the end, she must have decided it couldn't hurt after all, because she said, "Zahra, you'll go and relay her highness's request to her majesty."

"Yes, my lady," a pink-clad handmaiden replied, and she rushed off to see it done.

"Thank you, Fatima," I said, offering her a friendly smile, though I knew there was nothing that could save her now. She had chosen the wrong mistress, and that was going to cost her far sooner than she believed.

Fatima managed a stiff nod, but said nothing more. Evidently, she hadn't stopped to consider what the consequences might be for taunting the princess of Nizam.

I waited anxiously for Zahra's return, expecting at any moment that Arjun's forces might attack, or Sunil's, that warning cries would spring up in the fortress and I would be held at gunpoint by the guards. I had to get out of here before that happened. I had to deal with the men in the towers and I had to get Sanghar's men inside the palace. Everything depended on it.

As it happened, Zahra returned quickly, but she wasn't alone. Lady Asma herself was with her, and I hurried to stand respectfully, keeping my face covered with my dupatta and my head downcast like a properly chastened young maiden. She would know it for an affectation, but from the way she strode into the room, it was plain that she also viewed herself as a conquering heroine of sorts, so my submission was probably what she had envisioned.

"You wanted to speak with me?" Asma asked me, no doubt so she could have the joy of refusing my request in person.

"I would like to sleep, your majesty," I said, keeping my voice quiet and polite and deferential—and exhausted. I wanted her to think that I'd been broken, that I was giving up, surrendering myself completely to my fate. "Would it be possible for the guards to step outside so that I might have some privacy to undress?"

Asma pursed her lips and I was certain she was going to refuse me, which would make all this so much more difficult. But then she said, "I will permit you to undress and to go to bed in the privacy of your handmaidens and mine."

"Thank you, your majesty," I gasped, shocked that it had been that easy.

"*If*," she added, smiling like she'd just caught me in a trap, "you hand over your climbing shoes."

For a moment, I was angry, but then I realized that this was even more perfect. She would both have her suspicions of me confirmed and have a reason to believe that I was well and truly helpless at long last. That would give me the freedom I needed to act, I thought.

My shoulders slumped. I reached into my pockets and took out the climbing shoes, noting the way that her eyes widened behind the fabric of her dupatta, seeing the triumphant grin spread slowly across her face. I handed the shoes over. "I just want to sleep in peace, your majesty." My voice was thick with emotion, and I let my head hang. Maybe I was overselling it, but I didn't think so.

Asma snatched the shoes from me. "You were planning to run, were you?"

"No, your majesty, I just felt better with them, that's all," I murmured.

"Well, you won't be going anywhere now," she declared. "You may change without the men present, but they will return once you are suitably attired for bed."

"Thank you, your majesty," I said.

"Hmph." She sniffed and turned to go, but thought better of it after a moment, her eyes still flickering over the climbing shoes Karim had given me. "If you learn your place, Razia, and I mean truly learn it, then we can end these games, you and I."

"I'd like that, your majesty." I gasped, pretending to choke back a sob, thankful that my dupatta and my posture were doing a good job of hiding my face from view, so that she couldn't see the smirk I was fighting to suppress.

"Show me that, and we can talk," she replied.

"I will, your majesty," I promised.

"Fatima," Asma said, "you will step out and inform the guards when she is decent. I expect you to watch her closely."

"I will, your majesty," Fatima assured her, bowing to her as she left the room. Asma had motioned for the male guards to follow her, so that left Fatima alone in my chambers with just two other handmaidens, against eighteen of us. I liked those odds.

I removed my dupatta and gave Hina a significant look. She smiled, her hazel eyes lighting up. She knew just what I was asking for without being told, and I thought most of her celas did too. Had Asma forgotten that Hina was a mercenary captain, that her disciples were all zahhak-riding warriors? Maybe it was because they were all such disarmingly pretty ladies, and because they carried no weapons, but it was going to be the old woman's undoing.

"Let's help get Princess Razia ready for bed," Hina said, but the tone of her voice held an edge to it that I noticed, and that even her less observant celas seemed to notice too. Some of them went to fetch my clothing chest, others went to get my jewelry boxes, a third group went to get water and towels to help clean the makeup off my face. I sat on my cushion, letting the women remove the bangles from my wrists, and the tall necklace and the earrings, putting each piece away carefully in a hardwood box. All the while, I was looking into the mirror, watching as the celas who had gone to fetch water and towels crept up behind Asma's handmaidens. Their ajrak dupattas were wound into narrow ropes of silk, and they kept them stretched tightly between their hands.

When the moment came, it all happened in a flash of movement. The three celas threw their dupattas around the handmaidens' necks and pulled tightly, their collarbones standing out as they yanked with all their might. Other celas rushed forward, stuffing their sleeves or their skirts into the handmaidens' gaping mouths to muffle their cries. The women struggled, clawing at anything they could, kicking out with their legs, but they died quickly and quietly, just as I'd intended. Poor Fatima. She shouldn't have taunted me.

I stood up and stripped off my ajrak clothes, trading them for a black shalwar kameez. I moved with purpose, selecting a pair of simple slippers to protect my feet, making sure they were flexible enough that I could bend my toes in any direction I liked. They were the opposite of the climbing shoes Karim had bought for me, but that didn't matter so much.

"What are you going to do now?" Hina asked, and she sounded worried.

"We stick to the plan," I replied.

"But your shoes!" she exclaimed. She kept her voice low, but the urgency came through all the same.

It was Sakshi who laughed then, a surprising sound when she'd just witnessed three women being murdered in cold blood in front of her. She came up beside me and ruffled my hair. "My little sister didn't need special shoes to climb the cliffs of Shikarpur, or to steal from the wealthy havelis in Bikampur."

"They do help, though," I admitted. "I'll be a little slower than I would have been otherwise, but now Lady Asma will believe that I'm helpless, and that's the important thing."

Hina's eyes widened, and she shook her head ruefully. "I should have known. All right, your highness, what do you want us to do?"

"I want you to pick your three best actresses and dress them in the handmaidens' clothes. Hide the bodies wherever you can so the guards won't stumble across them. Put someone in my night-clothes and put her to bed just to be safe. The rest of your girls will need to be making ropes from clothes—as many as you can and as strong as you can. Dupattas, shirts, whatever it takes."

"And if the guards try to get in?" Hina asked.

"Have your false handmaidens tell them I'm not ready yet. If I'm still not back when they return a second time, then let them in, pretend everything is normal. Hopefully, I'll be able to get Sanghar and his men into the palace before that, though."

"Right," Hina agreed. She surprised me by embracing me. "Good luck, your highness."

"I'll be back soon," I assured her.

"You'd better be," Sakshi replied. "Lakshmi is counting on you, don't forget."

"I couldn't," I muttered. We hugged each other good-bye, though we didn't call it good-bye, and I headed for the balcony, intent on murdering two men and leading a rebellion.

CHAPTER 23

I crept onto the balcony, my slippers skimming the smooth surface of the marble floor, my body crouched low, keeping to the shadows formed by the tall sandstone columns, which blocked out the light from the brass lanterns hanging from the ceiling. Half a dozen worries were vying for a place in the forefront of my mind, but the most pressing was the problem of guards. Had Asma increased the tower guards, or were there still only two men guarding this side of the palace?

I slid on my belly across the open gap between the protective shadows of the columns and the low marble railing that marked the balcony's edge. I pressed my body tightly against the decorative stonework, peeking out through the finely chiseled rosettes, surveying first one tower and then the second. I swore under my breath. There were three guards in each tower now. Asma was taking no chances.

My heart pounded in my chest as I wondered what in the world I was supposed to do now. Sanghar Soomro's men were counting on me to get those guards out of the way so they could climb into the palace without being shot. Hina was counting on me to get those men inside silently so that she and her celas wouldn't be held hostage by the guards lurking outside my bedchamber. And Lakshmi, God, Lakshmi was in Ahura by now, all alone. And whatever designs Karim had on her, he would let Ahmed kill her once word reached them of my rebellion. I couldn't let that happen. I wouldn't let that happen.

So I did the only thing I could to prevent it. I rolled over the knee-high marble fence meant to protect me from plummeting to my death, and I dropped my feet and hips over the ledge of the balcony, my fingers getting tight grips in the railing's rosettes. My feet scrabbled against the sandstone buttresses for toeholds, and I found myself missing the reinforced toes of my climbing shoes as my cloth slippers did little to dampen the bite of the stone's sharp-edged cracks against my feet. Had I gotten so soft since my victory over Javed Khorasani? That worried me.

But the less time I gave myself to think, the better. I couldn't do nothing. I couldn't sit back and watch. I'd done that for weeks now; I'd played the part of the cowed damsel and I was sick of it. Tonight, I was going to free myself and free my sisters, and it didn't matter if there were three men in the guard tower or thirty. They were going to die.

Of course, that was easy to say, and harder to do. I wasn't sure, even as I began making my way along the wall, groping blindly for decorative lotus flowers and cracks in the masonry to support my weight, how exactly I was going to kill three armed men by myself. I was much less sure how I was going to do it silently. But it needed to be done. I prayed to God to give me the strength to see it through.

But even getting to the tower was no easy task. This wall was covered not with loopholes for toradars, but with fine screens so that ladies could look out at the water. That meant I couldn't risk climbing laterally across the wall. There was too much chance that some servant girl would be gazing out at the moon, only to see my body sliding across her marble jali. So, I had to lower myself into the water as I had the first time I'd escaped the palace, keeping my head barely above the surface of the waves and praying that no crocodiles found me.

It was hard, physical work, dragging myself through the water by my fingertips, each pull requiring me to jam my hands into crevices made slimy by algae. I couldn't go too fast, not without making noise. But going slowly was its own agony. My eyes were fixed on the guards in the western tower, visible beneath their brass chandeliers. The three of them were leaning on their toradars, chatting to one another, looking relaxed. That was something. A small advantage, though it meant that they would notice if I killed one of their number. My stomach was churning with anxiety as I reached the base of the tower. How in the world was I going to manage this?

I needed the right approach. I couldn't risk climbing where I would be seen by someone from one of the other guard towers. That meant climbing up the far southwestern corner of the wall. The curve of the circular tower would keep me just out of sight of both the men on the western wall of the palace and the soldiers manning the southeastern tower. But once I reached the top, I'd be visible, as would the murders I was planning to commit. How could I expect guards all along the wall to just not notice three of their number being killed? It was dark, sure, but they were standing full in the light of the chhatri's half dozen brass lanterns. There were probably sharp-eyed men and women in Kadiro who could have seen it.

I started climbing anyway. I had no plan. This was so stupid. My fingers were slick against the palace walls, from the slime and the damp of the alga-thickened water. My body was dripping wet, and the sound of all those droplets pattering against the tower and the surface of the lagoon was like a monsoon storm in my ears. How could the men on the tower not hear that? Were they completely deaf?

No. They were having a conversation. I couldn't quite make out the words, because they were speaking Mahisagari, but they were chatting quite happily with one another, and that was drowning out the sound of my dripping clothes. I hung there, my fingers burning, my leg muscles aching, scarcely able to breathe for fear that I'd make enough noise that one of them would finally take notice.

Even with the breeze stirring the hot desert air, it was a long wait for my clothes to dry enough that I felt confident climbing. I hadn't heard any cries from the tower, any trumpets sounding, so the dripping must not have been as loud as I'd imagined it, but even if I did make it to the top undetected, I still wasn't sure what I was going to be able to accomplish. Even though guards were rarely as well trained as princes, three grown men, armed and armored, would make for a fearsome set of opponents for me. I'd trained hard as a prince, but that was years ago now, and yes, I'd killed in the interim—once. And that had been some poor conscripted farmer who had been half-asleep at the time. What was I going to do against three alert men? I still didn't have an answer to that question, and I was halfway up the tower.

My mind spun itself in circles, imagining a half dozen possibilities as I felt for some new decoration I could cling to in order to lever myself up that little bit higher. I could shove one man off the tower, punch a second with my katars, and then the third would be alert, but he'd be alone. That might work. It'd make noise, but I didn't see any way around that now. If I could clear this tower, it might give the Zindhis a chance to get their boat up to my balcony.

And then what? Without me there to lower the ropes, or to tell Hina to do it, how were we going to get the men onto the balcony? Maybe she would do it herself? She was smart, she knew the plan. But even if that worked, what was I going to do? Did I really believe that after I killed three guards nobody was going to think to look for me as I crawled slowly along the wall back to a second tower to repeat the feat?

And even if I did manage to—my hand slipped in midthought. I squeezed hard with my left hand, my right dangling free, my legs burning as I engaged every muscle from my hips to my toes, struggling to pin myself against the wall. My heart was like thunder in my ears, and I was shocked I hadn't screamed in surprise. I was too high up to survive a fall. Stupid. I should have been focused on the climb. It was too dark to see what I was doing. I had to grab something fast, because I could feel my left hand starting to pull away from the slippery, smooth-glazed lotus it was holding.

I slapped the wall with my right hand, my fingers curling into a claw, my nails scraping the sandstone until they hit a tiny ledge. It was barely a fingerbreadth deep, but it was enough that I could pull against it with the muscles of my right arm, giving my left a little bit of relief.

I gasped for air, trying to keep it quiet, but the burning in my lungs was so urgent that it overpowered everything else. I hugged the wall, pressing my cheek against it as my body shuddered from pain and exhaustion and fear and the desperate need for air. And in the midst of all that, one thing leapt immediately to mind. I missed Arjun.

What a stupid thought. I was moments away from getting myself killed from distraction, and that was what my brain came up with?

I was tired. That was the other thing that entered my mind. I was tired of fighting all the time. I was tired of everything being such a struggle. I'd thought that was over after Bikampur, but then Karim had showed up, and this was even worse, even more hopeless. I was tired of being responsible for Sakshi and Lakshmi, tired of always having to have all the answers, tired of being constantly on my guard.

And I was physically tired too. My muscles were aching. My fingers hurt. And even if I succeeded here, there was every chance that Lakshmi would die anyway. I'd rather have died than live to see what became of her when Ahmed got word of what I'd done. If I'd thought for an instant that begging Asma would have saved Lakshmi's life, I might have just climbed to the top of the tower, surrendered to the guards there, and thrown myself on my knees in front of her. But I knew better. I'd backed myself into a corner with this plot. Either I would win it all or I would lose it all. There would be no quarter given or taken. If I gave up here, Lakshmi died, it was as simple as that.

I gritted my teeth and pulled.

She was *not* going to die. Her akka was not just going to give up and let that happen to her, not while she could still draw breath. If I had to swim the four hundred miles to Ahura, then I would swim. I wasn't going to leave her for Karim and Ahmed. She was counting on me. She trusted me. She believed in me. And so did Sakshi. And so did Hina. And Arjun and Sunil Kalani and Sanghar Soomro. They were all counting on me. Maybe I could have failed myself, but I wasn't going to fail them.

My hand hit the top of the tower, and I eased myself up until I could peek through the knee-high railing that surrounded the chhatri. The three guards were still standing together in the center of the dome, chattering away in Mahisagari, looking at one another. There was no way to attack one without the others seeing, and they had toradars in their hands. I didn't think they'd be able to get a shot off, not at such close range, but fourteen pounds of steel and wood makes for a pretty brilliant club, and that they would be able to accomplish.

I hesitated, but not from fear or doubt. I had to get this right. For Lakshmi. I couldn't fail here. Not now. Not when I was so close.

Fire rained from the sky to the east. Long columns of flame belched from shadowy forms circling over the fortresses guarding the harbor. Arjun! Arjun was here, and the attack had started.

"Fire!" one of the men in the tower shouted, and he pointed at the fortresses.

All three men rushed to the far edge of the tower to get a better look. They were knotted close together, their legs pressed up against the low railing, which only came up to their shins. This was the moment.

I threw myself up with more strength than I knew I possessed, vaulting over the railing, landing on my feet, and running for all I was worth. My footsteps were loud and squelching, but the men were talking to one another so frantically that they couldn't hear them. And anyway, it was too late. I hurled myself into all three of them, hitting them with every last ounce of strength I possessed.

The impact was so jarring that I felt like I'd been punched. Stars danced across my vision. But all three men lost their balance, toppling forward, shouting as they fell. I fell too, but not off the tower. I fell to the ground beside the marble railing, hiding myself from view just as the men splashed into the water, the impacts so hard that I knew there was no chance they'd survived. And even if they had, the armor they'd been wearing would drag them straight to the bottom of the lagoon.

I looked out from the railing's pierced decorations, struggling to see if the men on the other towers had seen what had happened, and I couldn't believe my good fortune. They were all too busy watching the attack of the fire zahhaks. They hadn't seen a thing.

But I had to get back to the balcony. Damn the other tower. Hina and her celas would be in danger. Sakshi would be in danger. The alarms were sounding everywhere. I had to get those Zindhi men into my bedchamber, and I had to do it now.

Sanghar Soomro and his men must have made the same decision, because I spotted boats sliding out of the darkness, propelled soundlessly by long sculls flapping back and forth like the tails of enormous fish. They were heading straight for the base of the wall beneath my balcony, and if I wasn't there by the time they arrived, then all would be lost.

There was no time to carefully climb back down the wall, and the parapets would be crawling with soldiers. But the rooftop was clear. I could run across it. I'd be visible to every guard in the palace, but it was too late to worry about secrecy now.

I scrambled to my feet and started climbing one of the chhatri's decorated columns, grabbing hold of the stone awning that shaded the guards from the force of the sun during the day. With a pull that made the muscles of my chest and back burn, I hauled myself onto the tiled dome, breathing hard, keenly aware of the shouts going up throughout the palace as guards rushed to and fro to try to make sense of what was happening.

I put them out of my mind as best I could, because I had to focus on jumping the gap between the roof of the chhatri and the roof of the women's quarters of the palace. They were separated by a ten-foot gap. It was a long way to jump, and I wouldn't get much of a run-up. The awning gave me at best five paces to work with. This was going to be close.

I didn't give myself time to think about it. I went to the corner of the tower and took a deep stance, leaning forward, preparing my legs for the explosive kickoff that I would need to see me safely to the other side. I knew that if I failed, I would slam my ribs into the hard stone roof at best, or fall fifty feet to my death at worst. But I'd come too far to give up now.

I sprang off with my legs, running for everything I was worth, watching my feet rather than my destination, so I would hit the edge of the roof with the ball of my foot, giving me the most powerful possible spring I could manage. I screamed through my teeth, heedless of the attention it might bring me. Nothing mattered if I missed.

For one exhilarating instant, I was flying. There was nothing below me but the glittering waters of the lagoon, nothing around me but the desert air. And then the roof of the women's quarters came rushing up in my vision and I realized that I'd missed it. I was dropping too fast. There was no way I was going to land on my feet.

I tucked my knees into my chest to avoid smashing my shins to bits on the edge of the stone awning. My feet hit hard, and there was no slack in my legs to take up the impact, so it jolted my whole body, all the way up to my head, which snapped painfully on my neck. I hit the rooftop in a heap, aching all over, dazed, the world feeling strangely off-kilter, like I'd suddenly stepped into a boat in rough seas.

I pushed myself up and ran all the same. A toradar cracked. Something whizzed through the air just behind me. I paid it no attention. My balcony was so close. I was almost there. And so were Sanghar Soomro's boats. They were pressing forward, and the men on the far tower still hadn't spotted them, because they were too busy watching Arjun's zahhaks attacking the fortresses at the mouth of the harbor. I knew only seconds had passed since the attack had begun, but it felt more like hours. I was so sure that I was going to be too late.

I leapt off the roof, onto the dome that overhung my balcony, sliding down it in my wet clothes until my legs were dangling off the side. I grabbed a decorative row of lotus blossoms with my fingers, swung my body back once and then forward hard, and let go, tumbling to the hard marble floor and landing flat on my back with a thud that knocked the wind out of me.

A figure loomed out of the shadows, and I raised my hands to defend myself, but she took them in hers and jerked me to my feet. Hina.

"You're crazy," she hissed.

"The ropes?" I gasped, fighting to catch my breath.

"We were only able to make one," she replied, gesturing to her celas, who were busy lowering it over the side of the balcony, tying it off on one of the columns.

"And the guards?"

"They ran off to deal with the attack," she replied, "but I would bet anything that Asma will be returning with them as soon as she figures out what is going on."

"We have to do something to stop them getting in," I muttered, but I wasn't sure what, not until I saw the lead boat rushing toward us, and I spotted all the swivel guns mounted along its railings. They were light. They could be hauled up easily. One of them might be enough to hold off a group of guards. It was worth a try anyway.

I rushed to the railing just as the boat reached the rope. One man was already taking hold of it, but I called down, "Tie a cannon to it first!"

"What?" Sanghar shouted back, horrified at the prospect of our taking a cannon and leaving his men in the boat, but there was no time to argue. One or two men with a toradar weren't going to stop thirty guardsmen, but a swivel gun loaded with grapeshot might.

"Just do it!" I hissed.

That got through to him. He tied off a cannon whose match cord was still burning merrily above the touchhole, and Hina and I hauled it up as fast as we could. It wasn't much heavier than Lakshmi, so it didn't take much time, but all the while the shouting was growing louder. And then the men in the guard tower to our left spotted us, and they fired their toradars, the long-barreled guns belching flame and white smoke.

Chips flew off the sandstone columns. Something nearly hit my face. I pulled the makeshift rope of silk dupattas through my hands as fast as I could, driven by a blind panic. There was nothing I could do to take cover, not until I had the cannon. The men on the tower were reloading, and behind me a cela shouted, "Hina, they're coming!"

The cannon crested the railing and I rushed to untie it, my shaking, stiff fingers fighting with the knot for what seemed an eternity. Once it was free I gathered it up in my arms, told Hina, "Get the men up!" and ran into my bedchamber.

I heard the jingle of the guards' armor, the pounding of their feet on the polished marble floors. They were right on top of us. I needed to find something to stabilize the cannon, but what?

My eyes landed on my bedpost and I slammed the spike at the base of the swivel mount right into the top of it, digging it in deep, fighting to make sure that it wouldn't come loose, or it would be more danger to me than to my enemies.

"You've crossed us for the last time, you little slut!" Asma herself screeched as she rounded the corner and entered my bedchamber's doorway, more than a dozen guards packed closely behind her. She froze, her eyes going wide as she took in the muzzle of the swivel gun aimed at her, the red glow of the match cord hovering over the touchhole, my finger on the trigger mechanism, my eye sighting down the barrel.

I grinned at her, savoring this moment, because who knew whether I would survive the night or not? As she reared back in terror, I said, in my most dulcet tones, "Good-bye, mother-in-law."

CHAPTER 24

I pulled the trigger. The burning match snapped down, burying a red-hot coal in a pile of fine black powder. There was a hiss, a stream of white smoke, and then a boom as loud as Sultana's thunder. The bedpost cracked from the force of the cannon's recoil as flames and smoke poured forth from the muzzle, which had been cast from bronze in the form of a fire zahhak's gaping maw.

A pound of musket balls tore through the hallway and everything in it, the lead shot punching through cloth and armor, flesh and bone, and carrying straight through into the marble wall beyond, gouging out thirty or forty holes, each one dripping with blood and gore.

I had never seen anything like the carnage the cannon had left in its wake. Nothing in that hallway could have possibly survived the wall of death that had been spewed out of the mouth of the bronze zahhak. Asma was barely recognizable as a person, the musket balls having torn the clothing from her body, and the flesh from her bones, sawing her completely in half and obliterating her hateful face. And each and every guard lay still, drenched in blood, their corpses covered with makeshift shrouds of shredded steel.

"Move!" Hina roared, shunting me aside from the rear of the gun. She was carrying a steel mug in her hand, and I didn't know what it was, not until she grabbed the D-shaped handle at the breech of the cannon and jerked free a matching mug, this one empty and smoldering. She tossed the used-up breechblock aside and slammed in the fresh one, twisting it so that it locked into place. She pulled back the lock, poured loose powder into the touchhole, and then pointed the muzzle at the hallway just as another troop of Mahisagari guardsmen came rushing into view.

They skidded to a stop, their eyes wide with horror as they took in the death and devastation in front of them, and then their eyes landed on Hina and the cannon, and all hope left them.

She let out a screech of malicious glee as she pulled the trigger. I pressed my fingers into my ears an instant before the bronze zahhak roared death for the second time in less than a minute.

A haze of white smoke hung thick in the air of the bedchamber. I pulled my fingers free from my ears, straining to hear the sounds of guards or muskets returning fire, but there was just an eerie silence. More distant shouts were still going up, but there was no sign that anyone had survived the cannon's second fusillade.

When the sea breeze cleared enough of the smoke to make out shapes amid the fog of war, my eyes widened in horror. There was a Mahisagari guardsman standing amid the bodies of his fallen comrades, his toradar leveled right at us. There was no time to think. I hurled myself into Hina, driving her to the floor just as flames spurted in front of us.

An angry sound hissed across my back, and there was a crack from the impact of lead against stone behind us. But he'd missed. That was the main thing.

I scrambled to my feet, fumbling to draw my katars as the guardsman dropped his toradar, drew his firangi and his buckler, and charged at us, screaming bloody murder. I got my fingers around the grips of the katars, sliding the second one free, gripping it with my right hand just as the guardsman slashed down with a shriek of fury.

I threw my left hand into the cut, letting the momentum propel my right fist forward. The firangi's sharp edge bit deeply into the good steel of the katar's blade, but I'd stopped his cut cold. His eyes were wide as my fist raced for his face, an eight-inch dagger projecting from my knuckles.

I had expected some kind of jolt of impact, but there wasn't one, and for a horrible second, I thought I'd somehow swung wide with my punch, but then my knuckles and the brass guard of my katar hit the man in the nose, and I realized that the blade had pierced through his entire skull with so little resistance that I hadn't even felt it go in. I kicked him in the chest, jerking my bloodied weapon free, averting my eyes from the narrow, bloody diamond that now connected his eyes through the space where the bridge of his nose had once been.

Hina was on her feet beside me a second later, and then I was startled to see ajrak-clad ladies rushing into the room from the balcony, carrying toradars, bhuj axes thrust through their sashes. They looked just like they had when I'd met them, all of Hina's celas ready for war at long last. They knelt down, pointing the muzzles of their weapons at the hallway, as men who looked like cutthroat bandits took their places behind them, their rifles projecting over the women's heads, creating a double line of barrels stacked one atop the other.

But nobody was coming, my ears told me that. The palace was in disarray, but the biggest danger now was to Lakshmi. If the messengers took off and got away, then they'd reach Ahura before

I could, and Lakshmi would die. I couldn't let that happen, not after we'd improbably succeeded at killing Asma and taking the palace.

"With me!" I cried, and I ran past the celas, the soles of my slippers slamming into the bodies of dozens of people coating the floor of the hallway, but I was sure-footed, and I burst out into the corridor beyond an instant later, searching for the guards I was sure were still ringing the women's quarters.

There! In the garden. Two dozen of them had formed up under the orders of a superior officer. They were trying to work out which way to go, but the minute they spotted me standing there in my black shalwar kameez, bloodied katars in my hands, they knew something was wrong.

"Kill her!" I understood enough Mahisagari to understand that. The officer thrust his firangi in my direction, and his men rushed to raise their toradars to send a volley into me that I knew I would never survive.

But the next thing I knew sixteen women were lining the railing beside me, their rifles already raised, and they got their volley off first. The sound of sixteen rifles going off at once was like the tearing of the fabric of reality itself. I was surrounded by smoke and flame, but I could still see the Mahisagari guardsmen below me. Almost two-thirds of their number toppled to the ground, stone-dead. God, Hina's celas were brilliant markswomen with those curious long-barreled Zindhi rifles!

But it wasn't enough. The officer was still standing, as were eight of his men. He shouted, "Shoot, damn it!"

They were stunned, staggered by seeing so many of their number killed, and they hesitated too long. The men reached us and poured another volley into the Mahisagaris, and they could hardly have missed, the range was so close and they were standing so plainly in the open. It was a slaughter. Every last man was hit at least once, most more than that. They shuddered from the impact of the musket balls, tumbled to the blood-soaked sandstone, and lay still.

"Hurry, we have to get to the zahhak stables!" I shouted as Hina's celas finished reloading their muskets, the men still slamming ramrods down the barrels, rushing to get themselves ready.

"Razia!" Sakshi shrieked, and to my shame I had forgotten to make sure she was safe, but she was holding a Zindhi rifle, her sweet face stained with gunpowder. She was pointing over the top of the distant gatehouse, and I saw the reason for her cry an instant later. A pair of acid zahhaks were rising up into the air. We were too late. We'd never catch them.

"If they escape, Lakshmi dies!" I screamed it so that nobody would be under any illusions as to the stakes. And then I flung myself over the railing, heedless of the ten-foot fall to the grass below. I hit with both feet, let myself crumple and roll, and was on my feet running an instant later like nothing had happened, sprinting for the gatehouse.

"With the princess!" Hina shouted, and I craned my head over my shoulder just far enough to see her take the same improbable leap, landing hard but getting to her feet and running after me. And then one by one all of her celas jumped, and Sakshi too, and I gritted my teeth and turned my head forward, my whole will bent on saving Lakshmi. If those women could follow me, then maybe there was some hope after all. If I could just get to the stables, I could climb onto Sultana's back and chase them down. She was faster than any acid zahhak and I knew where they were going. I would tear them from the skies as I had torn Asma from this world, that was a promise.

I raced toward the gates, my eyes fixed on the acid zahhaks climbing into the darkened sky, barely visible by the glint of the moonlight on their scales. If I didn't get to Sultana soon, they'd vanish. I had to get to her. Everything depended on it.

"Razia, no!"

I hit the ground just as a bullet whizzed overhead, Sakshi pinning me to the paving stone. It was only then that I saw what had been right in front of me—a mob of Mahisagari soldiers using the low hedges of the garden for cover, blazing away at us with their muskets. If not for Sakshi, I'd have been cut down. As it was, we might both be killed. Chips of paving stones were being kicked in our faces as they tried to shoot us, the smoke preventing them from seeing clearly enough to get a fatal shot.

We both rolled behind the rounded tower of the gatehouse, where Hina and her celas were waiting for us, along with Sanghar Soomro and his men. It was Sanghar who shouted, "You can't save your sister if you're dead, girl!"

I swore under my breath. It was over. Lakshmi was gone. I couldn't believe it. After all we'd been through, this was how it was going to end?

"Razia!" Hina shrieked, trying to break through to me. "We have to capture the palace first!"

She was right. I couldn't run off like an idiot. They needed me too.

"We take the parapets and we'll have them trapped in the open, just like before," I said, and I wasted no time in running up the stairs on the backside of the wall. The parapets were empty. Most of the men had gathered in the outer courtyards, and the ones who had been guarding the inner courtyard had been following Asma, and we'd killed all of them.

Hina's celas and my Zindhi soldiers followed me, taking up positions behind the tall merlons atop the palace wall, using funnel-shaped firing ports to shoot their muskets at the men hiding behind the hedges in the courtyard below them. It was a massacre, and that was before Sanghar Soomro himself slapped a swivel gun down into one of the spaces between the tall battlements and set it off, mowing down a whole column of men who had been rushing forward to join the fight.

More cannons roared. We had at least four swivel guns with us, and I knew more would be coming. The courtyard was quickly being cleared. There might still be a chance.

I searched the skies for the acid zahhaks, and felt a surge of hope as I spotted them to the west. They were pretty small, pretty hard to make out against the gray of the sky and the black of the water, but they were there. If I could just get to Sultana . . .

I chanced a look back into the courtyard. It seemed clear. It was clear enough, anyway. I ran down the steps and sprinted toward the stables, nearly slipping in puddles of blood as I picked my way over the corpses of Mahisagari soldiers. But before I could get to the stables, I saw something I couldn't explain—trails of white sparkling clouds in the air near the acid zahhaks, like the tails of comets.

In the distance, beasts screeched in pain and terror. The acid zahhaks' wings folded up, and the animals tumbled from the sky, a mix of dark shadow and bright white light, like snow on the mountains at night.

Snow. Ice zahhaks. Hope ran through my body like a tangible thing, making my skin tingle and my heart soar. "It's Tamara! She came!" I was suddenly aware that Sakshi was with me, and I wrapped an arm around her shoulders, pulling her close. "She came!"

"That's great, your highness," Hina told me, "but this fight isn't over yet." As if to prove it, she nodded toward the distant gatehouse, where enemy soldiers were rushing through by the dozens. God, there were so many of them, and we were in the open now. If it came to a gun battle, we would surely lose.

"Find cover!" I cried. I looked frantically for a place to hide, but there was nothing between us and the walls we had left except for open ground and mounds of bodies. What had I done? I'd been so desperate to save Lakshmi that I'd condemned us all.

"Too late!" Sanghar shouted, and he was right. The Mahisagari guardsmen were forming up into ranks, readying their muskets, and they had us badly outnumbered. Even with our cannons, we didn't have a prayer against them.

Just before death rained down on us, I heard a man shout, "For Jama Hina and Zindh!" The only trouble was, it wasn't any of my men.

CHAPTER 25

Sunil?" Hina gasped, looking around in confusion for the source of the voice.

Out of nowhere, a shadowy monster fell from the skies atop the Mahisagari soldiers. It crushed two men beneath its claws and bit another man clean in half, throwing the still-screaming torso into a fourth man, crushing him beneath the weight of his dying comrade. Atop the river zahhak's back, a man was shooting arrows one after the other, as fast as you could blink.

Some of the Mahisagaris screamed in terror, others turned to fight, but within a split second, five more zahhaks had plunged down into their midst, and then ten, and then I lost count. It was pandemonium as the animals bit and clawed their way through the ranks of the enemy soldiers, their riders shooting arrows or hurling javelins with startling rapidity. I immediately accounted every man a fool who had dismissed the idea of river zahhaks as useful in warfare.

But there was no sense standing around. I pointed forward and shouted, "Let's help them if we can, and secure the zahhak stables!"

A cheer went up from the Zindhis all around me, and we sprinted across the courtyard, vaulting hedges as we went. I ran for the zahhak stables, praying that Sultana was still there, still safe. I would never have forgiven myself if any harm had come to her. I was just on the point of reaching the entrance when a man stepped out of it and lowered his musket to kill me.

A bang went off near my ear that half deafened me, and the Mahisagari guardsman in front of me flinched back from the impact of the bullet and staggered, but was not killed. A bright red lehenga flashed past on my left, and a woman swung her empty rifle by the barrel, cratering the guardsman's skull with a vicious blow from its stock.

I hurried to catch up to her and was shocked to see that it was Sakshi. She'd shot the man and stove his head in with her musket? "Where did you learn to do that?"

"While you were dealing with Karim and his family, Hina and her celas were teaching me a few things," she replied. "Now come on, little sister, let's get our zahhaks just in case they're needed."

We ran into the stables together, and it was easy to see which zahhaks were left and which weren't. All the acid zahhaks were gone, the fire zahhaks too. There were still sixteen river zahhaks, though, and four thunder zahhaks, all made frantic by the shooting. Sultana was slamming herself up against the iron-reinforced wooden gate, trying to beat her way out to get to me.

"I'm here, girl!" I exclaimed, and I rushed forward and unfastened the stout lock, freeing her at last. She practically trampled me in her eagerness, pressing her whole head up against me, driving me back against the wall with enough force to knock the wind out of me.

"I'm okay," I told her, stroking her scales. "We're okay."

"We are," Sakshi agreed as she led a somewhat less worried Ragini out of her pen by the reins. She grabbed her saddle from the wall and got to work securing it. That was a smart move. When had Sakshi become the levelheaded one in a crisis? I grabbed my own saddle and tossed it over Sultana's back, securing it quickly and scrambling aboard. With my thunder zahhak beneath me, I could handle anything.

I urged her forward, and she raced out of the stables into a courtyard that was suddenly silent. White smoke hung low in the air, drifting on the wind. Bodies were everywhere, some torn apart by cannons, others by zahhaks, others full of arrows. Hina and her celas were gathered together with Sanghar Soomro and his men, facing a dozen river zahhaks. I recognized Sunil Kalani sitting on the animal in the center, the one closest to Hina. He was bowing in the saddle, saying something, but he broke off as I approached on Sultana's back.

He looked me up and down, and while he didn't exactly seem pleased to see me, he did seem impressed by what I'd achieved. "I was just telling her majesty that Kadiro is once again in the hands of the Zindhi people. Our army commands the town, and our allies from Registan seem to have taken the fortresses."

I didn't miss his phrasing, claiming that Kadiro belonged to Zindh and not to Nizam, but I wasn't going to debate it tonight. There was still too much left to do. Lakshmi still had to be rescued, and if we waited too long, it would be daylight before we could get to Ahura. But I couldn't just go rushing off blindly either, not when so much still needed doing here. And anyway, Sunil had given me an idea for how I might save my little sister.

"Is the palace secure?" I asked.

"My men are making it so," Sunil replied.

"As are mine, your highness," Sanghar added, favoring me with my title where Sunil hadn't.

"She's not our princess," Sunil grumbled.

Sanghar shrugged. "Maybe she is and maybe she isn't, my

friend, but after everything I've seen tonight, one thing I do know is that she's not someone we want to anger."

Hina grinned. "I'll say." She shook her head at me. "You're a madwoman, you know that?"

"Lakshmi is still in danger," I reminded her.

That wiped the smile from her face. She'd spent weeks with Lakshmi, and so had Nuri, the young cela who was standing with the others, holding a musket that was too big for her, but which she'd plainly spent the whole night shooting nonetheless. I was glad to see she wasn't hurt.

"We'll get her back, Razia," Hina said. "I swear it."

"I think I know how we might do it, but I'll need your girls, and I'll need as many zahhaks as I can muster. Arjun should be here as soon as the fortresses are secure. Then I'll know how many fire zahhaks we have. And I saw Tamara's ice zahhaks in the sky—they knocked down the messengers—but I have no idea where she is."

"You'll have every Zindhi flier in Kadiro, if that's what you need, your highness," Hina assured me.

"It may come to that," I allowed, because I wasn't sure how else I was going to get Lakshmi back.

"We'll get our zahhaks, then." Hina nodded to her celas, and the sixteen of them hurried to the stables to mount up, leaving me with Sunil and Sanghar and their soldiers. I didn't have the slightest idea where my Nizami guardsmen were now, though I supposed I could probably get a couple of Zindhis to handle the thunder zahhaks in an emergency.

Sultana twisted her neck skyward, and I followed her emerald eye with my own, straining to see what she'd spotted. Shadows coming toward us from the sky, their white-speckled undersides leaving me in no doubt as to their identity. Evidently, Sultana wasn't in any doubt either, because she set off at a gallop toward the far end of the courtyard where the ice zahhaks were alighting on one of the paved paths, running off their momentum with their rear legs before settling onto their wing claws.

One of the ice zahhaks turned her massive blue beak in our direction, her glacial eyes a perfect match with those of her rider. She leapt right at us, and it would have been terribly intimidating, what with her crest of white and black feathers, and the thick black ruff at the base of her neck for warmth, resembling the mane of a lion, but I knew better than to be frightened of Natia, and so did Sultana.

"Shall we dismount before they kill us both?" Natia's rider asked as our zahhaks danced around each other like a pair of overeager puppies.

"That would probably be for the best," I agreed, unable to contain a smile in spite of everything. My heart was fluttering almost harder than it had been when I'd been fighting. That had been life or death, but I found that the pain that relationships brought was equal to the sting of any sword. I hadn't seen Princess Tamara in seven years. I wondered what she would think of me now, knowing that I'd spent most of that time as a courtesan.

I slid from the saddle, landing hard on the paving stones, drawing myself up to my full height, and taking a deep breath. Just half a dozen paces away, Tamara had done the same thing. She was as dashing as I remembered her. I'd idolized her growing up, and it wasn't hard to see why. She wore her gold-trimmed green peshwaz like she was born to it, with a golden undergown that billowed out like the skirt of a lehenga, giving her a grace and a beauty that told the whole world she was a princess. But the khanjali thrust through the golden sash around her waist was proof that she was a warrior too, as were the flying goggles that now rested on her oversized fur hat, which must have been impossibly hot here in Zindh but was proof that she'd flown without pause, down from the mountains of Khevsuria, all the way here.

She was paler than I remembered, a real Firangi, though I'd gotten so used to living in Safavia that it seemed starker now after so long away. The same was true of her red hair, a brilliant copper color, not like the subtle mahoganies I saw so often in Daryastan. Her icy blue eyes were drinking in every detail of me too, and I supposed that was only fair. I'd changed more in the last seven years than she had. Of course, I wasn't exactly dressed like a princess in my sweat-soaked shalwar kameez, my face and hands blackened with gunpowder.

Tamara strode forward, crossing the distance separating us so quickly that it took me a little by surprise. I didn't know what she was doing, not until she wrapped her arms around me and held me tightly to her. "You're even more beautiful than I imagined you would be. It's no wonder you're having to use cannons to fight off your suitors."

I hugged her back, overjoyed that she didn't hate me for being what I was. "I thought you would come if I asked, but I wasn't sure . . ."

"Of course we came," she replied, her fingers tensing against my back. "Safavia isn't close, but it's not the other side of the world. We heard everything through Shah Ismail's network of spies, and Haider and I spoke of trying to find some way to help you. Then your letters arrived, and we jumped at the chance."

"Thank you," I whispered. "If you hadn't come . . ."

"You'd have found some other way to free yourself, I suspect," she said, patting my cheek. "But we did come. And we're here for whatever you need."

"Haider too?" I asked, glancing around, not seeing any sign of him.

"He's on his way. I expect he'll arrive shortly." She gestured back to the other Khevsurian woman riding an ice zahhak. "Do you remember my bodyguard, Ketevani?"

"Yes, of course." I nodded to the older woman, a bit embarrassed at having shown so much emotion. I was supposed to be a provincial ruler, not a child. "Thank you for your assistance. As soon as matters with Mahisagar are settled, I'll see to it that you are suitably rewarded for your efforts."

The Khevsurian woman wrinkled her pale nose and gave a toss of her head. "Child," she said, in Court Safavian, "I protected you when you were no taller than a newly hatched zahhak. You think I need rewards now?"

"You deserve them, Ketevani," I told her, remembering how much nicer she'd been to me than Sikander, though I supposed even that old man had now shown he could come around eventually. "For then and for today."

"Well, let's worry about that once Karim and his father are dead," Tamara suggested, with such fervor in her voice that I arched an eyebrow in her direction. "It wasn't just your letter, Razia. We heard about it soon after it happened. It was court gossip. Haider was furious, wanted to fly out to Nizam then and there, but it was impossible, of course. His father wasn't going to let him meddle with the crown prince of Nizam. But now we have a chance to set things right, and that's what we're here to do." She bit her lip. "We never should have let you leave Tavrezh."

"That wasn't your decision," I reminded her. God knew I hadn't wanted to leave either.

"All the same, we're here now." She put her hand on my shoulder and gave it a gentle squeeze.

"And you're going to roast in that hat," Sakshi warned, having ridden over on Ragini's back. Her Court Safavian was a bit rusty, as she'd only really used it during our poetry recital lessons, but I thought it was passable for a girl who had been born on a farm.

"And who might this be?" Tamara asked.

"Sakshi is my elder sister," I told her. "From the dera in Bikampur. She's saved my life more than once, and she's the finest musician you'll ever meet."

Tamara offered Sakshi the smile that had won me over so thoroughly in my time in the Safavian court in Tavrezh. "If she's your little sister too, then we must be family."

"In that case, welcome to our home, sister," Sakshi replied. "I'd offer you tea and snacks, but our youngest sister is being held hostage in Ahura, and it will be up to us to rescue her."

Tamara's eyes widened, and she looked to me for confirmation. "This is true?"

"It is," I said.

She sighed and shook her head. "Razia, there's a lot of zahhaks in Ahura. Haider said there were at least twenty, maybe more."

I frowned. Twenty was more than I'd expected, but it changed nothing. I had to get Lakshmi back. I opened my mouth to say as much, but just then I caught sight of eight zahhaks fluttering to the ground about fifty paces away—six fire and two thunder. I recognized the two zahhaks in the lead at once. The thunder zahhak was Roshanak, which meant that the tall, broad-shouldered prince riding in her saddle was Haider. But the fire zahhak beside her was Padmini. I'd have known that proud face anywhere.

I ran to them, heedless of how tired I already was, how shattered my body felt from the falls and the fighting. The only thing that mattered was that Arjun was here.

CHAPTER 26

Arjun was just sliding down from the saddle when I hit him like a cannonball, knocking him back a pace as I threw my arms against his neck and pressed my body close to his.

"I'm so glad you're here, my prince!" I gasped out, but those were the only words I could think to say, because the emotions I was feeling were like a pure physical need that defied the usual descriptors. To say that I'd missed him would have elided the disgust at Karim's caresses, the despair I'd felt each night wondering if I'd ever see Arjun again. But now he was here. Whatever else happened, I wouldn't lose him too.

Arjun's strong arms wrapped me up so tightly that they pulled my feet free of the ground. He pressed his forehead against mine so hard it hurt. "I'm here," he whispered, as if to assure himself of that fact as much as me. "I'm here. And I'm never leaving you again." He let go of my body to take my cheeks in his hands, tilting my face up so that we were staring right into each other's eyes. "I promise."

He leaned in and kissed me then, our lips meeting with an urgent pressure in spite of the hundreds of people gathered around us. A few of the men chuckled, but their laughter reminded me that Arjun didn't know what was coming next.

I pulled away suddenly, and the wounded look that brought to his face tugged on my heartstrings. I placed my hand on his cheek, taking comfort from its warmth, from the roughness of his whiskers scratching my palm. "My prince, this isn't over yet. Karim has Lakshmi in Ahura."

I expected to see shock or worry flicker across his face, but instead his eyes narrowed into an expression of hot rage. "Then we go to Ahura, and we get her back."

His determination lit a fire in my heart. This was what I'd been missing these last few weeks—a man who was truly my partner in all things, who shared my loves and my fears, my joys and my sorrows—and most importantly, my battles.

"Getting into Ahura isn't going to be easy," a man's voice warned, from just a pace or two to my right.

My eyes had only been for Arjun, but now I looked and saw a grown man who had, until that moment, still been a lanky boy in my mind's eye. Hard muscle had filled out arms and legs that had once been all pointy knees and elbows. His jaw had grown strong and square, and his smooth cheeks were now covered in thick copper whiskers, the color a vibrant red that bordered on orange, like an old maulvi who used henna to dye his hair and beard. Prince Haider of Safavia had his father's sharp, dark eyes, and much of that man's strength and bearing. If I hadn't known that he'd come all this way for me, I'd have been worried that he'd changed in his mind and his heart as much as in his body.

"Your highness," I said, keenly aware that I must have looked like some beggar girl off the streets in my frayed and soiled shalwar kameez, with my dirty face and sweat-stained hair, "I'll never be able to thank you enough for coming to me in my time of need."

Haider crushed me against the hard cobalt scales of his zahhak armor, the embrace momentarily startling me into silence. "I'd never have left my little sister with a man like Karim."

"Then you know why I must go to Ahura," I replied. "Lakshmi is eleven. She's the same age I was when . . ." My voice caught in my throat as fear and rage rose up to close off my windpipe. The thought of Karim touching her . . . I just couldn't bear it. It made me squeeze my fists with an impotent rage that needed to find an outlet or I thought I might explode.

"We'll get her," Arjun assured me, his warm hand landing on my shoulder. The strength I felt in his fingers helped me to relax a little. With Arjun here, and Haider, and Tamara, and Hina, and Saskshi too, we would be able to save her.

"Then we should move," I said. "There's not much time. It's an eight-hour flight to Ahura, and if we don't leave now, then we won't make it before sunrise, I don't think."

"With thunder zahhaks, flying flat-out, we can make it in six," Haider corrected. "I can lead you there. Ahura was a Safavian island until recently, after all."

"Then lead on, your highness," I replied, nodding to Roshanak, the thunder zahhak who had been staring at me the whole time, waiting for me to pet her, no doubt wondering why I was spending so much of my time lavishing my attention on human men.

I was surprised when Haider shook his head. "We can't just go flying in there. I left it earlier today, having watched to see what forces Ahmed Shah could bring to bear, and the news isn't good. He has at least a dozen fire zahhaks from Jesera in addition to the dozen or so acid zahhaks."

"Twenty-four?" Tamara gasped, having stood by listening this whole time. "There's no way we could defeat so many, Razia, and he would chase after you."

"If we can't defeat them, then we're all dead," Sakshi reminded her. "Razia killed Karim's mother with a cannon. We captured their fortresses. They won't let this stand. Lakshmi will be executed and Sikander too, and then we'll all be next. We have no choice but to fight, whatever the odds."

Hina sighed, having stood by with her Zindhi comrades, listening to all this. "If only our river zahhaks had breath like a thunder zahhak or a fire zahhak, we'd have them outnumbered."

"Maybe we can," I said, the plan having formed in my mind the moment I saw Sunil Kalani shooting arrows at the Mahisagari guardsmen from his animal's back.

"What do you mean?" Hina asked.

"It's nonsense," Sunil Kalani muttered. "She's not a sorceress."

"It's not nonsense!" boomed a deep voice standing near the fire zahhaks. We all looked over to see Udai Agnivansha, maharaja of Bikampur, striding toward us. "It means the girl has a plan, fool! And when Razia Khanum has a plan, you listen."

My cheeks burned, but I couldn't suppress a smile all the same, my heart swelling with pride. I bowed my head. "Thank you for coming to me in my time of need, your majesty."

"You're family," he replied, putting a big, weather-beaten hand on my shoulder. "Now, what's this plan of yours to gift a fire zahhak's breath to a river zahhak?"

"It's right there, your majesty," I replied, nodding to one of the swivel guns that was leaning up against a tree, its barrel cast to resemble the neck and head of a fire zahhak, its beak yawning wide to spew flames. "Those swivel guns can be reloaded from the breech, they weigh less than Lakshmi or Nuri, and Hina says that a river zahhak can fly with a small passenger. So, instead of passengers, what if we put those cannons on the fronts of the river zahhaks' saddles?"

Hina's hazel eyes went wide with wonder. "That might work . . ."

But Sunil Kalani shook his head. "You'd never hit anything with it, your majesty. Combat in the air happens too quickly. We've tried it with our rifles for years. We know it doesn't work."

"But the cannon is different, Sunil," Hina told him. "It shoots a spray of musket balls, a pattern the size of a man. You don't have to aim exactly—if you just point it in the right direction, a whole swath of sky will be filled with a pound of lead."

"But you can't fly and aim at the same time," Sunil protested. "We've tried this!"

"Sunil is right, your majesty," Sanghar agreed, though he sounded reluctant to admit it. "You'd never be able to maneuver against the enemy and draw a bead on them, especially not with something as heavy as a cannon."

"So we don't let it move," I said, drawing confused looks. Of course they were confused, they'd never flown thunder zahhaks or fire zahhaks before, they didn't understand how it worked.

Sakshi did. She exclaimed, "Of course! You treat it just like a thunder zahhak!"

Hina cocked her head, surprised that Sakshi could see what she didn't, despite her many more years of experience on the back of a zahhak. "I don't understand . . ."

"When you dogfight with a zahhak, you don't aim their neck to shoot at an enemy, you aim the whole zahhak," I explained. "You fly at the enemy and only when you're pointed at them do you shoot. If you put the cannon in a fixed position, so that it always shot its pattern straight ahead, say at a distance of a hundred yards in front of your zahhak's nose, then all you would have to do is point the zahhak at your opponent and pull the trigger."

Hina, Sanghar, and Sunil all stared at one another, mulling that over. It was Hina who asked, "Well?"

Sunil shrugged, but Sanghar said, "It could work, your majesty."

"Well, there's one way to find out," Hina declared. She walked over to the cannon, picked it up, and brought it to her zahhak. When nobody else moved, she snapped, "Well, don't just stand there, help me get this thing mounted properly!"

While dozens of Zindhi men and women converged on Sakina to help attach the cannon to the saddle, Haider said, "That's clever, Razia, but even if it does work, that doesn't solve all of our problems. Ahura is a fortress, it's crawling with Mahisagari soldiers, and the bulk of their fleet is in its harbor. How do you expect to get in and find your sister?"

"I sent Sikander with her, and I ordered him to hang an ajrak dupatta from the window after nightfall to mark the room she's in," I replied. "I'll fly to the fortress, land on the roof, and climb down to her window."

"And how will you get back to the roof?" Tamara wondered, scrunching up her nose.

"Lakshmi and I will climb the walls. We'll leave a rope for Sikander. He's old, but he's strong; he should be able to manage."

"Climb the walls?" Haider's eyes widened, and he looked from Arjun to Udai to Sakshi, seeming totally surprised that none of them saw fit to comment on the outlandishness of that plan. He shook his head. "Little sister, someday you're going to have to tell me all that you've accomplished since you left Safavia."

"Someday soon I will, your highness," I replied. "But we don't have that much time tonight."

"We don't," Sakshi agreed. "I'll go find your climbing shoes. You're tired, you'll need them. I'm sure Lady Asma has them in her quarters."

"See if you can find my katars too," I suggested. "Karim and his father took them from me."

"I'll have a look around," she promised. She motioned for a squad of Zindhi soldiers to follow her as an escort, and they obeyed so quickly that it brought a smile to my face. We were going to make a princess of her yet.

"She really grew up on a farm?" Tamara asked in disbelief.

I nodded. "She's special."

"If all hijras can scale walls like they're stairs, fly zahhaks, and issue orders like that, then one wonders why you haven't conquered the world yet," one of the Registani fliers quipped.

"We're working on it," I shot back, drawing laughs from everyone around. It helped to ease some of the tension in my chest. The less I had to think about Lakshmi being stuck in Ahura, the better.

I decided to see how Hina was getting on. That would give me something useful to do. But as I approached Sakina, it didn't look like the Zindhis needed much assistance from me. They'd mounted the cannon on the zahhak's front saddle pommel, and they were working on giving it two positions: an upright position for when the zahhak was on the ground, since her neck was in the way of the barrel, and one that would be lowered to shoot once the animal was airborne. That was clever, as were the metal hooks they'd devised to hang extra mug-shaped breechblocks from the sides of the saddle for easy reloading. They'd even thought to add wide leather straps to the saddle itself to help absorb the shock of the cannon's recoil. Even now, old men with years of sailing experience were working hard with awls and strong canvas thread to sew the straps into place, their deft fingers moving so swiftly that it beggared belief.

"If we're going to truly test it, we'll need a target," Sunil was saying.

"What about a bedsheet?" I suggested.

"A bedsheet, your highness?" he asked, with a good deal less scorn in his voice than he'd shown me up till this moment.

"I'll take a bedsheet up on Sultana, flying in front of Hina, and I'll release it into the slipstream behind me as I make a hard turn. Once I'm clear, she shoots it. That'll test if she can hit something in the air or not, and it will give us a chance to see what the bullet scatter looks like on the cloth."

Sanghar shook his head, grinning. "Like holing an enemy's sail."

That got all of the Zindhis nodding together. I didn't know anything about naval combat, but it seemed to please them, so I said, "I suppose."

Hina quirked an eyebrow. "Could it be that there's something you don't know everything about?"

"I'll leave the matters of sailing in your capable hands, your majesty," I replied, bowing my head to her.

She grinned. "Sanghar, have one of your men fetch a white bedsheet. We have to test this quickly if we're going to save her highness's sister."

"Right away, your majesty," Sanghar agreed.

While they went to deal with that, I noticed that my fellow fliers had drifted over to watch Sakina's saddle be outfitted with a cannon and breechblocks. Arjun was scratching his chin, his brow furrowed. I recognized that expression.

"You have thoughts, my prince?" I asked him, wrapping my arms around one of his, taking strength from his warmth.

"Questions," he corrected, nodding to Sunil Kalani. "If you can carry passengers, then why not just have the passenger shooting a rifle at the enemy while the other person flies the zahhak?"

"We can't carry a grown man with a rifle," Sunil replied. He frowned at the reinforced saddle, with the weight of the cannon and five extra breechblocks. "Even this much weight is pushing our luck, and it's not as heavy as you are, your highness."

"But if you could carry a passenger with a weapon, he can shoot just fine," Arjun pressed.

"She can, your highness," Hina agreed, and I noticed how she'd feminized the sentence. "Sometimes I would go hunting with my brother on the back of his zahhak when I was little. He'd let me shoot gazelles while he handled the flying. They were moving targets, and not easy to hit, but I was a good shot."

"We do the same thing in Registan for sport," Udai agreed.

"How many of these cannons do you have?" Arjun asked, nodding to the gun in question.

"With us?" Sanghar shrugged. "Each of my boats carried a dozen. So nearly fifty."

"As did mine," Sunil added. "And my count was closer to two hundred. More than enough to outfit all of our zahhaks."

"What are you thinking, my prince?" I asked him, though I thought I saw where his mind was going, and I thought it was brilliant.

"You haven't figured it out yet?" he teased.

"I didn't want to steal your thunder," I replied.

"No, it wouldn't do to repeat yourself," he agreed, earning an eye roll from me. "But it occurred to me that the great weakness of fire zahhaks is their tremendous strength and size."

Sunil arched an eyebrow at that. "Size and strength are to be considered weaknesses?"

"In the air they can be," he said. "A fire zahhak can't turn as tightly as a thunder zahhak, can't climb as swiftly. In a one-on-one fight, a fire zahhak almost always loses to a thunder zahhak or an acid zahhak if the odds are even. They're tremendous animals for attacking fortresses, fleets, and armies, but in aerial combat they are second-tier."

"It's true," Udai agreed. "Much as we love our animals, and take great pride in them, they are always at risk when facing lighter, faster zahhaks in the air."

Haider added his voice to the mix. "In Safavia we're blessed to have both thunder zahhaks and fire zahhaks, but the fire zahhaks are used primarily to attack our enemies on the ground, while the thunder zahhaks protect them in the air. Even against the best fire zahhak flier, Roshanak and I can get around on their tail feathers in two turns at most. Can't we, girl?" He gave the thunder zahhak in question a very fond pat.

"So, what if getting on our tail feathers was just as dangerous as flying in front of us?" Arjun asked, gesturing to the cannon. "What if we used double saddles with a gunner facing backward, using the swivel mount to let him take careful aim? A river zahhak can't carry so much weight, but a fire zahhak could."

"I wouldn't want to line up a shot behind a fire zahhak if I had that thing pointed at my face," Tamara murmured, glancing to Haider for his thoughts.

Haider was nodding right along with her. "It wouldn't have the range of a thunder zahhak's lightning, but acid zahhaks have to get closer, and so do ice zahhaks. A cannon that could shoot a hundred yards could hit them just as easily as they could hit you . . ."

"That would give us a huge advantage in the fight to come," I allowed, "but how long would it take to modify your saddles?"

"We flew with double saddles in case we needed to get you and your sisters out of the palace," Arjun said, gesturing to Padmini, who wore the double saddle he and I had ridden together so many times before. "With some sharp knives and some of these Zindhi sailors and their sewing skills, we could get it done in a hurry."

I frowned. I would need Padmini to get Lakshmi out of Ahura, and at least one more animal for Sikander. There was no way we could get them into the zahhak stables to claim their mounts, not with guards crawling all over the place. If I waited to outfit these saddles, and the sun came up before I could get to Lakshmi . . .

"My prince, if this must be done, it must be done right this instant. Lakshmi's life depends on it."

"Then we'll get to work immediately," he said, resting his hands on my shoulders and rubbing them gently. "While you're testing Hina's cannon, we'll have all six of our saddles modified. We already know it will work, because every nobleman in Registan has hunted from a double saddle before. We just never had these small ship-mounted cannons, because we don't have any water."

"If this works, Razia, it could change the whole balance of power in the world," Haider said. "There are so many zahhaks all across the continent without breath. Once word of this gets out, kingdoms will be desperate to arm them."

"If it works, then Jama Hina will be one of the world's great queens," I agreed, noting the looks of shock I received from the Zindhis gathered around me. But Hina didn't look surprised.

"You will always have a home here, your highness," she assured me.

"I know," I said, but this wasn't the time for that conversation. When Ahmed and Karim were dead, we could talk about Zindh and its freedom, but until then it was premature. I left everyone to their work, instead going to collect Sultana, to make certain that she was ready to fly.

I found her lying on the surface of one of the lotus ponds, cuddled up against Natia. The bigger ice zahhak had used her breath to freeze the water solid, and now Ragini and some of the river zahhaks were testing the cold, hard surface with their noses, attracted to the soothing cold on a hot desert night, but most of them having never seen ice before.

"The poor thing gets hot quickly in this climate," Tamara lamented, and I could have said the same thing about her. Though she'd doffed her fur hat, sweat had plastered her red hair to the top of her head and was pouring in rivers down her face. Her cheeks were bright red, and she had unbuttoned her undergown down to the tops of her breasts in an effort to keep cool, though it didn't seem to be working.

"You get used to it," I assured her.

Tamara shook her head. "No, I think we belong in the mountains." She lay down on the ice beside her zahhak, shivering and sighing with relief.

"It's a shame Natia isn't a little bigger; you could throw a cannon on her too," Haider said, coming up behind us.

Tamara shrugged in response to that. "Ice zahhaks may not have the size of fire zahhaks, nor the speed of thunder zahhaks, but they do everything well. And they're fiercest on the ground." She reached up and petted the end of Natia's enormous hooked beak for emphasis. It was designed for crunching through frozen prey and tearing giant chunks off of them. I shuddered to think what it would do to soldiers on the ground. River zahhaks had delicate snouts in comparison, and even they were capable of biting grown men clean in half.

"I've missed the two of you terribly," I told them, now that we had a moment alone together.

"Once all this is over, you'll have to visit my summer palace in Tamtra," Tamara offered. "I always wanted to show you the waterfalls, but they wouldn't let you leave Safavia. Now you can go where you please."

"If I can convince my father not to execute me for this," I muttered.

"We won't let him do that," Haider declared, placing his firm hand on my shoulder. "We grew up together, Razia, and I've always considered you the younger sister I never had. I promise you that I won't let your father hurt you."

"You really think Safavia would go to war for me?" I shook my head to show him how likely I thought that was.

"I think once this is over, you'll have a stronger force of zahhaks than any subahdar in Zindh," he replied. "And your father would be a fool to move against you then."

"I hope you're right," I whispered, but I wasn't as sure as he was. My father had seemed to want to protect me from Karim, at least a little, but when push came to shove, he'd let me be married off against my will to my rapist. How could I trust him not to hurt me when he was willing to do something like that?

"Razia!" Hina called, jarring me from my thoughts.

I turned and saw her riding toward me on Sakina's back, the cannon barrel pointed skyward to keep clear of the zahhak's long, sinuous neck. That neck would be held horizontal in flight, allowing the barrel to come down and face forward. The upper position would also make it easier to quickly reach the breechblock for reloading. At least I hoped it would. Whether a rider could really focus on flying and shooting a cannon at the same time remained to be seen. For that matter, I still wasn't certain they'd even be able to get off the ground when carrying so much extra weight.

"Do you think she'll be able to fly with all that?" I asked.

"She'll get in the air," Hina assured me. She tossed me a balled-up bedsheet, which I caught easily enough. It was big, but still scarcely a quarter of the size of a zahhak's wing area. That would make it a good test. If she could hit this, she could definitely hit an enemy flier.

I saw the way Hina's celas had gathered to watch with their river zahhaks at their sides. Sunil's men were pressed in close too, as were Sanghar's fliers. The look of desperate hope on the face of every Zindhi in the courtyard wasn't lost on me. For centuries, they had been conquered by outsiders because their zahhaks lacked breath. But if this worked, then they might for once be able to choose their own destiny. I didn't know what that meant for me, for my relationship with my father, for my future, but I knew that it was the right thing to do.

"Sultana, we have to fly now," I told my zahhak, who had fallen asleep beside her old friend. She opened one groggy eyelid, her emerald eye finding me at once, and when she saw that I was beckoning her, she perked right up. With a yawn that exposed teeth bigger than my hands, she sank her wing claws into the ice and levered herself up with practiced ease, not slipping despite the slick surface. She stretched, shook out her wings and her tail, and then padded over to me with a prance in her step, ready to get to work.

"That's my girl," I told her, giving her a kiss on the nose before climbing into the saddle and strapping myself in. I petted her neck scales a few times, and then took up the reins and nodded to Hina to let her know that I was ready.

"After you, your highness," Hina said, sweeping her hand toward the clearest path across the courtyard, one that was long enough to let a zahhak run up to speed before bounding her way into the air.

"Let's go, Sultana," I said, giving her the forward pressure on my seat to get her moving forward, tapping her neck gently with my heels to let her know it was time to take off.

She needed no more urging than that. With a surge of her powerful wing muscles, she threw herself into a headlong gallop down the path, taking several long bounds before springing up, beating her wings, and kicking off with her crane-like rear legs. It was a moment of violent action, followed by a stillness that nothing else in the world could rival as we began to fly.

She beat her wings hard, jarring me in my seat as we climbed to get over the walls of the palace; but soon they were far below us as we made a lazy, spiraling left-hand turn through the night sky.

How I had missed this. Being kept away from Sultana had been one of the worst parts of being engaged to Karim. It had been like running away from home all over again. But now we were reunited once more, and after I won this battle, we'd never be separated again, I would make sure of it.

I twisted in my seat to see how Hina was getting on. Sakina's takeoff run was longer than usual, but her bigger wings and her lighter body helped to compensate for the weight of the cannon, and I was surprised how easily she got herself into the air. She looked less buoyant than usual, and I knew that to some degree her performance would be impaired by the weight and drag of the gun and its breechblocks, but she was still an exquisitely maneuverable animal, thanks to that forked tail of hers and those pointed wings, which were broader than my Sultana's, giving them even more lift.

I leveled off and let Hina catch up, taking a position directly behind me. I knew this was a test of an idea, that I wasn't in any real danger, but still my heart skipped a beat when that cannon lowered into position, the muzzle pointed right at my back, the match cord glowing bright yellow thanks to the force of the slipstream blowing on it and making it even hotter than it would have been otherwise. It was plain Sultana was nervous too, because she kept sneaking glances behind her at Hina, and at me. She made a chittering noise, which I knew from long experience was her way of saying, "Hey! Are you going to do something about that?"

"It's all right, girl, it's just a test," I told her. I picked up my trumpet from the saddle and blasted out a simple note, since I wasn't sure if Hina knew the proper calls for Nizami fliers.

She responded with two blasts on her own trumpet to let me know that she was ready.

"All right," I muttered. "Here goes nothing." I took up the bedsheet, holding it by one corner of the fabric, letting the rest of it snap in the breeze like an enormous flag billowing up behind us. Once I was sure it would catch enough air to make for a reasonable target, I let it go and jerked hard left and down, leaning my body in that direction, telling Sultana to dive and turn with everything she had.

Her cobalt neck scales flared wide like the hood of a cobra as her wings rolled and her tail feathers lifted up. A weight settled upon my neck and shoulders, crushing down on my spine, forcing the blood from my eyes as we dropped into a tight, spiraling dive. All the while, I looked up, keeping my eyes on the cloth, which was fluttering in the breeze, spread wide, seeming to hover in space.

The boom of the cannon wasn't nearly as deafening in the open air as it had been in the confines of the palace corridors, but the smoke and fire billowing out of the muzzle of the cannon resembled the real flames of a fire zahhak to some degree, and it was close enough to Sakina's head that in the darkness, it almost looked to my eyes like the zahhak had been shooting the fire from her own mouth.

The cloth suddenly bunched up, as if it had a string tied to it and someone had jerked hard on it. With less surface area, it began to fall a bit faster, though it was still quite slow, and it was easy enough to keep below it.

Evidently, Hina had the same thought, because she had at once pitched up into a climbing turn, all the while yanking the smoking breechblock from the back of the cannon, hanging it on one of the saddle hooks, and slamming a second home. She lowered the cannon just as she reached the apex of her climb, Sakina describing a diagonal loop through the sky that put her nose right back on the cloth, but coming from the opposite direction.

The cannon barked a second time, and the bunched-up cloth shuddered and twisted and started to fall even faster, but Hina wasn't done yet. She jerked the breechblock free as Sakina pitched up into yet another diagonal loop. This time, though, the cloth was falling fast enough that by the time Hina got the cannon ready again, they were pointing almost straight down at the palace courtyard, and rather than risk shooting and hitting our comrades accidentally, she ordered Sakina to tuck in her wings, and they dove so swiftly that Hina was able to reach out and snatch the cloth out of the air an instant before Sakina snapped her wings wide once more, pulling up sharply to save them from plowing into the paving stones at two hundred miles per hour.

My heart was thumping away in my chest. Hina was whooping from the back of her zahhak. Far below us, hundreds of Zindhi men and women were cheering. There could be no doubt at all. It worked. Now we just had to hope that they could get the saddles ready in time to stand against Ahmed Shah and his zahhaks, and I had to hope that there was enough darkness left to save my baby sister.

CHAPTER 27

Flying over the ocean at night requires nerves of steel. Even with a mostly full moon and a cloudless sky, the water beneath me was pitch black. We had long since lost sight of the coast. If not for Haider's assurance that he could lead us to Ahura without getting us lost over the ocean, I never would have taken such a risk as flying directly. But this saved us at least two hours, and we were short on time as it was. I prayed to God it would be enough.

Behind me, Padmini was struggling to keep up, using Sultana's wake to help give her the lift she needed to stay aloft. Her double saddle had been cut in half, with the front put in the back so that it faced in the opposite direction, allowing the flier and the gunner to share the same high backrest. One of the bronze cannons was mounted directly in front of the rear-facing seat, which also had extra breechblocks hanging from hooks, just like Sakina's saddle had. The same modification had been made on the saddles of the rest of the Registani fire zahhaks, and four of the six of them carried the extra weight of men in their new rear gunner seats. They were keeping close formation to reduce the strain of flying at such an unnaturally high speed.

To my left and right were five thunder zahhaks, ridden by Haider and his wingman, my sister Sakshi, and my two Nizami guardsmen, who had survived the battle because Asma had imprisoned them in an out-of-the-way place. But they were free now and eager to fly against the Mahisagaris for the sake of honor. And just off their wings were Tamara and Ketevani riding on their ice zahhaks, which had an easier time keeping up with thunder zahhaks than the Registani fire zahhaks did.

Fourteen zahhaks was quite the aerial armada, but if Haider's reports were accurate, we'd still be badly outnumbered when the time came to fight. I'd given orders to my Zindhi fliers to meet us on the coast of Safavia due north of Ahura, where there were high cliffs that would be easy to spot from the air. But I hadn't had time to wait for them to outfit all of their thirty-two zahhaks with cannons. The men and women had been working rapidly, at least half a dozen working on each saddle to make the process go faster, but it took time that Lakshmi simply didn't have. If we were lucky, they would get to the coast in time to help us. If we weren't . . . well, then I was sure I would think of something.

The plan was simple. While the other zahhaks provided high cover to keep the Mahisagaris from pursuing us, Arjun, Udai, and I would land our zahhaks on top of the fortress, which Haider had assured me was built like a single giant tower, in the Firangi style. We'd probably have to kill a few guards, but Sultana and Padmini could do that quickly and quietly enough if we took them by surprise. Then I would tie off a rope to the battlements, rappel down to Lakshmi's window, get inside, wake her up, and she would climb with me while Sikander used the rope. They would get in the gunner positions in the saddles, and we would all fly together north toward Safavia to rendezvous with the river zahhaks from Kadiro.

It was a strong plan, I thought. If Sikander marked the window like I'd ordered him to do, then I would know just where to go. And with the rope speeding things along, I thought we could probably be in and out of the fortress in less than ten minutes. If we were lucky, Karim and Ahmed wouldn't even realize what we'd done until morning, and by then we would be long gone, on our way back to Kadiro. Then we could have a battle at our leisure, maybe even sending a message to my father for his support. If it was a choice between joining Mahisagar against me, or joining me against them, I thought he would pick me. At least I prayed that he would.

But that was putting the cart before the horse. I had to get Lakshmi out. That was the main thing. I just hoped that I wasn't too late, that Karim hadn't hurt her already. I thought Sikander could keep her safe, but he was one man, and he'd be surrounded by loyal Mahisagari men. If Karim wanted to hurt Lakshmi, he could, and there wasn't much Sikander could do to stop it. That thought, more than anything, had me keeping a white-knuckle grip on Sultana's reins as we soared over miles and miles of perfect darkness.

"Just like old times, eh?" Haider asked me as he glanced across the gulf between us, his voice dim from the roar of the slipstream, but audible nonetheless. It was remarkable how well you could hear another person in the air when there were no walls or trees to block the sound.

"Oh? I don't seem to recall us assaulting any fortresses when we were children, your highness," I replied.

"You don't remember our assault on Zahedan?" He sounded surprised, and not a little wounded at that.

"That was a game, your highness," I reminded him, because I did remember.

"It was a competition, and we won," he replied. "You had a head for strategy even then."

"Is that why you picked me for your team when nobody else would?" I asked.

"One of the reasons," he allowed. "You were also the best zahhak flier I'd ever seen. The other boys wouldn't admit that, because they didn't want to believe that a girl could do anything they couldn't, and you acted like a girl, even when we were in public."

I shrugged. "Couldn't be helped."

"No," he agreed, "it couldn't. But my point is that your little sister is in good hands with you planning her rescue. If I were in need of rescuing, I couldn't imagine anyone else I'd rather have coming to my aid."

That brought a warm glow to my heart in spite of all the uncertainty. "If you ever do need me, Haider, I'll be there for you, as you have always been for me."

"I know. You think I came here to help you? This is an investment in my future." He flashed me a mischievous grin, and I rolled my eyes in response, but it felt good for somebody to tell a joke, because I thought my chest was going to explode from the fear I was feeling, not knowing what had become of Lakshmi. I would have clutched at anything to take my mind off of that, even if it was only for an instant.

An instant was all the reprieve I got, because a moment later I spotted four orange lights glowing on the horizon, and their number increased steadily with each passing second, until they resolved into the windows of a tall tower of black volcanic stone, the white lime mortar providing an outline to what would have otherwise been nothing more than an inky shadow illuminated by torchlight.

I took a deep breath and gritted my teeth. This was it. I had to find the ajrak cloth waving from one of those windows, and then I had to get to Lakshmi. Everything depended on it. I glanced to Haider. "You'll keep us covered?"

"No zahhak will get within a mile of your little sister, you have my word on that, Razia."

I nodded, and after that fear robbed me of my voice. It was everything I could do to steer Sultana straight at the tower, the pressure of my hips in my seat urging her onward with every last ounce of speed. I was frantically scanning the windows for some sign of an ajrak cloth. It should have been bright enough for me to spot, and it was long, it would be waving in the sea breeze. Why couldn't I see it?

A thought occurred to me then that made my insides churn. What if Sikander hadn't been able to do it? What if he'd been imprisoned, or killed? Or what if the cloth had been spotted by the Mahisagaris, and they'd punished them for it? What if I was already too late to save Lakshmi from the fate I had suffered at Karim's hands six years before?

"Razia!" Haider called. He was pointing ahead of him. "Second light down from the top on the left!"

My eyes snapped to the spot he'd named and I breathed a huge sigh of relief. There it was, an ajrak cloth floating in the breeze. I wasn't too late. Sikander had done as I'd asked. Lakshmi was in that room, and I was going to get her out of it no matter what.

I leaned low to let Sultana fly that much faster, snapping the reins, letting her know that if there had ever been a time in her life to fly swiftly, this was it. Her wings beat a blur on either side of me, and we rocketed past Roshanak, diving toward the top of the tower. I really should have done a proper reconnaissance, should have waited to count the guards, but I had plenty of time to spot them up there if there were any. I thought most of them would be on the ramparts lower down.

We were screaming out of the sky at such a tremendous speed that without my flying goggles, I'd have been blinded by the wind tearing past me. As it was, I was sure that we'd be invisible to whatever sentries the Mahisagaris had placed around the fortress. The first warning they got of our arrival would be a zahhak slamming into them, crushing them into paste.

As it happened, there were two men on the roof of the fortress, patrolling lazily, each man staying on the opposite side of the top of the square tower from the other. I aimed for the man nearest to me, lining him up so that Sultana could take his head off and keep flying directly into the second man. She knew what I wanted. Her maw gaped, and the next thing I knew there was a sharp impact, and blood spurted past me, and then there was a second, harder impact, and we were soaring skyward, half of a man hanging from Sultana's tightly closed mouth.

We wheeled back toward the tower and landed atop it at about the same moment that Padmini came fluttering down with Arjun, and Udai joined him with his zahhak a second later. Sultana spit out the half-eaten Mahisagari guardsman, covered in blood and slime, and then looked back at me, half grinning, her emerald eyes inquiring as to whether or not she'd done a good job.

"You're the best girl," I told her, giving her pats on her neck, but only for a moment before my worries for Lakshmi consumed me again. I slid out of the saddle, taking the rope I'd brought with me. I rushed to the ramparts, making sure that I picked the right spot, directly above the window with the ajrak dupatta hanging from it, and then I set about tying the rope off on one of the tall merlons of black volcanic stone, wrapping it tightly and knotting it securely. Sikander's life would depend on this rope, and maybe mine and Lakshmi's too. It couldn't fail.

When I was finished, I moved to throw myself over the side of the wall and rappel down to get my sister, but Arjun stopped me with strong arms around my waist. He leaned in close, kissed me on the cheek, and whispered, "I'll be right here waiting. You get your sister. I love you."

"I love you too, my prince," I replied, and I kissed him back, pressing my lips to his for a single moment before rushing over the wall to get Lakshmi back. Until she was safe, I couldn't rest, couldn't focus on anything else. The thought that she was hurt, that Karim had raped her or beaten her or killed her, was so overwhelming that it consumed every ounce of my attention.

I had tied the rope off so that it had two ends dangling free, reaching just below Lakshmi's window. I now wrapped them around myself, forming a makeshift seat for my hips, holding the extra rope in my left hand, letting my right hand hold the part attached to the stonework. And then I sat down over the edge of the wall, kicked off, and started moving down as quickly as I could without slicing through my own legs with the burning friction of the rope.

It took no time at all to get to Lakshmi's window, since it was so close to the top of the tower, but I hung above it for a moment and listened carefully. There was a chance that my plan had been betrayed, that enemies might be lurking inside. I didn't want to risk getting killed now; then Lakshmi really would have no hope left at all.

What I heard broke my heart. Crying. She was sniffling and crying. Had Karim hurt her? I was going to kill the bastard!

I let loose the rope, unwinding it from my legs, holding on with both hands, and then I lowered myself, swinging at the same time, bursting feet-first through the window, landing easily on the stone floor in the middle of a small bedchamber, my katars whisking from their scabbards. I pointed my bladed fists at the first man I saw, and was startled to find Sikander sitting beside Viputeshwar, Sultan Ahmed's chamberlain, in tall-backed chairs, the pair of them sobbing like little girls. Or at least they had been, until I had burst in on them. Now they were rushing to stand and draw their swords.

"Sikander?" I gasped.

"Your highness!" he exclaimed, forgetting all about his sword as he came forward and embraced me tightly. "I'm so glad you're safe!"

I couldn't hug him back because I was holding my katars, but I was too confused to embrace him anyway. "Have you been crying?"

"What?" He let me go and frantically wiped at his face. "I . . ."

"It's my doing, your highness," said Viputeshwar, though his eyes were red and puffy and he had tracks of tears running down his dark, wrinkled cheeks and into his white beard. "Sikander and I were having a talk about you."

"About me?" I frowned, wondering what he meant by that, and wondering what he was doing here in Lakshmi's bedchamber in Ahura, but none of that really mattered. What mattered was getting her out before someone noticed us. I shook my head. "Well, whatever conversation you were having, it's over now. We're leaving, and if you try to stop us, I'll kill you."

"Your highness!" Sikander exclaimed, suddenly horrified at the thought of killing a man. I wondered what had happened to the man, if perhaps he was an impostor.

Viputeshwar held up a hand for calm. "Sikander was telling me what Karim did to you six years ago. I didn't know. I'm so sorry."

"Is that your way of saying that you're with us?" I asked.

"If you'll have me, your highness," he replied, bowing deeply from the waist.

"Once Karim and Ahmed have joined Lady Asma in the grave, we'll talk about it," I assured him.

Sikander's eyes widened. "She's dead?"

"She is," I affirmed. "And Kadiro is ours."

"How?" he wondered.

"There will be time to tell you later," I said, and I would tolerate no more distractions then, because Lakshmi was still sleeping soundly in her bed, looking so peaceful. She was safe. God, I would give Sikander such rewards for keeping Karim away from her if we all survived this.

I sat on the bed beside her and stroked her hair gently, knowing that would wake her up, but it wouldn't scare her. Sure enough, she cracked an eye open and caught sight of me, her vision a bit dazed at first, but after a second she sat upright and threw her arms around my neck. "Akka!"

"Shh . . ." I whispered. "Karim can't know I'm here. We have to leave now, okay?"

"Is Sikander coming with us?" she asked.

"He is," I agreed.

"Good." She smiled, and I wondered at that. But I supposed he'd kept her safe in a scary new place. He'd protected her. He hadn't beaten her or yelled at her. He'd been the bodyguard that he never was for me.

"We're going to have to climb out," I whispered. "Arjun is waiting up there with Padmini to take you with him."

"Prince Arjun is here?" She seemed thrilled by that for a moment, but then she frowned. "But what about Mohini?"

I took a deep breath, because this was the hard part. "We'll have to come back for Mohini."

Lakshmi shook her head. "No, Akka, we can't—"

I held a hand over her mouth, because she was shouting. I pulled her up against me tightly. "We can't shout. Prince Karim will kill us. His father will kill us. We have to be quiet, okay?"

I let go of her mouth when she nodded her agreement, but that didn't stop her from voicing her protest in quieter tones. "Okay, but I'm not leaving Mohini!"

"Lakshmi—" I began, but I was interrupted by Viputeshwar.

"If I may, your highness, I might have a solution," he said, keeping his voice soft and quiet.

I frowned. Viputeshwar had been kind to me, but he had raised both Karim and Ahmed from children. He was loyal to Mahisagar, and I had murdered his queen and admitted as much in front of him.

He seemed to sense my thoughts, because he said, "I know you don't think you can trust me, your highness, and I can't blame you, but I ask you to remember what I told you about my sister, remember how I felt then when I told you that story, and realize that Sikander just told me tonight what Karim did to you, what he has been doing to you."

My mind went back to that conversation, weeks ago in the palace of Rajkot, and I remembered the rage in his eyes, the anguish in his voice, and the strength in his arms when he had spoken of the client who had murdered his sister. The one he'd had butchered like a goat. I nodded then. Maybe I could trust him. "What is this solution of yours?"

"Lakshmi is a hostage here, it's true," he said, "but I am not, and neither is Sikander. Ahmed and Karim both believe that Sikander is committed to this alliance. I could take him to the stables on the pretense of caring for the zahhaks. No one will challenge us. We will take Mohini and Parisa, and we will fly them wherever you need them."

"The coast due north. There are cliffs."

"I know the place, your highness," Viputeshwar assured me.

"And you can fly an acid zahhak?" I asked.

"I can, your highness," he said. "And Lakshmi has already shown me Mohini. We've become acquainted. And Parisa will prevent me from being eaten if Sikander is there."

"Okay," I agreed. "The two of you get to the stables now. I'll get

Lakshmi to the roof. She can ride Padmini back to the cliffs, and then get Mohini back." I looked to Lakshmi. "All right?"

She bobbed her head. "Yes, Akka."

I sighed, glad to have that settled, because it meant we'd have two more zahhaks for the coming battle. "You two get moving. Stay safe. I'll get Lakshmi to the roof." To her, I said, "Put your climbing shoes on."

She hurried to do it while Viputeshwar smiled and shook his head ruefully, and Sikander just seemed confused. He bowed his head to me. "I feel like I don't know you at all, your highness."

"You don't," I agreed. "But if you get Parisa and you help me fight Karim and Ahmed, I'll give you the chance to learn as much about me as you like, Sikander."

"I would be honored, your highness." He hugged me again, like he had when I was little, and it broke my heart, but I tried not to show it. I had to stay strong. I had to get us out of this mess and then I could think about how I felt about things. Until then, I needed to keep focused on the mission, needed to get Lakshmi somewhere safe.

I hugged Sikander back and whispered, "I'll see you shortly." Then I let him go, and he and Viputeshwar stepped out of the room, closing the door firmly behind them.

"All right, sweetheart," I told Lakshmi, taking her hand and leading her to the window. "We're going to have to climb up to the roof. It's not far, but I want you to use the rope, so tie it around yourself the way your tutor taught you, okay?"

"Yeah, okay, Akka," she agreed, rolling her eyes, like she couldn't believe what a fuss I was making about having to climb a heavily defended watchtower in the dead of night under threat of almost certain death. I smiled. She was growing up.

She tied the ropes with as much aplomb as I had shown, and then stepped to the edge of the window, preparing to start her climb. But at that moment, I heard the metal handle of the door rattling against the stone wall, and I turned, expecting to see Sikander or Viputeshwar returning for something they had forgotten. Instead, I heard a very familiar voice saying, "Lakshmi, honey, are you asleep?" And Karim Shah stepped into the room, a familiar, hungry look in his dark eyes.

CHAPTER 28

Razia!" Karim gasped, his eyes going wide.

My katars were in my hands in an instant, my fists clenched tightly around their handles, rage in my heart. I'd been right. I'd been right the whole time. I looked over my shoulder to where Lakshmi was standing uncertainly on the ledge of the windowsill, and I said, "Lakshmi, sweetie, you need to climb. Akka will handle this."

Lakshmi nodded, and she started climbing. She knew that Karim wasn't her friend, had known it for a while now. As she disappeared up the tower, I watched Karim draw his sword from its scabbard, his lip curling with scorn.

"You think you can fight me?" he scoffed, puffing out his chest, as if to show me how much bigger and stronger he was. Not that he needed to. I was fully aware of how dangerous he was. His mistake was not knowing how dangerous I was.

"I killed your mother," I told him, because I knew that would unhinge him, that it would get in his head and make him sloppy. "I blew her away with a cannon. There's nothing left of her but sludge."

The stunned look on his face told me that he hadn't realized I'd taken Kadiro. He'd thought this was a desperate escape attempt, that I'd sneaked out of Kadiro in secret to get Lakshmi out of his clutches. Well, I seized the opportunity to land the first strike, and I punched straight at his hateful face with my katars. He barely managed to parry the punch with the hilt of his sword, but that left him open, and I punched for his chest with a strong left that he hadn't expected.

Karim twisted and staggered back, taking the punch as a slice that opened up a wide gash on his biceps, red blood spilling across his skin and staining his green sleeve dark brown. And then the little coward cried, "Guards!"

I punched again and again, driving him back toward the door, forcing him to frantically parry and stagger away from the razor-sharp points of my katars. In the tight confines of the room, I had every conceivable advantage with my two short weapons against his one longer one, and that advantage doubled when we reached the doorway, where he didn't have room to take a swing. But I wasn't trying to kill him. Oh, if I could, I would have, but I heard the footsteps in the hallway, and I knew my window for escape was closing fast. They'd be able to shoot me off the wall if I had to climb back up, rope or no rope. And the longer it took me to get away, the higher the odds that they'd saddle their zahhaks and attack. Even with the altitude disadvantage, our top cover couldn't stop all of them.

So I threw one last punch for Karim's neck to get a little space, and then I raced for the window as fast as my feet would carry me. He was stumbling back, so it took him a second to reverse direction, but then his long legs ate up ground faster than I'd thought they would. I was at the window, but with the katars in my hands there was no way to climb without throwing them down, and if I did that, I'd be helpless.

Karim kept his distance as guardsmen came rushing in, holding swords and shields. No toradars, that was a piece of luck. They must have thought they'd be worthless in such close confines. But even without muskets, they would cut me to pieces before I ever found my first foothold on the wall. I could see that now. There was no way out.

"Did you really kill my mother?" Karim growled, his whole body shaking with rage, his sword twitching from the tension in his fist.

I briefly considered lying, but I knew it wouldn't work, so I just smiled and said, "I did. And I enjoyed it. And Kadiro has been taken. All of your men are dead. Did you really think I would marry you? I'd rather die."

"Well, you'll get your wish," he assured me, leveling the point of his sword at my chest, though he was several feet too far away to thrust it home. "You can either surrender and die swiftly, or you can fight and die slowly. Your choice."

He wasn't wrong. I was going to die. I saw that now. This had been one desperate act too far. I had been too reckless. But I'd saved Lakshmi. Arjun would care for her like his own sister. Sikander would protect her. Hina would treat her like a little princess in a newly freed Zindh. They didn't need me anymore. They would be okay.

"Your choice, Razia," Karim growled, taking a small step forward, his men following his lead, cutting the distance just that little bit shorter. "Quick or slow, what's it going to be?"

I considered that for a moment, and then I realized that there was one last chance. One last hope. I stepped back, pressing myself up against the window, making sure that I was well positioned for what I was about to do, and then I sheathed my katars, noting Karim's triumphant grin. But before he could step forward to plunge his firangi through my heart, I said, "If I'm going to die today, Karim, then it's going to be on my terms—not yours." And I flung myself out the window.

CHAPTER 29

Sultana!" I shrieked at the top of my lungs as I tumbled backward out the window, snatching the rope and swinging along the side of the tower, kicking with my legs, running as far as I could before the rope went taut. I braced myself for what was coming.

"Sultana! Here, girl!" I cried as men began poking their heads out of the windows of the tower to see what was going on. The sun was just starting to peek above the horizon, and I saw the muzzles of rifles appear. I couldn't stay here any longer. I had to let go. So I kicked off hard, and I swung.

The wind roared in my ears and pulled at my clothes as I raced in a sweeping arc beside the tower, holding the rope with both hands, my legs dangling free below me. I accelerated, faster and faster, until the rope pulled me skyward once more, and I let go, the momentum carrying me clear of the tower, hurling me out into empty space. I screamed Sultana's name one last time out of sheer desperation, and then I spread my arms wide, bracing myself for the long plummet to the ground.

But the ground vanished, replaced by bright blue scales, and my arms went around a familiar neck, holding on for dear life as azure wings spread wide, catching the wind and pulling us higher and higher into the sky. I let loose a cry of sheer, panicked joy, heedless of the muskets shooting at us, knowing they didn't have a prayer of hitting us, but then Sultana beat her wings and nearly jostled me off her back, and I realized that if I was going to survive, I was going to have to find some way of getting into my saddle. The trouble was, if I loosened my grip on her scales at all, I was sure I was going to fall. But even I didn't have the grip strength to make it all the way to shore clinging to my zahhak's neck scales.

I chanced a look behind me at the saddle, so tantalizingly close, and yet so impossibly far away. It was just a few feet. I thought I could get to it if I just eased myself back, but if I slipped off . . . I shuddered to think about what would happen if I did that. But my fingers were burning, and my muscles were aching. If I didn't try it now, I'd never survive this.

I took one or two quick breaths to work up the courage, and then I relaxed my grip on Sultana's scales, pushing myself back toward the saddle. I expected to slide smoothly and gracefully back to the base of the saddle, and then I'd be able to work my way into it and secure myself with the straps, but that wasn't what happened at all. Instead, the wind shoved me right off the side of her neck, and into open air once more.

I waited for the rush of the wind, for the plummet earthward, but what I got was a sharp set of teeth snatching me out of the air. I cringed, stifling a scream, horrified and frightened and sure that I was going to be the only zahhak rider in history to be devoured by her own mount, but somehow none of Sultana's teeth cut me. She kept such fine control over her jaw that aside from my whole midsection being covered in her slobber, I was none the worse for wear.

I couldn't believe it. I was so thrilled to be alive and so shocked I wasn't dead and so scared and so happy all at once that I just started crying as she carried me away in her mouth, flapping over the water without a care in the world. Of course, clutched in her jaws, I could see that jammed in between two of her teeth were the tattered bits of cloth and the shredded flesh of the Mahisagari guardsmen she'd bitten a few minutes earlier, and I felt both a little sickened at the sight, and profoundly grateful that I'd been so good to her when she was little.

"Razia?" Arjun exclaimed. "Are you all right?"

I glanced up, somewhat mortified to see Arjun, flying with Lakshmi in his rear gunner's seat, atop Padmini's back just a few feet off Sultana's wing. Of course, I was seeing them all upside down because that was the way Sultana had grabbed me, but I was lucky to be seeing anything at all, considering the circumstances.

"Hello, my prince," I said, giving him a sheepish wave. "Yes, I'm fine."

"That was so amazing, Akka," Lakshmi shouted at me, "until you fell off!"

"Yes, she should definitely have practiced that part a little harder," Arjun agreed, and he was smiling now that it was clear I wasn't hurt, though the anxiety in his voice would have been hard to miss.

"Razia, are you hurt?" Sakshi cried as Ragini dove down, flaring her wings and the scales of her hood to slow herself enough not to go flying right past us.

"No, Sultana is very gentle when she wants to be," I said, frankly not believing it myself.

"Well, the Mahisagaris aren't going to give us much time to regroup," she warned, casting a glance over her shoulder at the fortress of Ahura, where a colorful cyclone of red and green zahhaks was swirling up from the courtyard. We were several miles away, but it was a long flight to the coast, and if we gave up our altitude to land and regroup, there was a chance we might not be able to get it back again, though I thought I had a plan for that.

I looked around for Sikander and Viputeshwar, breathing a sigh of relief when I spotted them on the other side of Sultana's head, though it hurt to lift myself up enough to see over her, and she seemed to not like it when I moved, her grip on me tightening ever so slightly, the pressure of her teeth a painful but ultimately harmless warning—the sort of thing she might do to one of her babies if she'd felt the need to carry it in her mouth. Of course, I wasn't armored like a zahhak, so I went limp rather than risking a sterner rebuke.

"Is everything all right, your highness?" Sikander shouted.

"Fine!" I shouted back, heaving a very audible sigh. I crossed my arms over my chest, uncomfortable, and a bit embarrassed, but mostly just grateful that I was alive, and so were my loved ones. Whether any of us survived the day, though, that was an open question.

"You're crazy!" Tamara shouted as she dove down to join us, with the rest of the top cover. She looked to Sakshi and asked, "She's really always like that?"

"Always," said Sakshi, her stern disapproval evident even through the roar of the slipstream in our ears.

"When I heard you scaled the cliffs of Shikarpur bare-handed, I didn't really believe it fully," Haider confessed to me, Roshanak flying about a dozen feet above me, so that I was looking straight up into his face as he looked down into mine. "But now I'm half-convinced you simply leapt to the top like a hero from a fairy tale."

"I'm flattered," I said, "but I climbed like an ordinary mortal."

"She climbed," Arjun agreed, his goggle-shrouded eyes lingering on my face, a smile spreading across his lips, "but not like a mortal, and certainly not an ordinary one."

My cheeks burned, and I vowed that if we survived all of this, I was going to make up for all the time we'd lost these last few weeks. I would find us a tall tower where nobody could interrupt us, and I wouldn't come out for at least a month.

"So do we have a plan, your highness?" Sikander asked, and I realized I hadn't told him anything yet. He didn't know about the rebellion in Kadiro, and he didn't know about the cannons mounted on the river zahhaks, though he was looking with interest at the ones on the backs of the fire zahhaks flying with us.

"We do," I replied.

He grunted. "I presume those swivel guns were your brilliant scheme?"

"Arjun's actually," I corrected. "He thinks they'll help the fire zahhaks survive better in a dogfight."

"He's probably right," Sikander allowed, "though it's not enough to make up for the difference in numbers. Even with Parisa and Mohini, we only have sixteen zahhaks to bring to bear against the twenty-four animals Sultan Ahmed can muster. At best it will be a murderous culling of the cream of both our forces, and at worst they'll gain the upper hand quickly."

"Which is why Hina and the other Zindhi fliers are on their way to meet us," I informed him.

"Flying river zahhaks?" It was plain that he didn't think much of that idea, but a moment later I heard a cry. "You put cannons on river zahhaks!"

"Thirty-six of them," I agreed. "If they get here in time, and the Zindhis can aim those guns as well as Hina did, then they'll be enough to overwhelm Ahmed and his allies. Which is why we will land on the cliffs, reorganize, and immediately fly east along the coast toward Kadiro, climbing all the while. The Mahisagaris will likely catch us before we can get back, but we want to give Hina every chance to reach us in time. Once the battle starts, it will be over in minutes. We need to do everything we can to make sure that the Zindhis get the opportunity to make their presence felt before it's too late."

I felt a little ridiculous, making plans like some great general whilst dangling from my zahhak's jaws, but orders had to be given, regardless of the circumstances. And at any rate, I rather suspected that as much hilarity as this story would elicit in the future, it would elicit an equal amount of awe. If I survived. I blew out a long slow breath to steady my nerves. Karim and his father had assembled a huge and deadly force, and Kadiro was four hundred miles away along the coast from the cliffs where we would be landing. Hina would have already left, I was sure of it, but even flying flat-out it was an eight- or nine-hour journey. There was every chance she wouldn't reach us in time, and even if she did, her zahhaks would be tired, as ours were. The Mahisagari animals, by contrast, looked fresh. They were already making up ground behind us. I wondered if we'd even make it to shore before battle was unavoidable.

And with Sikander having reclaimed his mount, and Lakshmi hers, either Arjun or Udai was carrying a cannon that would do him no good. That thought weighed on my mind, because the cannon would slow a fire zahhak down, reducing its ability to maneuver, and making it even more vulnerable to attack without a man to fire it. Viputeshwar could ride with Udai or Arjun, but he couldn't be in two places at once, and we had no gunners waiting for us onshore. I frowned. In a perfect world, we'd return to Kadiro and fight when we were fresh, but there was no way that Ahmed Shah would be stupid enough to let that happen. If we retreated, if we tried to hide ourselves away in a fortress, we would be slaughtered.

I stared back at the enemy zahhaks, formed up into two long lines across the sky. The acid zahhaks were closer to us, outrunning the fire zahhaks of Yaruba, which had climbed a little higher. I recognized the formation at once. It was the tactic I had devised for Ahmed Shah to use against the Firangi fleet, the tactic that had given him the victory that had led to all of this. He intended to catch us with his acid zahhaks, force us into a tight, turning fight, and then let his fire zahhaks strike down from above, their superior position enabling them to take easy attack passes at us without exposing them to danger in return.

I turned my head to look north, and was relieved to see the rocky outline of the shore in the distance, the brown cliffs looking fuzzy and indistinct thanks to a thin layer of white haze that hung low on the horizon. Our enemies were closing in, but I thought we might just make it.

"Only those who need to land should land," I shouted, so that I would be heard over the roar of the wind in our ears. "The rest of us will maintain top cover."

"I suppose that's you, me, and Viputeshwar?" Arjun asked.

I nodded, because that was the absolute bare minimum. "And your father, if he wants to free himself of that cannon's extra weight before the battle begins."

Udai Agnivansha nodded his agreement.

"Once we've landed and corrected our positions, we'll fly straight for Kadiro, climbing as we go. The rest of you will not descend to our altitude. Keep your height. We can't risk ceding a major advantage like that to Ahmed Shah."

"And what would you like us to do if he catches up to us, your highness?" Sikander asked.

"We take them head-on," I replied. "We'll aim ourselves for the fire zahhaks, forcing the acid zahhaks to climb if they want to meet us, and then we'll blow right through both of their formations. We'll keep running once we're past them, the thunder zahhaks taking the lead and climbing, while the fire zahhaks and ice zahhaks offer them a choice—attack the slower targets and risk getting killed from above, or chase the thunder zahhaks in a climbing fight they can't hope to match."

"The thunder zahhaks will give us the advantage in the head-on pass," Tamara allowed, nodding her head as she digested the plan. "And because they've broken themselves into two lines, they can't bring the full weight of their numbers to bear."

"We'll actually have them outnumbered at each moment in the fight," Haider agreed. He was smiling at me. "We may not even need those Zindhis, your highness."

"We'll need them," I replied, because I knew better than to believe that we could knock out eight of the enemy in two passes without taking any casualties in return. And even if we did that, it would do nothing more than even the odds. The fight would still be a bloody mess. I couldn't risk weakening Zindh and Registan in the same day. And if the crown prince of Safavia died defending me, the political fallout would be a nightmare.

But there was nothing I could do about it now. We were approaching the cliffs. I pointed at them, waving my hand to get Sultana's attention, and I said, "Down!"

She understood what I wanted immediately, curving her wings back and picking up speed, the slipstream battering the side of my body as we raced down toward the bluffs overlooking the sea. She alighted easily on the rocky desert ground, and set me down with a gentleness that I hadn't imagined possible from a zahhak.

I picked myself up, surprised to find that I was none the worse for wear, and was immediately greeted by Sultana's snout in my face. She sniffed at me, looked me over carefully, like a nervous mother. I stroked her scales, telling her what an amazing zahhak she was, what a perfect angel, how singularly wonderful, and she puffed out her chest and flicked her tail feathers in response, looking well pleased with herself.

I climbed into the saddle, securing my straps carefully so that I didn't end up falling off again, noting as I did so that Lakshmi was hugging Mohini's neck tightly, Viputeshwar was getting used to sighting down the barrel of the cannon in Arjun's rear saddle, and Udai was busy hurling breechblocks into the dirt. I glanced back at the southern horizon, startled by how close the Mahisagari acid zahhaks were to our own fliers orbiting high above us. There wasn't much time left.

"Lakshmi, get in the saddle and get airborne now!" I shouted. I gave Sultana's reins a shake to get her moving. She hurled herself off the cliff and into the air, strong beats of her wings propelling us higher and higher as we circled. I waited only as long as it took for Lakshmi, Arjun, and Udai to get their zahhaks into the air before pointing Sultana's nose to the east. We had to flee as fast as possible, and to pray that Hina and the Zindhi river zahhaks would reach us before Ahmed did.

CHAPTER 30

A bright line of white froth separated the glittering blue waters of the sea from the golden sands of the desert uplands that stretched east along the coast as far as Kadiro. My eyes were scouring every inch of land, water, and sky for the slightest hint of the indigo, white, and black wing feathers of a Zindhi river zahhak, but there was nothing. Twisting my head to look behind me, I saw that the Mahisagari acid zahhaks were all too clearly gaining on the slower fire zahhaks at the rear of our formation.

"If we're going to turn and strike, your highness, we should do it soon," Sikander warned from his place on my left wing. "Your zahhaks have flown all night. They're exhausted, and the longer we flee the worse it will be."

"We need to give Hina every chance to get to us," I replied, praying that I would see her this time when I looked east, but there was nothing. Just empty sky.

"I hate to say it, Razia, but we have to consider the possibility that she might not be coming," Tamara said.

"She's coming," I said, my voice holding far more certainty than I really felt, because I wasn't naive, I understood what Tamara was implying.

She made it explicit all the same. "She has Kadiro, she has an army, she has a way to use her zahhaks to defend herself from your father. She doesn't need you anymore, Razia. She might well sit this fight out, and then negotiate with the survivors from a position of strength."

"It's what your father would do, your highness," Sikander agreed.

"Hina is not my father," I snapped, but saying it didn't make her zahhaks magically appear on the horizon, and another quick look behind us told me that we had run out of time. If we let Ahmed Shah and his men get any closer, we'd never be able to organize ourselves properly for the head-on pass we needed to make to survive the battle.

"All right, we fight now," I declared. "On my call, we'll make a hook turn and fly straight at the enemy fire zahhaks, gaining as much altitude as we can manage. We'll do as much damage as we can before diving back east to make another pass on the acid zahhaks. Clear?"

"Clear, your highness!" they chorused.

My heart thundered in my ears as I took up my trumpet and brought it to my lips. This was it. Victory or death. I wasn't going to let myself be captured by Karim. I wasn't going to surrender to him. Either I would win or I would die. There were no other options to be had. I blasted out a single note on the trumpet, turning right, Sultana banking hard, an invisible force crushing down on me as we sped through the turn. I shoved the trumpet back into its saddlebag and steeled myself for the coming fight.

A dozen emerald-scaled acid zahhaks were racing toward us, stretched out in a long line across the horizon, but I aimed myself not for them, but for the fire zahhaks farther behind and at a higher altitude. Sultana was beating her wings hard, we were gaining altitude, but I could feel that we were slower than we should have been. After flying all-out to get to Ahura and rescue Lakshmi, and then flying a hundred miles more, she was exhausted. All around me, the other zahhaks who had made the same journey were doing their best, but their mouths were hanging open as they panted for air. Only Mohini and Parisa seemed fresh. By contrast, the Mahisagari animals had their beaks tightly shut, their wings flapping with perfect grace, their eyes fixed on us, gleaming, eager for the kill.

It wasn't just me noticing the danger. Sikander was grim faced. Haider and Tamara were looking at each other like it might be the last time, and I knew that Arjun was trying to catch my eye one last time too. Even Sakshi, who had never been in a battle before, seemed to know that this wasn't the way you wanted to enter one. If Hina had showed up, our morale would have been sky-high, but without any sign of the Zindhi river zahhaks, everyone knew what our odds were of winning this fight, and the zahhaks were sensing our discomfiture. They were looking toward their riders, one eye on the humans they trusted with their lives, and the other on the onrushing enemy.

I needed to give my fliers some hope, even if I wasn't feeling it myself. I needed to galvanize them. Because if we hit the merge like this, we were going to be incinerated by acid and flames alike. It occurred to me then that if I had one advantage at all, it was that my fliers were all trained in the same tradition. Just as Nizam, Safavia, and Khevsuria all spoke the same language in our royal courts, we all used the same trumpet calls in battle, and our zahhaks had been trained with them since birth, knew exactly what they meant and how to act when they heard them.

I reached into my pouch and pulled the trumpet out once

more, licking my lips to wet them. This had to sound good, or the effect would be exactly the opposite of what I intended. I took a deep breath, and I snapped the reins, urging Sultana ahead. She listened, beating her wings that much harder, surging ahead of the others in formation, so that every flier and every zahhak could see us clearly. I brought the trumpet to my lips with a trembling hand, but the notes I played were perfectly crisp and clear and as loud as I could make them.

The call was one I had heard from the time I was old enough to walk. It was a rapid series of ascending arpeggios that culminated in a piercing shriek that was meant to imitate the cry of an enraged zahhak defending its territory in the breeding season. A chill went through me at the sound of that call, because my whole life I had been taught that it meant one thing and one thing only—the time had come to fling myself at my enemies, to set myself upon them and destroy them. I could still remember Sikander's lectures on the subject. Of all the calls that a zahhak rider heard, that was the one she had to answer with the utmost attention, the one that required from her every last measure of her courage.

I was stunned to see the effect it had on Sultana. Her mouth had shut. Her wings were surging, her eyes were narrowed. She remembered. She knew what it meant. And so did the other zahhaks in the formation. They came racing up on my left and my right, azure-winged thunder zahhaks, their emerald eyes narrowed to slits as they waited for the order to spit lightning at their enemies. Tamara and her ice zahhaks were with us, their huge beaks clamped shut as they strained at their halters, their bodies pressing themselves into the attack. And while Padmini and the fire zahhaks of Registan were strangers to Nizami trumpet calls, the sudden intensity of the other animals around them galvanized them too. They were ready for this fight.

I put the trumpet back in its pouch for the second time in as many minutes, but my heart wasn't nearly as heavy as it had been a moment before. Now, as the acid zahhaks closed the last few hundred yards toward us, I thought we had a fighting chance.

"We blow a hole for the others!" I cried, though I didn't know if anyone could hear me. It didn't matter. They'd hear Sultana. I pointed her snout right at the Mahisagari zahhak directly opposite me. I thought it was Ahmed himself flying it. He was dead in front of me, coming on with everything he had. There were scarcely three hundred yards between us. He wouldn't have much time to dodge.

"Thunder!" I shouted.

Sultana's jaws yawned wide and every hair on my body stood on end as the static built in the air, the tingle of it on my skin making my heartbeat quicken. The air was torn asunder an instant later by an explosion that made the swivel guns of Zindh seem like children's toys, and a brilliant bolt of violet light crackled across the sky.

Ahmed's zahhak rolled hard right, banking sharply and diving away, narrowly avoiding being struck dead by Sultana's lightning. She turned and climbed, racing back toward me, but it was too little, too late. She'd never get a shot of her own. She was going to have to chase us again, and by then we'd have hit the fire zahhaks, just like I'd planned.

All around me, thunder cracked and bolts of lightning streaked across the sky. Indigo feathers and emerald scales exploded off one Mahisagari zahhak, and then a second and a third, as six thunder zahhaks let loose with everything they had. The center of the enemy formation disintegrated as riders banked hard away from the danger, creating a clear lane for us to surge through.

But the merge wasn't over yet. We crossed into the range of the acid zahhaks, and the half dozen animals that had held their formation spat globs of green, sticky poison at a speed that beggared belief. But at the same instant, the fire zahhaks of Registan and the ice zahhaks of Khevsuria returned fire with their own breath weapons, and for a moment I forgot that I was in a battle—I was struck by the awful beauty of glittering white trails of ice, hot streaks of fire, and glistening green orbs of acid all crossing over one another in a single patch of sky.

Though at least two of the acid zahhaks had taken aim at me, both of the shots missed wide, and Sultana carried on in her climb toward the Yaruban fire zahhaks, which were just a few seconds behind their Mahisagari counterparts. I glanced left and right and was startled to find that my formation was still intact. So far so good. We'd survived the first onslaught; now it was time for the second.

I didn't know who was riding the fire zahhak in the center of the Yaruban formation, whether it was Karim's cousin or his uncle or some other man, but I knew that if I struck him down, my fliers would take heart and his would be filled with fear. While adrenaline was carrying us through this battle, that couldn't last forever. Our zahhaks would tire and they would slow, and we needed an edge when that moment came.

"Get her, girl," I whispered to Sultana, making sure she was aimed at a particularly dark-colored fire zahhak, her burgundy scales contrasting sharply with the bright gold of her belly. As beautiful as she was, she needed to die. "Thunder!"

Sultana barked lightning once more, the bolt hammering the fire zahhak full in the face, blasting her right in the crest of thick scales that protected the back of her neck. I waited for her wings to crumple, for her to fall from the sky, but she just kept coming, and the men of Yaruba raised a war cry that was so loud it rang in my ears even hundreds of yards away. I'd just given them hope and stolen it from the heart of every flier in my formation. I cursed myself for my stupidity. Sikander had trained me better than to try to break through the heaviest scales of a fire zahhak.

"Shoot for their wings!" I shrieked.

"Thunder!" Sakshi cried, and Ragini let loose with a bolt of lightning that tore through the left wing of the fire zahhak opposite her, blood and feathers filling the air as the animal spun out of control, crying piteously all the while.

Now it was our turn to cheer. More lightning bolts licked over the surface of the sky, one finding soft belly scales and another taking off the wing of an unlucky Yaruban beast. Both shrieked in agony and plummeted toward the beach far below us.

I chanced a quick glance behind us before we reached the range of a fire zahhak's breath, and my stomach churned. The Mahisagaris had made up more ground than I'd expected. They were in good formation, ready for the fight. Even if we somehow managed to survive the inferno that awaited us, we wouldn't be able to dive away without showing the Mahisagaris our tail feathers. We were going to have to make a turning fight, which was the last thing I wanted when we were still outnumbered and our zahhaks were so tired.

But there was nothing for it now. Fire zahhaks began spewing their breath, and I knew the only way to survive was to dive, so I put Sultana's nose down, urging her on with snaps of the reins and pressure in my seat, my body bending low, like that would somehow make her go that little bit faster.

My mouth went dry as flames roared over my head, the skin of my face burning from the searing heat, the stench of brimstone filling my nostrils. I hunched over Sultana's neck, praying that we would make it through unscathed, half-certain that her tail would catch fire, or one of her wings, but suddenly there was clear air all around us, and the time had come to begin the fight in earnest.

We banked right, arcing across the sky, my head twisted

around to track the acid zahhaks still coming at us, close enough now that we couldn't charge at one another in formation like cavalrymen. Now it would be a series of duels, every zahhak and rider pairing herself against her opposite number. For me, that was Ahmed Shah. He'd been chasing me this whole time, and his zahhak was fresh, fast enough that I barely managed to get Sultana's snout around to face her before we crossed paths.

He broke into me and I into him, our zahhaks crossing belly to belly before bending themselves through tight arcs in the sky. I was looking straight up at him across the circle as each of us tried to edge closer to the other's tail feathers, but he was playing it smart. He had chosen to make our fight one of stamina rather than pure agility. He knew Sultana was tired, knew that maintaining a crushingly tight turn while keeping her wings flapping for speed was the hardest test of a zahhak's strength and endurance. And he was confident that my thunder zahhak would falter before his animal did. But he didn't know Sultana.

She dug into the turn, the force of her wingtips tearing open the sky itself, sending spirals of white vapor streaming off her primary feathers. I knew that we wouldn't be able to win this fight the conventional way, by gradually gaining the angle we wanted, and Sultana must have sensed it too, because she deployed her hood, the sudden increase in surface area providing a new source of lift that tightened the turn that much more. Suddenly, rather than our being stuck at opposite ends of the same circle in the sky, Sultana's nose started tracking toward Ahmed's tail.

I gritted my teeth and clung to the reins for dear life, the tightness of the turn putting a pressure on my body that seemed to multiply the weight of my limbs and my head. It drove the blood from my brain and the light from my eyes. I had to scream and tense my stomach muscles and my leg muscles, clenching down as hard as I could just to stay awake. But we were so close, so tantalizingly close. Ahmed Shah was just a few degrees off Sultana's nose. Another second, two on the outside, and we would have him.

Suddenly, the Mahisagari zahhak put on a burst of speed with her wings, and we stopped gaining on her tail. She tightened her own turn, racing around the circle, and my heart sank as I realized that I'd been duped. We'd never had the energy to catch her. He'd been playing us for fools, tricking us into giving it everything we had. And now he had us right where he wanted us. We were spent, and he was fresh, and the next thing I knew, I had the gaping maw of an acid zahhak lining up for a shot on Sultana's tail feathers.

CHAPTER 31

No, I wasn't going to let it end this way. I couldn't. Not after everything we'd been through. I was not going to let Ahmed Shah steal my life from me.

There was nothing left to do but make him miss. I pulled hard on the reins, directing Sultana tighter into the turn, and lower. If we didn't have the energy to tighten the turn ourselves, we'd use God's energy to do it for us. The moment her nose dropped below the horizon, our turn tightened, our speed shot up. At the same instant, Ahmed Shah took his shot.

A bright blob of acid zipped between Sultana's right wing and her tail feathers, somehow missing the both of us by inches, but my stomach clenched. That had been close. Even with the dive, we weren't getting away from him the way we should have been. And now Sultana was scared; her mouth was hanging open. She was looking behind her as the acid zahhak stayed glued to us through the turn. I could have sworn that her emerald eye flickered to me in that moment, pleading with me to find us some way out of this mess I'd put us in, but the trouble was, I didn't know what to do.

The smart thing would have been to use the vertical, to roll to try to force Ahmed in front of us, but Sultana didn't have the energy for that, any fool could have seen that. She was half-dead with exhaustion. If we tried to go up, we'd be too slow, and Ahmed would drill us right in the back and burn us alive, but if we kept spiraling down, we'd run out of altitude eventually, and then we'd be low and slow, unable to turn, and we'd be just as dead.

I twisted in my saddle, looking frantically for a friendly flier, but all around us it was chaos. Zahhaks of every description were swirling together in the sky, and it was practically impossible to tell friend from foe. There was no one here to help us. We were completely alone.

Ahmed's zahhak spat acid again. I pulled hard on the reins, praying that it would be enough. Sultana's hood was fully extended, her tail feathers slamming up to tighten the turn as her wings twisted, rolling us into a dive that aimed her snout right at the glittering waters of the sea.

The acid streaked past us—another miss. But there wouldn't be a third. We were diving now, and that made it dead easy for Ahmed to roll in right behind us. I pulled us into a right-hand turn, but it was too little, too late. He had the angle. He had the speed. His zahhak was fresh. There was nothing left to do.

Sultana's head twisted slightly, and her wings pounded the air. She'd seen something, but what? I traced back a line from her pupil to a patch of sky above and behind Ahmed's onrushing zahhak, and at first I saw nothing at all, but then, an instant later, there was a blur of blue and black and white, and a fork-tailed zahhak with her wings bent into sharp sickles streaked in behind Ahmed's tail feathers, a brilliant bronze zahhak aimed right at him. Hina hadn't abandoned us after all.

A burst of fire and smoke erupted from the cannon, and Ahmed Shah exploded in a shower of blood and bone, feathers and fragments of saddle. His beautiful acid zahhak went limp and fell away as Hina worked to reload her cannon, jerking out the smoking breechblock and replacing it with a fresh one.

She pulled up alongside us, grinning, and I could just make out her words across the roaring gulf of air between us. "It's the same cannon!"

"What?" I shouted, looking behind us to make sure our tails were clear.

"It's the same cannon that killed Asma! We killed both his parents with the same gun!" She was cackling with glee at that poetic justice, but I was mostly grateful to be alive.

"Thank you for not abandoning us," I shouted back, because she could have. Tamara hadn't been wrong about that.

"Never, your highness," she replied, her smile hardening into an expression of grim determination. "We're with you till the end."

I looked around us, trying to make sense of the fight, and I couldn't believe my eyes. Everywhere I looked, fork-tailed river zahhaks were blasting away at acid zahhaks and fire zahhaks with their cannons. More cannons were firing from the tails of Registani fire zahhaks. And there were ice zahhaks flying still, and thunder zahhaks too. We were winning!

"Come on, girl, let's finish this," I told Sultana, turning her back into the fight. She seemed to have the same sudden surge of joy that I did, recognizing the Zindhi zahhaks as our friends come to help us in our time of need. We raced at Hina's side at a pair of Mahisagari acid zahhaks who had spotted us and were diving down to kill us. I recognized them at once—Karim and Jamshid.

"Thunder!" I screeched, making sure Sultana's nose was pointing right at Karim and Amira. She seemed to know who it was, and what I wanted, because she spat her lightning bolt straightaway, the flash of light and roar of thunder filling the air between us.

But Karim had pitched up at the last second, rolling down to take us from above. I pulled up into him, expecting that we would pass one another by and start our turning fight, but at the last second I realized that Karim had no intention whatever of passing me by. He was aiming Amira straight for Sultana on a collision course.

I kicked up my legs, throwing myself back into my seat, giving Sultana the command to fight with feet and claws and teeth. At the last instant she pitched up, lashing out with her feet and her wing claws just as Amira slammed into us, the impact knocking every conscious thought from my mind. I saw emerald scales, teeth and claws, and then we were falling far too fast.

Something was wrong. Sultana wasn't righting herself. Amira was tumbling beside me, out of control. Was she dead? We were spinning too fast. I lost track of her. The white line of foam separating the yellow sands of the beach from the blue waters of the ocean was spinning like the blades of a windmill in a gale. I lost track of what was sky and what was water and what was ground.

"Sultana!" I screamed her name. I pulled on the reins. But she wasn't answering me. Her emerald eyes were lolled back in her head. Was she dead? God, it couldn't be. "Sultana!"

It was too late. We hit the shore with a splash, but the water was only knee-deep and the impact was unlike anything I had ever felt before. I screamed from the pain. My saddle straps snapped like the thick leather was nothing more than tissue paper. My legs burned and my back ached, but it was my heart that hurt most of all. Because Sultana didn't scream. She didn't move. She just lay there, neck curled up, her snout half-buried in the ocean waves. Her eyes were closed, like she'd gone to sleep, but I knew the awful truth. She was gone.

CHAPTER 32

I crawled out of the saddle, tears in my eyes from the pain in my heart, and in my body too. I could hardly walk. Something was wrong with my legs, or my back, it was hard to know. I struggled to hold myself upright in the surf, but my every thought was bent on Sultana. I stroked the scales on her face, praying she would open her eyes like she always did in the stables when I did that. I looked for some sign that her nostrils were moving, that she was smelling for me, but there were no signs of life at all.

"Sultana, no!" I dropped to my knees in spite of the pain, and I clung to her, pressing my face against hers, willing her not to be dead. "Wake up," I pleaded. "You have to wake up, sweetheart."

"Razia!"

I looked up to see Karim staggering through the surf toward me, his firangi held tightly in his hand. Behind him, up on the shore, Amira lay in a twisted heap of broken feathers and shattered limbs. He'd hurled her at us, intent on killing us both out of spite. And poor Sultana, she'd given her life for me at the last moment.

"I'm not going to let him get away with this, girl," I promised her, kissing a sleek cobalt scale, still warm, almost like she was still alive. But I knew those scales would be cold soon enough. She was gone, and I was going to make damned sure that I didn't live in a world without her that still had Karim Shah in it.

I jerked my katars free of their scabbards and struggled to my feet, my legs not wanting to work. My back was alive with pain. It was lancing through my ribs and darting along my hips, shooting down my thighs. There was something wrong with me, something serious.

Karim saw it. His eyes lit up. He was hurt too. He was limping, but he didn't look the way I did, stooped over, hardly able to put one leg in front of the other from the pain.

"I'm going to enjoy taking everything from you," Karim growled. "My only regret is that you won't be alive to see what I do to your little sister."

"You'll never touch her," I replied, my grip on my katars tightening. "She's safe now, with half a dozen nobles willing to protect her with their lives. And you have nothing. Your father is dead. Your mother is dead. And you'll die today too, whether by my hand or Arjun's or Hina's. It doesn't matter. You're finished. Mahisagar is finished. You lost."

"So did you," he replied, smirking at Sultana's corpse behind me. "And now you'll die by my hand."

"We'll see," I replied, because the pain in my lower body and in my heart didn't leave much room for clever retorts. I just gritted my teeth, gripped my katars, and lurched forward through the surf, one plodding step at a time.

Karim splashed forward, his silk dhoti clinging to his knees and thighs. He lunged at me, thrusting the point of his firangi at my heart, but I beat it aside with my left katar and punched with the right.

If we'd been on dry ground, if I'd been healthy instead of hurt, I'd have driven it right through his black heart, but with my back alive with pain, with the water slowing me down, the point of my dagger never got within six inches of him. He jerked his firangi back and thrust again and again at me, using his superior reach to force me to parry frantically just to keep the sharp steel from piercing my flesh. Every instinct told me to retreat, to fall back, but that was the wrong move. I had to keep moving forward. I had to close the distance, but it was hard to make my legs answer me. Something about that fall had left my hips feeling strangely numb.

Karim grinned. He saw that I wasn't moving my legs, and he suddenly stepped forward, thrusting for my face, forcing me to batter his blade aside, but it wasn't there. I swung my katar wide with everything I had, expecting it to clash against his sword, but when it didn't make impact, my back twisted and I screamed.

I landed on my hips in the surf, my body trembling from the pain. I could barely feel my legs. Was I paralyzed? Was this what that felt like?

Karim lunged at me, his firangi darting for my throat. I managed to batter it aside, pushing off the sand with my feet, the water taking some of the pressure off my body, as it was deep enough to float atop. I propelled myself back with two kicks, but it was a feeble effort, and Karim was laughing at me.

"This is too perfect," he sneered. "You were so full of yourself. You thought you were so smart, and so strong." He speared my right arm with his firangi, and this time there was no blocking it. I heard the point hit my bone, and blood flowed hot and fast down my arm as he jerked his blade free. But it didn't hurt. It was just hot and numb. I knew it would hurt later—if there was a later.

He thrust again for my chest, but I did catch this one with my left katar, beating it aside to stay alive another second more. But without any way of hitting back, I knew it was hopeless. I couldn't carry on like this. He drew back to stab me again, and I kicked water into his face, the salt stinging his eyes. I pushed myself back through the surf until I hit something firm and unyielding. Sultana's body.

I nestled myself against her as Karim stalked toward me. I was going to die, but somehow being with Sultana made it okay. I wished I could have said good-bye to Arjun and Sakshi and Lakshmi, but there was something fitting about dying here with Sultana. We'd been children together. She had been my oldest and firmest friend. And I wasn't sure I wanted to live without her anyway.

I sheathed my katars, because there was no sense in prolonging the inevitable. Karim noticed, and his eyes widened slightly.

"If you think I'm going to make it quick, you're fooling yourself," he ground out through clenched teeth, his dark eyes smoldering with hate.

I forced myself to shrug, to show him none of the fear I was feeling. I turned my thoughts away from him, to my sisters and to Arjun. It would have been so nice to have lived in peace with them for a little while. But they would have the peace and safety I had never known. I'd guaranteed that when I'd given Hina the power to protect her homeland, and when I'd brought Haider and Tamara here. Sakshi and Lakshmi would be spoiled for choices when it came to building a new home. And that was all I'd ever really wanted anyway.

Karim was standing over me, his sword tracing a line from my lips to my navel, the sharp point just barely kissing the surface of my skin, without tearing it open. "Where shall I cut you first?"

I said nothing. If I was going to die, then I would die well.

"You're so proud of that pretty face of yours. Well, when your precious Arjun finds your body, he's going to be disgusted by you, I can promise you that. What shall I take first? Your nose? An eye? Yes, I think one of those pretty green eyes will make for a fine trophy."

I saw the tip of his sword move toward my right eye, and then I just saw a shadow. At first, I thought I was blind, that he'd done it, but then I was aware of feathers and scales between me and Karim. Sultana's wing.

Karim reared back in shock as Sultana's head rose from the sea, water dripping from sparkling sapphire scales, her emerald eyes wide and alert. They knew. Somehow, she'd seen what he was doing to me, and it had brought her back to herself. Karim thrust at her with his sword, and I screamed, but she bit the blade, snapping it in half like it was made of rotten wood. Then her head darted forward and she bit again, and when she pulled away, Karim's legs toppled into the water, his entrails dangling from her teeth.

Sultana pointed her nose skyward, relaxing her jaw, loosening her throat, and the better part of Karim Shah slid straight into her stomach.

CHAPTER 33

My eyes flickered across the creamy marble ceiling, inlaid with lapis lazuli, turquoise, and jet river zahhaks streaking through the skies. If I was going to live in Kadiro for the rest of my life, I thought I might have a stoneworker inlay some golden cannons atop the animals' backs. It would make a nice touch.

I half expected to drift back to sleep, but there was a spasm of pain in my back before that could happen, and I had to grit my teeth to keep from crying out. The doctor said that it would heal, he thought. It was already better. The pain in my legs had stopped, and there was no numbness. I wouldn't be paralyzed. I just had a pain in my lower back that came and went with varying degrees of ferocity. At the moment, it was clawing at me like a frenzied zahhak in the breeding season.

"Arjun?" I looked around for him, my eyes scouring the cushion-covered wooden beds that had been placed beside mine for visitors, but there was nobody to be found.

"He was called away for a few moments, your highness." Sikander came to my bedside at once. He'd been standing watch near the doorway, but now he sat beside me on my bed, putting his hand over mine. He must have felt the tension in my muscles, because he said, "It's the pain again, isn't it?"

I managed a slight nod in response, but I knew that if I spoke I'd make it sound worse than it really was. It was getting better. I just had to keep it together for a few more days.

"I'll fetch the doctor," he offered, his hand slackening and pulling away, but I tightened my grip around his fingers.

"No," I gasped. "Stay."

Sikander's brow furrowed in alarm, but he eased himself back down onto the bed. "Your highness, if you're hurting I should fetch the doctor. He can give you something for the pain."

I shook my head. "I'm tired of being drugged witless. It's just a little spasm. It'll be gone in a moment."

He frowned, but he didn't insist on getting the doctor; that was something. He just let me squeeze his fingers until my knuckles were white without a word of complaint or any sign of pain on his part. Maybe my grip wasn't as strong as I thought it was. It certainly wouldn't have been with my right arm, which still ached ferociously whenever I moved it, though it always seemed to pain me less than my back.

"It would only take me a moment to fetch the doctor, your highness," Sikander whispered, using his free hand to stroke my sweat-soaked hair back from my brow.

I shook my head and let myself relax a little against the mattress. "No, it's already easing. Just distract me."

"And how shall I do that?" he asked.

"Tell me a story," I replied, half teasing, smiling in spite of everything.

Sikander didn't smile back. His jaw clenched, and for a moment I worried that I'd sounded too effeminate for him. He'd always got that same look on his face when I was a child and I'd asked for something I wasn't supposed to have, or when I'd begged him to tell me the story of Razia Sultana once too often. I let go of his hand and curled my limbs in close. It was a stupid reaction, but I was reminded of my childhood so overpoweringly that it was almost a reflex.

Sikander didn't miss my reaction, and the tension fled his face. He looked away, but I thought I saw tears glistening in his eyes. He choked out, "I'll fetch the doctor," and stood to go.

"No, wait." I reached for him, struggling to sit up, but that sent a flare of pain through my hips and down my legs that had me plastering myself against the bed and gasping for breath.

"Your highness, you're not supposed to get out of bed yet!" Sikander exclaimed. He pressed my shoulders down with gentle hands. "The doctor says if you move too much, you'll set back your recovery."

I sighed as the pain passed, though the nausea it had provoked in my stomach took a moment or two longer. When it finally dissipated I took a few slow, steadying breaths, and glanced up at Sikander, who was holding my hand, his dark eyes full of worry. "How about that story?"

He let out an exasperated noise that was half sigh and half laugh, shaking his head in disbelief. "What story shall I tell you, your highness?"

I considered for a moment, and the answer came to me sooner than I'd expected. "When I came to rescue Lakshmi in Ahura, you and Viputeshwar were crying. Why?"

His cheeks reddened slightly. "It's not a very interesting story, your highness. It's nothing you don't already know."

"I want to hear it anyway," I insisted, because I'd never in my life seen Sikander cry and now I'd seen it twice—once in Ahura and once just a moment ago, when his eyes had been brimming with tears at the way I'd reacted to him.

"Well, when we arrived in Ahura, I kept close to Princess Lakshmi as you ordered," he began, and I immediately found myself smiling. Princess Lakshmi? Did he really call her that, or was he just saying it for my benefit? The way he paused, confused by my reaction, gave me the answer.

"And?" I pressed, gesturing for him to continue.

"And Viputeshwar came to serve us once we'd been shown to Princess Lakshmi's chambers," he said. "At first I tried to keep him away from her, but he was very kind to her, and he treated her with respect. When I remarked on that, he told me the story of his sister, the same story he told you when you arrived in Rajkot for the first time. He told me of how she'd been murdered and how the greatest regret of his life was not being there for her in her moment of need."

He sucked in a sharp breath, closing his eyes and rubbing my hand with a strength that frankly surprised me. "And I told him of my greatest regret. I told him how I treated you as a child, and how when you called for me, when you needed me most, I . . ."

Sikander looked up at the ceiling as if by tilting his head he could somehow get the tears to flow back into his skull. "I know you can never forgive me, your highness, but—"

"That's not true," I interrupted.

"What?" he asked, his head snapping around, his glassy eyes staring into mine.

"Sikander, you've never asked me to forgive you," I reminded him. I didn't say what I could have said—that he'd never admitted to having done anything wrong. Not until today, and even now it was indirect, an admission of regret, but not of wrongdoing.

For a long moment, he was totally silent, just staring at the bedsheets, and I wondered if he would actually ask for forgiveness or not. I had just about given up hope when he said, "I don't think I ever really understood how courageous you are until today."

"Today?" I asked, wrinkling my nose in confusion. "What do you mean?"

"Until this moment, I didn't realize how much courage it took to . . ." He trailed off, fighting for the words that he'd probably never needed before in his whole life. He sighed with frustration. "It's one thing to fly into battle, your highness; it's something else to ask for forgiveness when you don't deserve it."

"It's not about deserving it, Sikander," I replied. "It's about having the courage to ask for it."

He pursed his lips and nodded. "You shame me with your wisdom, your highness." He stroked the back of my hand with the rough pad of his thumb and said, "I'm so sorry for what I did, and what I didn't do when you were a child, your highness. When I told Viputeshwar what I'd done, when I told him how badly I had failed you, do you know what he said?"

I shook my head, holding back the tears that were threatening in my eyes now, because he'd finally said he was sorry. He'd finally admitted it was wrong. God, I'd waited so long to hear those words. It was like something suddenly solidified in my heart, as if the world were suddenly rectified, because it meant I wasn't crazy. I hadn't been wrong to be hurt by what he'd done, I hadn't been wrong to be who I was.

"He said that his sister was dead, but my daughter was still alive," Sikander whispered.

"Your daughter?" I wondered why I'd never heard of her before. I'd thought the man had never married. Had he been living a secret home life that he'd never told me about? If he had been, I didn't know where he would have found the time.

Sikander took one look at my confused face and gasped out,

"Forgive my presumption, your highness. I know that I'm just a servant to you, but . . ."

I realized then that he'd been talking about me. I reached forward and placed my hand over his. "No, you've never been a servant to me, Sikander. You've always been family. I just . . . you've never called me that before."

"I'm sorry for that too, your highness," he replied. "I'm sorry for so many things. You should never have suffered the way you did in Nizam. You should never have been forced to run away from home. Any fool could have seen who you were, and that there was no changing it. But I think it wasn't until I came here, until I saw you as you are now, that I realized how much stronger and more powerful you are this way than you were living the lie we forced upon you. Will you forgive me, your highness?"

I nodded, because I could scarcely trust myself to speak. When the words did come, they were thick in my mouth, tears rolling in long lines down my cheeks. "Yes, of course I will. All I ever wanted was for you to ask. For you to be proud of me rather than ashamed of me."

"Your highness," he said, taking both of my hands in his, "I've never been more proud of anyone in my entire life than I am of my bold, brilliant, beautiful daughter."

I laid my head back against the pillow with a sigh of relief that brought with it even more tears. "I never imagined you'd say something like that to me."

"You must have thought me a very great fool, then, your highness," he replied, "because no one could have watched you these last weeks and seen what you've accomplished and think anything less."

"Have we heard back from my father?" I wondered, because I didn't think he would look on my activities in quite the same light. I'd disobeyed him. I'd killed our allies. Granted, I'd also captured

Rajkot and Khambat, and all of Mahisagar with them, to say nothing of Ahura, but it was going to be tricky to hold them without help from my father's soldiers. For now, the Mahisagaris had sworn allegiance to me, and their three surviving acid zahhaks had been added to my personal stables, but I wasn't sure how far I could trust the Mahisagari fleet to obey me. I'd named Viputeshwar the subahdar of Mahisagar, and he was in Rajkot even now, attending to matters, but who knew if the Mahisagaris would get it into their heads to rebel?

Then again, with thirty-six Zindhi cannon zahhaks on our side, and a pair of Yaruban fire zahhaks being gifted to Arjun in exchange for peace, I thought we probably were a more ferocious power in the air than we had been before. So I knew I had the power to crush any rebellion swiftly. The trouble was, doing that would just weaken me further. I needed soldiers I could rely upon if I was to keep my lands safe, and at the moment the Mahisagaris, while the most numerous, had the least reason to be loyal to me.

"We have not heard from his majesty, your highness, but I imagine he will arrive in person any day now," Sikander replied. "But you needn't fear him. I will make certain that he understands all that you have accomplished."

"May you have better luck than I have," I whispered, because I'd never been able to convince my father of my worth, though that hadn't stopped me from trying, however foolishly.

"You shouldn't be worrying yourself over such things now, your highness; you need to rest and heal." He stroked my hair again, fondly, like he had when I was little and he was putting me to bed. "You should try to sleep if the pain has passed."

"I'm tired of sleeping," I whined. "I want to *do* something."

"You don't think you've done enough?" Sakshi asked as she strolled into the room, Lakshmi at her side and Nuri trailing not far behind. They were all safe and sound. We'd lost not a single flier in the battle. I wasn't sure how that had happened, but it was probably Hina's timely intervention that accounted for it.

The thought of the battle reminded me of an ache in my heart. "How is Sultana?"

"She's fine, Razia," Sakshi assured me as she sat on the other side of my bed from Sikander, Lakshmi piling in beside her. "I took her up for a flight today, and she's completely healthy. She just knocked herself out from the impact, that's all. But there are no broken bones. The veterinarian assured me that there's nothing wrong with her."

"I want to see her . . ." I whispered, overwhelmed with a rush of confused emotions, mostly gratitude that she was alive and had saved my life, but guilt too. So much guilt.

"As soon as the doctor says *you're* healthy, you'll be able to see her," Sakshi promised. "But you have to stay in bed until your back is healed. As it is, it's hard enough to keep her from trying to land on your balcony."

"Maybe you could move me to the roof so I can see her?" I suggested.

She pursed her lips and nodded. "I suppose we could set up an awning. If it will keep you in bed."

"It will," I lied.

She rolled her eyes, knowing me too well to be fooled. "I'll arrange it. But for now, try to get some rest."

"Is Arjun around?" I asked hopefully. Sikander had said he had been called away, but ever since the battle I hadn't wanted to be separated from him for long. I knew it was probably exhausting for him, but not nearly as exhausting as it had been living so long under Karim's thumb.

"He and Hina are handling the emissary from Jesera," Sakshi said, "but they should be finished soon."

"There's an emissary from Jesera, and I wasn't told?" I demanded, and I tried to sit up, but both Sikander and Sakshi held me down so I couldn't.

"You need to rest," Sakshi said. "Arjun and Hina are more than capable of negotiating the final terms of peace with Jesera. You've spoken with them about it, they know your mind, and they are clever enough."

"You flatter us," Hina quipped as she and Arjun breezed into the room.

"My prince!" I exclaimed, though I couldn't sit up to see him with my sister and Sikander still holding me down.

"Are you trying to get out of bed again?" he demanded, struggling to sound harsh and serious, but unable to keep the smirk off his face.

"Akka wants to lie on the roof so she can see Sultana," Lakshmi explained.

"Oh, she does, does she?" Arjun asked, ruffling Lakshmi's hair. "Well, what do you think we should do about that?"

"I think we should let her," Lakshmi answered, which brought a smile to my lips. "Sultana is worried about her too. She's always smelling me when I go into the stables if I've seen Akka first."

"Me too," Sakshi agreed.

"Then we'll have to take her up to the roof," Arjun decreed.

"Thank you, my prince," I said, staring fondly into his eyes, wishing my back were up to more than just the occasional kiss or handhold these last few days.

He came to my bed, and I was surprised and pleased when Sikander stepped back so that Arjun could be the one to sit beside me. He reached out and placed his hand on my cheek, the warmth of his palm helping the pain to melt away. "I'd intended to tell you this in private, but perhaps it's better if everyone hears."

"Hears what?" I asked, my voice rising a note in alarm. There was something about the way he was looking at me. It was serious, whatever it was.

"I asked my father to send a letter to your father," Arjun told me.

I frowned. "Why on earth would you want to send a letter to my father? What sort of letter?"

"A letter asking for your hand in marriage," he said. "What else? Do you really think I'm going to wait around and miss my chance a second time?"

"After what happened to her last unwanted suitor, I wouldn't worry myself over that too much," Hina quipped, grinning mercilessly at the fate that had befallen Karim and his family.

But I was staring up at Arjun in shock and wonder, my heart swelling in my chest until it was physically painful. "You want to marry me? But what about heirs?"

He shrugged. "I don't care about any of that, and my father agrees with me. He's behind this proposal. If you're willing, that is."

"Willing? My prince, I can think of nothing I want more." I reached up to kiss him, but he leaned his face down so I wouldn't have to.

"Then we'll see what your father says, and if he doesn't like it, we'll devise a plan to conquer Nizam and hold him hostage until he agrees," Arjun replied.

I grinned. "I'd like that, my prince."

"I thought you might." He kissed me again, lingering longer this time. "But for now, let's get you to the roof so you can stop trying to sneak out of bed to see Sultana."

"All right," I agreed, and I lay back against the cushions and actually relaxed for a change, thoughts of marrying Arjun swirling in my head.

CHAPTER 34

"Viputeshwar reports that things seem to be moving smoothly in Mahisagar, your highness," Sikander told me as I sat under my canopy on the roof of the palace, Sultana curled around me, her neck and shoulders helping to support my back, which still didn't much care for sitting up straight unaided.

"The fleet is ours?" I asked.

"It is, your highness," he agreed. "And the zahhaks Hina dispatched have been on constant patrol, making sure no one gets any ideas about invading."

"And the riders I requested for the three acid zahhaks we captured in Ahura?"

"Viputeshwar has selected three girls from the local hijra deras in Rajkot," Sikander said. "They're all well educated, all young and eager, and they speak Daryastani. He says they should arrive any day now."

"Good," I said, turning my attention to Hina, who was sitting just a few feet away, on a cushioned dais of her own. "And Zindh, your majesty?"

"Zindh is secure, your highness," she replied. "All of my emirs have sworn oaths of loyalty to me as the rightful jama, and they all agree that we will permit Zindh to remain a subah of Nizam so long as you are the subahdar."

It was a strange arrangement, I had to admit. I had promised Hina that she would be the queen of her own land once again, but we'd both known that my father wouldn't permit a Zindhi bid for independence, especially not now that the river zahhaks had been made so valuable, though I wondered if he had heard about it yet. At any rate, I would be the nominal subahdar, but in effect that simply meant that Hina provided certain tax revenues to my father's court, and ruled Zindh as queen, while I was permitted to live in Kadiro or Shikarpur as I liked. In exchange, she would fight for me in times of war and I for her. I thought it was a mutually beneficial arrangement, though there was one oddity yet to be worked out.

"Have you decided how you will manage the succession?" I asked, as she couldn't have children of her own.

"The men of Zindh have agreed that from now on, a chosen cela of the Talpur dera will become the new jama once I am gone, and thenceforth in perpetuity."

My eyes widened and a smile spread slowly across my face. "A hijra dynasty?"

"Just so," Hina agreed, and she was smiling too. "A first in the world, I think."

"And hopefully not a last," I replied.

With Zindh secured, my eyes fell on Arjun and my happiness grew, because I knew that the letter had been sent from his father to mine concerning the prospect of marriage, though I had not the slightest idea how it would be received. I still didn't know why my father hadn't arrived yet. Nizam wasn't so far from Kadiro. He could have been here days ago. Why hadn't he been?

"And matters in Jesera, my prince?"

"Settled," Arjun assured me. "Jesera agrees to be your protectorate in exchange for peace, and in exchange for your guarantee of their borders against any assault from the other Yaruban emirs. The merchants there have named you emira officially, though they rule the city among themselves."

It was a good arrangement. It would bring us money, and the investment was light enough—zahhaks and ships. Those had come from Hina and Viputeshwar. Four cannon zahhaks now flew over Jesera, along with a pair of fire zahhaks. It wasn't nearly the force they had lost in the battle, but that couldn't be helped. And anyway, I'd taken two of their zahhaks and given them to Bikampur in thanks for Udai's assistance, and to strengthen my alliance with Registan. That was more important at the moment than the fate of Jesera.

Last of all, I looked to Haider, who was seated with Tamara on a dais to my left. "Has your father accepted the gift of Ahura in exchange for peace?"

"He has," Haider agreed. "The messenger arrived this morning. He is honored by the gift, and by the letter you sent him, and will always consider himself a second father to the princess of Nizam."

I raised an eyebrow, while Tamara suppressed snickers. "He didn't really say all that, did he?"

"He did, actually," Haider replied, which shocked me, because his father was cut from much the same cloth as my own. "He may not accept a hijra in his own household, but he knows how to play the game of politics as well as anyone, and so long as you're gifting him islands, he will be happy to send you pretty gowns and call you a princess."

"Well, I regret that I have no more islands to gift him," I quipped. To Tamara, I said, "And I regret even more that I have nothing substantial with which to honor Khevsuria's support beyond my eternal gratitude."

"Razia, it was a joy to help you," Tamara said, "if only so I could see Sultana carrying you eighty miles in her mouth."

I gave my zahhak some very fond pats as everyone laughed. Sultana seemed to know we were talking about her, because she cracked open an eye and swiveled it lazily around the rooftop before deciding that whatever it was, it wasn't worth getting up for when she was lying so comfortably in the shade. She settled back down with a snort through her nostrils and curled a little more tightly against me.

"Is that it, then?" I asked, scarcely believing that both of my provinces were under control, that my borders were secure, and that I had a wealthy merchant protectorate across the ocean that had agreed to my terms. There was no crisis left to stamp out? God, whatever would I do with myself?

A trumpet blared high above us, stirring me from my self-congratulatory thoughts. Sultana's head perked up. She recognized the call as a sighting of unknown zahhaks approaching. We both waited for the type and the number, and when I heard it called out, I knew who it was. Sixteen thunder—my father and his entourage had arrived.

"Hina, have the patrols maintain their altitude and keep their distance. They will permit my father to land here in the middle courtyard," I ordered.

"Yes, your highness," she agreed, but she didn't actually lift a finger. She relayed the order to a cela, who used her trumpet to send the message.

"Is there anything we can do, Razia?" Sakshi asked. She had been sitting patiently with Lakshmi, though she had already given me her reports on my household, which had become her responsibility.

"Have refreshments brought, please," I said. "My father will be hungry and thirsty and so will his men. If I want him to approve of this marriage, it'll be better if he's in a good mood."

"I'll have the servants bring food and drink at once." She stood up, tugging Lakshmi to her feet too. "Come on, let's make sure that Razia's father has enough nimbu pani that he's friendly."

"I don't think we have that much, Akka," Lakshmi said in a voice that was so serious it earned laughs all around the pavilion.

"Sikander, have you kept my father apprised of all of these developments?" I asked.

"I have, your highness," he assured me. "I presume he left Nizam this morning. If that's the case, then he would have received all the information covered today, less the news from the Safavian messenger."

"Good," I murmured, as that was less that I would have to explain. "I suppose we should go and greet him, then. It wouldn't do for a daughter to force her father to come to her like a supplicant."

I stood with a grimace, my back aching fiercely. I wondered if that would ever go away. I knew it hadn't been that long since the injury, and the doctor said the prognosis was good, but there was a part of me that worried I'd never be able to climb again, never be able to fly a zahhak again. The pressures on the spine in a dogfight were immense. If I'd tried it just then, I'd probably have ended up crippled for life. And that was to say nothing of the pain in my arm, or my groin. I was lucky the wounds had both hit bone, and hadn't hit any organs or ligaments, but they still stung.

Arjun took my arm and helped me down the stairs, toward the courtyard, where my father's zahhaks were landing in neat rows. I was surprised when I was met on the bottom step by Sultana, who had leapt off the roof, landing in the courtyard in front of me.

The poor thing was so worried about me these days. Keeping a firm grip on Arjun with one hand, I used the other to stroke Sultana's snout. "I'll be all right, girl."

"You really shouldn't be walking," Sikander muttered, standing just a pace behind me.

"I can't lie in bed all day," I replied, trying to ignore the "Why not?" that came in return.

My mouth went dry as I approached my father, who was standing behind Malikah in the courtyard, seeming a little surprised not to see me in the diwan-i-am, where court was normally held. He spotted me slowly making my way toward him, clinging to Arjun's arm, with a big thunder zahhak hovering close by, and he rushed over, moving faster than I'd expected.

"Should she be walking?" my father demanded the moment we were close enough to speak to one another without shouting.

"That's what I said, your majesty," Sikander answered. "And no, she shouldn't be. The doctor wants her in bed as much as possible."

"If I thought there was a chance of keeping her there, your majesty, believe me, I would have tried," Arjun said. "But, as I'm sure you've realized by now, she has a mind of her own."

"She always has," my father admitted, his tone changing to one that was tinged with an array of emotions I couldn't quite sort out, not with the pain in my back taking up so much of my attention.

"I've been holding court on the roof to be near Sultana, Father," I explained. "Please, join us."

He scowled. "You shouldn't have come down to greet me. Do you want to walk again, or not?"

"I am walking, Father," I pointed out.

"You know what I mean," he said, and he was looking me over with far more concern than I'd ever seen from him before.

I was so bewildered I didn't know what to do or what to say. After a moment, though, I thought I understood. I glanced to Sikander. "What in the world did you write in those summaries I asked you to send to him?"

"I sent a full report of everything that happened from beginning to end, your highness," Sikander replied, "drawing on what I saw, but also conversations with Princess Sakshi and Jama Hina and Princes Haider and Arjun. And the doctor's notes, of course, and what you told us of your encounter with Karim on the shore north of Ahura."

The mention of that made my father's eyes widen slightly and his jaw tense. He noticed Sultana standing there, and he reached out and petted her on the snout. "You've been a very good zahhak," he told her, just the way he always praised Malikah when she did well.

"She has," I agreed. I didn't know what my father and I would agree on concerning what had happened, but we could agree on that at least.

He scowled. "If we're going to meet on the roof, then we should go. You shouldn't be standing around like this. If you want to marry her, boy, you ought to take better care of her." He aimed that last at Arjun.

Arjun and I exchanged confused glances, though I thought I understood a little of what was going on here. Sikander had said something in those letters. Or maybe it was many things. He must have told my father everything, what Karim had done to me, what I had done to him, what he'd been planning to do to Lakshmi, how close he'd come to accomplishing it. My father had never been an easy man to live with, but he wasn't a rapist like Karim either. In fact, when it came to women, maybe he was a little sentimental. After all, he hadn't remarried after my mother had died. It was an oddity many men had remarked upon. Most rulers had more than one heir. My father should have married again, but he never had, and he never spoke of my mother either. I wondered sometimes why that was.

Going back up the stairs was harder than going down them had been. I gritted my teeth against the pain that lanced through my hips as I took the first two steps, but it faded almost immediately, because my father took my other arm and lifted hard, so that I didn't have to bear much of my weight on my legs and back.

"How long has she been like this?" he demanded of Sikander.

"Your majesty, this is the best I've seen her since the battle," he replied. "She and Sultana were both nearly killed. It was just sheer luck that they landed in shallow seas and not on hard rocks. Another hundred yards north and neither of them would have made it."

My father set his jaw, but said nothing until I was safely settled on my cushions on the dais once more, Sultana having returned to take up her place as my backrest, curling in close behind me, her snout making a very comfortable armrest for my wounded right arm.

No sooner had we been seated than refreshments arrived. I sipped at my nimbu pani with a sigh of pleasure, and was grateful that my father seemed to be enjoying his too. My other courtiers had departed, to give us the chance to speak alone, and I was glad for that.

My father noticed. "Haider not here?"

"He's here, Father," I assured him. "As are Tamara and Hina."

"Good. I always liked Haider and Tamara," he said.

I raised an eyebrow, because that was half-true. He'd liked them until he'd found out they'd let me prance around the Safavian court as a princess for two years while he was fighting a civil war, but I didn't want to rehash that old argument. Like I'd said, he would be more likely to agree to the marriage if he was in a good mood, and I was starting to think that he was. Or at least he was amenable to the idea.

"You've been kept up to date with developments here, Father?" I asked, because for the moment he'd seemed content to sip his drink and eat a few snacks.

He nodded. "It was very clever, the way you defeated Ahmed Shah. And the act of putting swivel guns on river zahhaks . . ." He actually smiled. "I would have loved to have been there to see the moment thirty-six river zahhaks with cannons strapped to their backs destroyed Ahmed Shah's entire force of zahhaks."

"He didn't get to see it himself. He was chasing me, and Hina cleared my tail feathers. Without her, he'd have killed us. Sultana was too tired." I patted her head gently. "I shouldn't have pushed us that hard . . . it was almost a disaster."

"Karim would have killed Princess Lakshmi if you hadn't, your highness," Sikander reminded me.

"I'm told that not a single zahhak was lost," my father said. "Is that true?"

"It is, Father," I admitted, and I allowed myself a slight smile then, because it had been a tremendous victory. "We killed sixteen of the twenty-four they brought against us. Three acid zahhaks and five fire zahhaks survived. Of those, the three acid and two fire were taken as tribute. Two fire zahhaks remain in Jesera, the fifth having been used as a messenger."

"And we've added Mahisagar to the empire, their fleet intact, and taken Jesera as a protectorate . . ." he murmured, shaking his head in disbelief. "And Ahura has been gifted to Safavia to secure peace—was this accepted?"

"It was, Father," I replied. "Shah Ismail told me to consider him a second father, and said that there would be peace between our lands."

He stroked his mustache, still trying to take it all in. "In a stroke you have brought us a new subah, and revenues from the richest trading port in Yaruba. Only Registan and Virajendra stand independent now."

"And Registan wishes a marriage alliance, your majesty," Arjun reminded him.

"I don't care what Registan wants," my father replied. His lively green eyes flickered over to me. "What matters is what my daughter wants."

"I want to marry Arjun, Father," I answered, because it had been the only thing on my mind since he'd asked me.

"Then you shall," he said.

I couldn't believe it was that easy. After everything we'd been through, he was just going to give me whatever I wanted? I frowned. "That's it? No negotiations? No demands? No conditions?"

He sighed heavily, and nodded to Arjun and Sikander. "If you please, I'd like a few moments alone with my daughter."

"Of course, your majesty," Sikander agreed.

Arjun was more reluctant. "She isn't well, your majesty," he warned.

"I'm fine," I protested, but Arjun didn't move.

He stared my father down instead. "This is the best day she's had since the battle. Only two drafts of opium."

"Sikander has made the situation clear to me, Prince Arjun," my father said, favoring him with his title for the first time in my hearing. "As I have said, I will consent to your father's marriage request, because my daughter wishes it. And I am grateful you are concerned for her well-being. But I am still her father, and I would speak with her alone."

"I'll be fine, my prince," I said, resting a hand on Arjun's knee.

Arjun grunted at that. He kissed me on the cheek and said, "We'll be right downstairs if you need anything."

"Thank you, my prince," I told him, though I watched him go with some reluctance. Private conversations with my father always made my stomach churn, even if he was acting strangely today.

"Do you love him?" my father asked me once they were gone.

It was not the question I'd been expecting, but I nodded cautiously all the same. "I do, Father. I know you don't approve, but—"

He held up a hand to forestall my arguments. "I agreed, didn't I?"

"Why?" I asked, because none of this made any sense. How had he suddenly come around to the idea of my marrying Arjun? Why was he so concerned for me now when he never had been before?

"Sikander," my father said, the name coming out as an exasperated sigh. "He sent me a summary of what happened here. A very, very detailed summary. And he also attached a personal letter in which he resigned himself from my service and told me that from now until the end of his life he would serve you and you alone."

"Me?" I gasped, having not heard any of that from the man himself.

"You," he agreed. "He told me that you were his daughter, his only child in this world, and that he would fail you no longer. He told me that you were twice as courageous as I was, and orders of magnitude more intelligent. He said that you would make the finest sultana in the history of the world, and that if I weren't so blinded by my own prejudices I would have seen that for myself."

I shook my head in disbelief, bewildered that the man was capable of writing such a letter, capable of expressing his feelings so clearly. "And you haven't killed him yet?"

My father smiled. "It occurred to me, momentarily. But he made a good argument. After all, I never had to single-handedly scale palace walls to deliver missives, never had to organize a secret rebellion, never came up with a stratagem half so clever as mounting light cannons on river zahhaks. The results spoke more clearly than any letter."

"Ah." That made sense. He saw an advantage in being nice to me. I was good for the empire now.

"But that wasn't what really got to me," he admitted, and his voice had gone quieter than I'd ever heard it.

"Oh?" I asked, wondering what else Sikander had put in that letter.

"He said that the fact that you looked just like your mother should have made me cherish you more, not less. And he told me about a man named Viputeshwar, your new governor of Mahisagar. He told me about a conversation the pair of them had. And he said that my wife was gone, but her daughter was still here, her spitting image, so like her in mind and body, and that if I didn't stop punishing her for being a daughter instead of a son I would lose her forever. In fact, he said, I nearly had. He told me what Karim did to you on the beach."

I shrugged with one shoulder, so as not to tug at the stitches in my right arm, but my throat was tight. My mind was going in a thousand different places, and the only question I had was such a stupid one, but I had to ask it anyway. "Do I really look like my mother?"

"So much so that it hurts sometimes," he admitted.

"Is that why you've always hated me so much?" I wondered, tears spilling down my cheeks.

"I've never hated you," he said, and when it was plain that I didn't believe him, he sighed. "I was angry with you, because you were my heir, the product of the union of myself and the only woman I ever loved. And I thought you were a broken, foolish deviant, and it killed me inside to see it. I thought that you had stolen from me the one chance I'd been given on this earth to have a son and an heir I could be truly proud of."

That just made me cry harder. I'd always known I was a disappointment, an embarrassment, a black mark of shame on my father's otherwise spotless record, but I'd never heard it put so damningly. And he wasn't wrong. I had stolen from him the chance at having the son and heir of his dreams by being born the way I had been. No wonder he could hardly stand to look at me.

"I'm sorry," I whispered.

"You're sorry?" he asked, his confusion plain on his face. "For what?"

"For being this way, obviously," I answered, gesturing to my pretty peshwaz and my dupatta and all of it. "God knows I tried so hard not to be. I wanted to be someone you could love. I wanted to be someone you could be proud of. I prayed every night that God would remake me so that I would be, but he never did."

"I'm glad he didn't," my father said.

"What?" I asked.

"I'm glad he didn't answer your foolish prayers," he told me. "I've seen how your cousins turned out. I've seen my own brothers, whose avarice and ambition outstripped their abilities time and again. They could never have accomplished what you have. They will never accomplish what you will accomplish. You will bring greatness to this family and this empire that will be spoken of for generations to come. My name will be a footnote when set beside yours, I see that now. You may be a girl instead of a boy, but you're the heiress I always dreamed of and more. And Sikander was right, I should have seen that from the first, but I was too certain that I knew best, too fixed in my eyes, too closed-minded to understand. But now I understand. You are my wife's daughter, and you will go on to do great things in this world if I get out of your way and let you."

"I never wanted you out of the way . . ." I protested. "Just the opposite."

"Another reason to value daughters more highly than sons, then," he said, and it took me a moment to realize he was making a joke. I couldn't remember the last time he'd joked around me. Maybe he never had.

He put his arm around my shoulders, and I flinched away from the sudden touch, which sent shooting pains through my spine. I choked back a cry of agony and fought to catch my breath.

"Are you all right? Do you need the doctor?"

My father was holding me close, keeping my back carefully supported so the pain would subside. I didn't know what to think about that. Maybe it was best I didn't think at all. The last thing I wanted was to question this beautiful dream until I woke from it.

"I'm all right," I said, though I knew I didn't sound very convincing.

"You're tired and you're hurt; we'll keep this brief," he said, still holding me in a way he hadn't since I was small enough to ride in his zahhak saddle with him. "I intend that Hina will be recognized as a subahdar in her own right, as will Viputeshwar. She will rule Zindh, he will rule Mahisagar."

"You're taking my provinces?" I couldn't believe that he would do that to me. It didn't make any sense at all.

"You'll be too busy to govern them," he said. "As the crown princess, you will be my coruler of the empire, because one day you will be its sultana. The first reigning sultana since the last time a Razia took the throne."

"And Arjun?" I asked.

"He will be your husband, but you will rule Nizam," he replied. "And your sisters, they will be elevated to princesses of the blood. I will acknowledge them as my own children."

"Because of a letter from Sikander?" I asked, still scarcely believing that such a small thing could have changed so much.

"Because of a letter from Sikander," he agreed. "Now you should rest." He reached up and stroked my hair. "You need to heal if you're going to be ready for the wedding. I want to hold it in Nizam, and you'll need to be able to ride for that."

A wedding to Arjun. Coruler of Nizam. I shook my head in disbelief. After everything I'd been through, it felt like a dream come true.

CHAPTER 35

The wedding had been like something out of a dream. My sisters, Tamara, Hina, and all of her celas had come the day before to do my mehendi, and though Hina and Tamara had tried to make me blush with their ribald advice, they'd forgotten that I had been a courtesan for longer than I'd been a princess and that I knew a thing or two about how to please my man. Then we'd signed the marriage contract, just Arjun and me, my father and his father, and Sakshi and Lakshmi because they'd insisted. It was witnessed by my father's chief cleric, and we'd signed it in the temple beside the great marble mausoleum that my father had built for my mother while I'd been away in Bikampur. The sight of it had robbed me of breath.

But none of that had compared to the wedding itself. Arjun had come riding in on Padmini, the poor thing totally covered in golden-embroidered scarlet cloth. His father had arranged for a procession of dancers, shenai players, and drummers to march chorus alongside Padmini's somber march through Nizam's streets and my father's fortress. Thunder zahhaks had flown overhead, shooting bolts of lightning to commemorate the occasion, and Sikander had led me to the tent to complete our public wedding vows to one another—a concession to Arjun's family. After that, there had been so much drinking and dancing and eating that it had all become a bit of a blur.

Now my eyes were clear, because Arjun and I were alone at last, back home in Bikampur. I'd symbolically flown home with him like a proper bride, and his mother and his sister had led me into our bedroom and sat me on a mattress festooned with flower petals, my dupatta draped over me so that Arjun could unwrap me when he arrived. He'd taken his time, which was traditional, if a bit annoying. But he was here, right in front of me, his strong hand brushing aside the gauze-thin scarlet silk of my dupatta, just like in all those storybooks I'd been so fond of as a child.

"You look so beautiful tonight," he told me, his palm cupping my cheek as he stared into my eyes. "All day, in fact. It took every ounce of my self-control not to ravish you in the temple."

"I don't think that would have gone over well with my father's clerics," I murmured, but I loved the idea, because I hated my father's clerics. They'd preached against me for years, though I supposed there was some small revenge in forcing them to attend to my wedding ceremony.

"No," he agreed, leaning forward and planting his lips against mine for a moment. "I don't think it would have."

I reached up and twined my arms around his strong neck, pulling his body against mine, grateful that I didn't wrench my back in the process, but I thought my injuries had finally healed. It had taken a month. I kissed his neck, and then his jaw, working my way to his mouth. "You have no idea how long I've been waiting for this."

"Oh, is this your first time?" he teased as he eased me back against the mattress, the hard muscles of his arms supporting my back with a tenderness that had come from watching me whimper and grimace for weeks on end.

"My first time not having to worry about Lakshmi barging in on us with a nightmare, or Shiv telling us that he's taking the bed, or Father showing up with a new suitor? Yes," I answered.

He grinned and started working loose the loops and knots holding my peshwaz shut. "Well, we should enjoy tonight, then, because it's only going to get worse."

"Worse?" I raised a quizzical eyebrow, wondering what on earth he meant by that.

"You've got three Mahisagari girls coming to you to learn how to fly zahhaks. You'll have Lakshmi back in no time to 'help.' And I know you, you'll want children of your own someday too. I'm not sure how we'll get them, but they'll be along eventually, even if they're just more girls like you in need of rescue."

"You're right, my prince," I agreed, stroking his hair with my fingers, using my nails to send little shivers of pleasure into his scalp that I could sense in my fingertips.

"And you'll be the coruler of Nizam," he added. "Your father will want you enlarging the empire against its enemies. And your uncle will try to have us both killed, as will your cousins, no doubt."

"No doubt," I agreed, but I was smiling, because they were the furthest thing from my mind.

Arjun pressed his forehead against mine. "But in spite of all that, I want you to make me a promise."

"Oh?" I asked, still massaging his scalp in the way I knew he liked best. "And what promise might that be?"

"No more adventures for a little while?" he suggested.

"I'm afraid I can't make that promise, my prince," I replied.

"No?" he asked.

I shook my head, biting my lower lip to suppress a big grin.

"And why is that?" he demanded, with a mock sternness that reminded me of a sweet puppy trying to learn to bark.

"Because I had planned to take you on quite a grand adventure this evening," I said. "But, if you'd rather we didn't . . ." I shrugged my shoulders and started wriggling my way out from beneath him.

I had scarcely moved an inch before his arms came down on either side of my shoulders, hemming me in. He leaned low over me, his voice husky. "All right," he said. "I suppose one more adventure couldn't hurt."

ACKNOWLEDGMENTS

If first books are surreal, unexpected successes, then second books are definitely heart-wrenching slogs. I've heard many authors say that the second book is the hardest, and I feel like that was true with *Gifting Fire*. But I was lucky to have so much support in bringing this project to fruition.

To my parents, especially my mom, who reads every word I ever write—thanks. You're the best.

To Maya Deane, thank you for letting me copy and paste random pieces of this book to you over Facebook Messenger so that I would feel like I was on the right track. I really needed a sounding board on this one and you delivered.

To Hallie Funk, Jeremy Van Mill, Sara Vega, and Nathan Eckberg, thanks so much for your support at a time when I really needed it. Without you, I definitely would never have managed to get this book in on time. Your inspiration and assistance are so appreciated.

To my friends Amrita Chowdhury, Ujaan Ghosh, Aarzu

Maknojia, and Sneha Bolisetty, thank you so much for your advice, suggestions, and continued support.

To Katherine Pucciariello, I so appreciate your beta read on this book. Your excitement for it was infectious.

To Peter Brett, thank you for believing in *Stealing Thunder* enough to blurb it, and thank you for the countless hours of handholding and advice sharing over the last eighteen months. You have made the transition from first-time author to second-time author so much less painful than it would have been otherwise.

To Brigid Kemmerer, Kerry Kletter, Rob Hart, E. E. Knight, Myke Cole, Anita Kushwaha, and so many others in the literary community who helped to signal boost *Stealing Thunder* in the midst of a pandemic, I can't thank you enough for your retweets and your enthusiasm. It really meant the world to me.

To my incredible editor, Kristine Swartz, thank you for bearing with me on rewriting the entire novel in the edits phase. I know that must have been a lot of extra reading for you, but I'm really grateful you gave me the freedom to do that.

To my brilliant publicist, Alexis Nixon, from meeting me on a street corner for New York Comic Con to arranging appearances online during COVID-19, you have given me so many opportunities that I never imagined I would get. Thanks so much!

To Jessica Plummer and the rest of my marketing team, I can't thank you enough for handling the advertising side of things, which I'm definitely not the best at. It has been a huge stress relief to have you working with me, and I really appreciate all that you have done for *Stealing Thunder*, and all that you will do for *Gifting Fire*.

To my agent, Andrea Somberg—you are the best! I really appreciate your always having the time for me when I need you, giving me fabulous career advice, and giving me this opportunity to put these books out in the world.

To Deepti Gupta, thank you for being Razia's voice in *Stealing Thunder*. Your support for my work has been so tremendous and so appreciated.

Lastly, thank you to everyone at Penguin Random House for believing in this project and helping put it out in the world. It's been an incredible opportunity to actually see my own books on store shelves for the first time in my life, and I'm so grateful to have experienced it because of your belief in my work.

GLOSSARY

PEOPLE

Ahmed Shah *(Ah-med Shah)* [starting off easy]—sultan of Mahisagar

Ammi *(Uh-me)*—name for Varsha; it's a word literally meaning "mom," sometimes used by hijras when addressing their gurus

Arjun Agnivansha *(Ahr-joon Ugh-nee-vuhn-shuh)*—devastatingly handsome prince of Bikampur, and Razia's chief love interest

Arvind Singh *(Ahr-vind Seeng)*—son of Govind Singh, a noble of Bikampur, and a skilled zahhak rider

Asma *(Uss-muh)*—wife of Ahmed Shah and sultana of Mahisagar

Disha *(Dee-shuh)*—Razia's sister from the dera

Firangi *(Fih-rung-ee)*—a foreigner from the west

Gayatri Agnivansha *(Gai-ah-tree Ugh-nee-vuhn-shuh)*—Arjun's mother and the maharani of Bikampur

Govind Singh *(Go-vihnd Seeng)*—a noble of Bikampur who possesses an overly large golden peacock statue

Haider *(Hay-dur)*—crown prince of Safavia

Hina Talpur *(Hee-nuh Tahl-poor)*—rightful jama of Zindh

Humayun *(Hoo-mah-yoon)*—Razia's father, and the sultan of Nizam

Jai *(Jive* without the *v)*—a eunuch servitor at the palace in Bikampur

Jaskaur *(Jahs-kohr)*—Razia's sister from the dera

Javed Khorasani *(Jah-vayd Kor-ah-sah-nee)*—subahdar of Zindh, and an enemy of Udai Agnivansha

Karim Shah *(Kuh-reem* [but roll your *r* a bit] *Shah)*—son of Ahmed Shah, prince of Mahisagar, and all-around jerk

Lakshmi *(Luck-shmee)*—Razia's little sister in the dera, a former prince of Kolikota, and a brilliant zahhak rider

Nuri *(Nur-ree)*—one of Hina's celas

Pir Tahir *(Peer Tuh-heer)*—a local religious cleric in Shikarpur

Rashid *(Ruh-sheed)*—the younger of Razia's two cousins, and son of her uncle Shahrukh

Razia Khan *(Rah-zee-uh Khan)*—former crown prince of the sultanate of Nizam, now the subahdar of Zindh

Sakina *(Suh-kee-nuh)*—a famous jama of Zindh, for whom Hina's zahhak is named

Sakshi *(Sahk-shee)*—Razia's older sister in the dera, and the finest sitar player in the world

Salim *(Suh-leem)*—Razia's deadname, used by jerks

Shahrukh *(Shah-rookh)*—Razia's uncle, and a powerful subahdar

Shiv *(Shihv)*—a eunuch servitor at the palace in Bikampur (the nice one)

Sikander *(Sick-under)*—the master-at-arms of Nizam, and one of Razia's least favorite people

Sunil Kalani *(Su-neel Kuh-lah-nee)*—a local emir of Zindh

Tamara *(Tah-muh-ruh)*—crown princess of Khevsuria

Tariq *(Tah-rick)*—the older of Razia's two cousins, and the subahdar of Lahanur

Udai Agnivansha *(Oo-day Ugh-nee-vuhn-shuh)*—maharaja of Bikampur, and father of Arjun

Varsha *(Vahr-shuh)*—Razia's guru, a mother-like figure who runs the Bikampur dera; often called Ammi by her celas

Vikram Sharma *(Vih-kruhm Sher-mah)*—Bikampuri noble who possesses a lovely khanda

Viputeshwar *(Vih-poo-t(h)esh-wahr)*—grandfatherly courtier in Rajkot fort

PLACES

Bikampur *(Bee-kahm-poor)*—a city in Registan ruled by the Maharaja Udai Agnivansha

Daryastan *(Duh-ree-ah-stahn)*—the subcontinent on which the story's principal action takes place

Kadiro *(Kuh-dee-roh)*—chief port city and historic capital of Zindh

Kolikota *(Koh-lee-koh-tah)*—the coastal city where Lakshmi was born, currently part of the Virajendra empire

Lahanur *(Lah-huh-noor)*—a Nizami subah to the north of Zindh, ruled by Razia's cousin Tariq

Mahisagar *(Muh-hee-sa-grr)*—a sultanate on the west coast of Daryastan, ruled by Ahmed Shah and home to Prince Karim

Nizam *(Nih-zahm)*—the capital city that lends its name to the sultanate of Nizam, the greatest empire in northern Daryastan

Rajkot *(Rahj-kot)*—a fort in Mahisagar

Registan *(Reh-gih-stahn)*—a desert land famous for its warrior kings, its beautiful fortresses, and the wealth that flows through it on its way to or from the sea

Shikarpur *(Shee-kahr-poor)*—capital and largest city of Zindh

Virajendra *(Veer-uh-jehn-druh)*—a major empire to the south of Nizam

Yaruba *(Yuh-rooh-buh)*—a desert land to the west of Daryastan

Zindh *(Zind)*—a subah of the sultanate of Nizam to the north and west of Bikampur

TERMS

cela *(chay-lah)*—a disciple of a guru living in a hijra dera

crore *(kror)*—ten million

dera *(day-ruh)*—a hijra house

dupatta *(doo-putt-uh)*—a scarf or shawl-like garment worn by women to loosely cover their hair

haveli *(hay-vay-lee)*—a mansion or townhouse

hijra *(hee-jurd-uh)*—a member of a community of transfeminine individuals who were assigned male at birth

jalebi *(juh-lay-bee)*—a dessert made from a sweet batter deep-fried in pretzel-like twists

jam *(jahm)*—a Zindhi king

jama *(jah-muh)*—a Zindhi queen

kameez *(kuh-meez)*—a long tunic with slits along the sides

katar *(kuh-tahr)*—a punch dagger with an H-shaped grip and a triangular-shaped blade, often used in pairs

khanda *(kuhn-dah)*—a word meaning sword; it normally refers to one with a straight double-edged blade, usually with a spatulate tip and basket-like hilt

kurta *(koor-tuh)*—a long, tunic-like garment, similar to a kameez

lakh *(lahk)*—one hundred thousand

lehenga *(lehng-uh)*—an outfit consisting of a tight-fitting, midriff-baring blouse, a full A-line skirt, and a very large dupatta wound around the body for modesty

maharaja *(muh-hah-rahj-uh)*—the title given to the ruler of a Registani city-state

mirza *(meer-zuh)*—an honorary title used as a surname granted to Nizami princes of the royal line

nirvan *(nir-vahn)*—a surgical procedure that removes the genitals

paisa (pl. paise) *(pay-suh;* pl. *pay-say)*—a small monetary denomination equal to one one-hundredth of a rupee

rupee *(roo-pee)*—a common monetary unit, usually minted in the form of silver coins worth one hundred paise

samosa *(suh-mow-suh)*—a savory, deep-fried snack of pastry stuffed with a spicy filling

sari *(sah-ree)*—a long piece of cloth wrapped around the body as a garment, usually paired with a petticoat and blouse underneath

shalwar *(shuhl-vaar)*—a pair of loose-fitting trousers usually paired with a kameez or kurta

subah *(soo-buh)*—a province

subahdar *(soo-buh-dahr)*—a provincial governor

talwar *(tuhl-vahr)*—a word meaning sword; in the weapons trade it refers to a single-edged, heavily curved sword with a short hilt and disc-shaped pommel made for slashing attacks

toradar *(tore-uh-dahr)*—a matchlock musket

zahhak *(zuh-hawk)*—one of several different species of large, feathered, flying creatures, which are ridden by Daryastan's nobility

zamorin *(zuh-more-in)* [a corruption of Samoothiri]—the hereditary ruler of Kolikota

© Spencer Micka Photography

Alina Boyden is a trans rights activist, author, and PhD candidate in cultural anthropology. As an ACLU client, her case secured health care rights for transgender employees in the state of Wisconsin. Her work in cultural anthropology centers on the civil rights struggles of transgender women in India and Pakistan, and consequently she divides her time between the United States and South Asia. When she's not writing, traveling, or working on her dissertation, she spends her free time indulging in two of her childhood passions—swordplay and flying airplanes.

CONNECT ONLINE

AlinaBoyden.com